THE ROMANCE AND ENCHANTMENT OF VALENTINE'S DAY FROM FIVE ACCLAIMED REGENCY AUTHORS

MARY BALOGH won the *Romantic Times* Award for Best New Regency Writer and the Reviewer's Choice Award for Best Regency Author in 1985, and the *Romantic Times* Award for Best Regency Author in 1989. She lives in Kipling, Saskatchewan, Canada.

KATHERINE KINGSLEY was born in New York City and grew up there and in England. Her impressive debut in 1988 with the publication of *Wild Rose* was followed by three more highly acclaimed Regency novels. She is married to an Englishman and they live in the Colorado mountains with their son.

EMMA LANGE won the *Romantic Times* Reviewer's Choice Award for Best New Regency Author in 1988. A graduate of the University of California at Berkeley, she and her husband live in the Midwest and pursue, as they are able, interests in traveling and sailing.

PATRICIA RICE won the 1988 *Romantic Times* Award for Best Historical Regency for *Indigo Moon*. She lives in Mayfield, Kentucky.

JOAN WOLF is the author of the highly acclaimed trilogy about the making of modern Britain, which includes *The Road to Avalon*, *Born of the Sun* and *The Edge of Light*. She lives with her husband and two children in Milford, Connecticut.

A REGENCY VALENTINE

Five Stories by

Mary Balogh

∾

Katherine Kingsley

∾

Emma Lange

∾

Patricia Rice

∾

Joan Wolf

A SIGNET BOOK

SIGNET
Published by the Penguin Group
Penguin Books USA Inc., 375 Hudson Street,
New York, New York 10014, U.S.A.
Penguin Books Ltd, 27 Wrights Lane,
London W8 5TZ, England
Penguin Books Australia Ltd, Ringwood,
Victoria, Australia
Penguin Books Canada Ltd, 2801 John Street,
Markham, Ontario, Canada L3R 1B4
Penguin Books (N.Z.) Ltd, 182–190 Wairau Road,
Auckland 10, New Zealand

Penguin Books Ltd, Registered Offices:
Harmondsworth, Middlesex, England

First published by Signet, an imprint of New American Library,
a division of Penguin Books USA Inc.

First Printing, February, 1991
10 9 8 7 6 5 4 3 2 1

"Golden Rose" copyright © Mary Balogh, 1991
"The Secret Benefactor" copyright © Julia Jay Kendall, 1991
"Lady Valentine's Scheme" copyright © Emma Lange, 1991
"Fathers and Daughters" copyright © Patricia Rice, 1991
"The Antagonists" copyright © Joan Wolf, 1991

Contents

Golden Rose

by Mary Balogh

WINTER WAS ALWAYS a dreary time of year in Bath. There were few visitors except those whose poor health had driven them there to drink the waters. And the season usually brought the famous spa its fair share of wind and rain and leaden skies. Spring was on the way by the time February came, but still, it came slowly and was evident only in a few tantalizing glimpses of primroses and snowdrops.

But the Master of Ceremonies, whose task it was to see that every resident and every visitor was suitably entertained despite the season and the weather, made an interesting announcement at the beginning of the month that boosted the spirits of almost everyone, young and old alike.

A masked ball was to be held at the Upper Assembly Rooms on St. Valentine's Day, February 14. Even that detail was interesting enough, since few people can resist the lure of a costume party and the chance to dress up and don a mask. But there was more.

Each gentleman was encouraged to send a valentine to the lady of his choice with the request that she carry some favor of his to the ball to be reclaimed at the end of the evening. In the true spirit of the festival, the card was to be anonymous.

Ladies were asked to reply to the valentines. In the event that they received more than one, they were asked to choose. Each was to carry only one gentleman's favor to the ball.

Bath was agog with the news. Most people thought it all a splendid idea, though there were, of course, criticisms. How was a lady to know if her gentleman admirer was respectable? If she had more than one valentine, how was she to know which came from the gentleman she preferred?

But most agreed that the whole mystery surrounding the game added excitement and fun and romance to one of the dullest months of the year.

"What if a poor lady wears a brooch from a gentleman she abhors and discovers the truth only when it is too late?" Lady Copeland asked her brother as they sipped tea together one afternoon in her downstairs salon on the Circus, one of Bath's most prestigious residential areas.

"It's a deuced foolish idea," Lord Westbury said. "There's scarce a soul here below the age of forty. What do we want with cavorting about a ballroom wearing masks and sending ladies expensive gifts when they don't even know whom to thank?"

"It is a very romantic idea, of course," Lady Copeland said with a sigh. "But there should be some way in which the gentlemen can hint at their identity. I can remember the time when I had three valentine cards in one year. To this day I don't know which one came from Alistair and who sent the others. It was most provoking."

Her brother snorted and suffered a coughing spell for his pains. He thumped his broad chest and turned purple in the face.

"Emily, dear," Lady Copeland said, turning to her young companion, who was seated quietly behind the tea tray, "another cup for Lord Westbury." She waited for the worst of the coughing to subside. "Besides,

Stanley, there are some younger people in Bath. Our nephew, for example.''

His lordship sipped loudly on his tea. "Roger will think it deuced silly, take my word on it," he said. "He don't want to be here to start with, and wouldn't be if Jasper had not insisted. Roger is determined to be bored. When I called on him this morning at the White Hart, he was still in bed and had the effrontery to growl at me."

"Then this ball will be just the thing for him," Lady Copeland said. "What did he do, anyway, that our brother would send him away from London?"

"Nothing serious," Lord Westbury said after taking another noisy sip of his tea. "He didn't kill a man or anything like that. Caught between the sheets with a lady, I gather—by her husband."

Lady Copeland coughed delicately. "Do remember Emily, Stanley," she said. "Emily, dear, you may take the tray back to the kitchen if you will be so good."

But before the girl could get to her feet, Lady Copeland's butler was at the door announcing the arrival of the Honorable Mr. Roger Bradshaw. The young man himself followed close behind. Tall and handsomely built, with thick dark hair that fell in a heavy lock over one eyebrow, he looked on the world from a pair of dark gray eyes with ironic humor.

"Aunty!" he said, striding across the room to take both of Lady Copeland's hands in his own and plant a kiss on her cheek. "What the devil are you doing living quite at the top of the world here? Trying to hobnob with the angels, are you?"

"It was a deuced foolish thing to take lodgings all the way up here, Adeline," Lord Westbury said. "Having to take a chair instead of a carriage, and being bounced and jounced uphill like a barrel of pork.

Why couldn't you stay in Laura Place like last year, eh? You were quite comfortable there.''

"Uncle Stanley," Roger said, extending a hand to his uncle. "Did you really call on me this morning, or did I dream it? Mornings are not always my best time, I'm afraid.''

"How are you, Roger dear?" his aunt asked. "Do take a seat. And how did you leave your dear father?''

"Hastily," Roger said with a grin, seating himself, "and decided to come to Bath to pay a call on my favorite aunt.''

"Your *only* aunt," she said matter-of-factly. "Yes, Emily, dear, thank you. I'm sure Roger will appreciate a cup of tea after his climb. I assume you walked, dear?''

Roger took his cup of tea from the hand of his aunt's companion, looked at her absently, and then returned his eyes for a second look. "Present me, please, Aunty.''

"Miss Richmond," Lady Copeland said, "my new companion, Roger. Her father is our neighbor, Sir Henry Richmond. They have such a large family that they were able to spare Emily to bear me company. This is my scamp of a nephew, dear," she added. "Roger Bradshaw, my brother's son—Viscount Yardley, that is.''

Roger got to his feet and made the girl a bow. She still had not sat down after taking him his tea. She curtsied while his eyes examined her slender form in its neat gray dress and her golden hair, which framed her heart-shaped face with shining smoothness and was confined in a knot at her neck.

"Ma'am?" he said.

"You'll have to get used to early mornings, Roger," his uncle was saying. "It won't do for you to miss the promenade in the Pump Room. It begins at seven o'clock.''

Roger winced. "Barbarous!" he said. "Do I have to? But there is precious little else to do in Bath, is there? Where is that scallywag of a grandson of yours, Aunty? In Bath, is he, or have you packed him off back to school?''

"Dear Jasper," Lady Copeland said fondly. "He could not possibly survive at school, Roger, especially at this time of year. He is so susceptible to chills. I fear sometimes that he is consumptive.''

Lord Westbury gave a bark of what sounded like derisive laughter, though it soon turned into another coughing bout.

His sister looked at him disapprovingly. "I tried to persuade Harriet and Nigel to take the boy to Italy with them this winter," she said, "but they would not. He would doubtless interfere with their pleasures. But I would not send him back to school after Christmas. He is about the house somewhere. I could not find him to come to tea. He has no appetite, poor boy. You may remove the tray now, Emily, dear.''

Roger waited for two minutes before getting to his feet. "I'll go in search of Jasper," he said. "I'll see if he has forgiven me for the thrashing I gave him last summer when he cut the white tassels off my Hessians.''

"You ought not to have done that," Lady Copeland said. "The boy is delicate. Besides, Harriet had a fit of the vapors that lasted all of an hour. And then she had the migraines for two days.''

Roger grinned and left the room.

"Gone to look for Jasper!" Lord Westbury said scornfully. "Does he think we were born yesterday, Adeline? I would look to that little girl of yours, if I were you.''

"Emily?" his sister said. "She is too shy by half, Stanley. She could be a beauty if she would allow herself to be. And she seemed to be a girl of some spirit when she was in the country. I believe she finds it lowering that her father is impoverished and she must take employment. Poor dear. I have hopes of finding her a husband one of these days."

"Roger won't have matrimony on his mind," her brother said. "Not with someone's companion, Adeline."

"If he grows troublesome," Lady Copeland said, "I shall give him a sharp setdown, Stanley. Or perhaps Emily will prove to have more spirit than she has shown thus far in my employ. She is quite a dear girl, I do assure you."

Emily Richmond took the tea tray to the kitchen and paused to commend the cook on the little currant cakes that had been on it. Then she had to wait, smiling, while the cook explained to her at great length how her grandmother had passed the recipe on to her mother and how her mother had passed it on to her.

Emily did not chafe at the delay. She did not mind her employer's company. She could sit cheerfully through a whole day alone with Lady Copeland when it was necessary to do so. But she hated it when there were visitors. Always she was introduced as Lady Copeland's companion—her employee, that was. She never knew quite how to behave.

She had refused two offers of marriage from two perfectly worthy gentlemen at home before Papa had finally taken her aside and explained gently to her that with three other daughters and four sons all growing up behind her, he could not afford to take or send her anyplace where she was likely to meet a suitor to her liking. Papa had not reproached her for refusing those offers, but she had felt mortified and penitent. If she had only known!

She must have been incredibly naive not to know, since their neighbors the Copelands obviously did. Lady Copeland asked for her companionship to Bath just a couple of weeks after Papa had had his talk with her. And though she had been very tactful and had made it seem that Emily would be doing her a favor by going, it was very clear that it was employment that was being offered. There was an "allowance" involved—pay for services rendered.

Emily had accepted, though Papa had assured her that things were not at such a bad pass that she needed to enter service.

She had come to Bath determined to find herself a husband just as soon as possible. And she was not going to be as foolish as she had used to be, looking for love, that special something that all girls dreamed of. Respectability would be enough.

Perhaps Mr. Harris would be the one. He made a point of greeting Lady Copeland at the Pump Room almost every morning, though Emily always suspected that it was she who really drew him. He was an amiable gentleman, no older than forty, if that old, and perfectly respectable, if a little dull.

She would not aim high. Though her father was a baronet, he had committed the unpardonable crime of becoming impoverished. And she herself was in employment. She could certainly not aim for someone like the Honorable Mr. Roger Bradshaw, for example, though he had looked at her a few minutes before with definite interest and though her heart had quite turned over within her under his scrutiny.

He was a man to be despised, anyway. He had been sent away from London by his father to avoid scandal.

He had been caught in bed with another man's wife. What sort of a man must he be?

She was walking from the back stairs along the dark hallway beside the main staircase, her eyes lowered to the tiles, when she became aware that someone was ahead of her. When she raised her head, it was to find the object of her disapproving thoughts coming toward her. He met her beneath the bend of the stairs.

"It was a large tray," he said. "I'm sorry that I am too late to help you with it."

He had a way of looking very directly at a person, Emily thought, as if he saw far into her soul. And he stood just a little too close for comfort. She resisted the urge to take a step back.

"It was not heavy," she said.

She had never known a flirt. She had only ever had experience of earnest and straightforward gentry and tenant farmers. This man was a flirt, she knew instinctively, and he had come to flirt with her. Her heart fluttered at the same time as she recognized exactly why he did so.

"Miss Richmond," he said, smiling slowly at her— without a doubt, he knew what effect crinkled eyes and white teeth had on the female sex—"I am new to Bath. What does one do here for entertainment?"

Emily's heart began to beat up into her throat. She had always thought the idea of eyes dancing was a silly one. But his eyes danced. "There is the Pump Room," she said. "And there are the Assembly Rooms and the shops and the abbey and private concerts. And Sydney Gardens when the weather is not too cold."

Had he moved? She had not seen him do so. But he must have, because that backward step could no longer be avoided. Except that somehow she must have stepped sideways instead of back, because the slope of the stairs was now at her shoulder. She was in the shadows beneath the stairs and he was blocking the way back into the open hallway.

"And which places do you frequent?" he asked her. "What would you recommend?"

No, she would not become silly or fluttery or show him in any way that he had discomposed her. She looked him calmly in the eye and willed the breathlessness from her voice. "Lady Copeland likes to spend an hour in the Pump Room each morning," she said, "and some time strolling on the Crescent in the afternoon if the weather is good. She likes to take tea at the Assembly Rooms during the evenings."

His lips twitched. They were very sensuous lips, she thought, and then realized with dismay that she was staring at them. They were disturbingly close. He had placed one hand flat against the wall beside her head. His voice was low when he spoke—but then it was only a few inches from her ear.

"I shall have to develop a taste for the waters and for early mornings, then," he said, "starting tomorrow. And for strolling and sipping tea."

His eyes on hers were very disturbing, but they became even more so when they looked up to her hair and down to her mouth.

She swallowed and could think of not a single thing to say. He was closer—his coat was almost brushing her bosom. And his eyes were steady on her lips. She passed the tip of her tongue across them nervously. Her heart was beating right up into her ears.

His lips were parted when they met hers, warm and moist and lightly exploring, tasting, inviting. She spread her hands flat against the wall behind her and wondered if her knees really would buckle under her. There was a sudden throbbing ache between her legs and a tightening in her breasts. His tongue followed the same path her own had traveled a moment before.

She lifted her hands and pushed firmly against his chest. Dear God. Oh, dear God.

"I beg your pardon," she said, her eyes on his cravat, "but I think there has been some misunderstanding. I have taken employment, sir, because my family is impoverished. I have taken *respectable* employment." She put some emphasis on the adjective.

His voice was still low. She did not look up to see if he laughed at her. "Then I beg your pardon too," he said. "I did not mean any disrespect."

Not much, she thought, her embarrassment and confusion turning to anger. He had merely thought to dally with her because she was a servant. He had merely hoped to seduce her.

But her anger as she walked past him—he had stepped to one side—and made her way back to the salon, trying not to hurry, was directed as much against herself as against him. She could easily have avoided his kiss. He had not exactly grabbed her and thrown her against that wall. Was it what she had heard about him that had fascinated her? Had she been intrigued, wondering what it would be like to be kissed by a rake?

Well, if that were so, she had found the answer. It was quite gloriously wonderful, that was what.

She heartily despised herself.

Roger stood in the hallway, his hands clasped behind him, his eyes on the tiled floor. Ah, delectable. All soft, feminine warmth. And for one moment he had thought she was his. No, not *thought*—she had been his. For one moment before she remembered that she was a virtuous woman.

A shame. A decided shame. He needed some diversion in Bath if he were not to go insane within a week.

"Psst!"

The sound came from the general direction of the front door, though there appeared to be no one in the hallway except himself.

"Psst!"

More specifically from the direction of the large aspidistra plant to one side of the door.

"Jasper," Roger said, "if you think I am going to slink back there to share secrets with you, think again, my lad. Come on out. What are you hiding from, anyway?"

The aspidistra rustled and a red-haired, freckled boy of about twelve stepped out from behind it. "*Whom* is more to the point, Rog," he said. "If I had been anywhere to be found, I would have been made to sit politely through tea, saying, 'Yes, Great-Uncle Stanley,' and 'No, Grandmama,' until I wouldn't have been able to enjoy the cakes."

"And it is so much more satisfactory to hide behind a plant than to stay in the schoolroom or wherever it is you spend your time upstairs?" Roger said.

"I'm very glad I did," Jasper said. "I should tell Grandmama what I just saw, Rog. She wouldn't like it above half."

"Wouldn't she?" Roger said. "Be my guest, Jasper. Shall I hold the sitting-room door open for you?"

"That's what I always hate about you, Rog," the boy said cheerfully. "You'll never let a fellow make a decent bit of pocket money from blackmail."

"That's not what you hated me for last summer," Roger said. "For how many hours was it you couldn't sit down after I had finished with you?"

"Oh, two or three minutes," the boy said airily. "I've had worse from Papa. You shouldn't be mauling Emmy about like that, though, Rog."

"Fancy her yourself, do you, lad?" Roger said. "A word of advice. Forget it. She's of a breed known as virtuous women. She's not worth the energy expended on wooing her.''

"I like Emmy," Jasper said. "She's the only grown-up I know who treats me as if I'm human."

"You had better be thankful that your grandmother doesn't treat you as a human," Roger said. "You would be at school at this very moment if she did."

Jasper grimaced. "And don't I know it," he said.

"So what am I to do for entertainment around here?" Roger asked. "Any ideas?"

"Meaning what females are available?" Jasper said. "Not many, Rog. Most of them must be eighty if they're a day. There are the Misses Traviss."

"Plural," Roger said. "Do they come separately? I never did like more than one at a time."

"No," Jasper said. "Always together, Rog. And one has teeth that stick out and the other a chin that sticks in."

"Marvelous!" Roger said. "I can see I'm going to have a wonderful time."

"What did you do?" Jasper asked. "Grandmama said you wouldn't have come here at this time of year if you didn't have to. Was it over some female?"

"Never you mind," his cousin said. "So it's the Traviss sisters or the octogenarians, is it?"

"There is the Langtree woman," Jasper said, "but everyone's after her, Rog. Men swarm around her like bees around a flower. I can't see why. She must be thirty at the very least. She does have one asset, though. She has great big . . .'' His hands made expressive cupping gestures a few inches from his chest.

"Does she, by Jove?" Roger said.

"You wouldn't want to be part of a crowd, though, Rog," Jasper said.

His cousin raised one eyebrow. "No, I certainly

would not," he said. "If I like what I see, Jasper, I'll roust the opposition."

"Send her a valentine," Jasper said.

Roger frowned.

"It's going to be all the rage here," Jasper said. "Masked ball, secret valentines, special favors, and all that nonsense. What a bore! I'm not going to be so silly when I grow up, I can safely promise." He settled into giving an interested Roger full details of the approaching ball.

"Great!" Roger said. "All the trappings of intrigue and high romance and no women below the age of eighty except one virtuous woman, two horsey females, and a queen bee—with a bosom. I can just see myself having such a grand time that I'll never want to go home."

"You wouldn't care to take me to a confectioner's for cakes, would you, Rog?" Jasper asked halfhopefully.

"Why not?" Roger said. "It sounds as if that might be the closest I'll get to excitement during this particular sojourn in Bath."

"Super!" Jasper said with some enthusiasm. "You go and tell Grandmama. And it was your suggestion, mind. I'm too sickly even to think of food."

"Quite so," Roger said, looking at the sturdy build and moon face of the boy. "I can quite see why she thinks you might be consumptive, Jas. I'll have to make her a present of a pair of spectacles before I leave here. Wait here, then. I'll be back in a trice."

It lacked a few minutes of half-past seven when Roger strolled into the Pump Room the following morning. He paused in the doorway to look about him. The long, high room was fairly crowded despite the season and the drizzling rain outside. And Jasper's comment of the day before that there was scarce a soul there below the age of eighty seemed not much exaggerated.

Roger sighed and wondered what on earth he was doing there. It was true that his father had advised flight in that blustering way of his that took no account of the fact that his son was now seven-and-twenty and no longer seventeen. It was even more true that he himself had thought discretion the better part of valor. He had not known that Ruby was married until she had shrieked out the dramatic words "My husband!" while he was still too busily occupied with his pleasure to have noticed the third person in the room. For honor's sake he had waited one day in case the injured husband wanted to challenge him. Then he had left.

But why Bath? Of all places in England, Wales, or Scotland that he might have chosen, why had he come to Bath? Just because Aunt Adeline and Uncle Stanley were there and his father had suggested it as a destination? Or for some other reason? Because he had been unconsciously reaching out for something quite new and different, perhaps? Something a little more meaningful than the life he had been living for the past seven or eight years? Ach, what nonsense. Roger sighed again.

His uncle was conversing with two other men as portly as he. All three of them held glasses of the waters. One of them was drinking and showing by his facial contortions that he did so more for his health than for pleasure.

His aunt was talking with a gentleman who must be almost the infant of the gathering. It was possible he had not yet reached his fortieth year. As Roger watched, the man turned and bowed to Emily Richmond, offered his arm, and went promenading off about the room with her.

She was still dressed in gray. She probably wore it always. Her nightgowns were probably gray and enveloped her from her chin to her longest toenail. She probably covered that golden hair with a gray nightcap. Perhaps sometimes she made a daring switch to a different color—brown.

What a waste, Roger thought, his eyes following her as she moved down the room away from him. She had a neat little figure, one that would feel sweet pressed between a man and a mattress. Her hair was the color of sunshine and would doubtless dazzle the eyes of the beholder if it were allowed to appear from beneath the gray bonnet and to be released from that ruthless knot at her neck. Her eyes were thickly lashed and large and an interesting shade of hazel. They were the sort of eyes one could drown in if one allowed oneself to. And her mouth—well, her mouth was eminently kissable.

But she was a virtuous woman. What a dreadful waste! It was not as if she lacked sexuality. There had been a definite something when he had kissed her the day before, a something that he had felt in his loins. But of course it was unvirtuous to show passion, especially with a stranger beneath the stairs. When she finally married, she would probably deny herself all pleasure and lie quite decorously still for her husband.

Well, if she were his, she would not be allowed to get away with it, he thought.

"Psst!"

Confound it, where was the boy?

"Good Lord, Jasper," Roger said, raising his quizzing glass to his eye and turning to the shadowy corner to his left, "What are you doing up at this unholy hour? Does your grandmother drag you here kicking and protesting every day?"

"No, no," Jasper said, "but it is by far the most

entertaining part of the day, Rog. I like to see 'em drinking the water, and I like to see 'em sitting in it up to their necks.'' He indicated the long windows down the left side of the room, which overlooked the King's Bath and the few brave souls whose health demanded more drastic measures than a mere glass of the waters.

"Interesting," Roger said, sounding anything but interested.

"You've been so busy ogling Emmy," Jasper said, "that you haven't even noticed the Langtree woman. There she is in the middle of that cluster of idiots.''

Roger looked and waited patiently for someone to move so that he could see the lady in question. He pursed his lips a few moments later. Ah, yes, a definite attraction, a definite possibility. Her charms were many and obvious. He suspected that the red hair did not owe all its glory to nature, but it was glorious nevertheless. Her clothes were expensive and flamboyant and did nothing to hide the mature charms of her body.

And Jasper had been right again. A man might never look into the face of a woman who was the owner of such a bosom. Who would ever want to raise his eyes higher?

"She's a widow," Jasper said, "and rich. She keeps 'em all dangling on a string, Rog. If I were you, I wouldn't lower myself to be just one of many.''

"I'll keep your advice in mind," Roger said, not removing his eyes from the beauty. He did glance about at her court, too, and noticed that one of her followers was an acquaintance of his. He strolled across the room, acknowledging his aunt in passing—she was conversing with an elderly couple.

"Ah, Poindexter," he said when he had come up with the group, "pleased to see you.''

He was introduced to Mrs. Langtree, though he did nothing to press his attention on her. He was too experienced a player of the game of dalliance to make that mistake. While he talked with Poindexter, he and the lady covertly examined each other. And he was not displeased with the result. She signaled interest in that way experienced women had, without either a word or a significant gesture passing between them.

And he was interested too, though at close quarters he guessed her age to be somewhat closer to forty than thirty. She wore cosmetics, carefully applied. The neck of her peacock-blue dress, daringly low for morning, gave hint of a deep cleavage. At her neck she wore a heavy gold chain with a large gold rose pendant—an expensive bauble given her by the late Mr. Langtree, perhaps. Or by some grateful lover.

Roger took his leave after five minutes. Without once talking to each other beyond the initial greeting, he and the lady had established that they would both be at the Upper Rooms that evening to take tea.

Perhaps this stay in Bath would not be quite the utter bore he had anticipated earlier, after all, Roger thought. He bowed to his aunt and uncle and Miss Richmond, all standing together on the spot where his aunt had been the whole time, and addressed his thoughts and his steps to the White Hart Inn and his breakfast.

Emily watched him go and was glad he had not come closer to talk with Lady Copeland or Lord Westbury. Instead he had been paying court to Mrs. Langtree. Of course. It was thoroughly predictable that he would do so.

Her eyes had followed him unwillingly almost the whole time he was in the room. Perhaps it was because there were so few young men in Bath, she thought. Yes, perhaps that was the reason. If there had been dozens more, then she would not have noticed Mr. Bradshaw at all.

Not much she wouldn't! His form-fitting green coat and biscuit-colored pantaloons and black Hessians left no doubt whatever in the mind that his splendid physique owed nothing at all to padding. And then, of course, there were his thick dark hair and handsome face. Emily sighed at her own foolishness and was pleased to find that Lady Copeland was making a move to leave the Pump Room.

"Time for breakfast," she said firmly, as if someone were about to argue with her. "Come along, Emily, dear. Will you join us, Stanley? And where is Jasper? I hope the dear boy has not got lost."

Jasper was still in his corner, feeling in dire need of his breakfast. But he had observed with interest the way Cousin Roger's eyes had followed Emily about the room and the way hers had later followed him.

Interesting, Jasper thought. Virtuous Emmy and rakish Rog. Very interesting!

Drinking tea at the Upper Assembly Rooms was very little different from drinking tea in one's own or anyone else's drawing room except that it could be done in a more public setting and gave one a fine excuse to don one's evening finery and look critically at everyone else's.

Emily did not possess a great deal of finery. She had with her only two gowns suitable for evening wear, and both were woefully old and sadly unfashionable. But even so, it felt good to change from the drab gowns she wore in the daytime and dress more becomingly.

She was wearing her gold-colored gown and sitting beside Lady Copeland, observing the scene around her. Mrs. Langtree was sitting across the room, holding court to three gentlemen. Emily felt a faint envy.

How did some women do it? she wondered—attract so much male attention, that was. Mrs. Langtree was neither very young nor particularly pretty. She did have a figure, of course. Emily thought rather regretfully of her own slender curves.

Mr. Bradshaw had not yet arrived. Mr. Harris had, and was making his way across the room in the direction of their table. He had paused to pay his respects to a group of acquaintances. He had actually strolled with her that morning and conversed amiably with her the whole while—though quite impersonally. She was not at all sure that he was especially interested in her. Or she in him, for that matter, though that was quite off the point. For Papa's sake, she could not afford to try to choose with her heart.

If there were any choice to make. Emily sighed inwardly. There seemed to be so few eligible gentlemen in Bath.

"Angela has already had two valentines for the ball," Mrs. Krebs was telling Lady Copeland, "and knows very well which two gentlemen sent them. The problem is to know who sent which. Should she wear the heart-shaped brooch, or should she carry the lace handkerchief? It is quite a dilemma, I do assure you, ma'am."

"It would be as well to choose the one she finds prettier, I suppose," Lady Copeland said.

Mrs. Krebs tittered. "Perhaps there will be more," she said. "There is more than a week left."

"One would wager that Mrs. Langtree will have many more than two to choose among," Mrs. Arnold said. "Quite a headache for her, I would guess."

"Have you received a valentine yet, Miss Richmond?" Mrs. Krebs asked.

Emily smiled. "No, ma'am," she said.

"But it is very likely that she will," Lady Copeland said, patting her hand.

It would be so wonderful, Emily thought wistfully. So wonderful to have a card or a note from a gentleman and a request to wear a certain something to show that she was his valentine. She smiled at Mr. Harris as he came up to their table, and listened to him talk with the other ladies. He made no move to converse privately with her.

And her eyes were on Mr. Bradshaw, who had just arrived and was standing beside Mrs. Langtree's table, talking with her. He looked very splendid dressed in silver knee breeches and black velvet coat with a very white neckcloth and white lace over his hands.

Mrs. Langtree would receive a valentine from him, doubtless. And surely she would accept if she knew from whom it came. He was by far the most handsome gentleman in Bath. How wonderful it would be, Emily thought, her mind drifting into a dream of herself in the ballroom, carrying some favor of his, waiting for him to come to claim it and her. He would come to dance with her, and he would smile that crinkle-eyed smile he had given her the day before—was it just yesterday? And he would tell her that he . . .

Emily was jolted back to reality when her eyes met Roger's across the room and she realized both the direction of her thoughts and her ignorance of what was being said at her table.

"I shall hope to see you in the Pump Room in the morning," Mr. Harris said, rising and bowing to all the ladies seated there. He looked directly at Emily and smiled.

Would he send her a valentine? she wondered. And suddenly she wished that the Master of Ceremonies had not had such an idea. For although it was marvelously romantic, it was also cruel to those women who would not receive even a single valentine. And how humiliating it would be to attend the ball if one had nothing from any gentleman to display. She resolved not to go under such circumstances, even if she had to feign a headache on the evening.

"Ah, Aunty," a voice said from behind her shoulder. "I knew as soon as I saw that elegant turban room across the room that it could belong to no one but you. Miss Richmond?"

"Impudent boy," Lady Copeland said fondly. "Sit down, Roger, and have some tea. Let me present you to Mrs. Krebs and Mrs. Arnold."

Roger did not anticipate that sipping tea and gossiping in the Upper Rooms would be a wonderfully exhilarating experience, but when in Bath, he had thought with amused resignation as he dressed carefully for the evening, one must do as the people of Bath did—drink tea.

Perhaps he would have avoided the entertainment had he not had a definite purpose in going. But he did. Without either word or sign, he and Eugenia Langtree had agreed to meet there.

He approached her table with a feeling of some self-mockery. His tastes did not normally run to women ten years his senior or to those of voluptuous charms. He preferred women of more subtle appeal. But if Bath was to be bearable for a few weeks, he needed some diversion—some long-lasting diversion. The pleasure of bedding this particular woman would have to be worked for. She knew the game as well as he and would not give herself for the asking. He would find amusement in the challenge.

"Do you plan to attend the Valentine's Ball, sir?" she asked him after both of them had spoken only with the other gentlemen about her for a few minutes. Her voice was low and seductive. She glanced up at him provocatively from beneath darkened lashes.

"Only if I can feel persuaded that it will bring me some, ah, enjoyment, ma'am," he said, returning look for look.

She smiled and turned her attention to another of her admirers. Never more than a hint at a time. The woman played the game well.

He would send her a valentine the next day. He glanced to the bare flesh above her bosom, where the gold rose still hung on its heavy chain. Yes, he could be content to play the game for nine days more. Then, though, he would expect some reward, some action.

He did not realize that his gaze had shifted to a table across the room until he found himself locking eyes with Emily Richmond. She lowered hers immediately.

Well, he had been wrong. She did not always wear gray, it seemed. That gown she was wearing was thoroughly virginal, with a neckline that ended in a small frill beneath her chin, and long, straight sleeves. And it certainly followed none of the current fashions that he was aware of. But the dull gold of its color, matched with the shining gold of her hair, made her look rather like an angel. A pale angel.

He felt a certain breathlessness, looking at her. And yet again a regret. For he had not mistaken the matter. He was experienced enough with women to know that there would be no assailing the virtue of Miss Emily Richmond. She would give herself—or part of herself—on her wedding night, and not a moment sooner. And he had no interest in wedding nights.

He must pay his respects to his aunt, he thought as he strolled across the room. But after doing so he found himself with the unspeakable pleasure of sitting at a table with four women for the following ten minutes, making conversation with them—or with three of them, to be exact. Emily Richmond sat mute to the left of him. And to his astonishment, he found that he could not turn his head easily and include her in the conversation. He totally ignored her, just as if she had not been the main reason for his seating himself there.

He was behaving like a gauche schoolboy!

"Roger," Lady Copeland said at the end of the ten minutes, "you may call my carriage, dear. It is time to go home."

He jumped to his feet, glad to put an end to the evening. He was back five minutes later, offering to escort his aunt and Miss Richmond to the waiting carriage.

But confound his aunt, he thought two minutes after that. Did she know every single person in Bath? And must she pause to exchange pleasantries with every last one of them on her way out? She waved him and Emily on, declaring that she would be with them in just a moment.

He took the girl on his arm and escorted her outside. The cloak she had donned, he was satisfied to see, was gray. Her hand on his arm was as slim as the rest of her, her fingers long, her fingernails short and well-manicured.

And what the deuce was he to talk about with a virtuous girl he had tried to seduce just the day before?

"Have you lived all your life in the country?" he asked her abruptly. What a profound question!

She looked up at him with those eyes he had already conceded it possible to drown in.

"Yes," she said, "every moment of it until one month ago, when I came here with Lady Copeland."

"And were you sorry to leave your home?" he asked.

She thought for a moment, as if she considered her answer of some importance. The girl clearly was not used to the shallowness of polite conversation. "I think more sorry to realize that I have grown up than to leave home," she said. "I am the eldest of eight children and it was time to step out on my own and make my own life. That was a little sad and a little frightening."

"Was yours a happy home?" he asked.

"Yes." She smiled and looked down at her hands. "Yes, very."

"If you have lived with parents and seven brothers and sisters," he said, "you must find your life here very bleak."

"Oh, no," she said, looking up at him sharply. "Lady Copeland has been very kind to me. And life is never dull with Jasper."

He chuckled. "Has he told you of the time when he cut the tassels from my Hessians?" he asked. "Sparkling white tassels from *new* Hessians, I might add. I was inordinately proud of them."

"No," she said, her eyes laughing up into his. "Did you catch him?"

"I did," he said, "and when I had finished with him, I believe he did not know if it would be less painful to remain absolutely still or to try dancing a Highland fling."

"Oh, dear," she said, laughing, "he committed the worst of all sins—he got caught. I shall have to take him home with me for a while to learn some lessons from my brothers. Particularly Gregory."

"Do you miss them?" he asked her.

The smile faded from her eyes and she nodded abruptly. "Yes," she said.

She was looking at her hands again and he knew that she had suddenly become aware that she was alone with a rake. He wanted to reach out a hand to touch hers and assure her that he would do her no harm. He clasped his hands behind him instead and noticed her shiver from the cold. He stepped to his right to shield her from the wind.

Where the blazes was his confounded aunt? And since when had he found it difficult to make conversation?

"May I hand you into the carriage?" he said on sudden inspiration. "It will be warmer inside."

"Thank you," she said, and put her hand in his. It was icy cold.

Well, at least, he thought, she had had a happy childhood with a large family. Even if she was impoverished and forced to work for her living now, she had had that. His only brother had died with his mother of smallpox years and years ago, and he had not seen a great deal of his father after that. Only tutors and schools and valets.

She had that, at least. And talking about her family had made her face light up with warmth and humor and affection. But poor girl. The very happiness of her childhood and girlhood must make life harder for her now. He released her hand and reached for a carriage robe to tuck about her.

"So sorry to have kept you waiting, dears," Lady Copeland said from behind him.

Yes, he was sorry too. *"Have* you kept us waiting?" he said. "It has seemed the merest moment. Good night, Aunty." He kissed her cheek and helped her into the carriage. "Miss Richmond?"

"Good night," she said softly from the shadows of the coach.

The following day was a fine one, the sky an almost clear blue, the wind a mere breeze, and the sun almost warm for the time of year. Half the residents of Bath, it seemed, converged on Sydney Gardens during the afternoon.

Jasper was strolling along one of the paths, trailing along in the wake of his grandmother and great-uncle, Roger and Emily. They were paired up that way, too. Jasper had watched in glee the discomfiture of Roger and the dismay of Emily when they had realized that they must walk together, her arm drawn through his.

It was great sport. Jasper slunk into the shadow of a bush for a moment while his grandmother paused briefly to greet an acquaintance—he did not fancy being chucked under the chin by yet another elderly lady and called sweet with his red hair and round face and freckles. *Sweet!* Jasper shuddered. His mother was the one to blame, with her bright red tresses.

Yes, it was great sport. It was as clear as the nose on his face that the two of them fancied each other. Except that Emmy was not at all Rog's type, nor he hers. It would serve Rog right, too, if she could net him somehow. Parson's mousetrap would be fitting punishment for that humiliating thrashing the summer before—Rog had not even had the decency to bend him over a chair, but had taken him over his knee. "Spanking" was the humiliating word that leapt to mind. Yes, it would serve him right.

Of course, Emmy deserved better. Except that there was no better in Bath. There was that Harris fellow, of course, who fancied her but kept his distance. But he was far too old and poker-faced for Emmy. She deserved someone more to her liking. Rog? He was handsome, of course. Jasper would kill for looks like that when he grew up, especially that careless lock of dark hair over the eyebrow. And Rog had been his idol until he had proved himself to be a man without a trace of humor over those silly tassels.

Ah, well. Jasper scuffed his feet through some loose

stones on the path. Sometimes he thought life would be more interesting if he were at school. Rog had told him earlier that he wanted to see him before he went home. What was that all about? he wondered.

Lady Copeland stopped for a lengthy gossip with two ladies and then announced to her hangers-on that she was returning for tea with Lady Harper and Miss Harper. Stanley must come with her. But there would be no room for the others in Lady Harper's carriage. Would dear Roger be so good as to see Emily and Jasper home?

"It would be my pleasure, Aunty," Roger said.

"There will be no need at all for anyone to accompany us," Emily said brightly. "Jasper and I will be each other's chaperons."

They both looked rather as if a noose had been placed about their necks, Jasper thought, glancing from one to the other. His grandmother and great-uncle were already disappearing along the path.

"Take us for cakes before we go home, Rog?" Jasper asked.

"You'll be popping right out of your clothes if you eat many more, my lad," Roger said.

"I really must be getting home," Emily said simultaneously.

"Please, Rog?"

Roger looked at Emily. "Shall we humor him?" he asked her.

"Please, Emmy?"

She hesitated. "On condition that I hear not one whisper about a stomach pain for the next week," she said, smiling at him.

Jasper marched ahead of them on the long walk to his favorite confectioner's on Milsom Street. They said scarce a word to each other, he noticed, except to make foolish comments on the weather and even more foolish comments on the houses and carriages they passed on the way. Silly pair.

He took mercy on them during tea, telling them between bites of the three cakes he wheedled out of Roger all the hair-raising scrapes he had got into at school.

"I'm surprised you have ever had a chance to get into trouble at school, Jas," Roger said. "I thought you were always too sickly to attend."

"Naw," the boy said. "I'm there all term when Papa is home. I'd have to have the pox before Papa would let me stay away."

"Your papa has just gone up in my esteem," Roger said dryly.

But conversation was no longer labored and stilted. Roger told a few stories of his own from university days, and Emily talked about her brothers and sisters and their escapades—and some of her own.

"It must be great to be part of a large family," Jasper said wistfully.

"Yes, it must," Roger said at the same moment as Emily said, "Yes, it is."

"You have a crumb on your chin, Em," Jasper said.

He watched her turn scarlet as she brushed ineffectually at the wrong side of her chin. And he watched with even greater interest as Roger took his napkin and brushed the crumb away for her. Poor Emmy, he thought. If there were a brighter color than scarlet, she would be it.

Roger insisted on walking all the way back uphill to the Circus with them, though Emily protested that there was no need for him to do so. His eyes followed her as she ran lightly up the stairs when they were inside the house, and he turned to Jasper and drew a folded sheet of paper from an inner pocket.

"Would you care to make a delivery for me, Jasper?" he asked. "I'll make it worth your while."

"A sovereign?" Jasper said.

"Half."

"It's one of those stupid valentines, I suppose," Jasper said. "The stationers are probably doing a roaring trade these days."

"It's a valentine," Roger said, "for Mrs. Langtree. You know where she lives?"

"On Great Pulteney Street," Jasper said.

"On no account must you say who sent it," Roger said. "And ask if you are to wait for an answer. Will you do it?"

"I suppose," Jasper said, taking the paper in one hand and holding out the other, palm-up. "Payment in advance, though."

"Fair enough," Roger said, digging into a pocket and coming out with half a sovereign. "Today or tomorrow at the latest?"

"Trust me," Jasper said.

Five minutes later, after Roger had gone and he was safely snug behind the aspidistra plant, Jasper was delighted to find that the paper was not sealed but only folded over four times. Dear Rog. He had obviously forgotten what it was like to be twelve years old. Jasper unfolded the paper.

"My fair Golden Rose," he read. Great Jupiter, but any self-respecting schoolboy could be excused for wanting to vomit.

My fair golden rose,
    You must know how I admire you, how affected I was by your beauty at the Pump Room yesterday morning, and how dazzled by your loveliness at the Upper Rooms last evening. You must know why I can think of you only as my golden rose, though the word "my" is doubtless presumptuous. Will you be my valentine at next week's ball? Is it too much to expect—to hope—that you will single me out from all others?

Will you make me the happiest of men by wearing a real golden rose for me if I send it you on the day? I am, madam, your anxiously awaiting servant.

Really, Jasper thought, it was too embarrassing even to be funny. But he tittered anyway and held his nose—one never knew when old poker-face, the butler, might appear in the hallway and shoo him upstairs to the schoolroom. Old Rog! Old Rog and his golden rose.

Mrs. Langtree a golden rose? Jasper frowned. He could not quite see the logic of the name. Now, if it were Emmy . . .

If it were Emmy. Jasper read quickly through the letter again. Great Jupiter, it could be Emmy too. It could well be.

He folded the paper, stuck it none too reverently into a pocket, and sat back against the wall, his knees drawn up to his chest. He frowned in thought and then grinned. If it were Emmy, indeed.

It would serve Rog right, too.

Emily was getting ready to accompany Lady Copeland to a concert that evening at the home of Mrs. Adler in Sydney Place. Her blue dress would have to do, she thought, staring at it in the mirror and brushing absently at her hair. It was at least a little more fashionable than the gold, with its scoop neckline and short puffed sleeves.

She piled her hair on top of her head with both hands and pulled a few strands free to frame her face. No, it would not do. She was not attending any entertainment to draw attention to herself. She brushed the hair smooth again.

She had turned female heads that afternoon, all right. But only because she had been on the arm of the most handsome gentleman in Bath. And she had been so tongue-tied and so uncomfortable that she had not been able to enjoy the sensation at all.

And that crumb on her chin! Could Jasper not have made discreet gestures so that only she and he would have known the dreadful truth? Drat the boy. But then Mr. Bradshaw had doubtless noticed already and had been laughing inwardly at her.

Oh, dear, she must not think of Mr. Bradshaw. Not again.

There was a scratching at her door.

"Come in," she called, and Jasper's head appeared around it.

"Are you decent, Emmy?" he asked. "I have something for you, and I didn't think you would want Grandmama to see it."

"What do you have?" she asked, setting her brush down on the dressing table and smiling at him.

"This," he said, holding up a folded piece of paper and waving it in the air. "I think it's one of those valentines, Em."

"For me?" she asked foolishly. "But who gave it to you?" She reached out her hand.

"Aw, I'm not allowed to say, Emmy. It's all a secret, remember?" he said.

"It's from Mr. Harris, isn't it?" she said, looking closely at him. "He gave it you to give me."

"My lips are sealed," Jasper said.

"Provoking boy," she said. "It's from Mr. Harris. There is no one else it could be from. It is from him, isn't it?"

Jasper shrugged. "Perhaps he signed it," he said. "Perhaps he broke the rules and signed it."

She unfolded the paper hastily and glanced to the end of the letter. "He didn't," she said, lowering it to her lap. "Oh, Jasper, are you sure he said to give it to me? Are you quite sure?"

"There is only one Emily Richmond that I know," Jasper said. "If you have an answer, I'm supposed to take it tomorrow morning. I'll see you, Emmy." And he whisked himself from the room.

Emily sat with the paper in her lap. A valentine. She had had a valentine. From Mr. Harris. She was so happy, she could have danced about the room. She did not do so, but spread the paper on her lap and smoothed her fingers over the folds. She had begun to think that perhaps he was not interested in her after all. That morning he had not come near either her or Lady Copeland in the Pump Room.

She had not been unduly upset. Try as she would, she could not feel any real enthusiasm over a possible relationship with the man. But to have a valentine! To have one gentleman in Bath single her out for public attention at the ball! But she must not jump to conclusions. Perhaps it was not a valentine after all. Perhaps Jasper had misunderstood. She lowered her eyes to the paper, half-afraid to read.

Large, bold handwriting. Not quite what she would have expected from neat Mr. Harris. Golden rose. She could feel her heart thumping. Fair golden rose. He admired her beauty. Was she beautiful? She would know why he thought of her as his golden rose, he wrote. Did she?

Emily looked up and stared unseeing at the back of the door. Her old gown? Her hair perhaps? Had she looked like a golden rose to him? She smiled slowly. What a lovely compliment. A golden rose. She liked it.

Would she be his valentine? Would she wear a real golden rose of his at the ball? But where would he get a real rose in February?

Mr. Harris was quite a romantic after all. She would not have suspected it. And he admired her. He must be a little like her, she thought, shy in company. Not that she was shy by nature, but she was unused to life in a town and unused to life as a servant. He must be plain shy. Oh, he could hold a polite conversation, it was true. But he must find it difficult to express his feelings in words.

He did very well on paper. Would she be his valentine? Oh, yes, indeed she would. On the night of the ball, everyone would see her carrying his golden rose and would know that one gentleman had singled her out for his gallantry. They would see him claim her hand for a dance and claim his rose.

Oh, she did not care that he was dull Mr. Harris. She did not care at all. She would be going to the ball, and she would be carrying a gentleman's favor. She must reply. But what would she say?

And what time was it? She was going to keep Lady Copeland waiting if she did not hurry. She folded the letter carefully and laid it inside her jewelry case. Then she lifted her brush again and pulled it ruthlessly through her hair.

Her *golden* hair. Golden rose. She smiled at her reflection.

Roger did not stay long in the Pump Room the following morning. Jasper, he was pleased to discover, was hiding away in his usual corner and extracted a crumpled note from about his person when asked for it. He held firmly to it, though, until Roger had paid him another half-sovereign.

"It's a good thing I don't intend to set up a clandestine correspondence with the lady," Roger said. "I would be a beggar in no time. Have you been paid double, Jasper? Did Mrs. Langtree pay you too?"

"No," Jasper said.

"Did she know you?" Roger asked. He hoped so,

as he had no intention of allowing the lady to remain in the dark about his identity.

"Don't know," Jasper said.

"A word of advice, Jas," Roger said. "Go home and back to bed, and when you get up later, get out on the other side of the bed."

He missed Jasper's smile of glee as he turned away.

Roger strolled out into the Pump Yard and wandered toward the abbey. The game was progressing well, but he did not want to approach Eugenia Langtree until he had read her letter. He lifted it to his nose. Surprisingly, it was not perfumed. He had expected it to be. The paper was not sealed. He opened it and looked down at it. She had a small, neat hand—another surprise.

> Dear Sir,
>   I was honored to receive your letter yesterday and will be even more honored to be your valentine at the ball next week and to carry your rose. I shall look forward eagerly to the occasion.
>
>   Golden Rose

Roger chuckled as he folded it again. What a strange, formal little note for the woman to write. Mrs. Langtree honored? And eager? The words did not quite ring true.

Of course, she had probably had a dozen such notes and was being cautious until she had somehow worked out in her mind just which had come from whom. It was time to enlighten her—without breaking any rules, of course. He reentered the Pump Room.

She was surrounded by her usual court. But this morning she went so far as to present him with a languid hand, which he raised to his lips.

"Bath becomes tedious, Mr. Bradshaw," she said. "Will this ball liven our spirits, do you suppose?"

"I imagine it will be all we hope it will be, ma'am," he said, looking very directly into her eyes. He reached out a hand and touched briefly with one finger the pendant on its chain about her neck. "A distinctive work of art," he said, looking back up into her eyes. "A gold rose. You wear it always, ma'am?"

Something flickered in her eyes. "It is a pity it cannot be red, is it not?" she said. "But the goldsmith's art does not extend to any other color."

"But how could one improve on gold?" he said. "It is an exquisite rose, whatever the color."

She smiled at him. He bowed and turned away. And saw Emily Richmond at the other side of the room, standing beside his aunt.

Ah, she wore dark green today. It suited her, though as usual the outfit was not in the height of fashion. Not that she needed to be in fashion. She would look quite exquisite in a sack. He looked at her with even more regret than he had felt two evenings before as he approached her. For although she was a virtuous woman, she was not a mute and a dull one as he had first thought. There was a sweetness and a brightness hidden only just beyond the surface of her demure manner.

He had seen it the day before when they had taken tea with Jasper. She had laughed and been genuinely amused at both Jasper's stories and his own. He would have expected her to be disapproving. Of course, she had also made that comment the night before about Jasper having committed the unpardonable sin of getting caught in his misdeed. The stories she had told of her own family had been ones of mischief. And her face had been full of fun and animation—until that ass Jasper had spoiled it all by drawing attention to the cake crumb on her chin. He had been enjoying the mental image of himself leaning forward to kiss it off.

"Good morning, Aunty," he said as he came up to them, raising a careless hand to indicate that he did not wish to interrupt her conversation with two ladies. "Good morning, Miss Richmond."

"Good morning," she said.

But she was her prim and demure self again, despite the becoming green outfit. He took his leave of her after just a couple of minutes.

Sweet little Emmy. It was a shame that circumstances had forced her away from her family. Some fortunate man should marry her one of these days and start giving her children of her own. He surprised himself with the stab of jealousy he felt for the unknown man.

Emily was out shopping two days later with her employer when, as often happened, Lady Copeland met some acquaintances and was borne off to take tea with them. Since they already had several parcels to carry, Emily was excused and left to return home alone.

She really did not mind, even though she had five parcels to stumble along with, two of them quite bulky. For one thing, one of the parcels was hers. When Lady Copeland had heard that she had received a valentine, she had insisted on buying Emily a domino and mask for the ball.

"There is no question at all of hiding one's identity, of course," she had said. "That is not the point of masked balls. The point is to look mysterious. What color would you like, dear?"

Emily had chosen a midnight blue to wear over her gold-colored gown. She had been relieved to find that Lady Copeland was not annoyed with her but really very pleased indeed.

"I cannot think who it can be," she had said, "but

obviously you have a secret admirer, dear. We will hope that he will be eligible.''

"Mr. Harris?" Emily had suggested.

But Lady Copeland had frowned. "I think not, dear," she had said.

But it had to be Mr. Harris. There was no one else. At least, she thought rather wistfully, no one else who would wish to make such a public statement of admiration for her. There had been someone eager to seduce her on one occasion, of course.

There was another reason why she did not mind being left to carry the shopping home. She had been presented with a rare afternoon to herself. She did not have to return home immediately. Even Jasper was not with her. He had gone riding with Lord Westbury. She turned her footsteps toward the abbey. It was her very favorite place in all of Bath.

It was as she was stepping out of the abbey an hour later that Roger ran almost headlong into her.

"Don't tell me," he said. "That is Miss Richmond behind all the bandboxes. And let me guess again. Every last one of them belongs to my aunt, and she has abandoned you to carry them up the hill to the Circus alone.''

She smiled, he was interested to note. "One of them is mine," she said.

"Is it?" he said. "This one?" He took the largest bandbox from her and dangled it from one finger by its pink ribbon.

"No," she said.

"This one, then." He took the other bandbox from her and dangled it from his other hand.

"No," she said, indicating one of the smaller parcels. "This one."

He inserted one of his forefingers through the ribbon loops of both boxes and held them at his side. He offered his free arm to Emily. Why miss an opportunity that had been offered to him on a platter? Eugenia was still playing games with him, and undoubtedly would until the night of the ball. When he had taken her walking in Sydney Gardens earlier, two of the rest of her court had also arrived there, clearly by prearrangement.

When she had taken an arm of each of them, he had remembered another appointment and taken his leave of her, and she had looked at him with approval. He was not accustomed to being only one of several strings to a bow and had no intention of becoming accustomed to it.

Emily was flustered. He intended to escort her home? She would be alone with him for half an hour?

"We do not have Jasper here to play chaperon," he said when he saw her hesitation. "But in the open street I believe you can feel safe, ma'am. I am unlikely to attack you in a public place."

She flushed. He was laughing at her. She took his arm—and felt her breath quicken. What could she talk about?

"What shall we talk about?" he asked. "The weather?"

They talked about it for a few minutes.

"That exhausts that," he said when silence fell between them. "What next? The beauty of Bath? It is lovely, is it not? Do you not admire it excessively?"

They talked about it for a few more minutes.

Roger was amused. She was so obviously uncomfortable to be in company with a rake, no one else with them to support part of the conversation. He might have felt the discomfort too, as he had a few evenings before outside the Upper Rooms. But there were daylight and sunshine today, and they were walking, not merely standing still awaiting the arrival of his aunt. And he was content to feel the pull of an attraction to her.

But he wished there were some way to get past that quiet, demure manner that she wore as a mask. He wished he could see her laughing and talking again, her eyes full of life and merriment, as they had been at the confectioner's when they had had Jasper with them.

"Are you going to tell me what is in your parcel?" he asked. "Something frivolous, I hope. Or is it an unmentionable?"

Emily felt herself flushing at his final words. What if it had been? How embarrassed she would be. But being reminded of the parcel lifted her spirits. She smiled down at it.

"It's a domino," she said, "and a mask."

"Ah," he said, "then you are going to the ball, are you?"

"Yes," she said.

He looked down at her. And quite unwittingly he had accomplished what he had been wanting to do. She was looking glowingly happy, breathtakingly lovely.

"You are to be someone's valentine?" he asked.

She looked up at him, and he felt that familiar drowning sensation. "Yes," she said.

He could sense the suppressed excitement in her. She looked quite radiant. He felt a surge of gladness for her. And a surge of something else too—envy. Jealousy.

"And who is the fortunate gentleman?" he asked.

"Oh, I don't know," she said. "His letter was anonymous."

"But you can guess?" he asked.

She smiled at him again. "Yes," she said.

"If you are to be at the ball," he said, "I will have

a chance to dance with you. Will you reserve a set for me, Miss Richmond? Or is your card full already?''

She laughed. ''Oh, no,'' she said.

She had never been any good at flirtation. She should not, of course, have admitted that she knew from whom her valentine came. She should have made it seem as if it might have come from any of a number of admirers. And she ought not to have admitted so quickly and emphatically that her dancing card was not full—indeed it was quite, quite empty.

Except that it was no longer so. He had asked for one set. Mr. Bradshaw. The most handsome gentleman in Bath or even in all England, perhaps. How she envied Mrs. Langtree. The lady would doubtless have many valentines, but somehow surely she would find out which was his and choose it. How could she not?

How wonderful it would be to be Mr. Bradshaw's valentine. Except, she thought, sobering, being such would doubtless involve something quite different from a mere dance and a reclaiming of his favor and perhaps an offer of marriage a few days later. She could imagine very well what he would expect of Mrs. Langtree if she chose to be his valentine. She flushed at the thought.

It was doubtless Harris, Roger thought. He had not seen any other man hanging about her. Harris. He was too old for her. Too dull. She deserved better. Who? Himself? His lip curled into a smile of self-mockery.

He might have sent his valentine to her instead of to Eugenia, with whom he had no interest in anything beyond a good bedding. He might have given Harris some competition. But no. It would be too dangerous to play with the affections of someone like Emily Richmond. It was far safer to stick with a game whose rules and methods he knew from long experience.

Dangerous? he thought, frowning. Dangerous for whom? For her, certainly. And for himself?

When they reached the house on the Circus, Roger went inside with Emily and deposited the two bandboxes on a table in the hallway. The butler, who had opened the door for them, shambled back to the servants' quarters again.

"There," Roger said, "my good deed is done for this week." He grinned at her. "What? No Jasper? He is not hiding behind the aspidistra, is he?"

"Oh," she said, smiling, "you know about that hiding place, do you? No, Lord Westbury took him riding."

She had set her parcels on top of his as she spoke, and untied the strings of her bonnet. She pulled it off her head. But somehow the back of it caught in the pins that held her hair in its knot at her neck. There was a tinkling as several pins fell to the tiles, and her hair cascaded down about her shoulders.

Roger, standing a mere couple of feet from her, felt as if a fist had just caught him in the chest, robbing him of breath. It was pure gold silk. And suddenly she was transformed before his eyes from a prim and lovely lady to a beautiful and voluptuous woman.

"Oh," she said ineffectually. She was transfixed by the look in his eyes, unable to think clearly enough to move.

"Golden silk," he said huskily, lifting a hand to take one lock between a thumb and forefinger. "Emmy, what a crime to keep it so disguised." His eyes strayed to her lips. She licked them as she had once before.

But before he could lose his head entirely, she lifted her arms sharply and caught back her hair. "The pins came out," she said foolishly.

He stooped down, picked them up from the floor,

and set them in her outstretched palm. "An embarrassment to make you forget about the crumb on your chin, doubtless," he said, grinning at her. "Good day to you, Miss Richmond."

He let himself out of the front door. Thank goodness she had moved when she had, he thought, taking several deep breaths of fresh air. He would have made an ass of himself by kissing her again. But not in the way he had kissed her before, exploring, asking with his mouth if she was seducible. He knew she was not seducible. He would have kissed her with genuine desire, genuine affection.

Good Lord, had he really called her Emmy? Jasper's name for her? He hoped she had been too embarrassed to notice. What the devil had he been about, going all to pieces merely because her hair had fallen down?

Emily stood in the hallway holding her hair back with one hand and stabbing at it with the pins in the other. She had been inviting his kiss. She had been standing there foolishly, her hair all about her, knowing that he was about to kiss her, and wanting it. Had she turned thoroughly wanton?

She frowned suddenly, and her hands paused about their futile task. He had called her Emmy. Not even Emily, but Emmy. Papa's name for her and Jasper's. He *had* called her Emmy, hadn't he? She had not imagined it?

Roger had six golden roses delivered to his hotel room the morning of the ball—at an exorbitant cost, considering the fact that it was February and not June. He had ordered six so that he might be sure that at least one of them would be the exquisite bloom he hoped for.

He was looking forward to the evening, though not with quite the warm anticipation he had expected. The truth was that he was restless to be gone from Bath. Perhaps he would have left already if he had not sent that valentine and received an affirmative reply. Now he must stay, at least for tonight, and probably for a few days longer.

He had no doubt that he would spend the night with Eugenia Langtree, and that would doubtless whet his appetite for a few more such nights.

He had no fear of failure. She had accepted his valentine and doubtless knew that it was his. Both of them had made several veiled references to roses during the past few days, though each of them had kept the rules and had not come out quite into the open. He had spoken of sculptured gold pendants and she of red roses, her favorites.

They were coming close to ending the game and having at each other with all the energy they had kept carefully leashed for more than a week. A few times in the past few days she had sent away her other admirers on some pretext and granted him a few minutes of her time. Never longer. If she did not move away from him after that time, then he moved away from her. Appetites grew greater with abstention or the merest nibbling at desired foods, he had found from experience.

And yet for all the success of his endeavors and for all the closeness of the final consummation, there was a certain flatness about the game that he had been experiencing with disturbing regularity over the past several months. What was the point? he asked himself in unguarded moments. He would bed Eugenia until they were both sated, and then he would move on to another woman. And nothing significant would have happened beyond the beddings themselves. His conversations with the woman would be as light and insubstantial as they always were with his mistresses and casual amours.

On the whole, he thought, looking carefully at all six roses and selecting the one he would send with Jasper when the boy saw fit to put in an appearance, he would be quite happy to have the evening over and done with.

There was a knock on his door.

"Come in," he called, and Jasper came breezing in.

"I say, Rog," he said, seeing the open box of roses, "are you going to have six of 'em? They'll be scratching one another's eyes out, won't they?"

Roger grinned. "It would not have done," he said, "to have ordered only one, just to find that it was withered and scrawny. What would the lady think?"

"I see your point," Jasper said. "So I'm to take one to the Langtree woman? This will cost you a whole sovereign, I suppose you realize."

"And another when you come to report that the lady accepted it, I suppose?" Roger said dryly.

"Naw," Jasper said. "I'm not greedy, Rog."

"On your way, then," Roger said, placing the single rose alone into the box and setting a small card beside it.

He watched the door of his room long after Jasper had disappeared through it, slamming it behind him. He wished it were going to a different woman, one more suited to the romance of the occasion. He wished there were not just sex to look forward to, but romance.

One corner of his mouth lifted in self-derision. Romance? Him? He had always scorned any such thing, and carefully avoided any situation that might lead any lady to think he was romancing her. Any woman with whom he had ever consorted had known that romance was the very last thing on his mind. Sex pure and simple—his only object in his dealings with women.

And was he now dreaming of romance just because it was St. Valentine's Day and there was to be a masked ball that evening and he had just sent a real rose to his valentine? Somehow the occasion and the rose seemed wasted on Eugenia Langtree—and on his own intentions toward her.

If it were Emmy, now . . . He should put the thought from him without more ado. But it was too sweet to think of her and what might have been. What might have been if he had been a different sort of man, if he were more the type who might be worthy of her. Or if he had approached her differently from the start. He could not now imagine how he could have looked at her that first day and thought that perhaps she would be available for dalliance.

He had seen her a fair number of times in the past few days and had even sat beside her for a whole segment of an evening concert. He could not now recall who the performers were. His attention had been taken up entirely with the woman who had sat quietly enthralled at his side. There had been none of the restlessness that was common in women—and men, he supposed—when forced to sit through a musical recital: no playing with a curl or a fan, no looking about to see who else was present, no attempt to hold a whispered conversation either with him or with his uncle at her other side. Just total concentration on the music.

So very typical of Emmy.

He was quite in love with her.

Roger looked down at the five roses in his hand and began to rearrange them absently. Where had that thought come from? And what a ridiculous thought! He did not believe in love. He would not recognize love if it formed itself into a fist and punched him in the nose.

But he was in love with Emmy. How very stupid of him. It was high time he left Bath. Perhaps after all he would satisfy himself with one night in Eugenia's arms and take himself off the next day—while he still had some traces of his sanity left.

It was an anxious day for Emily. The letter Mr. Harris had written was clear enough—she had read it many times. And her answer had been clear. It had been delivered—she had asked Jasper. It was foolish, then, to worry that nothing would be delivered to her that day. No golden rose. Of course it would come.

But he had behaved no differently to her since writing that letter than he had before. A few times at the Pump Room he had greeted her and talked with Lady Copeland and Lord Westbury. Once at the library he had paused to recommend to her a book she had just withdrawn from a shelf. And one afternoon on the Crescent he had taken her on his arm and strolled with her for five minutes.

But there had not been a flicker of a sign that she was more than an acquaintance, no hint that he had written that note to her inviting her to be his valentine. No hint that to him she was his golden rose.

Of course he could do none of those things. There were the rules, which most gentlemen would keep, out of a sense of honor and of fun.

But even so, she had looked with some unease all week for something in his manner that would indicate a fondness for her. She had seen nothing.

Of course, it was foolish to believe that he was planning to make her an offer just because of that letter. The Valentine's Ball was merely an entertainment, the invitations and the favors merely a game to brighten up the dull ending of winter. It was foolish to expect more than just a pleasant evening.

And did she want more? She felt a certain cringing from the thought of marrying Mr. Harris. There was something almost cold-blooded in contemplating marriage with a man she scarcely knew and for whom she felt no tenderness at all, merely because she was the eldest daughter of an impoverished family and must marry or spend her life in employment.

But if the rose would only come, she thought, pacing her room while waiting for her hair to dry, then at least she would be saved from humiliation. Lady Copeland knew that she was to be someone's valentine. And of course Jasper knew. And oh, dear, Mr. Bradshaw knew too. She had told him so.

The rose must come.

She spun around to face the door when there was a light knock, and schooled her voice to calmness as she called to whoever was on the other side of it to come in. Jasper's head appeared.

"Are you decent, Em?" he asked. "I've got something for you."

She felt her whole body sag with relief. "What is it?" she asked.

He whisked his hand from behind his back and held out a long white box to her. "This," he said, "from a certain gentleman who wishes to remain anonymous." He grinned cheekily.

"Oh," she said, "already? It is only early afternoon yet."

"See you later, Em," Jasper said. "I have to go and hide. Grandmama has this strange notion that my hair needs cutting." He was gone.

Emily scarcely noticed his leaving. She opened the box with trembling fingers. Oh, it was exquisite. Quite exquisite. One large golden bud nestled among dark green leaves. She lifted it almost reverently from the box, thinking to take it to the washstand and stand it in the water jug until the evening. But she paused. There was a card in the box.

That large, bold handwriting again:

My fair golden rose,
    Wear this for me at the ball if you have a care for my happiness. I anticipate a night to outdo all other nights.

She smiled and held the card to her heart. Oh, it was so very romantic. Surely the man must have depths of feeling that she had not seen on casual acquaintance. Surely tonight and in the coming days he would reveal that hidden side of himself and she would feel with him what she felt now merely holding his rose in one hand and his card in the other.

She continued to hold the card after she had put the rose in water. If only, she thought, wandering to the window and gazing sightlessly out on the sweeping circle of tall houses surrounding the central garden of the Circus. If only it could have been from someone else. And if only that someone else could have been a different kind of man. And if only she could have been someone of more social significance, not just a lady's companion.

How silly she was to have fallen in love with him, to have come to live for those almost-daily and all-too-brief sights of him. How very foolish and rustic of her. For if she had only had a little more experience of town and society, surely she would not have done something quite so naive as to fall in love with a libertine.

But no matter, she thought with a sigh, turning to prop the card on the table beside her bed. At least she was acting with good sense even if her heart was going its own foolish way.

Golden Rose. She must concentrate on that. She was going to be Mr. Harris' golden rose that evening. And now it was certain. She did not have to feel any more anxiety. His rose had arrived and was even now standing in water on her washstand.

Emily twirled into a sudden pirouette on the carpet and then laughed self-consciously at herself, just as if she had an audience.

Lady Copeland was always a punctual person. She and Emily were almost the first to arrive in the ballroom at the Upper Assembly Rooms. Emily felt fit to bursting with suppressed excitement. She was wearing her dark blue domino over her gold-colored evening gown, and the matching blue mask. Lady Copeland's maid had styled her hair, piling it high on her head and allowing curls to trail along her neck and over her temples.

The rosebud, now just beginning to open, had been threaded into her hair. There had been a discussion in the downstairs salon about what she should do with it. It would be too awkward to carry it, since there was to be dancing. When pinned to her domino, at Lady Copeland's suggestion, it weighted down the fabric. Everyone had a good laugh at Jasper's suggestion that she carry its stem between her teeth. Finally it was decided that she would wear it in her hair.

She felt pretty for the first time in a long while. For four years, since she was sixteen, she had been much admired at home. And there had been those two marriage proposals. But somehow when one became a lady's companion, at least in Bath, one became virtually invisible. She had not once felt pretty until this evening.

There was very little danger of being a wallflower at one of the Bath assemblies. The Master of Ceremonies was meticulous about his job of finding partners for all the young ladies. So Emily danced with Julius Caesar and with a Cavalier and a Viking warrior.

She noticed Mr. Harris' arrival—he was not dressed in any costume—and looked eagerly across the ballroom toward him. But he did not immediately approach either her or Lady Copeland. There was no hurry, though. The gentlemen were not to reclaim their favors or unmask their ladies until much later in the evening.

In the meantime it was entertaining to look around at the other ladies to see what favors they had about them. Some were obvious—lace handkerchiefs, peacock fans, posies of flowers. Others perhaps wore earrings or brooches or necklaces sent by their valentines.

Mrs. Langtree carried a single long-stemmed red rose in her hand. It looked too perfect to be real. Emily had not been close enough to see if it was. But she felt a dreadful stab of jealousy, especially when Mr. Bradshaw arrived.

He was quite unmistakable, dressed all in black—long black domino with black knee breeches and waistcoat beneath, black mask, the only relief the white lace over his hands and his white stockings. He was standing in the doorway looking about him when Emily noticed him, tall and slim and broad-shouldered. He looked long and intently at Mrs. Langtree.

Emily felt a terrible sense of desolation and gave herself a mental shake. This was one of the most exciting evenings of her life, and she was not going to spoil it by sighing for a man she should have been looking on in scorn. She was Mr. Harris' golden rose and wore his favor in her hair. She had his letter and his card to prove that he cared for her, even if only for this evening. She must be happy with what she had and not dream of the impossible.

She smiled brightly when Mr. Harris bowed before her and Lady Copeland, asked her if he might dance the next set with her, and proceeded to converse with her employer until the set began to form.

He looked at her appreciatively as they began to dance. "May I compliment you on your looks, Miss Richmond?" he said. "You are all blue and gold."

"Thank you," she said, looking into his eyes and watching them stray to the rose.

"The flower is lovely," he said, "but quite outshone by your hair."

"But it is beautiful," she said, "and real, though this is only February."

"Ah," he said, smiling, "a valentine."

She felt herself flushing. "Yes," she said.

They scarcely spoke after that, but concentrated on the steps of the dance. When he returned her to Lady Copeland's side, he said nothing about dancing with her again. But then, of course, he did not need to do so. He would automatically dance with her when the gentlemen were given the signal to claim their valentines.

There was a great deal of laughter and excitement in the ballroom. But Emily wondered if any of the ladies felt quite as full of eager anticipation as she. Even if he was just Mr. Harris, she would pretend for this one evening that he was a knight in shining armor. She smiled at the thought.

"You are enjoying yourself, Miss Richmond?"

She turned her head sharply to find that Mr. Bradshaw had approached without her even realizing it. The black of his domino made him seem even taller and more imposing than usual. The mask accentuated the brightness of his gray eyes.

"Yes, I am," she said, hearing her own breathlessness with some dismay.

"Good evening, Aunty," he said to Lady Copeland. "Can you manage without your companion for a time while I dance with her?"

"You don't think I came here tonight just to have dear Emily sit beside me, do you, Roger?" she said. "Foolish boy."

"Just so," he said, and turned to Emily. "Miss Richmond?"

"Thank you," she said, putting her hand in his and feeling that she would surely suffocate. It is just a dance, she told herself. Think of Mrs. Langtree's red rose. Think of your own golden rose. Think of Mr. Harris.

"A golden rose," Mr. Bradshaw said quietly. "Very appropriate."

"Yes," she said.

"A valentine?"

"Yes."

"From Harris?"

"Yes," she said, "though he has not said so, of course."

"Of course," he said. "He is a fortunate gentleman."

Roger stood in the doorway of the ballroom looking about him. He was obviously late, though he had been congratulating himself on being early. He had forgotten, of course, that if one did not arrive promptly at Bath entertainments, one was likely to miss them altogether. Even tonight's ball would be over by eleven o'clock. Not that he minded that. The night would be correspondingly longer.

Eugenia Langtree was immediately noticeable, clustered about with her usual court, though several of them looked dejected, Roger noticed with some amusement. She was dressed as Queen Elizabeth, an appropriate choice, given the redness of her hair. She was carrying a long-stemmed rose in one hand.

Roger looked intently. Even across the width of the ballroom he could see that it was in full bloom and a very dark red. As he watched, the hand holding the rose lifted slightly in greeting, and when he looked up, it was to find her watching him across the room, a smile on her face.

Well. One of his rare losses. They had both played a game, but it seemed that it had been a different game. He had expected them to be mutual winners. She obviously had intended from the start to be the sole victor. Or perhaps she wished to prolong the game, play cat and mouse with him for another week or more. However it was, the message was unmistakable. For tonight she had decided to snub him and favor someone else.

Roger stood where he was and waited for the onslaught of disappointment or anger or amusement. He was surprised to find that he felt nothing. Except perhaps a little relief. There would be nothing to keep him in Bath any longer. He would be able to leave the next day.

Yes, there was definitely a feeling of relief. He needed to get away, though he supposed he should stay away from London for a few weeks or even months longer. But he could not stay in Bath either. His heart was beginning to ache, which was a remarkably silly way of describing his feelings. But then, the feelings were remarkably silly too.

She was there already, standing beside his aunt, since the dancing was between sets. He had not needed to look to see if she had arrived. He had *felt* her presence as soon as he entered—another remarkably silly idea. But it was true. When he did finally glance briefly and sharply in that direction, sure enough—there she was in a midnight-blue domino and mask, her hair curled and golden, a touch of greenery threaded into it.

Well, she was there, and he felt like a breathless schoolboy. And embarrassed because he had backed her into the shadows below his aunt's staircase less than two weeks before and made some veiled and quite inappropriate suggestions to her and kissed her.

He had to get away. He needed to get away. He strolled across the room to Eugenia Langtree. The rose, he saw at close quarters, was made of silk.

"Your majesty," he said, making her an elegant bow, "may I commend your condescension in favoring your subjects with your presence?"

She touched him on the sleeve with the rose. "Mr. Bradshaw," she said, "you are late. It is a good thing this rose is not real or it would have wilted even before your arrival."

Ah, so she thought to rub salt into his wounds, did she?

"How could it wilt when in the presence of such dazzling beauty?" he asked. "Are you free to dance?"

"Absolutely not," she said with a sigh. "I am spoken for for the next three sets at least. However, sir, I daresay we will contrive to dance with each other later." She smiled at him.

He bowed to her as she was led onto the floor for the next dance. He watched her throughout the whole of it and saw only Emily, who was dancing with Harris.

He was being thoroughly foolish, Roger thought. He should leave immediately and see to the packing of his trunks so that he might be on his way early the next morning. There was no longer a reason to stay. But he had asked Emily Richmond a few days before to reserve a set for him. Besides, it would be unmannerly not to greet his aunt.

He waited until the music ceased and it was possible to move across the room without being bowled over by the dancers. She was standing beside his aunt, her head turned slightly away from him. She smiled as he approached, though he did not think she had seen him.

She looked more lovely even than usual. The domino and the mask added mystery to her appearance, and her hair was curled about her face. He had a sudden memory of its cascading down about her shoulders several days before.

He asked her for the next dance and was granted it. And so he would have one final chance to enjoy her company, he thought as he led her onto the floor, before leaving the following morning. She turned to face him fully as the music began.

And he felt as if he had stepped suddenly from reality into some bizarre dream. Nestled among the green leaves in her hair, almost unnoticeable against its brighter gold, was a perfect golden rosebud. He felt for one moment as if there were not enough air to breathe. It looked just like . . . But it could not be.

"A golden rose," he heard himself saying. "Very appropriate." Golden hair. A golden gown beneath her domino.

"Yes," she said.

"A valentine?" But it must be. Girls did not wear real roses in their hair in February.

"Yes," she said.

"From Harris?" He found himself holding his breath.

"Yes," she said, and there was no doubt in her voice, "though he has not said so, of course."

Pure coincidence. It must be. And it made perfect sense. Emily Richmond was a golden rose, far more golden than the flower in her hair. It looked far more appropriate in her hair than it would ever look in Eugenia's hand. Though it was not the same one, of course. It could not be.

Unless . . .

Where was that fiend of a boy? But no, even Jasper would not have dared such a trick. There was too much likelihood that Emmy could get hurt by the deception, and Jasper was fond of Emmy.

Was it Harris'? Would Harris come to claim her when the time came? She evidently was confident that it was so. And she wished it to be so. He could recall quite vividly her look of radiance five days before when she had told him that she had a valentine.

It must be Harris'. Jasper had had recent experience with the heaviness of his hand. He would not have risked an encore so soon, surely.

Damnation. Twenty thousand damnations!

"You dance well," he said. "Did you have much opportunity to dance in the country?"

"We have many neighbors who like to socialize," she said. "But even apart from that, Mama loves dancing and has taught us all, much to the disgust of my brothers. Edgar is the only one who has thought of a way of escape. He learned to play the pianoforte and is needed to provide the accompaniment while the rest of us dance."

Her eyes were sparkling and her lips smiling. He had noticed before that it was possible to drown in her eyes. Now he was aware too that there was grave danger of becoming enmeshed in her hair, captured beyond all hope of escape. There was a poem . . . He frowned. A sonnet about the poet becoming ensnared in his lady's golden hair. He had always thought the poor man a fool, though he could not for the life of him remember who the poet was.

Now he was behaving just as foolishly.

He bowed and withdrew at the end of the set. But he could not leave the ball as he had planned to do. He had to wait and see. That was not his rose, of course. It was Harris'. But even so . . .

He sought out his uncle, found him with a group of men who had no intention of dancing for the whole evening but who had set about putting the world to rights, and joined in their conversation.

Eugenia was smiling his way, the silk rose to her lips. Emmy was dancing with King Louis XIV, who looked as if he must have two left feet.

At half-past ten the Master of Ceremonies took the floor between sets to make an announcement. An expectant hush fell on the room.

"Gentlemen," he said, "the next dance will be a waltz. Claim your valentines, if you please."

The hush gave way to a babble of voices and laughter. A few squeals. The orchestra began to play a waltz tune.

Roger had moved away from his uncle. He stood in the doorway alone. Eugenia looked at him, raised the rose to her chin, and smiled. He was aware of the smile turning to astonishment when Poindexter stepped in front of her, took the rose from her hand, and lifted away her silver mask.

Astonishment? Was it possible that she did not know, that she had mistaken the red rose for his? He could recall that during the past week when they had talked of roses, she had always spoken of red roses.

But his attention was not really on Eugenia. He was

watching and not watching Emily. Harris was across the room from her and seemed engrossed in a conversation with an elderly couple. He made no move to cross the room. And no other man was approaching her.

There were several couples on the floor already, waltzing. Ladies all about him had relinquished trinkets and were submitting to having their masks removed.

Emily was standing alone beside his aunt.

Lord. Oh, good Lord!

He went into action.

Emily was aware of Mr. Harris across the room. At first she thought he was being polite, waiting for one of the people with whom he stood to finish what she was saying. But he did not even look across at her. And she could not look directly at him.

A lady to her left squealed, and one to her right laughed. There was movement all about her. Gentlemen were leading their partners onto the ballroom floor and beginning to waltz with them.

Emily stood tense and cold, unable to move a muscle. He was not going to come. For some reason he had changed his mind. She felt as if she were trapped in some dreadful nightmare. How would she bear the humiliation?

She felt suddenly as if everyone must be looking at her. In pity. With derision. She turned jerkily away. She could not even remember for the moment where the nearest door was. But a hand on her arm detained her.

"Emmy?" he said, his voice uncertain, questioning.

And she turned back to find herself looking into gray eyes behind a black mask.

She looked lost and bewildered, he thought. She

really had believed it was Harris. She would be less than pleased when she discovered the truth. He hoped that by the time he got his hands on one Jasper Copeland he would have thought of a more deadly punishment than a severe spanking.

He lifted both hands and gently disentangled the rose from her hair. And then he lifted the mask away from her face. He had not taken his eyes from hers the whole while.

"Ah, how splendidly you kept the secret, Roger, dear," Lady Copeland said, but he did not hear her.

He threaded the stem of the rose through a buttonhole of his domino, pulled off his own mask, and held out a hand for hers.

"Come waltz with me, my fair golden rose," he said.

My fair golden rose. It was he. For one moment she had thought that he was merely being kind, having seen her humiliation. But it was he. Emily put her hand in his and allowed him to lead her onto the dancing area and take one of her hands in his and set his other hand at the back of her waist.

They began to dance, eyes on each other's eyes.

She looked pale. But beautiful beyond words to describe.

"You." Her lips formed the words, though he did not hear the sound.

"Are you disappointed?" he asked. He wondered if she could hear the words. He had been afraid to say them.

She shook her head very slightly after a few moments.

He did not want to hold her away from him as propriety demanded. He wanted to hold her against him, that shapely and supple body against his own, his cheek against her golden curls, his eyes closed. He wanted to move to the music together with her, feeling her, warmed by her—not forced to look down at her and into her eyes, which she did not move from his own.

He did not want to see or to know what a terrible trick had been played on her. Poor Emmy—thinking she was being courted by a sober and respectable citizen like Harris and discovering that she was being toyed with by a rake.

"Golden," he said. "A pure golden rose."

"Was it my dress?" she asked him.

"And your hair," he said. "And you, Emmy. All golden and beautiful and valuable beyond price."

Her eyes widened and he had to resist more than ever the urge to pull her against him, to avoid the sight of those eyes. And what had he been babbling?

She was in a dream. The most wonderful dream of her life, and as with all good dreams, she held on to it consciously, willing herself not to wake up. Not yet.

She should not be dancing with him like this, their eyes locked together, totally unaware of anything or anyone else around them. She should not allow him to say such things to her. But this was a magical time. He had chosen her—freely chosen her—to be his valentine. To him she was all golden.

He made her *feel* beautiful. He made her *feel* valuable beyond price.

She would not let go of the moment. Tomorrow, yes. Tomorrow would be February 15. Valentine's Day would be over and ordinary life would resume. But not yet. The golden rose in his buttonhole had not even begun to droop. She was his golden rose and she would remain fresh and lovely for him until the next day.

She smiled.

And Roger felt that his hands might well be trembling. He held a very delicate and beautiful flower in them and he felt that he could only do it irreparable damage.

The music ended far, far too soon. Surely it must have been the shortest set of the evening. In all of the week and more since she had received his letter, Emily had not once thought past the moment when he would make himself known to her. Oh, she had assumed that it would be the beginning of a serious courtship and possibly the herald to a proposal of marriage. That was when she had believed the sender to be Mr. Harris, of course. But she had never thought of what would happen at the ball after the moment when he would come to claim her.

He took her by the elbow and led her back to Lady Copeland. Was it all over, then? Would he bow and leave her now? Was the dream over, and cold reality already about to take its place?

"Roger, dear," Lady Copeland said as soon as they were within earshot, "you may go have my carriage brought around to the door, if you will be so good."

"It will be my pleasure, Aunty," he said. His hand tightened on Emily's elbow. "Come with me?" he asked her.

She had no thought to refusing, even though doubtless it would be highly improper to go. But this was not a night for propriety.

"Do take your cloak with you, dear," Lady Copeland said placidly. "Make sure that Emily puts on her cloak, Roger. I would not have her take cold."

"Trust me, Aunty," he said.

Several people's carriages had arrived, it being a well-known fact that in Bath all good citizens returned home at eleven o'clock. Most were at the side of the Assembly Rooms, waiting to be summoned to the doors. Their coachmen stood in small groups, talking.

Roger and Emily strolled along the length of them between the carriages and the building, unseen by the gossiping coachmen, until they reached Lady Copeland's carriage. Somehow they were hand in hand, Roger noticed, their fingers laced together. They walked in silence while he fought an inner battle with his conscience and his better nature.

She was a young innocent. A sweet and lovely innocent. She did not need to become tainted with the likes of him. She deserved someone better.

But whom? Amazingly, she seemed to have attracted no admirers in Bath. Because she was so quiet and unassuming and dressed so plainly? Because she was a lady's companion? Although her father was Sir Henry Richmond, she was in reality a woman in service.

Would she ever find the husband she deserved?

He had nothing to offer except a wild and unstable past. And a fortune, of course. And the expectation of a viscount's title at some time in the future. Security for a girl from a large and impoverished family.

They stopped by unspoken consent when they came to his aunt's carriage, though neither made a move to pass between the carriages in order to attract the attention of the coachman.

Almost without his willing it, his arm was about her waist, turning her to face him, bringing her at long last against him. She did not resist. She lifted her face to look up at him. Inviting his kiss? Emmy.

"Emmy," he said, his voice low, one hand smoothing over her hair. Her hands reached up to his shoulders. "Emmy."

Her lips were closed when his own touched them, and cool from the night air. But they were soft and responsive. They parted to his coaxing, and moved over his. Her arms were about his neck, one hand in his hair.

He probed gently with his tongue at first, but when her mouth opened to receive it, he plunged inside to the heat and moistness of her, his tongue circling hers, teasing the soft flesh beneath until she whimpered in his arms.

He was lost to conscience and good sense and propriety. He wanted her. God, he wanted her. Even through the folds of her cloak and her domino and the dress beneath, he could feel the heat and the softness of her and the enticing curves. He wanted her. Sweet Emmy.

Emmy. Beautiful, quiet, gentle, affectionate, fun-loving, innocent Emmy. His rose. His golden rose. Brighter by far than the rose that was being crushed between them. He wanted her, yes. But not just for his bed. There too, but not just there.

He wanted her for his life. She had become his hope, his lifeline, his promise of salvation. He wanted her for all his life and for eternity after that.

His kiss gentled. His arms cradled her.

"Emmy," he murmured, lifting his mouth away from hers and kissing her softly once more, "you feel it too, don't you? Say you'll be mine."

Something shut down behind her eyes as she looked up at him. "No," she said. "Don't spoil it. Oh, please don't spoil it. Don't let me know that that has been your motive all the time. Please don't."

He captured her hands against his chest as she pulled away. "No," he said, "don't misunderstand, Emmy. I'm not trying to seduce you. I am ashamed that I ever tried. I would never do it again. Forgive me. I have no business compromising you like this. We had better find my aunt's coachman and go back inside. Let me call on you during the daytime in a more proper manner. May I?"

"If you wish," she said, but her eyes were wary.

He could say no more. Not then, when his blood was up. How old was she? Eighteen? Nineteen? It was hard to tell.

He took her hand in his and they said no more until they were back at the doors into the Assembly Rooms. But she pulled back on his hand.

"Please," she said, looking up at him, not quite meeting his eyes.

He bent his head toward her.

"Please may I have the rose?" she asked.

He took it from his buttonhole and handed it to her without taking his eyes from hers. "I am afraid it is probably somewhat bedraggled," he said. "And even at its best it was not one fraction as lovely as you, Emmy."

"Thank you for choosing me as your valentine," she said, her voice breathless. "It has been the most wonderful night of my life."

She whisked herself through the doors ahead of him, not even waiting for him or a doorman to open them for her.

She wished he had not said that about calling on her during the daytime, Emily thought, holding the pressed rose carefully on the palm of her hand and touching the bloom lightly with the forefinger of her other hand. If he had not said that, she would not have expected him and the four days since the ball would not have been so long and so dreary.

Not that she had really been expecting him, of course—or not to visit her personally, anyway. But when a person says something like that, one cannot help but expect him, even when one knows that he will not come.

Lady Copeland had been called downstairs by a visitor. And so, left alone for a few minutes, Emily had been unable to resist the urge to take the rose from between the pages of a book and gaze at it. She had spent the last four nights with the book hugged in her arms. And though it had been very embarrassing and very forward of her to ask him for it, she was not sorry she had done so. She had this one memento of the most wonderful night of her life.

She wished she had not told him that, though. It was very gauche of her to have done so, and doubtless had frightened him off even if he really had intended to call on her.

Jasper said he had gone away, disappeared from Bath without a word to anyone. Jasper had followed her about more than usual in the past few days, a look of dejection on his face.

"Are you sad, Em?" he had asked once.

"Sad?" she had said, smiling at him. "Why should I be sad?"

"Because the ball is over," he had said, "and you don't have a beau."

She had laughed at him. "But I had a pleasant evening," she had said. "That was all I looked for."

"Are you sorry it wasn't Mr. Harris?" he had asked, his eyes troubled.

"Gracious, no," she had said. "It was very obliging of Mr. Bradshaw to have chosen me for his valentine."

"Besides," Lady Copeland had added, looking up from the letter she was writing, "I would have been very annoyed if it had turned out to be Mr. Harris. He is a married man."

She had said no more, and Emily had asked no questions. But she had been shocked again by her own ignorance.

She looked down now at her flower and smiled. At least she had memories. Wonderful memories. She had relived that kiss a thousand times during the past four nights. She had not known a kiss could be like that. She was quite sure that it had been shockingly improper, but it had been very wonderful for all that. She slipped the rose between the pages of her book again as the door opened.

"Ah, how foolish of me," Lady Copeland said, stopping just inside the door and patting the pocket of her dress. "I left my handkerchief in the salon downstairs. Be so obliging as to fetch it for me, Emily, dear, will you?"

Emily got to her feet and smiled. A few moments later she was running lightly down the stairs.

After talking to Lady Copeland, Roger wandered out into the hallway as she went upstairs to send Emily to him. It was deserted.

"Jasper?" he said without raising his voice. "Are you there?"

There was silence for a moment, and then a rustling from behind the aspidistra plant.

"Is it safe to come out?" a voice asked.

"Relatively," Roger said. "I have other things on my mind at the moment than thrashings."

There was another rustling and Jasper appeared in the hallway. He was grinning. "Now I can blackmail you, Rog," he said. "Em would probably be very interested to know where that letter and rose were really destined to go."

A moment later his toes were dangling a tantalizing half-inch from the floor, the lapels of his coat clutched in his cousin's fists.

"Let me be fast and clear on this point, my young lad," Roger said. "If Emmy *ever* learns the truth, your rear end will be in grave danger of the worst thrashing of its life. Do you understand me?"

"Yes, Rog," Jasper said briskly.

"If you care for her," Roger said, lowering Jasper until his big toes were scraping the floor, "it should not be just the threat that will keep your mouth shut."

"No, Rog," Jasper said.

He was lowered until he was able to stand flat on both feet.

"What I really came out here to say," Roger said, "was thank you, you fiendish little brat. Depending upon the events of the next half-hour, I may be eternally in your debt. Let's not exaggerate this too much, though. Suffice it to say that I owe you something."

"Cakes?" Jasper said hopefully.

"Perhaps later," Roger said. "Back to your hiding place, now." He returned to the salon, closing the door behind him. He was standing with his back to the fire when the door opened again and Emily came hurrying in.

She stopped when she saw him, and turned pale. Her eyes grew large.

"My aunt knows I am here," he said. "She sent you to see me."

She stared at him.

"Your father knows too," he said.

She frowned in incomprehension. "Papa?" she said.

"I have been to see him," he said. "And your mother and all seven of your brothers and sisters, who talk enough for twice as many. It is no wonder you are so quiet. It must have been difficult to get a word in edgewise."

"You have been to see them?" She was looking at him rather as if he had two heads, he thought.

"I have your father's permission to ask you to marry me," he said.

Her hands crumpled the gray fabric of her dress at the front. Her face was suddenly flooded with color.

"You did not compromise me," she said. "I went willingly with you, and no one saw or knew about it."

"I want to marry you," he said. "It has nothing to do with the fact that I kissed you rather intimately outside the Assembly Rooms. I want to marry you, Emmy, because you are the most beautiful and the most precious thing in my life. *Thing!*" He laughed softly. "I have practiced this over and over in the last four days, and I cannot remember a word of what I planned to say."

She looked at him, handsome and rather dusty in his riding clothes. And for the first time she realized that he had come as he had said he would. And he was asking her to marry him. The fact was beginning to register on her mind.

"But I am very dull and very ordinary," she said.

"If you were a man," he said with a faint smile, "I would call you out as a consummate liar. You are golden, Emmy. I cannot think of a better word to describe you. You shine from within like the sun. A rose cannot even begin to compete with you."

"Oh," she said.

"Emmy," he said, "I have nothing to offer you except money and position and security. I am twenty-seven years old, and I have wasted my youth in gambling and drinking and rioting and . . . debauchery. I don't know why you would even think of accepting me, but I am offering myself. Will you have me?"

She hesitated. She could not quite understand. What was the attraction? Why would a man like him, who had everything, want her? There could be only one reasonable explanation.

"Is there nothing else?" she asked. "Nothing else you can offer me?"

He smiled, a look of mockery on his face. "Only my love," he said, "for what it is worth, Emmy. I have never given it before. That at least is untarnished.''

He was still standing in front of the fire, she just inside the door. But her face lit up from the inside, so that he found it difficult to remain where he was. She leaned slightly toward him, though she did not move.

"You love me?" she asked.

"I love you, Emmy," he said. "Will you have me?"

She was the one who moved finally. She came hurrying toward him, wide eyes gazing into his.

"You love me," she said. "Can it be true? And you have been all the way to ask Papa for me?"

He was not sure who had reached for whom, but they were suddenly in each other's arms, his wrapped about her slim waist, hers about his neck. Without the barrier of her winter cloak and the domino, she fitted against his body as if she had been made to rest there.

He kissed her, opening her mouth with his, running his tongue back and forth across her lips and up to the soft flesh behind them.

But he would not lose touch with reality. If all went well, he would have a lifetime for that. He drew her even closer, afraid that he might yet lose her.

"If we are betrothed," he said, "this is only slightly improper, Emmy. If we are not, it is unpardonable. Are we?"

"I love you," she said. "Roger, I love you."

"Despite everything?" he asked, looking into her eyes. "Despite that ghastly first encounter?"

She smiled. "I spent days dreaming of it," she said.

He grinned. "Hussy," he said. "What have you dreamed of in the past four days?"

"You," she said. "You taking the rose from my hair. You waltzing with me. You kissing me. I have pressed the rose so that I will have it with me always."

He lifted a hand to smooth lightly over her hair,

which was in its usual simple style. "Will you marry me, Emmy?" he asked.

She nodded. "Yes," she said. "Oh, yes, Roger."

"I won't need any pressed roses, then," he said. "I will have the real thing to hold in my arms for the rest of our lives. I can't change my past, Emmy, but I'll treasure you for the present and all of the future. I promise most solemnly."

"And I you, Roger," she said, smiling eagerly up into his face. Her cheeks flushed. "Kiss me again. As you did after the ball."

"Anything you say," he said, rubbing his nose lightly against hers, "my fairest golden rose."

He kissed her. Not in quite the same way as he had kissed her four evenings before. But she did not complain, either while he was busy doing it or later.

But by then so much time had elapsed that it was probable she had forgotten her request.

The Secret Benefactor
by Katherine Kingsley

"PAXTON CERTAINLY is very large," Aubrey said with
a touch of humor as her eyes traveled over the massive
front of the castle that seemed to have no end, at least
not one that was in sight. She had seen many large
buildings in her travels, but this was one of the largest,
competing easily in size with Versailles, although she
much preferred the Yorkshire setting. Aubrey was not
particularly impressed by grandeur or opulence, but
she did appreciate architectural soundness, which Paxton Castle possessed.

"It is one of the largest residences in the country,"
replied Miss Graham, "the original stonework origi-
nating in the twelfth century. I trust you observed the
shell-keep on the motte. The keep was increased in
the early fourteenth century, which is evidenced by the
towers. This was once a powerful stronghold, and the
third earl was well aware that he commanded the eastern route into England. The earldom was first established in 1309, by the by. The castle was restored to
its present condition in the seventeenth century by the
second duke after a fire partially destroyed it. I believe
there is a particularly fine conservatory, and the
chapel—"

Aubrey smiled. "Miss Graham, I daresay the headmistress in you will never disappear for even a moment, but rest assured that I do know the history. Years

77

ago you gave a most elucidating series of lectures addressing all of the most important properties in the British Isles, and Paxton was very thoroughly included. I know it is a great favorite of yours.''

Miss Graham sniffed and straightened her skirts as the carriage pulled up in front of the massive stone steps that led to the vaulted entrance. ''One can never know enough about these things, especially if one is to be an assistant headmistress. The very history of Britain is written upon stones such as these. Paxton has a library that is nearly one hundred feet long, housing one of the finest collections of books and manuscripts in Europe. As you know, the duke is a renowned scholar, who has greatly added to the collection, an admirable avocation.'' She paused only to draw breath. ''If more people paid attention to collecting things of rare and lasting value and less to frivoling their money away on empty pleasures, the world would be a much better place. Scholarly pursuits are far more admirable than the pursuit of pleasure.'' She firmly skewered an escaping pin into the neat gray bun at the back of her head.

Aubrey, suppressing a sigh, declined to comment. For the last nine years Miss Graham had been a combination of mother, companion, and teacher to her, and she had learned long ago that when Miss Graham decided it was time for a lecture, that was what it would be. A two-way discussion was not what she had in mind. As Aubrey descended the lowered steps after Miss Graham, she wondered what had prompted the homily. Miss Graham surely could not be thinking that she had suddenly become interested in frivoling. Perhaps she was concerned that spending a week at Paxton would decide Aubrey against accepting her offer, forever ruined by luxury and mingling with her betters.

* * *

"My dear Aubrey, how wonderful this is!" Annabelle said, her hands outstretched as she came across the great hall toward them, her lively gait not measurably slowed by her advanced pregnancy. "I've been counting the hours till your arrival! I am so delighted you could join us!" She pulled Aubrey into her arms and gave her a fierce hug, then laughed. "My immense proportions make embracing difficult, do they not? And, Miss Graham—I am so pleased you both could join us. I know the weather is not all it might be, given it is February, but we could think of no better time for a small party. We've been starved for company, and in truth, I could not wait to see my friends. Confinement is so dreary, I cannot tell you. It is a good thing I did not tell Harry of the coming child for the first months, or he should have swept me home immediately, and I should never have traveled as far as Turkey! I must tell you all about it, and you must tell me everything that has happened to you since we saw you last."

Despite the enormity of the hall with its cathedral-like air, Annabelle completely filled it with her glowing personality and Aubrey was immediately reminded of what had first drawn her to the unconventional duchess.

"You are looking well, your grace," Aubrey said with her characteristically shy smile, but her eyes were dancing with laughter.

"Aubrey! I shall positively expire if you insist on such formality at this late date. It is hard enough having to endure it from the rest of the world, but I thought at least you would not plague me with it."

Aubrey laughed. "I suppose that meeting on the steps of the Parthenon was not conducive to formality, whereas arriving at your ducal seat puts one more forcefully in mind of such matters.'' Aubrey saw the flash of shared memory in Annabelle's eyes and the corresponding grin of understanding. Miss Graham was not as given to informality as Annabelle and would have keeled over in a faint had she known some of the things Annabelle and Aubrey had done together when she hadn't been there to observe.

"Yes, I can see your point," Annabelle said, as if they had never shared a single impropriety in their lives. "Paxton is rather large, isn't it? I was quite taken by surprise myself when I first saw it, despite how well Harry had described it. Never mind, there are all sorts of wonderful things to see and do, and you shan't have a moment of boredom."

"It was very kind of you to have us, Duchess."

"Oh, not in the least!" Annabelle said with a smothered laugh. "It is you who should be thanked for taking the time to visit me. Now, come and let me show you to your rooms. You'll want time to rest and change before dinner."

"You mustn't trouble yourself, your grace," Miss Graham said firmly. "Surely in your condition you would rather the housekeeper or a footman . . ." She trailed off delicately, her meaning evident in the expression on her face.

"But I would enjoy it, Miss Graham," Annabelle solemnly replied, clearly not prepared to go that far in appeasing Aubrey's companion. "You really mustn't feel you need to cosset me, for fresh air and all the exercise I can manage keep me feeling fit. I don't mind in the least; in fact, it gives me pleasure." She slipped her hand through Aubrey's arm and headed toward the stairs, and Miss Graham, who disapproved of such a modern attitude, but who could hardly argue with a duchess, gave another sniff and followed.

* * *

Aubrey took advantage of the two hours before dinner to have the rest Annabelle had suggested. After washing, she slipped under the warm coverlet that had thoughtfully been laid at the end of the enormous bed and closed her eyes, settling herself for sleep. It had been a fairly long progress from Bath to the north of Yorkshire, and the roads had been none too good. Aubrey was accustomed to long hours of traveling and did not mind bumpy roads overmuch. But she had not slept well the night before, worrying about Miss Graham and her proposition, knowing she could not postpone her decision for much longer. Miss Graham had already been very patient with her, and it would not be fair to keep her waiting. Perhaps being at Paxton would help to clarify her thinking, give her some time not to think at all, simply to live for a last few precious days. Annabelle was sure to provide a much-needed diversion.

She remembered in great detail the day they had met, holding it as a particularly cherished memory. She'd clambered dusty and hot to the top of the Acropolis, having left Miss Graham and their guide far behind, not caring in the least about the berating she was bound to receive later. She wanted the moment to be her very own. Her hair had long before escaped from her hat in abandoned tendrils, the thick dust turning the blond to gray, and she'd hiked up her skirts to her knees to make it easier to climb. And then she'd finally reached her goal, the Parthenon itself, and there had been another figure, someone about the same age as herself, as dark as she was fair, sitting on the steps, her skirts also hiked up about her knees, her bare legs stuck out akimbo.

"Hello," the other woman had called in a completely unconcerned fashion, as if she and Aubrey had known each other a lifetime. "Would you like an orange? I have some extras and you must be parched."

Aubrey collapsed on the steps beside her and gratefully accepted the offering. "Thank you," she said, tearing into the sweet, tender flesh, too thirsty for any other civilities.

"It will grow cooler soon. Have you ever seen such a wondrous sight in your life? I could sit here for a year."

"Mmm," Aubrey agreed through a mouthful of orange pulp, "there's nothing like a good ruin to set one up, but this has to top them all. I could sit here two years at the very least, possibly three if my appetite wasn't bound to interfere. It is a shame to be ruled by such mundane matters. You haven't another orange, by any chance, have you?"

Her companion shot her a look brimming with surprise and amusement, and then she burst into laughter. "I'm Annabelle Calderon and I think I'm terribly happy to have met you."

Aubrey, normally fairly reserved with strangers, found herself instantly responding to Annabelle's warmth and humor. When she met Annabelle's handsome husband, who appeared a half-hour later with a pocketful of plants, his blond hair just as dusty as her own, she found him equally as easygoing.

She was sad to be parted from Annabelle when the time came to go their separate ways, the Paxtons to Turkey, Aubrey and Miss Graham to Italy, but they swore that they would be in touch when they had both returned to England. And now here she was, and it was very wonderful to know that nothing had changed. That had been her biggest fear, that it had been Greece that had exerted the magic, and when they met again, everything would have descended to the level of the ordinary. But one look and word from Annabelle, and she had known that wasn't the case. It was all just as it had been.

Aubrey had one last precious week before she had to make her final decision, and who knew what could happen in a week? Miss Graham would say that she was thinking in an irresponsible manner, but she didn't care. With the rest of her life stretching before her in a long, unexciting line, she could afford a few last days of dreaming.

Her eyes finally closed in sleep.

The drawing room was abuzz with conversation when Aubrey finally found it, having lost her way only three times, a major accomplishment for someone with no sense of direction. She took a moment to check her appearance in the long Italian mirror on the adjacent wall, glad there were no footmen immediately in sight. But all appeared in order. There was not a sign of the cobwebs she'd run into when she'd somehow ended in a deserted corridor, nor was there any evidence of the soot from the coal room as she had attempted to make her way back. All was as it was supposed to be.

She gave one last distracted sweep of her hand down the front of her blue velvet dress, settled the Kashmir shawl, which had somehow become askew in her wanderings, more stylishly around her shoulders, and took a deep breath. She couldn't help wondering whether the duke would remember that they'd once been on comfortable terms, if not exactly friends, or whether he might have reverted to ducal type now that he was ensconced in his castle. Annabelle hadn't reverted, but then, she hadn't been born to the elevated position, and anyway, one could never tell. She'd learned that particular lesson after her father had died; people might behave toward you one way under one set of circumstances and behave completely differently once those circumstances had changed. One learned to make quick adjustments.

Annabelle's merry laughter rang from within the drawing room and Aubrey's heart lightened at the sound. She stood on the threshold for a moment in order to acclimate herself before entering, a practice which had always helped to ease her initial shyness. The large room was filled with people, all chattering away gaily, and Aubrey strained for a sign of someone she might know. Her eyes finally found the slightly built duke, who stood with his back half-turned to her. He was addressing a comment to Annabelle, who sat on the sofa, listening with quivering lips to her husband's story, her hands resting lightly on her swollen abdomen. It was a warm and friendly picture, and Aubrey felt instantly comfortable, and actually quite excited to be out in society.

"Aubrey, there you are at last!" Annabelle exclaimed, glancing up and holding out a hand as the duke turned toward the door with a welcoming smile. "I can't possibly get up once I'm down, so you must come to me, I fear."

"Good evening, your grace," Aubrey said, moving into the room and curtsying to the duke. "It is indeed a pleasure to see you again."

He bowed. "The pleasure is very much ours, Miss de Salis. My wife has most particularly been awaiting your arrival, and I hope that your presence may settle her, for I fear our poor child has been badly jarred about, given all of my wife's excess energy."

Annabelle gave her husband a superior look. "Nonsense, Harry. If you were in an interesting condition, you wouldn't give it a moment's thought. In any case, I am equally jarred about by all of the baby's excess energy, so we are perfectly in accord. Now, where is that dragon of a companion, Aubrey? I must say, I feel like a child still in the schoolroom when she is about.''

Aubrey gave Miss Graham's excuses, for Miss Graham had decided that she most assuredly had the headache and would retire early to bed. "I am sure," Aubrey added with a smile, "that if you looked, you would find her in your library, your grace, cataloging. Libraries are a private passion of Miss Graham's, and I'm sure yours was the only reason she agreed to accompany me here, for she does not enjoy large gatherings overmuch.''

"Really? But how delightful. And I must tell you that I would be everlastingly grateful to Miss Graham if she took it upon herself to catalog the library, for the task is far beyond my solitary abilities. I never seem to be able to keep up with it. Come, let me introduce you to our friends, for I am sure that you will feel most comfortable. They are mostly of the same mind we are, if a trifle older. I'll be back directly, Annabelle.'' He leaned down and planted a most unconventional kiss on her forehead, and she smiled up at him.

"I'm bereft," she said, laughing. "Actually, Harry, I long to engage in a tryst, so do take yourself off.''

"Do amuse yourself with Kincaid, here. Kincaid, tryst with my wife while I'm gone.''

He took Aubrey around the room, making the introductions easily and with no fuss. And then suddenly, all of the names and faces faded away as one figure in particular separated from the crowd and swam into Aubrey's slightly unbelieving view. She blinked hard, but he was still there, looking nearly the same as when she had tearfully bidden him farewell ten years before. The room might have parted as neatly as the Red Sea, for all she was aware of anything but him before her.

For a moment she thought her years of fantasizing

about George must have finally affected her brain, as Miss Graham had always warned would happen when one indulged in daydreaming. But he was definitely real, there was no doubt about it, for no matter how hard she continued to blink, his face did not waver and reconcile itself into that of a stranger's, as had happened so many times in the past. If there was one thing that convinced her of her sanity, it was that he had changed. She tried to quiet the thudding of her heart and concentrate, to adjust the old image to the new one.

He was tall, but she wasn't certain if he was taller than when she'd last seen him, for she had grown too. His dark head was bent in careful attention, his slightly hooded eyes gravely focused on an older woman who was speaking intently, waving one beringed hand about in the air. She knew that attentive gaze well—so well. How often had he bestowed it upon her, all the times she had offered him a leaf, a flower, or a particularly fine rock, and once a snail for his careful inspection.

He was as immaculately dressed as he had ever been; even as a child he'd been fastidious in his dress, a trait which somehow had always gone well with his innate gravity. His black coat was superbly cut to fit his shoulders, his linen brilliantly white, his black pumps without a speck of dust, his pantaloons creaseless.

But he had lost a certain sharpness, an angularity she remembered; his long, thin nose now fitted his face more easily, for his features had filled out. That was it—it was the strong line of his cheek, the defined jaw, the ease of his posture. His shoulders were broader, squarer, and he looked more muscular overall. Age had not only mellowed him, it had turned him from a youth into a very attractive man, and oddly enough, he was not altogether unlike the idealized version she had created for herself.

Now, as she watched him, his thin mouth took that slow curve upward in the achingly familiar, slightly sardonic expression he'd always worn when he was privately amused, and they might have been children again, for Aubrey knew just what he was thinking of the old woman, and she wanted to laugh.

Despite his strongly masculine appearance, he was really just as she remembered, as familiar as if it had been only days instead of years since they had been parted. And it was absolutely, astonishingly wonderful to see him again.

And then, as if feeling her eyes on him, he looked up and saw her.

Aubrey grinned, her eyes filled with a combination of welcome, happiness, and her own astonishment.

But George's eyes held nothing. He seemed to freeze. She saw that his long fingers had tightened on the head of his cane until his knuckles whitened. And then the moment had vanished and he smiled at her briefly and dismissed himself from the old woman. He started across the room.

Aubrey had never before thought of George as anything but George, but part of the physical reality of George had always been his crippled leg, for it had affected so many aspects of his life. And yet he was walking across the room with only a slight limp, certainly not the difficult, pained gait she was familiar with. She looked harder. Both his legs looked exactly the same to her, the muscles equally developed, and she hardly thought that any amount of padding could effect such an impression. She could not quite believe the change, but she put it to the back of her mind for the moment, too happy to see him to have any extraneous thoughts interfere.

Harry turned as he approached. "Ah, there you are, George. I'd like you to meet one of our newest—"

"I am acquainted with Miss de Salis," George said in his rich, curiously melodic voice. Aubrey had forgotten its beautiful timbre, and it sent a shiver down her spine, hearing it again after all this time. "How have you been keeping, Aubrey?" he asked, taking her hand and bowing over it.

"George." It was all she could find to say, for a lump had risen in her throat: the memories brought on by his immediate presence were far too many and too complex to be able to sort through at that moment. All she managed to register was that she was very, very happy to see him, and that for some reason her heart was hurting terribly. "George," she said again, and swallowed, then blushed as she realized that the duke was observing them with interest.

"I see that you and Mr. Asquith are old friends. How very pleasing," he said easily. "In that case I shall leave you to renew your acquaintance, for I am sure you have no need of me." He slipped away before Aubrey could respond. She only then realized that her hand was still in George's, and she squeezed it.

"It's been so long," she said, her voice faltering only slightly. "Since Aldershot. Are you still at Havenstone?"

George inclined his head. "My father is still at Havenstone. I have been living here at Paxton these last eight years."

"Oh . . ." Aubrey felt completely tongue-tied. "You're looking very well."

He smiled slightly and removed his hand. "And you're looking all grown-up. What were you when last I saw you? Twelve or thirteen?"

"I was fourteen," said Aubrey, feeling inexplicably hurt that he didn't remember. "And you had turned nineteen only days before. It was at my father's funeral."

"I do remember that much, Aubrey," he said gently. "I would not forget such a difficult time. But," he added with another smile, "it looks as if your life has taken a turn for the better since then, if your glowing looks are anything to go by. You've grown into a most beautiful woman, Aubrey. I confess I am surprised to find you are not yet married."

"Thank you, but I have no wish to marry," she said, matching his light tone, but secretly terribly pleased that he thought she had grown beautiful. Miss Graham had never encouraged her to think of herself as anything more than passable, and as for George, he had so often teased her about her pixy face, forever smudged with dirt. "I am so unfashionable that I would marry for nothing but love, but I find that I am unconscionably fickle. In any case, I have been far too busy to marry."

"Oh?" George said with a rise of his eyebrow. "And what is it you have been far too busy doing?"

"Teaching school, and for the last two years, traveling. The benefactor who put me through the seminary was kind enough to sponsor the trip. It was an extraordinary experience, seeing other countries and cultures."

George regarded her soberly, one long finger resting on his cheek. "I see. I begin to understand what brought you here to Paxton. You are not the only person who has contracted this particular disease. I imagine you must have met the duke and duchess on your travels?"

"Oh, yes, I did, and, George, it was the most marvelous thing!" She launched with enthusiasm into an account of her meeting with Harry and Annabelle, and she forgot that she was supposed to be behaving like an adult. It was as if the ten years had completely dissolved, and she was speaking again to her child-hood friend, with no constraints between them.

"I am delighted to learn you have become such friends," George said when she had finished. "Your being here will be a tonic for Annabelle, for she is in need of a cheerful friend just now. I imagine I will see you about, Aubrey. It has been very enjoyable coming across you again, for I'd wondered what had become of you. You'll excuse me—there are some people I must speak with."

Aubrey felt as if she had just been firmly dismissed, and with a great rush of embarrassment she realized that in her enthusiasm she clearly had been forward, horribly so. She wanted to sink into the ground. "I beg your pardon, George. Please forgive my lack of manners. I hadn't meant to keep you. It was just so wonderful seeing you after all this time."

"Not at all." George gave her a slight bow and moved away, and Aubrey made her way back to Annabelle, crushed by how much George had changed from the way she'd remembered him.

But then, what had she expected? Should he have gathered her up in his arms and called her his "funny-faced little gosling"? Should he have laughed and pulled a lock of her hair, as he had always done? Or perhaps he should have tossed her up over his shoulder, with a laugh and a smack on her bottom, the way he had done when she was very small. Yes, that would have been truly appropriate behavior for the occasion.

She laughed at herself and went to find Annabelle, her heart singing to have rediscovered her dear friend, and looking forward to all the time she might spend with him during her stay. Had she thought something exciting might possibly happen? To have found George after ten long years, with nothing but daydreams to

hold her together until now, was beyond happiness. It
was true joy.

The Honorable George Asquith, renowned for being
cool, calm, and collected under even the most hair-
raising of circumstances, was in a thoroughly rattled
state. He paced his room one more time, not a habit
he was normally prone to.

"Dear heaven," he murmured, running his hand
over his brow. He poured himself a generous measure
of cognac from the crystal decanter on his desk, then
lowered himself into his armchair, taking a long drink.
Then, putting the glass down on the table next to him,
he placed the tips of his fingers together, attempting
to collect his thoughts. They seemed to have scattered
in a hundred different directions, and he had to force
himself to focus.

Aubrey . . . all those years since he had last laid
eyes on her, her sweet pixy face grown even more
vibrant and very much more beautiful since childhood, delivering the promise that had always been
there . . . Aubrey was a woman full-grown. Aubrey
of the shining sapphire eyes and flaxen hair, Aubrey
of the impish laughter, the irresistible smile, the pen-
etrating observations—Aubrey was back.

And now she was at Paxton.

It had given him a terrible shock seeing her, for she
was the last person he ever would have expected to
have shown up on the doorstep. Actually the impact
had been more like a hammer hitting him over the
head. He had spent the rest of the evening waiting to
retire to his rooms in order to sort through his thoughts
in privacy.

His mind was crowded with images, vivid flashes of
memory brought on by seeing her again. He remembered her so clearly as a child, a wild, tousled angel

of a child, with an insatiable curiosity and constantly dirty knees. And how well he remembered Laurence, his hair as fair as Aubrey's. How often had he watched Aubrey sitting on her brother's lap as he read to her from a book of fairy tales, her adoring eyes watching him solemnly. But George could not think of Laurence just now, nor of any of the rest of it. He would not think of it. He would think only of the present. That was difficult enough in itself.

He sighed heavily. He might not have laid eyes on Aubrey from the day she had left Aldershot, but she had never been far from his thoughts. How was he to reconcile all that had happened between then and now? How on earth was he to behave toward her? There was so much she would never understand: his reasons for allowing her to think he had forgotten her, his reasons for continuing to keep his distance. And yet it was better to keep her in ignorance, for he would not see her hurt.

He took another sip of the cognac, feeling it beginning to steady his nerves. And, by God, they needed steadying. The past had just coming rushing up to meet him full in the face, and it was a rare man who could meet his past and emerge unscathed. And it was probably a rare man who could meet Aubrey as she appeared now and not be affected. *Why* had she not married? It made no sense to him, and he had always wondered, but to see her as she was now—it was unimaginable that she had not been snapped up. She fully deserved the happiness that having a family of her own would bring.

He finally rose, feeling bone-tired, and undressed without a thought to the state of his clothes, flinging them over the arm of his chair, not even noticing when his coat fell to the floor in a heap. He slipped beneath the cold sheets, the warming pan having long since lost its heat, turned on his good hip with another sigh, and rested his head on his elbow. But his bed offered no comfort, giving neither sleep nor peace.

"Did you sleep well?" Aubrey inquired of Miss Graham as they made their way down the great staircase to the hall early the next morning.

"Not particularly," Miss Graham replied with a customary sniff, "but then, these old houses always bring on the ague. It's the damp. However, it hardly matters. I am very pleased to be here, and I have a great many things to discover. I spent last night reviewing my history, but it is fairly incomplete."

She sailed through the front door as if she were a ship launching on a maiden voyage. "I thought we would start our exploration of the grounds here"—she pointed to a map she had drawn—"with the eastern bailey, as you can see. There was a gateway added to the curtain wall in the fourteenth century. Have I already mentioned it?" she asked, drawing her thin eyebrows down until they met in the middle.

"No, but that would be fine," Aubrey said, wondering how many hours they would be out wandering before Miss Graham remembered breakfast, and relieved she had remembered to pack her sturdy boots.

They stumped around some time before finally reaching the eastern bailey, Miss Graham constantly stopping to comment or point out some particular sight. Aubrey's mind had long since wandered, but she was brought abruptly back to her senses by the sight of George, who was standing just inside the keep, examining something above him, his breath appearing in little white puffs in the cold air. Aubrey, her heart leaping, thought he looked remarkably at ease, one hand pushed into the pocket of his coat, the other on his cane. His dark hair blew about his forehead as he called up, his words carried away by the wind. She saw that he'd been speaking to a workman as they approached and the gateway came into view.

She went straight over to him with the same directness she'd had as a child.

"George."

He felt a light touch on his arm and turned, startled. "Aubrey . . . good morning." Her smile was as bright as the sun and reached all the way into her eyes. It took him a moment to collect himself. "You are out and about early."

"It's such a lovely day, and I can never seem to sleep very much after the sun comes up."

"Yes. I remember." He smiled down at her, resisting the temptation to push the blowing strands of pale silken hair from her face as he'd always done. "You haven't changed much, have you?"

"Not much, no. But you haven't changed much either. At least not very much."

"Not very? I wonder what you find so very different?" he said, wondering uncomfortably if she was going to make note of his leg.

"You are more handsome, I think."

George was utterly taken aback, but he managed to speak casually. "Oh? I am flattered you should think it, although it is the first time to my recollection anyone has called me so."

"Don't be absurd, George. I have always thought you very handsome." She grinned. "But now you put me in mind of a fallen angel, dark and mysterious and beautiful in a fallen sort of way. Yes, that's it," she said, observing him with satisfaction, and George couldn't help laughing.

"I see. A fallen angel, beautiful in his fallen sort of way. As you wish, Aubrey. I see that your imagination has not altered either. By God, it is good to see you."

"Is it, George? Is it really? I missed you so, you cannot guess. I knew that my Aunt Prudence must have kept back your letters to me, and she would not let me write to you, and then when I left to go to the seminary, I tried to write, but my letters were returned. I felt so sad, George, for I had no idea how to reach you and knew you could not know how to find me either. It was the most terrible feeling in the world."

She looked so sad that George felt a terrible rush of guilt. "I'm sorry, Aubrey."

"But now you have turned up here of all places, and it's the most wonderful thing possible, better than anything even I could have imagined! I've thought so often of meeting you again. I thought maybe I would find you in Vienna, coming off a gondola, or in Paris, strolling on one of the boulevards, or even in Athens, contemplating a ruin. I always looked for you, hoping . . . But I'm being foolish," she said, noting by the oddly withdrawn expression on his face that she had said too much, and probably upset him. "It's absurd, isn't it, having Annabelle as my dearest friend, and not knowing that you and she were so well-acquainted."

"Aubrey, you are not foolish in the least. I can quite understand—" George turned in surprise as a middle-aged woman came pounding up behind them, looking exactly like a hunter about to bag her prey.

"Aubrey! What *are* you doing!" she said with alarm. "And who is this . . . this person?"

"Oh, here you are, Miss Graham," Aubrey said brightly. "I do not believe you have yet met Mr. Asquith."

"No, I have not." Miss Graham looked him up and down carefully, and George was quite sure she did not miss a single detail of his dress, down to his top boots and the cape on his greatcoat.

"Mr. Asquith was a close friend of my family's," Aubrey said quickly—looking slightly defensive, George thought. He could hardly see why.

"I see. It is a pleasure, I am sure," Miss Graham replied dryly.

George bowed, quietly amused, thinking it was certainly time to disengage. "The pleasure is mine, Miss Graham. If you'll excuse me . . ." He began to move away, but Miss Graham waylaid him.

"How is it you came to know the de Salis family, Mr. Asquith?" she asked severely.

"We once lived on adjoining estates, Miss Graham," he said pleasantly enough.

"I see. That would have to be Havenstone. Yes, of course. Asquith. I thought the name sounded familiar. Your father is the Viscount Asquith, is he not?"

"He is." His face betrayed no expression at all, as ever when anyone mentioned his father.

"Hmm. Miss de Salis has told me quite a bit about her life in Hampshire. I have looked after Miss de Salis since then. I owned the school where Miss de Salis had the last years of her schooling."

"Indeed?" said George. "How nice." Once again he attempted to move off, but it was not to be. Miss Graham peered at him slightly more closely. "Have you come up from Havenstone? It is quite a distance to travel."

"I have not, Miss Graham. I now live here. I am steward to Paxton."

"The steward . . . Oh! The steward! I see!" Miss Graham's eyes lit up. She instantly abandoned her line of questioning, clearly aimed at flushing out any hidden intent Mr. Asquith might have had toward Aubrey. "But how marvelous! I have been an avid student of Paxton's history. Perhaps you would be so kind as to answer some questions for me, for there is a great deal

I wish to know, and I am sure you must know the history in great detail.''

"I am familiar with it, yes,'' George said, his heart sinking. ''Please, if I may be of assistance . . .''

He was trapped, he knew. There was no way for him to escape, short of overt rudeness or the sudden occurrence of a natural disaster. He called to the workman that he would be back later and to continue without him. For the next two hours he obligingly walked Miss Graham around Paxton, showing her in detail the gatehouse and barbican, now under extensive reconstruction, explaining in minute detail the process. Miss Graham was in transports, her keen mind taking in everything. He tried to include Aubrey, who trailed slightly behind, but Miss Graham hardly gave him time to pause for breath before she fired yet another question at him.

"I cannot thank you enough, Mr. Asquith,'' Miss Graham finally said, shaking his hand vigorously as the tour concluded. ''You have been most informative, and most kind indeed to indulge my inquisitiveness. I must go and take notes before I forget a single word. You'll find something to amuse yourself, won't you, Aubrey?'' she said, clearly having forgotten that she'd ever had a suspicious thought of George Asquith in her head, and went marching directly off, leaving them alone together.

Aubrey turned to George, her face solemn. ''Thank you very much, Mr. Asquith,'' she said, curtsying. ''You were truly . . . truly . . . informative. Informative and . . . and very forbearing.'' Her nose wrinkled up and a laugh escaped, and then another. ''Oh, George, I do apologize. She really isn't so bad, she's just very dedicated.''

"Dedicated?'' George said with the flicker of a

smile. "My dear Aubrey, I'd say the woman borders on obsession. Is she always quite this purposeful?"

"Always. She will not be turned aside from anything she considers a worthwhile pursuit."

George nodded. "Yes. I can see it most clearly. She is very solid, in nature and in build. She is more persistent than a terrier, and twice as inquisitive, traits that might serve admirably in the schoolroom, but I can see that they could be quite trying outside of it. Have you been happy with her, Aubrey?" The expression in his eyes suddenly changed to something she couldn't quite read.

"Happy?" she said, considering as she strolled next to him. "I don't know if I would use the word 'happy' to describe the last decade. I have been looked after, and Miss Graham has been most dedicated. But nothing can be compared to how things were, not in terms of happiness. Then I had people to love, who loved me in return." She stopped abruptly. "Please don't misunderstand me. I am very grateful to Miss Graham. She has been very kind. But it is not the same as having a home and family of one's own."

"No, it wouldn't be. I quite understand." He paused for a moment, then continued. "I am sorry, Aubrey, that everything took such a bad turn for you. One can only make the best of circumstances, and one can make a new life for oneself, I have found."

"I see what a wonderful new life you've made for yourself. You have been very successful. You must be very happy."

He stopped and looked down at her. "Happiness is relative, Aubrey. Sometimes it is making the best of what one has. Sometimes it is accepting that certain things cannot be changed, nor called back." It was too damnably true, he thought. It was far too damnably true for his own comfort.

Aubrey raised her eyes to his and smiled, her lashes slightly wet, and he wanted to put his arms around her and comfort her, but he knew those days were forever at an end, no matter how strongly he wanted to bring them back just at that moment.

"You have always been so much better at acceptance than I, George," she said ruefully. "You were always the strongest one, the person who held the rest of us together. I don't know what I would have done without you when all was said and done. It broke my heart to have to leave you."

"You were very young." George couldn't take another moment of this particular torture; he almost wished Miss Graham back. He looked away from her, wishing he could simply vanish into thin air. "You really must excuse me. I should return to the bailey. I do have people waiting."

"Of course," Aubrey said, wondering why all the warmth had suddenly vanished from his eyes. "Thank you again for giving Miss Graham her tour."

"Not at all."

He turned abruptly and walked off as Aubrey watched him, his gait so much steadier, the cane no longer appearing as a necessity but more as an afterthought. And yet as he disappeared into the distance, Aubrey noticed something in the set of his shoulders, something weary and sad, and she wondered at it. She had always been exceptionally fine-tuned to George, and that was one thing that apparently had not changed. That there was something troubling him did not escape her, and she resolved to discover what it was.

Miss Graham was in even higher transports when Aubrey returned to the house. "Aubrey, dear, the duke has actually sought me out to invite me to assist him in the library! I can scarcely credit the honor he has paid me, and naturally I could not refuse. You understand that I must forgo any further social activities, and every minute must be put to the best use."

"You must not think of me another moment, Miss Graham. I know how wonderful an opportunity this is for you, and you can be of inestimable value to the duke, I am certain." Aubrey not only understood, she was also secretly relieved, for she had had very little respite from Miss Graham in all the years she had been with her. The longest block of time they'd been even marginally apart had been the month in Greece, when Annabelle had stepped in—one fragmented month out of nine years.

Aubrey later confided this slightly disloyal thought in Annabelle's private apartments as they were in the midst of reminiscing about their adventures.

"Oh, do you remember the Turkish baths!" Annabelle said, holding her sides in hilarity. "If Miss Graham had only known! She really would never have countenanced another moment of our being together."

"Certainly not," Aubrey said with feeling, rolling onto her back and observing the ornately painted ceiling, complete with cavorting cherubs, from the end of the canopied bed. "Miss Graham is under the impression that God gave us bodies so that they could be clothed at every possible moment as a mark of extreme piety. Oh, now I'm not being very kind. But really, Annabelle, you can't imagine how difficult it has been to share a room and never show an inch of flesh."

Annabelle went off into a fresh paroxysm. "Oh, but, Aubrey, God had a completely different purpose for Miss Graham's flesh than for yours," she said, laughing so hard she could hardly speak. "I'm sure Miss

Graham looks her very best covered head to toe, and God is pleased.''

Aubrey looked at Annabelle with concern. ''Annabelle, what about the baby? Should you be indulging in such hilarity?''

Annabelle responded by burying her head in one of the pillows of the massive bed. ''I . . . I'm fine,'' came her muffled voice. She finally looked up at Aubrey, tears streaming down her cheeks. ''My dear friend, don't you see how silly this combination of you and Miss Graham is? I know you are devoted to her, and she to you, but don't you think it is time for a change? You cannot spend the rest of your life changing inside your nightdress.''

''Oh, but we usually have separate rooms,'' Aubrey said reassuringly. ''It is only when we are traveling that we share.'' Aubrey's brow crinkled as Annabelle dissolved again, twice as hard as before, and she came to the conclusion that pregnancy had an extraordinary effect on the brain, for Annabelle had always had a highly developed sense of humor, but she'd never before approached lunacy.

Aubrey quickly changed the subject, moving onto ground she considered less likely to cause another upheaval. But oddly enough, she had a reluctance to approach the one subject she had been burning to bring up—George—and before she knew it, the afternoon had flown by and Annabelle's voice had become fainter and fainter, until Aubrey realized she'd fallen asleep. Aubrey crept out and went to her own room, reasoning she could discuss George with Annabelle when Annabelle was in a steadier frame of mind. The business of making a child was most assuredly an odd one.

Aubrey found dinner an amusing affair, for Annabelle and the duke had most interesting friends, also well-traveled, and the conversation leapt about in a diverse fashion, never dragging. Better, Miss Graham was not there to keep an eye on her, and she could relax and enjoy herself.

George arrived late, just as the doors were being opened, and he gave Aubrey only a cursory smile. During the meal she attempted a number of times to engage him in conversation, for he was sitting diagonally to her at the table, but he would not be drawn. He looked tired, she thought, although he behaved perfectly civilly. George had always had a gift for civility that masked whatever might be going on beneath the surface.

Sensitive to that, she did not push him any further.

But what happened after dinner she could hardly feel responsible for, nor understand George's behavior at all.

She was standing with a group of people, discussing the ethical concerns of Lord Elgin's removal of so many valuable pieces from the Acropolis. George was on the fringes of the group, close to the window, observing from what seemed to be his customary position.

"But, Sir Thomas, despite what was decided," Aubrey said emphatically, "I cannot help but feel that taking the frieze, not to mention the Erechtheum Caryatid and the other statues from the Acropolis, was very wrong. The Turks have no right to decree such a removal, whether they presently happen to occupy the country or not. Furthermore, I think the British Museum should return them to their rightful place."

"But, Miss de Salis," the beleaguered baronet said, "I was only saying that the marbles will be greatly appreciated in a country such as ours, whereas very few appreciative people will venture as far as the Acropolis. It is not as if Lord Elgin stripped the entire structure, after all. He merely brought a piece of civilization to the civilized, and the argument was all long ago laid to rest, was it not?''

''But it was laid to rest by a majority of people who had not seen the original sight, Sir Thomas. It's a question of principle. After all, suppose the Ottoman Empire persists in handing over any Grecian antiquity as long as someone offers a high-enough price? The country would be stripped of its own monuments.''

''I am sure that will not happen. In any event, Lord Elgin's defense of his actions was most sound.''

''But, Sir Thomas,'' Aubrey said insistently, ''had you ever seen the Parthenon, you would understand completely how wrong it is for the frieze to have been taken from it. It would be like . . . like stripping the gateway from Paxton and carting it off to the Louvre to give an example of early English stonework. And think: Paxton is only a few hundred years old. The Parthenon is many thousands of years older than that!''

She looked up and saw that George had been listening. He was smiling, his eyes filled with amusement, and she smiled slowly in return, knowing that he understood her perfectly.

And then suddenly his eyes lost their laughter and warmth and went completely blank. He turned away and gave some instruction to a passing footman, as if their silent exchange had never taken place. A moment later he left the room.

The laughter vanished from Aubrey's face. She was baffled, feeling buffeted back and forth between the few moments of ease and familiarity they'd had and the removed coldness of a stranger, the stranger he seemed so deliberately determined to deal her. It hurt terribly, far more terribly than she would have thought. She had never once in all of her imaginings thought that George would ever reject her.

She had a sinking feeling in the pit of her stomach as a very simple truth struck her. Maybe there was nothing wrong with George at all. Maybe it was all to do with her. It was entirely possible that she had been indulging in her perpetual habit of daydreaming and had convinced herself that she and George still shared an unbreakable bond, a bond that she alone had kept alive in her mind. But George, although he had not in any way been unkind, was simply not there in the same way. He had not stayed mired in the past as she had. He had moved on with his life, had put her and Laurence and Papa behind him, knowing that there was no point in dwelling on what no longer was. That had always been her flaw, holding on to the past. She couldn't go on making up the impossible, as she had for so many years. This was cold, harsh reality and it bore no resemblance at all to her fantasies. George did not care.

Miss Graham was right: she didn't belong here; she'd be far better off devoting herself to teaching.

"Miss de Salis?" Harry asked, lightly touching her arm. "What is it? You were in high spirits a moment ago. Has something happened to upset you? It was not Sir Thomas' withdrawal from the conversation, was it? I thought you dealt with him most admirably."

"N—no," she said as brightly as she could, swallowing back the tears in her throat. "I was just thinking how nice it is to be part of a group such as this. It will be difficult to go back to teaching school when I leave Paxton next week."

"But I understood in Athens that Miss Graham had sold the seminary," Harry said with considerable surprise.

"She did, before we went on our tour. She decided she could not pass up the opportunity of seeing all the historical sights she had been teaching others about for so long. But now that we are returned, she has resolved to start another school and would like me to be her assistant headmistress. It will be in Bath, a most attractive location. I have made up my mind to accept her offer.''

''But is there not something else you would like to do with your life, other than teach? You are very young to cloister yourself away.''

''I really have no other options. I must make my own way in the world—I cannot live off someone else's generosity forever.''

''Ah, yes—your benefactor. Annabelle briefly mentioned the situation to me. I hope you do not mind. But surely he does not begrudge you the funds to live as you are living now?''

''No. That is not the issue, your grace. It is a conclusion I have come to on my own. Mr. Dickens does not yet know.''

''You do plan on informing him before you make such a decision?''

''I will write to him in the morning to tell him that whatever responsibility he has felt should be at an end. His debt to my father must surely be more than paid by now. We share no blood tie, and he has no legal obligation.''

''I do not know the details of your arrangement with Mr. Dickens, but do you not think he would welcome the opportunity to discuss such a decision with you?''

''I will explain myself to Mr. Dickens in my letter. I hoped you would not mind franking it for me in the morning?''

''Not at all. My signature is at your disposal. Give your letter to a footman and he will see it is brought to me. I must naturally respect your feelings, although I cannot help but wonder if your decision is a sound one. If I were your benefactor, Miss Aubrey de Salis,

I would do everything in my power to see you happy, and I am not convinced that being a schoolmistress for the rest of your days is going to accomplish that. There are so many other things in the world that you might choose from. I am sorry,'' he said with a wry smile, for he could see she was uncomfortable. ''I am being presumptuous. I really do know so little of your situation—I must be badly in need of a sound debate. It happens to me every now and then.''

''Does it?'' Aubrey said with a laugh. ''How very distressing.''

''Usually I take it out on Annabelle or George, but Annabelle has gone to bed, and George appears to have vanished, so I'm afraid that leaves you, Miss de Salis, and you strike me as being a worthy opponent.''

Aubrey realized he was very gracefully moving away from a subject that had appeared to distress her, and she was more than willing to help him. ''I have no proper experience with debating, your grace. George and my brother used to study Socratic logic while I played around their feet, but beyond that I have not had much study in the field. I would not think to tangle with an eminent scholar such as yourself.''

Harry smiled and propped himself against the mantelpiece. ''I am delighted you hold me in such high regard, Miss de Salis, and I shan't say another thing for fear of giving myself away. But you have brought up a subject I am most interested in, and that is how you come to know my friend George Asquith. You say he and your brother studied together?''

''Yes. They shared a tutor for many years. George was like a member of the family.''

''I see. How very interesting—I had no idea, but then, I did not know George until he came up to university. He was two years younger than I, but we became immediate friends. We had quite a few things in common. I was a bit of a recluse, and George . . . well, he had his own reasons for keeping apart.''

"I wanted to ask," Aubrey said, coloring. "I mean, I didn't want to pry, but George—his leg is so much better. But I do not understand—he was born with it so terribly twisted. It plagued him terribly, and now you would hardly know there was anything wrong."

Harry smiled. "It is a marvel, is it not? George had a surgery last year—a very experimental surgery, but he was willing to undergo the risks involved, which, as you can imagine, were considerable. Still, the surgeon has an extraordinary reputation for success, and so the risk was acceptable to George in exchange for the result. It was not a very pleasant experience at the time, or so I heard from others who looked after him, but it worked well enough."

"How wonderful!" Aubrey said, her eyes shining again. "He was always so brave, but I know how his leg bothered him. Not just the pain or deformity, but the way people looked at him, the things they said behind his back—sometimes to his face. I . . . I always wanted to protect him, but he wouldn't have it. Instead he used the sharpness of his brain to defend himself. You should have heard some of the things he said to those who bullied or pitied him! His tongue had far more of an effect than fists ever could."

"He has refined the practice. George has one of the most subtle tongues I have ever come across, and very effective, I might add. I have never once seen anyone get the better of him. He wields his wit like the mightiest of swords, and his cane is just as effective when he chooses to use it."

Aubrey laughed. "I remember when he was younger, just after my father died, when the extent of Papa's debts was discovered, some of the village boys taunted me. You can guess the sort of thing. But

George was there, and he took them on with his cane, all three of them. Of course they were younger, and they were fools in the bargain, but George had them all howling in pain and running away in terror. I don't think I ever loved him more than I did at that moment. Afterward, he turned to me and offered his arm as if nothing had happened. He grew at least three more feet in my eyes that day.''

Her eyes darkened, and she gave a small twisted smile. ''It was one of the last times I ever saw him— George, my great protector. He was a hero to me; he always had been. He and Laurence, they were so wonderful together. Laurence couldn't get about much because of his bad heart, and there was George with his bad leg, but it never mattered. They were both intent on their studies, and I did enough running for all three of us and so reported all the things that were going on in the outside world, from the vantage point of a tree-top or the depths of the bottom of a lake.''

''It sounds a wonderful time.''

''Yes, it was. It truly was. George and Laurence were terribly close, but they never pushed me away, they always made time for whatever foolishness I brought to them. Whenever I came racing in the door, they would put away their books or conversation and listen to me as if what I had to say was of the utmost fascination.''

''I'm sure it was,'' Harry said with a little laugh. ''I am learning a great deal I did not know before about my old friend.''

''He gave all of us a great deal of happiness. My father loved George, as did we all. But then Laurence died, and it wasn't the same after that.''

''I'm sorry. Given how close you all were, it must have been quite dreadful.''

''Yes, it was a very bad time, even though we knew

it was coming. But George was wonderful to my father and me afterward, always there when we needed him. Always. He spent hardly any time at his own home, because his father would have nothing to do with him. It was because he wasn't perfect,'' she added with disgust.

"Yes, I know,'' Harry said with a frown. "George has no liking for his father. It has always enraged me, the way the man treated him. George was his only child, by God, not to mention his son and heir, and he could not bring himself to speak to him, not even to give him the time of day. And all because of the wretched circumstances of his birth. George could hardly help that he came out the wrong way round, nor that his mother died in the process. And his blasted father was so wrapped up in his own pain and anger that he never once recognized his child's physical suffering, let alone the emotional suffering he caused on top.'' Harry stopped abruptly and rubbed the nape of his neck, smiling apologetically. "I beg your pardon. I'm afraid I became carried away.''

"You do understand, don't you?'' Aubrey said very softly. "You really do.''

"I think so. George has since been to me what he was to your family. He has been a rock, a good friend, someone in whom I have always been able to confide, to trust with my soul, never mind my properties. George has been the best friend a man could ever ask for. And I have never found a way to understand him as well as he has me. Until perhaps now.''

"Now?'' Aubrey asked in confusion. "Why now?''

"Ah. I think you may have given me the key by giving me some of the details of his youth. He doesn't talk easily about himself, as you know, and so I was largely in the dark as to his life before university. He never mentioned any of what you have told me, a rather large error of omission, to my way of thinking. It indicates how much it must have meant to him.''

"Oh. Well, I'm delighted to have been able to help. I wish I could find a way myself to get through to George, somehow to find the way back to the friendship we had, but he doesn't seem to want anything to do with it." She looked down and twisted her handkerchief between her fingers, thinking of what he had said to her just that morning. "I suppose I remind him of a time he has put behind him and would rather forget."

"Do you think so? I shouldn't be so sure," Harry said, considering carefully.

"Why is that, your grace?" Aubrey said. "He has made it very clear that a childhood friendship has no place in his life. I would be foolish not to accept that. George has always been removed from the outside world, although I never thought he'd become so removed to me. But then, a great deal of time has gone by, and people change."

"George keeps very much to himself and his thoughts close to his chest, but I do not think he has changed very much from when you knew him, at least not given the ways in which you described him. In fact, I believe in some ways he is less removed than he used to be, now that the pain is not constantly with him, for he does not have to exhibit such control to keep us all from guessing at it."

"I am glad for that, truly glad."

"So are we all. But perhaps other kinds of pain are not so simple to rectify. George is a very complex man, and not always easy to follow. Ah, well, I suppose it takes a good sense of direction if one is going to go wandering in mazes."

Aubrey smiled. "Oh, dear. You have put your finger

on it exactly, your grace. I have absolutely no sense of direction! It's been a terrible curse.''

Harry grinned. ''Have no fear. I have an excellent sense of direction myself, even in the dark. And please, do call me Harry. I can't be comfortable when my friends insist on treating me as if I breathed rarefied air.''

''Very well, Harry,'' Aubrey said gravely. ''I would have no one accuse me of being top-lofty.'' She put out her hand and Harry shook it.

''So nice to be among friends,'' he said. ''If you'll excuse me, I'm going to go up and see to Annabelle.'' He wandered off, leaving Aubrey looking after him with an appreciative smile, thinking that her friend Annabelle was very lucky indeed to have such a fine husband.

George was in the conservatory, his very favorite place to be when he needed quietude. Usually he was in the position of seeking quietude because of the outrageous behavior of others. That had never disturbed him. His life revolved around Paxton, its activities, and its people, and that was how he would have it. But that peace had been shattered when Aubrey had come crashing right into the middle of it and upset his calm, ordered existence.

He moved over to the glass doors, heavy with condensation, and absently ran his finger in a straight line down a pane. Little drops beaded up and slipped down the path that he'd made. He had chosen his course and would not deviate from it. Aubrey had no place in his life, and he certainly had none in hers, no matter how strong his feelings. It was so damnably hard to keep that in mind, though, and he'd had a very bad shock tonight, as if yesterday hadn't held enough in the way of nasty surprises.

Tonight he had realized just how very much Aubrey had crept under his skin. It wasn't a pleasant realization. He felt like an idiot for having let his control slip as far as it had, to have lasted all the way throughout dinner and then to have allowed one unexpected, innocent, but astonishingly seductive smile to set his blood on fire. His loins had leapt to life embarrassingly unbidden and unwanted, even after everything he had told himself earlier. He might as easily have been a callow youth, for all the influence he had over them. It seemed a hopeless situation, for with memory they began to stir again.

His will seemed to be eroding from underneath him, and he could no longer rely on himself to keep his sangfroid in place. That morning had proved that to him quite conclusively. Aubrey was no more going to behave as if they were casual acquaintances than she was going to slip back to being ten years old. He had thought last night that he would be able to manage to be near her without falling apart, but he hadn't counted on that smile of hers with her heart in her eyes, as if she were handing herself to him with no reservations, as if she had no awareness that he was a man and she was a woman and the resulting repercussions of those facts.

"Oh, God!" he exclaimed with frustration. "Damnation!" He *was* a man, and although she might think nothing had changed, one thing had changed completely. He had always loved her, but now he wanted her. He wanted her more than he had ever wanted anything in his life, and this simple fact had taken him completely by surprise. It had never crossed his mind to consider Aubrey in that light, but how could he help it now, given what a striking woman she had become? And yet he could hardly let it matter, for he had no right to her at all, and he knew it all too well. He could well enough imagine taking Aubrey to bed, and the expression on her face, first of disgust, and then pity, as she saw his mangled leg and the long red, puckered scars where the surgeon had cut so deeply onto the muscle. But that did not bear remembering.

Instead he closed his eyes and desperately tried to remember Aubrey as a child, at five, at eight, even at twelve. It became too dangerous after that to think of her at all. But all that he managed to see was Aubrey as she had been tonight, Aubrey with her cheeks flushed, her face animated, her hair a golden halo around her head, a simple ribbon threaded through it, the outline of her long limbs showing through her dress, the swell of her full breasts above the neckline of her rose-colored dress, a dress the exact color of her lips. . . . He groaned and leaned his head on his arm. It really was hopeless. She wouldn't go away, no matter what he did. Perhaps he should be the one to leave. It seemed the only solution.

"George?"

At first he thought he was imagining it, but then he saw the hazy image of her reflection in the foggy glass, and he slowly turned around, pulling his composure about him like an old, familiar cloak.

"Yes, Aubrey?" he replied coolly, desperately willing his body to behave. "What may I do for you? Oughtn't you to be with the other guests?"

"I . . . I wanted some time alone. I didn't come looking for you, if that is what you are thinking, but since you are here and it was you that I was thinking about, I might as well talk to you."

"Yes?" he drawled. "Was there something in particular?"

"George, it is exactly this—the way you treat me, as if I were suddenly an utter stranger. I cannot understand it. I wondered if I have done something to offend you.'' She looked down and bit her lip, obviously trying to keep the tears from her eyes. ''I know that it has been a very long time since we have seen each other, and one cannot rely on a childhood friendship, but I cannot believe that you have changed so much that you can no longer talk with me. We used to be such . . . such friends.''

''Aubrey . . . Aubrey,'' George said, his heart breaking for the unhappiness that he had caused, but steeling his resolve. ''Please, sit down here and dry your tears.'' He led her to a settee, and leaning his cane against the wall, sat down next to her and prepared himself to lie his head off.

''I am not crying,'' she said, taking his handkerchief and wiping her eyes. ''It must be the humidity.''

''It must be,'' George said, unexpectedly wanting to laugh. ''But I am still most sorry to see you upset, Aubrey. I cannot think what idea you have taken into your head that indicates I can no longer talk to you.''

''You have been very cold,'' she said. ''Not all the time, but often, and it is most unlike you, so I thought perhaps you no longer cared.''

''Naturally I care, Aubrey.'' He forced himself on with difficulty. ''But many years have gone by since we were those two young people you remember, and we have both changed in many ways. I am no longer the young boy you knew, nor the raw young man. And you are now a young woman with a whole life ahead of her. There's no going back to the past, Aubrey, and it would be foolish to try to recreate the relationship we had then, for it would not fit into this world. You are too old to go dashing barefoot through the woods, and I am far too old to make up stories about fairy children living in those woods to entertain you. And in any case, we are most certainly at an age when we must observe the proprieties, which we are not doing very well at this moment.''

Aubrey's heart felt as if it had suddenly gone utterly numb, as close to dead as numb would take her. She wiped her eyes, then returned George's handkerchief. ''No, of course, you are quite right. I had forgotten about observing the proprieties. It was foolish of me, I suppose, to think that anything could be the same. I should have learned that lesson a very long time ago. Actually, I thought I had, until I saw you again. I suppose that brought everything back rather sharply, and so I lost my perspective. I see that now, and I will not ask anything more of you. But, George, you seemed so unexpectedly detached, and so I thought—''

''As you said, you thought you had done something to offend. No, Aubrey, believe me, you have done nothing at all save for being yourself, and that is a pleasure. It always has been, and I imagine it always will be. And now, if your mind has been put to rest, I have—''

''George,'' Aubrey said softly, cutting him off, ''I only wanted to say one thing more to you—no, actually two things. I will not speak again of anything personal after this. First, it has made me very happy to be with you again. Even if we cannot be the same as we once were, it has given me great happiness to be near you, for you have reminded me so strongly of Laurence and Papa, and there is nothing else in my life that has done that, not with Aldershot gone. Those were very fine and happy days, the best of my life, and you were an integral part of them.''

''Aubrey, don't—''

''Please, allow me to finish. You know that you were my favorite person in the world next to Laurence. You needn't have felt the same about me, for you were so much older than I, at least as old as five years' difference appears to children. But you were always so kind to me, and so considerate, and I want you to know now that I haven't forgotten a moment of what you were like and what you did for me. No, please don't say anything. I truly won't speak of it again. I know that that time is long over for you. The second thing is this, and I know you have never liked any mention of it, but I'll speak despite that. I have noticed how much your leg has improved. I remember well how it pained you constantly, and how brave you always were, and to see you so very much better also gives me great happiness. Good night, George. I shan't bother you again. But I did want to tell you how I felt. I'm sorry we can no longer be friends.''

She gave him a long sad look, then slipped away, her face wet with her tears.

George sat there for a long time after, turning his handkerchief over and over in his hand, trying to put the flood of emotions back into the place where they belonged, trying to put Aubrey back into the place where she belonged.

But Aubrey's simple honesty and warmth had reopened the old wound far too successfully, and memory with all of its attendant pain had been unleashed and washed over him as if time had stood still.

It wasn't just the memories—there were enough of those that were happy enough. It was the worst of them, the ones he had locked in some dark recess of his soul, the ones that chronicled the systematic stripping from him one by one of the only family he had ever known, of all the people he had ever loved.

George swallowed hard against the tight knot in his throat. Laurence's face swam before his eyes, his face as white as the sheets under which he lay, his gentle voice softly saying his good-bye, calling him his brother. And then, like turning the pages of a book, there was Lord de Salis the day he buried his son, the life gone out of him as surely as if he had died himself, turning wearily to George for comfort that could not be given.

And he remembered Aubrey just as clearly, poor Aubrey at her brother's funeral, and then at her father's, only ten months later. She'd been dressed all in black as she was taken away from Aldershot, tears streaming down the little face pressed against the carriage window. He had stood and watched until the carriage had become a speck in the distance, then disappeared completely from sight.

He clenched and unclenched his fists, searching for control, but it was too late. The tears came despite his best efforts, and he put his head in his hands, his entire body shaking as he gave himself over to them. George cried for the first time in ten years, for the first time since the day that Aubrey had left Aldershot forever, the last and most beloved of the de Salis family taken from him.

He cried for Aubrey, the sweet girl who had once been so full of joy and life and laughter, who should have had the world given to her, who now seemed so unexpectedly unhappy. He cried for Laurence, who had died so young, and he cried for Lord de Salis, who had been as much a father to him as he had ever known. But those were old losses, and finally, and with true grief, he cried for himself and what could never be his.

He made his way to bed in the cold, gray hours just before dawn.

Aubrey also found sleep elusive that night. She finally gave up, her eyes swollen with spent tears, her throat hot and dry, and she slipped out of bed, grateful for the warmth that still seeped from the embers in the fireplace. She bundled herself in a shawl, lit a candle, and fetched her writing materials. She had a difficult letter to her benefactor to write, and if she could not sleep, at least she could get it out of the way.

It took her well over two hours and a number of false starts to complete. She usually found it very easy to pen a letter to her dear Mr. Dickens, pouring her heart into the process, but this was the hardest letter she'd ever had to write. She'd become so very fond of him over the years that she was loath to hurt or disappoint him in any way.

He would no doubt think her ungrateful, for if he had not rescued her from her dreadful Aunt Prudence, where would she be today? No doubt still there, doing the mending in a back room somewhere. But he had rescued her, and sent her to Miss Graham's seminary, and it had made all the difference in her life. He had wanted so much for her to marry well, but she could hardly explain to him that there had never been any prospects of marriage on the horizon, were none now, and there never would be any.

Aubrey slumped in her chair and thought for a few minutes, then brightened. Mr. Dickens had insisted, after all, that she take the Continental tour to further her education—maybe he would understand if she put it in that light. She was going to put her education to good use. It was true, after all. She hardly need add that there was nothing else she was suited for—the penniless daughter of a baron might have some sort of social rank, but it counted for very little. Miss Graham had been very clear on that point.

Perhaps if she tried to convince him that it was what she really wanted to do, he would accept it more easily. He had been so very sweet, trying to push a dowry upon her, offering her a Season, all things she could not possibly accept, and so declined rather awk-

wardly; but it had not before occurred to her to tell
him that all she longed for in the world was to dedicate
herself to teaching. It might not be entirely true, but
it would spare his feelings.

She finally managed to complete her missive, not
without a few tears shed. As hard as it was to admit
to herself, reality was more difficult to face than she'd
thought. A most awful awareness had come upon her
in the conservatory as she'd felt her heart tighten in
her chest until it had truly felt about to break. George.
She'd known she had loved him always, for as long as
she could remember, and for so long it had never occurred to her that love could change to something so
different and so much more powerful. What had happened that could make her want his arms around her
so badly that she ached, that she wanted . . . What?
She didn't even know what this nameless longing was.
She only knew she wanted him in a quiet, most desperate way. It had also never occurred to her that
anything could ever again be quite so painful as losing
her family. George might just as well have died, for
all that she had any sort of tie to him.

But it could hardly matter now, she thought despon-
dently, twisting the loose strands of her hair around
her finger. In a few days her life would go back to the
same humdrum existence she had known at the seminary for all those long years. George would be forever
lost to her, far more lost than he had been all the years
she had fantasized about him, nurtured a secret hope she
would find him and all would be well.

She sat and stared at the letter on her lap until the
last of the embers faded to ash, forcing her back to the
warmth of her bed.

"You wished to see me, Harry?" George appeared
in Harry's study, only the very slight bruising under

his eyes attesting to his long night. Other than that, he looked his usual imperturbable self, and he stood just inside the door, regarding Harry quizzically.

"Yes, I did wish to see you." Harry leaned back in his chair. He'd had a most enlightening conversation early that morning with Annabelle and was prepared to put it to good use. In any case, it was St. Valentine's Day and he felt like playing Cupid. He pulled out his first arrow. "Please, sit down, George. I must confess, I have been concerned about you over the last few days. You have been looking tired, my friend. Is there any particular reason, anything I can do to help?"

George's surprise at the question was betrayed by only the slightest rise of his eyebrow. "Tired, Harry? How extraordinary. I was not aware of being anything but well-rested."

"Ah. I can see you are going to make this difficult. I should hardly be surprised. I thought that you might have something on your mind, for you have been unusually reserved recently and we have seen very little of you. All is well at Havenstone? Your father's condition has not deteriorated?"

"No one has informed me if it has, and I would hardly be losing sleep over such a thing. I imagine I'll be notified when he finally sticks his spoon in the wall, and not before then. But you surprise me, Harry. When did you begin worrying yourself over the state of my father's health?"

"I must confess," Harry said with a smile, "my only concern until now has been how soon your responsibilities at Havenstone might take you away."

"I hadn't thought of it. I imagine that in the event, I will hire myself a steward," George said wryly. "I cannot imagine I have given you any indication that I was about to leave Paxton. Is that why you have summoned me? You have heard some rumor to that effect?''

"No, I've heard nothing at all."

"Harry, you are behaving most oddly. Why do I feel as if we are engaged in a game of cat and mouse? If there is something you are leading up to, then say it."

"Very well. It is simply this. I believe something has happened to distress you, and I think you would feel better if you spoke of it. Come, George, whatever it is, you can rely on me. I have known you these many years and I cannot think how many times you have rescued me from one disaster or another. Let me return the favor and help you if I can."

George rubbed his forehead with a finger. "If I could, I would invent something plausible, but nothing occurs to me, Harry, and I'm not in the habit of lying to you."

"Do you mean to slight me, or do you simply not want to admit that you are as human as the rest of us?"

George inclined his head. "I have never thought to rise above my mortality, Harry. Perhaps it is because I have lived so closely with my imperfections for all of my life that I am acutely aware of their consequences."

Harry's amusement faded, and he wondered with alarm whether he had been wrong. "Has this to do with your health, George? If it has, then you must tell me. I will write to the man in Vienna and—"

"No, it's not that, Harry; please don't concern yourself. The surgeon you sent did an exemplary job, and as I told you, the pain has been much reduced. My health is really greatly improved, and I am most grateful to you."

Harry gave a relieved sigh. "You have nothing to be grateful for. It gives me the greatest of pleasure to see you so much better. And who knows? Perhaps in another few years Dr. Heigelbrow will have developed a perfect cure and you will be leaping hedgerows.''

George shuddered eloquently. ''Thank you, Harry, but I think I have had quite enough of Dr. Heigelbrow and his experiments, no matter how successful. I will be forever indebted to you, but I am quite content.''

''Well, if it is not your health, what then? I have never been accused of being a slow-top, but I must confess I am at a loss. You might as well give it up, George, for my persistence is legendary. I will have it out of you one way or another, and if I don't, then you know perfectly well that Annabelle will. And that, my friend, could lead to all sorts of unforeseen consequences.''

The corner of George's mouth twitched. ''For the love of God, Harry, please don't say anything to Annabelle, or I shall never have a moment's peace. I had not thought you would resort to threats. If you really must know, I have been under a slight strain. However, it is nothing of great importance, nothing to concern yourself about. The truth of the matter is that one of your guests has brought up some old memories, things I thought I had long ago laid to rest.''

''I see. It wouldn't be Miss de Salis, by any chance?''

''Yes, as it happens. But then, you were aware that we were previously acquainted, so I should not be surprised by your perspicacity.''

''I don't think I have ever managed to surprise you, George,'' Harry said sadly. ''So it won't surprise you if I tell you that Miss de Salis has told me quite a lot about your close connection with her family. Actually, I am glad her name has come up, for I wanted to speak with you about her.''

''Yes?'' George said as neutrally as he could manage. Aubrey was the very last person he wanted to talk about just now, and he couldn't imagine what Harry could possibly want to discuss.

"You know she has become a good friend of Annabelle's, of course, and Annabelle has had time to observe her relationship with Miss Graham. She's Aubrey's—"

"Yes, yes. I know who she is. And . . . ?"

"Aubrey told me last night that she plans to accept a post in Miss Graham's school. A permanent post, George, as assistant headmistress. I believe she is on the verge of giving Miss Graham her decision."

George leaned forward in his chair, his eyes sharp. "What sort of poppycock is this? I've never heard such an absurd idea!"

"Good. I was hoping you would take that approach. I cannot think of anyone else who might help to make some sense out of it, given that you once knew her so well. I think that I should give you some background so you might better understand what has brought her to this decision."

George leaned back in his chair, his eyes more hooded than usual. "Yes?"

"It begins and ends with Miss Graham, I believe. Aubrey was put under the woman's charge at a very young and influential age. She had no family, save for some dreadful aunt who had no interest in her."

"Yes, I know all of this. What are you getting at?"

"I believe that Miss Graham has played upon Aubrey's youth and vulnerability, causing her to think that the only productive life she could lead was the one Miss Graham offered her. I don't think Miss Graham's a malicious woman, only a bit shortsighted and absorbed with her own vision of the world."

"Yes . . . well, it's a vision that I don't think has

been very productive for Aubrey. She should have fallen in love and married long since.''

''Yes, I agree. But how could she? The way Miss Graham fends off the gentlemen, I don't think Aubrey's ever had much of a chance to engage in conversation, let alone to make a match. I have seen Miss Graham in action, you must remember, and she guards Aubrey like a dragon at the gate of a sanctuary.''

''Does she, by God?'' George said slowly, remembering Miss Graham's behavior of the previous morning and feeling the first stirrings of anger.

''Yes, she does. Which is why I offered Miss Graham a job in the library, reasoning it was the only way poor Aubrey would get a chance to breathe. I realized very quickly in Greece that if one dangles any sort of antiquity before Miss Graham, she's off like a shot, and Aubrey's left to fend for herself.''

''Yes, you're quite right,'' George said, sitting up straighter. ''She did exactly the same thing yesterday, wanting a tour of Paxton. Aubrey might as well have vanished from the face of the earth as far as she was concerned.''

''I'm hardly surprised. Distracting Miss Graham worked very well in Athens, which is abounding with antiquities, and so Aubrey was left to spend time with Annabelle, a distinct blessing. Annabelle's only regret was that there were no eligible young men around at the time, for she thought it might be the only chance Aubrey would have in years for some decent introductions. According to Annabelle, Miss Graham doesn't have a very high opinion of love or sex or reproduction. My wife also has the distinct impression that Miss Graham has neglected to inform Aubrey about the latter two. It is no wonder Aubrey has such a curiously childlike quality to her. She's utterly innocent.''

George put his head in his hands for a moment.

"Dear God," he said, then looked up. "I can scarcely credit what I'm hearing. I'm going to do murder, Harry, I swear it. She's had sole responsibility for Aubrey, and she's done nothing but try to strip every bit of joy from the girl, and for what? For what, I ask? Aubrey might as well have gone to a convent, for all it appears Miss Graham has prepared her for the world! It doesn't sound as if Miss Graham wants Aubrey to go out into the world at all."

"I suspect she is a lonely old woman who has become very attached to Aubrey and doesn't want to lose her. I doubt very much that she has any idea of what her attitudes have done to Aubrey. In fact, I imagine she thinks she has done a brilliant job of raising her. Aubrey is humble, modest to an extreme—certainly unaware of her own beauty—that is very obvious; she is without artifice, she is studious, and she is biddable, all high attributes on Miss Graham's list. Miss Graham has also banged it into her head—and this, again, according to Annabelle—that to desire anything but hard work and dedicated service to others is the height of self-indulgence."

"It's no wonder Aubrey refused a Season," George said, his voice shaking. "Miss Graham must have convinced her against it."

"I am sure. I am certain Aubrey would never have taken her tour of the Continent had it not been something that had irresistibly appealed to Miss Graham. And I am also certain that Miss Graham is behind this latest idea. The fact that it will suit Miss Graham very well to continue to have Aubrey at her beck and call probably hasn't occurred to Aubrey. From everything she's said, I think she really does feel truly obligated to Miss Graham."

"It probably also hasn't occurred to Aubrey that Miss Graham has been well-paid for her services all these years, and was given a free Continental tour as well,'' George said bitingly.

''Interesting. That aspect probably hasn't occurred to Miss Graham either. I am sure she thought it was only her due.''

''Of all the—'' George clamped his teeth down and rose, turning his back to Harry, for he did not want his face to betray him. But it was no good, for his knuckles gave him away, having gone completely white on his cane.

''It is rather sad, isn't it?'' Harry said to George's stiff back. ''A spinster trying to force a vital, beautiful young girl into her own puritanical image? Oh, I am sure Miss Graham did it for the very best of moral reasons. And Aubrey believes that Miss Graham and her school are the only options left to her because there has been no one to tell her anything else.''

George turned around and glared at Harry. ''I cannot believe Aubrey would think such a thing for a moment. You forget she has a benefactor, and I am sure he will not stand for this for a moment.''

''Ah, yes, the benefactor. I don't suppose you know anything about him? I didn't want to pry too much last night, and Annabelle drew a blank this morning, save that Aubrey's very attached to him.''

George found himself wondering what Aubrey meant by ''attached.'' ''I really don't know very much, Harry, only that he was an old friend of her father's, and there was some matter of a debt to the family. He has looked after her well-being for most of this time, although I'm beginning to think he has not done a very good job.''

''I can't imagine how he was to know what has been transpiring. It's rather an insidious sort of thing unless one sees it for oneself. But it's a pity you don't know more, for here is the gist of the thing: Miss Graham has put it into Aubrey's head that she has lived off this man's benevolence for far too long as it is. Aubrey now feels she cannot take another penny from him, that she must be fully independent of him. She wants to terminate the association. It's something to do with accepting charity, I believe, and repaying Miss Graham, and so on."

"I cannot credit this!" A vein throbbed in George's temple. "I truly cannot! Aubrey would never be so foolish as to cut herself off—she simply wouldn't be."

"But it is quite true. Aubrey would not hear a word from me to the contrary. She has written to the man to inform him of her decision. In fact, I probably have the letter right here." He searched through the pile of outgoing mail that had been brought for him to frank. "Yes, here it is. To a Jerome Dickens, Esquire, of 64 St. James's Street. George, what are you doing, man?" He stared incredulously at his friend, who had pulled the missive from his hand and was tearing it open. "George," he said in as serious a reproof as he had ever given him, "I really don't think this is at all correct. Please give that to me."

"Oh, hush, Harry," George said, sinking down in the chair and reading the paper intently. When he was finished, he threw it down on the table. It confirmed everything Harry had told him.

"Why in *God*'s name didn't I see it coming?" he said with disgust. "It should have been as clear as day—all the things she has said over the last two days, especially last night. I just heard what I wanted to hear, I suppose. Oh, damnation! How stupid could a man be?"

Harry regarded George mildly, his chin resting on his fist. "That's all very well and fine, and I'm delighted that you are taking such a passionate interest in Aubrey's affairs, but just how are you going to explain to Mr. Dickens that you not only pilfered his letter but also helped yourself to the contents?''

"I assure you, he won't mind."

"I beg your pardon, but if I were Mr. Dickens, I'd mind very much."

"Oh, for the love of God, Harry, don't be obtuse! I *am* Mr. Dickens. I have every right to read my own letter."

"You? *You* are Jerome Dickens? Good God!'' Harry stared at him for one incredulous moment, his agile brain leaping to all sorts of interesting conclusions, and then he crowed with delight. "The mysterious benefactor himself. You've been looking after Aubrey for all these years and she's never had an inkling? How absolutely marvelous! Of course, you're going to have to explain yourself, but I must say, it's a wonderful twist to the story, and quite typical of you, when I think about it. I should have thought of it myself. It's positively Machiavellian! You have surprised me, George. You well and truly have."

"Harry, do come down to earth for a moment, and it's not the least bit Machiavellian." George felt a complete idiot. "It's perfectly simple," he said, recouping his dignity with an effort.

"Whatever you say," Harry said, leaning back in his chair and folding his hands over his trim stomach, looking at George like a cat might look at a cream pot.

"And you can wipe that smug expression off your face. This is not amusing in the least."

"Certainly not," Harry agreed.

George raked a hand through his hair, an extremely uncharacteristic gesture, then remembered himself and smoothed it back down again as best he could. "I suppose I do owe you an explanation, although it's rather awkward. As you are aware, I have known Aubrey for many years. Her brother, Laurence, was a particular friend of mine. I was the same age as Laurence, and we shared a tutor. Lord de Salis didn't seem to mind having me underfoot all the time; Lady de Salis had died shortly after Aubrey's birth, and I suppose he was glad for the company we three provided him. But I digress. Laurence had always had a weak heart and he died when he was just eighteen.'' George paused for a moment and cleared his throat. ''It was very hard on Aubrey. They'd always been quite close, and then her father died less than a year later. I suppose it was the shock of losing Laurence—Lord de Salis never recovered from it, and the first chill he caught killed him.''

''What a sad story,'' Harry said sympathetically, thinking what a different and very unemotional version it was of the story that he had heard from Aubrey. ''How very difficult it must have been for Aubrey.''

''It was,'' George said, but did not elaborate.

''And what happened to Aubrey?''

''That was the terrible thing, you see. Lord de Salis was a good man, but not a very practical one, and when he died it was quickly discovered that he had been living on credit for some time.''

''Yes, I vaguely remember hearing something about a problem after his death. Bad investments on the 'Change, wasn't it?''

''Exactly. In any case, Aubrey was only fourteen, and was left completely on her own. The estate was sold to pay the debts Lord de Salis had left, so there was no money and nowhere for her to go, save to an aunt who didn't want her and who made her life a misery for the year she was there. I came to hear about it, and so I stepped in—Harry, you must swear you'll never let a word of this out of this room.''

''Of course not. I wouldn't think of such a thing. I

should be offended that you even mentioned it, but given your distressed state, I'll keep my ducal pride to myself.''

"Thank you. It's very important Aubrey never learn of my actions. By that time I was twenty, and I'd received a small inheritance from my maternal grandmother. I settled most of it on Aubrey in a trust, with the provision that she never know my true identity. She was only to know of me as Jerome Dickens, an old friend of her father's, and no more than that. I arranged for her to be sent to the seminary, where she could live year-round. She was meant to have a Season when she finished her schooling, but she refused, and now I finally know why. The rest you know.''

"Indeed.''

"That's all.''

"I see. You're quite sure that's all?''

"Yes,'' George said firmly. "What more could there be?''

"I have no idea. It is an interesting story and one that speaks eloquently of your good heart. And yet, my dear friend, you have not yet explained why Aubrey's arrival at Paxton has sent you into such a state.''

"Harry, for God's sake, can't you see? I know far too much about Aubrey's life in the years since her father died, certainly too much for someone who is not supposed to have had any knowledge of her since that time. Given the fact that we have been corresponding for all these years—''

"Corresponding as Mr. Dickens, not yourself.''

George regarded Harry impatiently. "I've just finished telling you that as far as she's concerned, I've had virtually no word of her since she left Aldershot. As her 'benefactor,' however, I've kept in close touch. From the beginning, Aubrey felt that if she had someone kind enough to aid her, the least she could do was to let him know how she was getting along. I've had her letters forwarded to me through my solicitor, whose address I use as Mr. Dickens. Naturally, I have always replied, although I've had to disguise my handwriting, for she would have recognized it. Ironically, because 'Mr. Dickens' has remained a virtual stranger, whom she knew she would never meet, she has written almost as she would in a journal, confiding many of her innermost thoughts—although not enough of them, apparently,'' he added with a frown. "So you see, knowing what I do about her, I might easily say something to give the entire thing away, and that I cannot risk.''

"But where is the risk? And why, George, are you so determined to keep your largess a secret?''

"For a man with a razor-sharp brain, Harry, you're being unusually dull. It's perfectly obvious. I have never wanted her to feel she has taken charity from me. She knew I didn't have all that much money of my own, or at least I wouldn't have until my father died—and he'll probably spend the entire lot just to spite me. She would never have let me use my grandmother's funds to support her, even though I kept enough back to complete my own education, and since then you have paid me more than well, so I did not particularly need it. It was easier to let her believe she was accepting money from a mysterious stranger who, she believed, owed her family an obligation. I did, in fact, owe the family a very great obligation, given the debt I will always owe her father for my education, never mind that I promised Laurence before he died that I'd always keep an eye out for his sister.''

"Ah,'' said Harry, thinking of what Aubrey had told him about the very wise Laurence. "A promise to keep. Even more significant.''

"Furthermore,'' George said, ignoring him, "if

word ever got out, Aubrey might be put in a compromised position. After all, there is only five years' difference in our ages, and the gossips might see the arrangement differently than it was intended, as absurd as such an idea would be. Now, do you understand?''

''Yes, I think perhaps I do. However, I learned some time ago that being honest can save one a great deal of unnecessary trouble and heartache.''

''But these are very different circumstances, Harry. I cannot upset Aubrey's life at this point, which is what would certainly happen if she learned the truth.''

''It hasn't occurred to you that she might have a positive response?'' Harry asked, wondering just how much George was hiding from Aubrey, and how much he was hiding from himself.

''A positive response? Harry, I have deceived her. I did it for her own good, but as I told you, she has been pouring her heart out on paper to someone she considers a benevolent stranger. She has accepted money from the same stranger, who has led her to believe that there was a financial debt outstanding. She believes she will never in her life meet this person. If I should suddenly announce that I am one and the same as her benevolent stranger, I can scarcely imagine her reaction. No, thank you. I would rather keep things exactly as they are. But thank you, Harry. You have been most helpful. I feel much clearer about the course I must pursue. I will write her a firm letter as Mr. Dickens, explaining why she must not accept Miss Graham's offer, and I will have a quiet word with her myself, pointing out some of the things you and I have discussed.''

''But, George, you've already convinced her that you no longer care one way or the other what happens to her. I'm sorry, but Aubrey told me that last night. That in itself only confirms what Miss Graham has told her about her situation, that she has no one in the world left who cares *but* Miss Graham, and nowhere else to go. You have a fairly large problem on your hands, the way I see it. I do in truth believe you are the only person who can set her straight, but I think there is only one way to do that. You must tell her the truth about your being Mr. Dickens.''

"Harry, I have just told you why—"

"And I have just told you why your reasoning is faulty." Harry reached into Cupid's quiver for his final arrow. "But even more important than that is to tell her how you feel about her."

George's head jerked up. He had gone suddenly pale. "What do you mean by that?"

"My dear friend, it is perfectly obvious to me that you are in love with Aubrey de Salis and have been for some time. It is also perfectly clear to me that she is in love with you, although whether she is aware of the fact, I do not know. Given those two factors, it seems to me that either you can both go through your lives miserable and apart, or you can find your courage and change both your lives for the good." He rose. "Think it over. I have business elsewhere. And by the by, George," he said as he was on his way out, "since I owe you a favor or two, I'll give you this last piece of unsolicited advice. I wouldn't use your bad leg as an excuse to save Aubrey from yourself. It's never mattered a bit to Aubrey, and in any case, your leg's nearly as good as new. It's high time you saw it that way yourself."

George heard Harry's cheerful whistle echoing down the corridor. It seemed to last forever, and then there was silence.

It was a particularly fine February that year, and Annabelle and Aubrey went out walking that afternoon in the garden to have the quiet coze Annabelle had suggested. She wasted very little time with trivialities before going straight to the point.

". . . So Harry told me everything about your childhood with George, and how close you'd been, and I was so happy for you to have found each other again! And then he told me that despite that, you were going to closet yourself away forever with sour old Miss Graham. I cannot understand you, Aubrey—we did everything we could to escape her in Greece. We were discussing it just yesterday, and you said nothing of any of this nonsense to me. How could you want to do such a thing, especially when you have George, and us? It doesn't make any sense at all, Aubrey."

"But it does," Aubrey said in protest. "I cannot think why you are both so up in arms over the idea. It was George, you see, who finally brought it home to me. I cannot continue to be an idealistic child, thinking that somehow, somewhere, all my dreams are going to come true. Do you know, when I was a child, I was quite determined I was going to marry George one day. It seems absurd now, I know, but I loved him so dearly, and I was so convinced he loved me. I think he probably did, as children do love, quietly and without conditions attached. I thought all I had to do was to wait to grow up. But then life comes along and shakes one around, and all those things one once so much hoped for turn out to be nothing more than a silly dream. It's such a shame, to lose all those wonderful illusions."

"Do you think they are truly lost, or do you think you have merely set them aside?" Annabelle asked, utterly fascinated by Aubrey's feelings for George.

"Oh, they are lost, I think. How could they not be? An illusion is an illusion, after all, nothing to do with reality. Life is quite harsh and does not take into consideration one's needs or desires. It simply sweeps along like a typhoon, and catches everything up in its path."

Annabelle chuckled. "It indeed does that. But sometimes what it catches up can be very interesting. I would hold on to some of those dreams, Aubrey, for life might be deadly dull without them."

Aubrey sighed. "Yes. Deadly dull, but at least safe, and I would also be doing some good to others, repaying what has been given to me."

"Aubrey, you sound positively pious!" Annabelle said on a laugh. "It doesn't suit you in the least. It's a pity you look so angelic, you know. I am sure people must be constantly fooled by you, but I know you're not the least bit angelic, and I'm very grateful for it."

"I'm so very glad you are my friend, Annabelle. It becomes so exhausting always to try to be good, and grateful, and attentive, and all those other dreary things, when underneath I'm longing to jump out of my skin, to dance. Do you know," she said suddenly, as if the thought had just occurred to her, "I have never danced the waltz." And then she blushed furiously. "I longed to when we were in Vienna, but Miss Graham would never have countenanced it."

"Oh, Aubrey," Annabelle said, "I really must take you in hand."

"You mustn't worry about me, Annabelle. I have a very rich inner life, even though Miss Graham would be horrified if she knew about it. My imagination is positively ruinous."

"Which is another reason why you must not make this decision, Aubrey. Your outer life should be just as rich as your inner life."

"But I cannot keep accepting charity from my benefactor, Annabelle. It isn't right. In any case, I have already been through all of this with Harry.''

_ "Yes, I know. But I was wondering, don't you think your benefactor might be hurt that you no longer need him?''

"What a peculiar idea! I should think he'll be relieved." And then she thought with a twinge of his wonderful letters, the letters that had sustained her through so many of the dark times. "I should think I will miss him far more than he will miss me. He is very good with words, and I have always felt as if I have a lifeline to a friend, even when things seemed very bad. He has a generosity of spirit, a finely honed mind, and a humorous but insightful outlook upon the world. I know it is foolishness to read all of that into him when I've never met him, but I feel somehow attached—''

"Oh, not at all," Annabelle said, settling herself with a sigh on the bench by the little fish pond. "I can see exactly how you would become attached to such a person. After all, you have lived a very solitary life since you were fourteen, devoid of most normal emotional contacts. I cannot imagine how it would be to lose a brother and then a father, then to be placed as a poor relation in the home of a cousin who despised you. We won't even mention Miss Graham and your years with her. It's no good to protest, Aubrey. I cannot like her. I am very happy that at least you have had Mr. Dickens as some sort of outside contact, even if it has been only through the post. If I were in your position, I would have made up all sorts of stories about him. It is all deliciously mysterious, after all. I should have made him into someone very daring—a sheikh, or possibly a highwayman, I'm not sure.''

Aubrey laughed. "I'm afraid that Miss Graham has insisted that he is most likely an old man, and most probably close to death, yet another reason I should ensure my future. She does try so very hard to keep me on the correct path, Annabelle, which cannot be easy with someone like myself.''

''Nevertheless, Miss Graham should let you daydream in peace,'' Annabelle said firmly. ''It's no good stifling a person's creativity.'' And then her eyes suddenly widened, and she gasped, her hand going to her abdomen.

''Annabelle? Annabelle, what is it?'' Aubrey asked in alarm.

''Oh, dear, Harry's going to be so very cross,'' Annabelle said in dismay. ''He did tell me just this morning not to go galloping around the garden.'' She gasped again and doubled over, unable to straighten for a full minute. ''I do believe the baby's coming, Aubrey,'' she finally managed to say. ''I've been feeling quite odd since this morning. We'd better go inside. I have a dreadful feeling it might be coming rather quickly.''

Aubrey, trying not to panic, helped Annabelle inside, turned her over to her maid, and had Harry summoned immediately, anxiously waiting for him outside Annabelle's room while the maid helped Annabelle into bed.

''Harry,'' Aubrey said as he came down the hall not five minutes later, ''thank goodness you're here! It's Annabelle. She says it's her time, and I think she must be right. There was . . .'' She blushed furiously. ''There was suddenly water everywhere, and she seemed to think that meant something.''

Harry gave her a sharp look, then disappeared inside. Two minutes later he was back. ''Ask one of the footmen to have the midwife summoned immediately, Aubrey, and tell him to find the housekeeper. We'll need hot water and blankets, a scissors . . . Never mind, she'll know. I don't think there's going to be time for the midwife. Ah, well, I reckon I can deliver my own child as well as the next person.''

Aubrey's lips went completely bloodless. "Oh," she said.

Harry smiled as if he delivered babies every day of the week. "Please don't faint, Aubrey. Annabelle will be perfectly fine. Now, off you go—you'd best hurry . . . and, Aubrey," he said as an afterthought, "after you've delivered the messages, go and find George. He should know, although there's nothing he can do. Tell him to look after you."

She nodded and hurried off, happy to have been given something to do and relieved that Harry didn't seem to feel her presence was in any way required. She had no idea at all about the process of birth, save that Miss Graham had hinted it was something far too dreadful to discuss.

She did as she'd been told, sending the household into a quietly controlled flurry, and she nearly ran George down outside the library, just as he was coming out. He managed to avert disaster by grabbing her by the shoulders.

"Aubrey?" he said, an amused question in his eyes, for she was in full flight and looked as if she had a dozen devils on her tail. "Where are you going in such a hurry?"

"George . . ." she said, panting for air. "I was looking for you. This house never seemed so huge, and I kept losing my way. But I've found you now, so it doesn't matter." In her concern for Annabelle she had completely forgotten that they were no longer friends.

"And why were you searching for me so intently?"

"Harry. Harry sent me."

''Harry . . .'' George's brow drew down. ''Why would Harry be sending you to me?''

''It's Annabelle. The baby. It's coming.'' She was still trying to catch her breath.

''I see,'' he said, releasing her. ''Has the midwife been summoned?''

''Yes, but Harry says she'll never be here in time, and he's planning to deliver the child himself.''

''Goodness. Typical Annabelle. She never does anything in the ordinary fashion, but then, neither does Harry, which is why they're so well-suited.''

''George, how can you possibly be so calm?''

''It's the only way I have ever been able to deal with the Calderon family. It's only my own affairs that seem to put me in a state of controlled panic. But as far as the duke is concerned, you mustn't worry. He is one of the most capable people I have ever known. No doubt he's delivered babies in India, or Arabia, or some such place. He wouldn't dream of delivering Annabelle if he didn't know something about it.''

''Oh.''

''Did he want me?''

''No. He said you were to look after me, although I can't think why.''

''Then that's precisely what I will do. Why don't we go to my rooms while we await news. I have something to give you which is in my study.''

''Yes. Whatever you like.'' She was silent for a few more minutes while they walked through another maze of corridors, somehow ending up in the west wing. She paid little attention to their direction, her mind busy with what was happening upstairs. But she knew she would never work it out on her own. Finally she took a deep breath and said, ''George, I've never been in a house where a baby is arriving.

What will happen?'' She gave him a shy, sidelong glance.

George smiled wryly to himself. It appeared that today was to be a day of a great many revelations, and he might as well surrender himself to the process. At least he had bearded Miss Graham and dealt with her to his satisfaction. Now there was just the matter of Aubrey left. Explaining birth was going to be far easier than explaining everything else to her.

He turned to a passing footman and said, ''Miss de Salis and I will be in my study, should the duke want me. Please alert me if there is any news concerning the duchess.'' He opened the door for Aubrey, and left it ajar, leading her to the comfortable sofa that sat against one wall. He continued to stand.

''George,'' Aubrey said uncertainly, ''surely it is far beyond the bounds of propriety for us to be alone together in your apartment?''

''I am sure it is. However, the servants know that I am a veritable pillar of propriety, and I am quite sure they will not give it a second thought. I certainly shall not.''

''If you say so.'' Aubrey wasn't at all sure she knew how to read George's mood at this moment, for he seemed to be behaving very strangely, and in a complete turnabout from the last two days. She imagined it had something to do with the impending birth.

''So, Aubrey. I suppose the procreation and parturition of children is another area of your education that Miss Graham has neglected?'' he asked, looking down at her.

''I know it is utterly absurd to be four-and-twenty and to be completely ignorant of such a basic thing, but I had no one else to ask, and Miss Graham does not think it proper for unmarried ladies to know of these things.''

"No. But then, you should not be an unmarried lady, my dear Aubrey."

"George, please. I had thought we were no longer to talk of personal matters."

George laughed. "Oh, and asking how a child is born is not a personal matter?"

Aubrey blushed a bright pink. "Yes . . . I suppose it is. I forgot."

"Aubrey, I promise that I will explain to you, for I can see you are quite right—there is no one else to do it, and it is something you should know. But there are other things we must discuss first."

"George, what is it?" she said with a perplexed frown. "You seem so different today. Yesterday you told me that we could not go back to the way things were, that everything had changed, *and,*" she continued, fixing him with a stern eye, "you said we had to observe the proprieties."

"I think I have finally come to my senses."

"I wasn't aware you'd lost them," she said, "although perhaps that's the best explanation of your attitude that you have produced so far."

"I wasn't aware I had lost them either. But I made the discovery that sometimes we truly are our own worst enemies, often acting from a misguided sense of what is right. Which leads me to the subject at hand. Aubrey, this morning I had a most disturbing conversation with the duke. He told me of the decision you had made regarding Miss Graham and her school. I was most surprised, especially when he gave me the details of that decision."

Aubrey looked down at her hands. "I wish he had not. I have already been lectured by Harry and Annabelle, and you cannot make me change my mind, George."

"Can't I?" he asked quietly. "I am not so certain."

Her eyes flew to his, and she colored at the tone of his voice.

"All I have ever wanted is for you to be happy, Aubrey. I cannot let you go through with this idiotic plan of yours, for I know you will be miserable. Therefore I am going to break a firm resolution I made to myself many years ago and interfere directly."

"You have no right to interfere anywhere in my life, George," Aubrey said angrily, by now thoroughly resenting the fact that she couldn't be left alone to make a simple decision, a decision that affected no one but herself. "You gave up that right ten years ago when you cut me out of your life. You certainly gave it up when you told me last night that we had no relationship at all. The only person who has any right to speak at all is my benefactor, for he is the only person who has truly cared about me all this time!"

"Precisely," said George, moving away from the wall and going to his desk. "I have a letter here for you from that very person."

Aubrey stared at him. "How could you possibly have a letter . . . ?" Her voice faded away as George handed it to her, and she could see for herself that her name was written on it in Mr. Dickens' cramped handwriting. "Oh. But I don't understand—he doesn't even know I am here, and my letter couldn't possibly have reached him."

"But he clearly does know you are here, and as for your letter, he read it this morning. I was there. He is well aware of this pigeon-brained scheme of yours. I suggest you read what he has to say."

Aubrey looked at George, a stricken expression on her face. "Do you mean he has been here all this time and I haven't known? Oh, I feel like such a fool!

Who is he, George? Was I introduced and didn't realize it?''

"You didn't realize it, no. But then, he didn't mean for you to know.''

"You know him, George? You speak as if you are well-acquainted!''

"I would say we are, yes. But that is neither here nor there for the moment. Please, read what he has to say. Perhaps that will change your mind.'' George turned away from her.

She shot a furious look at his back, meaning to take up the point with him afterward, and then opened the paper with slightly unsteady fingers and began to read:

My Dearest Aubrey,

By now you will have realized that I am at Paxton. I was most alarmed when you appeared so unexpectedly, for it was never my intention to make my identity known to you. However, I now realize that my decision has not been fair to either one of us, and it is time to make a clean breast of the matter.

It has come to my attention that you have not been happy with Miss Graham, and I believe I begin to understand better why that has been, having had an opportunity to observe Miss Graham for myself. The duke and duchess have also added their observations to my own, and the picture has become clearer. You said in your letter to me that you felt it was time to relieve me of any obligation I might feel. You said a number of other foolish things, none of which I find I can take with any seriousness. I don't believe that one vital point has occurred to you. I do not wish to be relieved of my obligation.

However, I can offer you an alternative to locking yourself away in a place where you would be unhappy, with a woman who has absolutely no understanding of you.

Marry me, Aubrey. Marry me and let me try to

make a happy life for you. I can guess at your shock at this moment, but please, let me explain myself. It is an explanation long overdue. I have never before told you this, but it is time you should know. I love you, my Aubrey. I have loved you for many years, although I did not realize the scope of that love until I saw you here.

That love began when you were as a child. (You did not realize, I know.) It grew as you grew, as I learned about you through your letters, which I have always cherished. But you see, I never thought of myself as someone who would ever marry. I certainly did not think of myself as a suitable husband for you.

And yet it has also come to my attention that you might return my regard and that I have been inadvertently hurting you by keeping the truth from you.

You need not give me an answer immediately, Aubrey, but I think it is time we speak together, you and I. I shall be waiting in the rose garden this afternoon. I am sorry there are no roses, but that cannot be helped. At least it is St. Valentine's Day, when lovers make themselves known to each other and pledge their troths.

You might be dismayed, and possibly very angry with me, but those are risks I must take. God willing, they will be worth it. But I will understand if you do not come, and I will understand if you choose to walk away from me.

Trust me, Aubrey, when I say that I love you with all my heart.

> Your devoted servant,
> J. Dickens
> (*alter idem*)

Aubrey dropped the letter to her lap, completely taken aback. She swallowed hard, for some reason suddenly wanting to cry.

"Well," said George, looking up from his desk where he was sorting through a pile of papers, "I hope Dickens said something that made sense."

"He made no sense at all," Aubrey said through a dry mouth. "George, what does *'alter idem'* mean? My Latin has never been any good at all."

"I believe it means 'another self' if directly translated," he said, writing something on the top page. "It also loosely translates as 'inseparable friend.'"

"Oh, I see. George, I'm going for a walk. How do I reach my room from here? I need to fetch my cloak."

"You're still wearing it," he pointed out. "Do go on, Aubrey. You're obviously very distracted. I will let you know as soon as I hear something about Annabelle. And then perhaps I will explain about the birth process if you still want to know."

"Thank you. George?"

"Yes?"

"Where's the rose garden?"

"Out the front door, to the right, down the hill, and over the bridge. You can't possibly miss it."

"Thank you. And, George?"

"Yes?"

"I'm furious with you for not telling me about Mr. Dickens being here."

"I beg your pardon. It never came up."

"I'll speak to you later."

"Indubitably." He went back to his writing, his hand moving over the paper in long smooth strokes, and Aubrey was sure he'd forgotten her.

She finally found the front hall after another series of false starts and went out into the fresh air, carefully turning right and looking for a hill. Fortunately it was just where George had said it would be, and she could see the bridge below. She paused for a moment, trying to collect her thoughts. She wished she'd had time to think more carefully, but she could hardly keep Mr.

Dickens waiting. As to what she was going to say to him, she had no idea.

She knew she was terribly fond of him. She also knew he was an old man, although his letter, which she still held clutched in her hand, had been written with the tenderness and ardor of someone much younger. Nevertheless, she could not think of a male guest at Paxton younger than fifty. His declaration of love had been touching, certainly shocking, but it was obviously very sincere. But did she love him? How could you love someone you had never met, at least not to your knowledge? And did she really want to marry someone she didn't truly love, especially a kindly old man?

She took a deep breath. Marriage would certainly save her from her predicament. She knew she loved George with all of her heart, but George did not love her anymore and never would again, so in that sense she was free. But marriage? Surely Mr. Dickens was misguided. Maybe if she told him everything, they could talk the situation over and come to some sort of satisfactory conclusion, for she could not possibly marry him under false pretenses. In fact, she wasn't the least convinced she could marry him at all.

She squared her shoulders and headed down the hill.

The rose garden was empty. The bushes stood in row after row of tilled earth, their thin branches bare, appearing far too fragile to hold the heavy burden of leaf and flower that the summer would bring. She looked down at her feet, feeling every bit as fragile, as if a stray puff of wind might blow her off her feet. She felt very small and frightened, and very much alone.

She stood there for a few minutes, wondering how long she should wait. Perhaps Mr. Dickens had given up hope that she was coming. Perhaps it was all to the good. She felt tears start to her eyes, and she turned her head to the side, wiping them away with the back of her hand.

"Aubrey?"

Her heart seemed to freeze as she heard the voice. For a moment she could not look up. Then she steeled herself, for this was why she had come, and she turned around.

But it was George who stood there, not Mr. Dickens at all. "Hello," she managed to say, trying to keep her voice steady. "Did Annabelle have the baby?"

"No. At least, not that I have heard."

"Oh. Then why are you here?"

"To see you. I'm glad you decided to come. I wasn't at all sure you would, but you've always been a brave girl."

"George, what are you talking about? I don't understand you in the least."

"Don't you?" he said with a little smile, but his eyes held anything but humor. "Would you rather I go? I told you I'd quite understand if you wished it."

She looked at him hard as comprehension slowly dawned. "Not you . . ." she whispered. "Surely not you?"

"Aubrey." His voice was choked. "Is it too terrible a disappointment?"

She couldn't move. She couldn't even speak. The years rushed away and she saw George, her George, the day she had left Aldershot, all the anguish he'd been so careful not so show to her revealed in his eyes as he held her close to him one last time. It all came clear in a great rush. He had not forgotten her, nor ceased to care.

"You have been Mr. Dickens all this time?"

"Yes," he said very simply.

"You were the one who took me away from Aunt Prudence?"

"Yes."

"And you have been the person who has supported me since, the person I have written to all these years?"

He sighed and looked away. "Yes."

She covered her face with her hands.

"Aubrey. Aubrey, my love, I am sorry for the deception. I tried to explain in my letter. It is why I wrote the blasted thing in the first place, rather than telling you to your face. I was hoping to prepare you for the truth. I do love you, very much, but to ask such a thing of you—I mean, such a thing as marriage—with all of the other things in the way, I didn't know how you might react. Especially to me."

Aubrey looked up at him incredulously. "Do you know," she said slowly, "I feel as if I should box your ears."

George smiled. "You do?"

"Yes. And I will tell you exactly why. I have loved you all my life, George Asquith, and you have known it. There has not been one day that has gone by that I have not loved you and thought of you and missed you. It wasn't just Papa and Laurence, and you know that also. It was what was between us, something special and precious, and you chose to make me think that you had forgotten me. You chose to couch yourself in the garb of some anonymous protector who owed a family debt. And I believed it. I believed it, George, and went through all these years feeling that you had abandoned me."

By now tears were streaming freely down Aubrey's face and her nose was running as well. George silently offered her his handkerchief and she took it from his proffered hand.

"And furthermore, there you were," she said, blowing her nose in a most unladylike fashion, "writing me such beautiful letters, and I didn't even know who they were really from, except I thought they were from an old man called Mr. Dickens! That's misrepresentation, or something like that, I'm quite sure. In any case, it's criminal, and you should be truly ashamed. And not only that, you made me believe you didn't love me anymore, that I meant nothing to you. If that is not misrepresentation, I don't know what is. I was miserable, George. And I wasn't going to accept Mr. Dickens' proposal—at least, I don't think I was."

"Are you quite finished?"

"Yes. I think so. I can't think of anything else except what a shock you have given me."

George didn't bother to reply. He took two steps forward and gathered Aubrey into his arms in one collective movement. "Aubrey. My sweet Aubrey," he said on a choked laugh, holding her tightly against his chest. "You are quite correct. I am a blackguard, the veriest sort of blackguard. Call me criminal, call me utterly lacking in conscience, call me anything you choose, but for God's sake, try to understand that I love you. Love can drive a man to extremes."

He set her away from him and looked down into her face, lightly holding her shoulders. "I may have behaved as an utter fool, but I did have my reasons. But the larger question is whether you can forgive me, Aubrey. Can you believe that I love you more than life itself, and always have?"

"Why?" she asked. "Why the need for such a charade? You must have known how I felt."

"It is not obvious to you? Aubrey, how could I feel

enough of a man to claim you in wedlock when I could scarcely walk across a room?''

''I can hardly see what that has to do with anything,'' Aubrey said, still angry with him despite the fact that her heart was nearly pounding out of her chest.

''Aubrey. There are things you still have to learn,'' George said in exasperation. ''I would have asked for you without hesitation had I felt I could give you everything you needed. The fact is . . . Never mind. Suffice it to say that I'm much better now.''

''Then why did you delay in coming to me?'' Aubrey asked. ''Harry said that you had the operation last year.''

George actually colored. ''I did not know that you would accept me as I am. I am not a very pleasing sight, Aubrey. The surgery left me with some bad scars.''

Aubrey shook her head in disbelief. *''This* is what has kept you from telling me the truth? Do you think for one moment I care about a scar or even ten scars you might have? Do you think I ever cared about your leg the way it was before, save for the fact that it pained you, George?''

''Aubrey, you do not know—''

''Nonsense. I know a great deal more than you think, George. I know that I love you, and if someone came along and chopped off both your arms and legs tomorrow, it would make no difference. I would still love you. I cannot understand why you have made such a fuss over a simple limp. Your leg looks perfectly functional to me, and if it took a few nasty cuts to make it so, then I am only grateful. I would think you would be grateful as well, instead of worrying about what I might think of it.''

George smiled and leaned his face into her hair.

"Be it on your own head, then, my love. I am to the point where I cannot fight you anymore. Only say you'll marry me, and I will be the happiest man on the face of the earth."

Aubrey looked into his eyes with all the love that she held for him. "Of course I will marry you. I only wish you had thought to ask me years ago."

George sighed. He could hardly believe his luck, for he had not been sure of anything until that moment. "I wish I had too. I am sorry, Aubrey. But as I said, I have finally come to my senses, although I do believe I am about to put myself out of them."

He took her face between his hands and gently lowered his mouth onto hers. Aubrey responded as if she had been kissing him all her life. Her arms went around his back and pulled him close and her lips molded themselves to George's as if there had never been anything else for them to do.

George groaned as he gave himself over to Aubrey's ardor, praying he could hold on to the last shred of his control.

And then there was a cannon shot, and another, and then a third, and Aubrey pulled away and looked at him with tremendous surprise.

"Does that always happen?" she said in wonderment. "I have always imagined what it would be like to kiss you, but I never imagined that."

George laughed. "Aubrey, my love, I hope one day to make you the happiest of women, but I cannot be held responsible for the gunfire." He looked up at the castle. "I believe that Annabelle has been safely delivered of a son. It's a Paxton tradition to fire the cannon when an heir has been born."

"Oh," she said as casually as she could manage, but her heart was near to bursting with happiness. "How wonderful. We should return then and offer our congratulations. And on the way, perhaps you will be so kind as to tell me how babies are born. I have some ideas, but it's all rather vague.''

George inclined his head, thinking with a silent laugh of life with Aubrey. ''Knowing you, my dear, I can hardly begin to imagine. But I'll do my best to enlighten you. I should start at the beginning. . . .''

Lady Valentine's Scheme
by Emma Lange

THE VISCOUNT ADDINGTON, Harold Charles Staunton, known as Harry to all, glanced down the long corridor he had traversed, before, satisfied no one watched, he slipped into the conservatory his grandfather had added to the family seat. A pungent, earth-scented smell filled the vaulted room, but Harry scarcely noticed as he sought out a young lady of slightly above average height, whose willow-slender figure and graceful carriage imparted elegance to the simple lime-green muslin she wore.

Alexandra Talbot smiled encouragement as she turned to him. "You needn't worry, Harry. No one comes to the conservatory—and," she anticipated the very objection he opened his mouth to make, "there's no use warning me your mama will fly up into the boughs if she finds us here unchaperoned. The mere sight of me has already placed her in the treetops. I must know why her reception was so cool. After all, she's not seen me in a year, and . . . you, too, Harry, seemed distracted."

For perhaps the first time in his life, Harry saw real uncertainty in Alexandra's eyes of deep, forest green. Instantly he possessed himself of her hand. "Dash it all, Alex! You must know I could not be happier to see you. I've never been apart from you so long in my life. It's only that . . ." Having known Harry since

153

they were both in leading strings, Alexandra was aware he'd not be hurried into speech and, summoning patience, waited until a loud sigh heralded that he'd come to the point.

"I did not wish to tell you, you see, but Mama has invited the Rutledges to Penthurst for Grandmama's birthday festivities!"

"The Rutledges?" As enlightenment dawned, her finely arched eyebrows lifted. "Ah! Miss Mary Rutledge, the heiress. Then Lady Sophy remains dead set against a match between us?"

Harry transferred his unhappy gaze to a nearby camellia. "Mama says we are too young."

"I am nineteen and you twenty-two, Harry. It isn't our youth she objects to. She never approved of Papa's decision after Mama died to raise me without benefit of a governess." Alexandra sighed. "And now she's my complete lack of portion to complain of as well as my ragtaggle manners."

"That's not true, Alex! She . . ." Uncertain why it was his mother did object to Alexandra and always had, Harry flushed. "That is, she says I . . . we were too affected by your father's sudden death, and . . . and she wants me to take my time to make the best choice. That's a reasonable attitude for any mother! She can't know I made up my mind ages ago. She wasn't there!" He gave a boyish laugh, and Alexandra smiled for no reason but that Harry was trying so very hard to reassure her. "That's better! You've only to smile, Alex, and she'll be won over. You are so beautiful."

It occurred to Alexandra that a large purse would weigh more heavily with Lady Sophy than beauty, but she stilled her tongue. "At least there is Lady Val to plead our cause," she said instead. A sudden smile curved her finely drawn mouth. "And Valentine's Day is her time of the year. Do you know, Harry, I think your grandmother even resembles Cupid?''

"Now, I wish you'll not go into that nonsense, Alex!'' Harry rolled his eyes. "It goes to Grandmama's head that she was born on St. Valentine's day.''

"And was named for the saint,'' Alexandra added, chuckling. "But, truly, she is the image of the Cupid in my locket. They've identical twinkling blue eyes, rosy cheeks, and the very same bow mouth. She only lacks his bow and arrow.''

"Egad! Grandmama with a bow and arrow. I don't doubt she would be more perverse in selecting her victims than Cupid's reputed to be!''

Alexandra's eyes twinkled. "You are being severe, Harry. She only likes to play matchmaker.''

"You take her part as she takes yours, Alex,'' Harry observed with an almost bemused smile. "She insisted her birthday celebrations last year were naught, with you in mourning for your father and unable to provide diversion.''

Unexpectedly, Alexandra responded with a dry look. "I rather thought Lady Val's eyes were twinkling suspiciously when she greeted me, but she wouldn't say what had her so amused. Do you know if she has some particular diversion in mind for me to provide, Harry?''

"Only the diversion of beauty,'' he replied at once. Alexandra cast him a swift smile for his gallantry, only to be disconcerted by the discovery that Harry's gaze was fastened upon her lips. Only slowly, for he had not so forgotten himself as to kiss her even when he had pledged to marry her, did Alexandra divine his intent. As he bent down toward her, her eyes went wide.

Her inadvertent start of surprise brought Harry up short. "Ah! Well!'' Flushed, he looked everywhere but at Alexandra. "Well, I believe we ought to be getting back. The Rutledges are to come at any time, you know."

Alexandra had met the Rutledges once before, and she was in no rush to renew the acquaintance. They were not particularly objectionable people, only exceedingly proper and dull, as were most of Harry's mother's friends.

"You go along, Harry. I imagine Lady Sophy will be relieved to have me absent from the welcome, and I wish to go up to Lady Val."

"You're certain?"

"Yes."

Alexandra's smile faded as soon as Harry had left her. She'd been counting on him, though it was true she'd not leapt to accept his offer of marriage. Harry had always been her playmate, tagging along behind her despite being the elder, and she'd never thought of him as a girl does of a husband.

In the end, though, she'd not seen what else she could do. Her cheerful, boisterous father had been a wagering man, but not an expert one, as the tide of debts that had rolled in after his death had attested. His man of business could allow Alexandra no more than eighteen months to raise the money to satisfy Jack Talbot's creditors. If she failed, and she had only three months left, her home, Beechfields, home to the Talbots for a century and a quarter, would be sold.

To save money, she had closed the house and gone to Yorkshire to live with her only relative. A kindly woman, her father's sister, Winifred, but poor as a church mouse and reclusive besides. Little wonder that Harry's offer had grown increasingly attractive the longer Alexandra resided on the bleak, lonely moors.

In the eyes of the world, of course, Harry Staunton was a remarkable catch. Not only was he heir to the very wealthy Earl of Richland, but he was also exceedingly handsome, with refined, almost beautiful features, thick, curling chestnut hair, and a pair of wide velvety brown eyes.

Though Harry's title meant little to Alexandra, his looks were pleasing, and his wealth appealed insofar as it would help her to keep Beechfields, but what weighed the most heavily with her was the knowledge that they'd suit. As Harry had been a comfortable playmate, so it followed he'd be a comfortable husband. He was devoted to her, Alexandra knew, and she could depend upon him.

The only difficulty was Harry's mother. As handsome and unyielding as a blade of steel, Lady Sophy would be a test for both Cupid and Lady Valentine, Harry's grandmother and Alexandra's godmother, and no matter that it was the time of year for young lovers.

"I do fear that sigh is entirely warranted, my dear. When she chooses her daughter-in-law, Cousin Sophy is just the one to dismiss spirited beauty in favor of pliable wealth."

"Oh!" A bolt of lightning could not have spun Alexandra about more rapidly. The filtered light in the conservatory was dim, but she saw him immediately, standing, or lounging rather, not five feet away, his shoulders propped against a marble column and his arms crossed over his chest. She met his dark blue amused eyes and stared. "Joss!"

His features were just as she remembered. Not so beautiful as Harry's, but well-formed and strong . . . and masculine, she found herself adding, now that she was older. He seemed taller to her, somehow, and broader-shouldered, though he was still lean as ever. He wore his black hair brushed back as carelessly as ever from his high forehead, but the sun of a hot climate had darkened his skin, and there were unfamiliar lines etched at the corners of his eyes. "You . . . you've changed."

"Is that all you've to say after four years, Alex? No welcome for the prodigal?"

Alexandra found then that Jocelyn Staunton's strong, white, slightly crooked smile still had the power to trip the beat of her heart. Then she recalled the last time he'd flashed it at her, before he cantered off down the drive at Beechfields to make his fortune in the world, never once glancing back at the girl who watched until he was out of sight.

But what had she expected? Joss had never played the lover with her. A foolish girl, she'd made too much of being called his "brat," of all things. She would not make the same mistake again. "A man's a fool only if he gets himself burned twice by the same match," as her father had used to say.

"Alex?"

She had stood staring too long. Joss's smile was even broader now. The old hurt goading her all the more because she'd thought herself beyond it, she replied tartly, "I apologize, but I find it impossible to summon an eloquent welcome when I am taken by complete surprise! And you ought not to have eavesdropped!"

"It is you, Alex!" Joss grinned. "Until that display of temper, I could not be certain, for if I have changed, you have undergone a metamorphosis. When I left, you were a skinny brat with little to distinguish you but torrents of unruly auburn hair and a pair of enormous eyes. But now . . ." He whistled half under his breath as he raked her with such a lazily appreciative glance that she—to her fury—blushed. Compounding his sins, Joss laughed again. "Only those flashing eyes are just the same. Do you realize, Alex, that you've the distinction of being the only woman who has ever beaten me?''

"I was a child of ten," she protested as stiffly as she could with such a twinkle in his eyes. "And I only gave as good as I got."

"You'd the advantage of a stick, which was most unfair, even if I was six years your elder, as I'd Harry arrayed against me too."

"Well, I thought you were being unfair to poor Harry."

"Poor Harry! He had deliberately impugned the honor of my first ladylove."

"Lily Bailey had no honor to impugn!"

"Lily!" Joss, disregarding her sharp retort, sighed reverently. "How could I have forgotten her name?"

"Well, you needn't think I remembered it after all these years," Alexandra lied without the least regret. She remembered not only the tavern wench's name but also every word Joss had uttered in her defense when Harry had termed her a loose doxy. "It so happens I saw Lily only yesterday when we stopped at the Golden Bull for refreshments before coming on to Penthurst. She is Lily Raikes now and has five children."

Joss clapped his hand over his heart in mock solemnity. "I always said the girl was made for motherhood."

Alexandra's defenses, weakened from his first smile, crumbled then. Ever, when he had teased her so outrageously, she had laughed. As she did then. "Liar."

Joss took no affront. His eyes on hers, he only smiled slowly, and suddenly Alex looked away. That lazy smile was new. Busying herself with a loose thread on her sleeve, she asked, "To what do we owe the honor of your visit, Joss? Certainly you did not return from a need to keep in touch. You never wrote once.''

''You wound me, Alex.'' She glanced up swiftly, to find she had been taken. There was no pain in his dark blue eyes, only a glint of amusement. ''I included my best wishes to you in my notes to Aunt Val, and that's quite a tribute to you. I did not do the same for anyone else. As to why I've returned, this Valentine's Day will be Aunt Val's seventieth, as every letter for the last two years has reminded me, and, too—''

A gurgle of laughter interrupted him. Lady Val was famous for the shameless ploys she used to force people out in the uncertain weather of February to attend her birthday festivities. This year there was to be a ball one night, a dinner party for Penthurst's guests on the eve of the day, and on her birthday, a great feast for half the neighborhood, villagers and gentry alike. ''Did she stoop to sending dire warnings about this being her final birthday?'' Alexandra laughed again when Joss nodded. ''Well, I am certain she is in alt . . . oh, have you seen Lady Sophy?'' she asked, as it occurred to her suddenly that Harry's mother's chilliness might have had more to do with Joss's arrival than her own.

But Joss had not encountered his cousin by marriage. ''The Countess of Richland has not yet had the pleasure of learning I am to be part of the cozy family group,'' he admitted with a dry smile. ''I don't doubt she'll be overcome . . . though likely with as little pleasure as when I was presented to her at the age of ten, and she took some seconds, perhaps two, to declare that I would be a 'pernicious influence' upon her precious Harry.''

Recalling the tall, proud, angular boy dressed in well-cut but exceedingly worn clothes, whom Lady Val had brought directly to Penthurst from his parents' funeral, Alexandra smiled faintly. "As I recall, you lifted your nose—which was arrogant even then—and gave her look for haughty look."

Joss laughed. "There didn't seem much else to do."

Or to continue doing, Alexandra thought to herself, for Lady Sophy had not warmed to the orphan, who had had, it must be admitted, a penchant for challenging authority. She had held that he belonged with all that remained of his family, his elder brother, Richard, to which Lady Val had replied with equal force that Richard Staunton was not fit to raise a flea, much less a nephew of hers who showed "all the promise his wastrel brother never did."

Caught between his mother and his wife, the Earl of Richland eventually devised a compromise: Joss was sent away to school for most of the year but did return to Penthurst on holidays.

"But I'd another reason for coming home." Roused from her thoughts, Alexandra looked to Joss and was struck anew by how assured he seemed. "I decided that after four years it was time I came to see if you'd kept my heart safe and sound."

For a half-second Alexandra forget to breathe. His heart! Surely he did not mean . . . And then he reached out to lift the heart-shaped locket she wore on a gold chain about her neck. "It is in better condition than the day I gave it to you."

She glanced down rather stupidly at the locket that had become such a part of her she'd forgotten it, then quickly, for she'd not have him know she had worn it every day for the four years he had been away, said, "I've no other jewelry left, actually. The rest went to pay Papa's gaming debts. Do you want it back?"

Joss allowed the pretty thing to fall from his fingers back to its place upon the muslin bodice of her afternoon dress. When his eyes met hers, their expression was enigmatic. "And deprive you of your only ornament, Alex? How cold you must think me." Embarrassed, she would have protested she meant no such thing, but he cut her off. "You've more need of it than I, as you seem to have given your own away to Harry— I judge, you understand, by how dispirited you sounded when you chided him for his tepid reception of you." Joss addressed Alexandra's back now, for she had turned abruptly away from him to pace to a bay window hung with ferns. When she neither denied nor confirmed his remark, he went on in the same cool tone, "Allow me to add: I'd never have thought you would be so foolish, Alex."

"You have been gone four years, Joss!" She addressed the window in a low, husky voice. "And you know nothing of matters here."

"I know enough. From what I heard, Harry's not changed in the least. If I were wagering on it, I'd say he'd drive you to distraction in a week, though with luck those great dewy eyes of his might not lose their appeal for as long as a fortnight."

"Dewy!" She spun around, only to find Joss sniffing unconcernedly at one of the velvety camellias that surrounded them. "Harry has beautiful eyes."

"And piles of money," Joss added, a mocking gleam lighting his eye as he straightened. "Always appealing, money, and that is not to mention his title. You would be a countess in time."

Alexandra dug her fingernails into the soft flesh of her palms. "You insult me! He is kind and steady and faithful. And it is for those qualities I would marry him, not his wealth, though I admit that after the last two years I have learned to value the security piles of money can bring."

Alex bit her lip and swung her gaze back to the window. She had said more than she intended. In the ensuing silence, she heard the stem of a flower snap and then Joss's step behind her.

"Alex?" She shot him a distrustful look from over her shoulder. "I did not mean to get your back up on my first day home. Truly, I meant to wait at least until the second. First I meant to tell you how very sorry I was to hear of Jack's death and . . . the way he left things for you." Unable to speak past the sudden lump in her throat, Alexandra only nodded. "He'd have been proud as the devil to see what a beauty you've become." Gently, with the merest pressure on her shoulder, Joss turned her about that he might tuck the camellia he'd plucked into her hair. "Truce?" he asked.

A faint misting of tears made the eyes she lifted to his sparkle like emeralds. "As long as you don't cut up at me over Harry, I'll cry truce with you."

Joss smiled slightly. "We're good for a few minutes, then."

"What kept you, Alex? You're the last to come down!"

Having little desire to discuss why it had taken her two hours and not one or even two but three changes of dress to make herself presentable, Alexandra smiled vaguely. "Oh, I'd unpacking to do."

But Harry scarcely heard her. "Joss has come back!" he exclaimed in an undertone.

In fact, Alexandra's eyes had at that moment come to rest upon Harry's cousin. Of the group gathered in the grand saloon, Joss was the only one facing the door. One arm draped casually along the mantel piece, he listened to some discussion Lady Valentine seemed to be leading. If Alexandra had ever seen him in evening dress, she had forgotten how very well he looked.

She forced her gaze to Harry. "I saw him earlier."

"When?"

"Harry! Bring Alex along, boy! We've been waiting an age for her."

Alexandra hid a sigh of relief as Harry hastened to obey his grandmother's command. He wore his "Joss" face, or so she had once labeled the sulky glower with which he had invariably greeted his cousin's arrival from school. Tedious then, the expression had not grown more pleasing with the years.

"Well! At least you kept us waiting to some effect, Alex," Lady Val observed, her bright, shrewd eyes twinkling as she swept Alexandra with a critical glance that might or might not have accounted for the flush that rose on Alexandra's cheeks. With a wave of her walking stick, Lady Val indicated the Rutledges, whom Alexandra greeted with a graceful curtsy, to which Mr. Rutledge in particular responded with an appreciative smile. His wife mouthed a pleasantry, while his daughter, resplendent in a gown of pale blue satin trimmed in yards of Belgian lace, smiled nicely. Taken aback by the girl's friendliness, Alexandra reminded herself that a girl who would bring twenty thousand pounds to her marriage could afford to be affable.

Lady Sophy acknowledged Alexandra's curtsy with a frosty, scarcely perceptible nod. Her peripheral vision excellent, Alexandra saw a flash of white, and knew Lady Sophy's cool reception had amused Joss, a belief she had confirmed when she bade him good evening and found his eyes alight, though he only replied, "Miss Talbot," in the blandest of tones.

"Come, sit by me, child," Lady Val directed, thumping the place beside her with customary peremptoriness. Alexandra was pleased to do so, until Harry, having fetched her a glass of ratafia, went to seat himself in the only place remaining. Then she saw Lady Val had left her grandson, unless he cared to stand with Joss, no choice of where to sit. The only place remaining was beside Miss Rutledge. Alexandra looked swiftly to Lady Val, but she was not to learn if her godmother, with Cupid's perversity, had decided to favor the heiress for Harry's bride. The older lady was smiling up at her nephew.

"Joss has been entertaining us, Alex, telling us of an attack upon his ship by pirates off the coast of Madagascar."

Alexandra realized her eyes had flown wide with alarm only when Joss assured her lightly, "It was only a skirmish. No harm befell us."

Lady Val snorted. "The pirates may not have inflicted harm, but the bandits who attacked you in India managed to get a ball in your arm!"

"Ah, well, that ambush brought a local prince to our rescue, and much good came of meeting him."

"I wonder what sort of good?" Lady Val demanded. "You went to the East to acquire more than adventures, I believe. Did this prince bring you the fortune you sought?"

The stir Lady Val's bald question created was visible, but Alexandra did not notice. Her gaze had shot to Joss. His grin was wry, dreadfully, damnably wry, and she did not need his words to tell her he had not come home able to rescue her from her father's disastrous legacy.

"While in the prince's company, I earned a fortune . . . in further adventures. They'll be worth a chest of gold at least when I am old and must entertain myself with my memories."

"Hmpf!" Lady Val scowled with patent displeasure. "Far better, in my mind, to have both!"

"To my mind," Lady Sophy pronounced, not quite managing to hide a certain cold pleasure over Joss's failure, "gadding about in search of . . . adventure, no matter the end result, is a dereliction of the duties one must assume when one matures.''

Alexandra glanced up at Joss to see if Lady Sophy's imperious drawl still had the power to set his back up. To her surprise, he looked more amused than put out. ''As I'd no responsibilities''—he shrugged his broad shoulders—''adventuring was as good a way as any to pass the time.''

''What do you think, Alex?'' Lady Val, apparently dissatisfied with her nephew's noncombative attitude, rounded upon Alexandra. ''Demonstrate you've something in that lovely head of yours! Was it the height of irresponsibility for Joss to hie off about the world for little gain, or ought he to have given up the experiences he contends were broadening in favor of dutifully staying at home as Harry has done?''

''I say, Grandmama! That is putting Alex in a deuced ticklish position.''

''Nonsense, Harry!'' Lady Val waved off her grandson's protest. ''Jack was putting the girl in ticklish positions from the moment she left the cradle. Come, Alex. What do you say?''

What Alexandra wished to say was that her father had never put her to so ticklish a test with such high stakes riding on her answer. Aware though she was of Lady Sophy's narrowed gaze, Alexandra also knew she was incapable of toadying—whether Joss were looking on, a sardonic smile lifting his mouth, or not.

''I think, ma'am, that had Joss stayed in England, he'd have joined the ranks of those restless, bored young men who waste their lives careening in flimsy curricles from London to Brighton in record time. At least now he's acquired stories to amuse us. As to his travels broadening him, however''—Alexandra glanced consideringly at Joss's well-filled-out shoulders before looking back to Lady Val—"honestly I cannot say if it was his travels or only time that did that."

Lord Charles's chuckle could be heard over his mother's, but Lady Sophy could not have been less amused. "It is not becoming in a young lady to be pert, Alexandra. Nor ought you to encourage such manners, *chère* Mama. They only discredit her. Ah, look! There is Moreton come to announce dinner. Harry, you will escort Miss Rutledge."

"Miss Talbot?" Joss stepped forward to offer his arm to Alexandra before Lady Sophy could determine his partner for him, and as the others went on ahead, he leaned down from his superior height to whisper wickedly, "I scored that round to you, Alex, but alas, it seems your opponent controls the prize."

"Harry is no trophy, and he is only being polite!"

"Harry is being dutiful. As always. If his mother insists, he'll end up with that insipid child."

"Do you truly think her insipid?" Alexandra brightened, for she had been rather set back to find Miss Rutledge far prettier than she remembered.

"Quite insipid . . . and entirely suited to Harry. They make a very nice couple."

Because they'd arrived in the dining room, Alexandra could not dispute the gibe, but she was able to contemplate how well Harry's brunet good looks set off Miss Rutledge's fair coloring. She was seated across from them, and Mr. Rutledge, her partner on her right, had little conversation that did not relate to his latest consuming passion. As snuff held not the least interest for Alexandra, she had the further leisure to remark how attentive Harry was to the heiress, and though she tried, she could not decide if it was mere politeness that animated his expression or some deeper feeling.

To distract herself she sought out her other dinner

partner, who was, as it happened, regarding her. She smiled. "Is it true, Joss, that you became the friend of an Indian prince?"

Joss's blue eyes narrowed fractionally. "Are you truly interested, Alex, or are you only seeking diversion from the cozy couple across the table?"

"I am making polite conversation at the dinner table—a practice it would seem you neglected to cultivate on your travels!"

Tossing her burnished head at him, she went back to Mr. Rutledge and a new lecture, this on snuffboxes, that dragged on until a footman, offering sole meunière, mercifully put an end to it. As Joss was, clearly, the lesser of two evils, Alexandra consigned her pride to the devil. "Joss?" She summoned the sweetest of smiles as she caught his attention. "Would not your princely friend properly be called a maharajah?"

The gleam that suddenly lit his eyes gave Alexandra to understand Joss knew very well why she had deigned to speak to him again, but for one reason or another, he did not take issue with being used as a diversion from Mr. Rutledge. "Yes, in fact. But how is it you know the proper form of address for a maharajah, Alex?"

"Lady Val had books on India sent down from London."

"I am flattered you were sufficiently interested in my travels to read them."

"You needn't be! I've an inquiring mind and read about the Americas, the South Pacific, and China as well," she informed him to his patent amusement. That she had read three times as many books on India as on all the other countries combined, she saw every reason not to add. "Tell me about India. Are the forests really inhabited by troops of monkeys?"

"It is the thick, nearly impenetrable jungles they

inhabit, along with marvelous birds all the colors of the rainbow, and snakes bigger around than your''— his glance dipped briefly—"waist. And elephants and beautiful sleek tigers.''

"How lucky you are to have seen such things!'' Abandoning her meal, Alexandra turned her sparkling green eyes fully upon him. "Though I'm not certain I should care to see a snake broader than I am, I would dearly love to see all the rest. Don't you fear England will be dull as ditchwater now?''

"Oh, England has its points of interest.'' Her heart, of it own accord, raced, but was proved a most vain as well as foolish organ when Joss added, "And I speak the language here, of course.''

"Ah. Of course.'' She looked down at the peas she'd scarcely touched. "Is that why you left the maharajah's court? Because you did not know the language?''

"No, Kassim spoke fluent English. He'd an English wife.''

She looked up, surprised. "An English wife?''

"When you've thirty-five wives, a few exotic nationalities here and there . . .''

Alexandra had read of harems, actually, and knew that among the followers of Islam it was perfectly acceptable for a man to take as many wives as he could support. But she had not made the leap of imagination required to place Joss in a setting where there were troops of women who had, as it seemed to Alexandra, only one purpose in life. As a blush began to rise in her cheeks, caused as much by the thought of Joss in such a setting as by the thought of that single purpose, Joss, seeming able to read her mind, began to smile.

The sight of that knowing expression gave birth to an overpowering desire to throw him off-stride too. "I see. And what of you, Mr. Staunton?'' Alexandra asked with wide-eyed innocence. "While you were at this Kassim's court, did you adopt the age-old wisdom: 'When in Rome . . .'?''

Alexandra would not soon forget the thrill of satisfaction she experienced when Joss threw back his head and laughed aloud, or as loudly as was possible at a fashionable dinner party in England. "Minx! I ought to rap your knuckles for that indelicate question.''

"Well?" As it happened, she rather wanted to know.

But Joss was proof against her wide green eyes. "You are prying, Alex," he reproved, only to laugh again when she pretended to pout. "Now, enough of repaying me in my own coin—yes, I admit to provoking you. I shall return to your original question. I left Kassim's court without regret because life with any eastern potentate can be precarious. One may be in favor on Tuesday but quite, quite out by Wednesday.''

Knowing when enough really was enough, Alexandra allowed the change of topic. "And I take it the consequences of falling from favor are more potent than having to suffer the cut direct from Prinny?''

Joss regarded her with approval. "Refreshingly perceptive, Alex. Falling from favor in an instance with which I was familiar meant the fellow lost not recognition but his head.''

"In that case," she retorted dryly, "I should say you were quite wise not to linger, however beguiling the local customs.''

"There you are laughing again!" Lady Val peered around Joss to include Alexandra in a smile that belied her sharp tone. "Include me in your amusement, if you please. It is my birthday, after all.''

As Joss related a highly edited account of their exchange, Alexandra took the time to glance around the table, and was not displeased to find Harry's attention upon her and not Miss Rutledge. She did not much care for his glower, however, and summoned as appealing a smile as possible to banish it.

She succeeded almost instantly, and when she turned to serve herself from a platter of roast pheasant, she felt quite pleased with herself. All too soon, however, her warm glow evaporated, for she glanced up to see Joss watching her, a look in his eye she'd never seen before.

"Be warned, Alex," he said, his voice low but not so low she did not hear the steel in it. "I'll not be used to pique Harry's interest."

She opened her mouth to protest, but Joss, declining her the privilege of a reply, turned to Lady Val. Alexandra stiffened. He was being absurd. While they'd talked, she'd not thought once of Harry. The unwelcome realization caused her to worry her lip.

Mr. Rutledge, seeing she was free, seized the opportunity to describe at tedious length a snuffbox he'd captured almost literally out from under Prinny's nose. Alexandra smiled politely but heard almost nothing he said. From the corner of her eye she watched the shoulder Joss turned to her.

As the courses continued to arrive, and still Joss kept his attention upon his aunt, anger warred with dismay in Alexandra's breast. She had every right to be glad Harry had noticed her! Joss was in the wrong. Oh, but fie on him! She did hate for them to be estranged! She always had.

"Why the sigh, Alex? Have you discovered another impediment on the road to becoming the Countess of Richland?"

Alexandra's eyes flashed. After ignoring her for three-quarters of the dinner, he had remembered her only to mock her! Never, even were she to roast in hell, would she admit that sigh had been for him.

"I was only thinking that the evening ahead will be

tedious, for Miss Rutledge is to entertain us on the piano.''

''Ah. And because you ever evaded that poor man Jack dragged in to be your music master, you'll not have the opportunity to show off your glorious auburn head bent low over the keys. A bitter pill, I'm sure, and not sweetened a whit, I imagine, by the knowledge that Harry will not be seated cozily by you, but will be close by your rival, turning her pages for her.''

''You could perform the service,'' Alexandra shot back, resentment of Joss's cutting tone winning out over pleasure for the compliment he had paid her. Later, perhaps, she would recall he had said she'd ''glorious'' hair.

''I could, but unlike Harry, I'm not the least dutiful. In fact, I'll not be on hand at all. I'm off after dinner to sample the quality of play at the Golden Bull. I understand from impeccable sources belowstairs that it is still excellent.''

''You enjoy gaming that much—that you would go out on your first night home?''

''Careful, Alex. You sound as if you're practicing for the role of Sophy's daughter-in-law.''

''Oh! You are hateful! I only . . . Oh, never mind!''

Now it was she who turned a shoulder, but as Mr. Rutledge was occupied on his right, Alexandra had to make do with studying her wineglass.

And, therefore, was keenly aware that Joss studied her for what seemed an eternity. ''I believe I've misjudged you, Alex,'' he said after a moment. ''And though I think indignation becomes you remarkably, I am not so selfish that I'll allow that flush to continue to stain your cheeks merely for my own pleasure.'' She darted him an exasperated glare, as she felt the heat in her cheeks rise further. He grinned, but his voice held no humor when he added quietly, "You needn't be concerned that I'll bankrupt myself, Alex. I always play within my means."

But not fairly, Joss, not fairly! You mean nothing by that dratted lazy, crooked, appealing smile, and you know it. She sniffed. "As I know all too well, that is what every gamester says, Joss."

Alexandra, to her satisfaction, had the last word on that subject, at least, for Lady Sophy rose then, signaling it was time for the ladies to withdraw.

"Do you know me, my beauty?" Alexandra whispered, throwing her arms around a sturdy mare she herself had raised in what seemed another lifetime. "Shall we go for a ride home?"

"I see you still talk to horses, Alex."

Alexandra swung about, showing her surprise. "I did not expect to see you up and about so close to sunrise, Joss. Did you not game the night away after all?"

The only answer she received was the evidence of Joss's clear eyes, for he only grinned before he glanced up at the sky, blue but for a few white, puffy clouds. "I am up to enjoy that clear sky, my dear. It's the first one I've seen since I returned. And," he added with real pleasure, "to enjoy the hint of spring in the air. Lord! How sweet it is. There is no spring in India, you know, only beastly hot weather or beastly rainy weather."

Alexandra tilted her head. Her thoughts all on her reunion with Clytie, she'd not noticed how soft the breeze, indeed, was. Half to herself she murmured, "I wonder if the snowdrops are out on Granger's Hill."

Joss heard and glanced at her over the strong neck of a mettlesome stallion a groom led out to him. "Shall we see?"

"I think not." Alexandra's reply came quickly, almost before the mare shied a few steps. "Clytie's taken exception to your mount, and I would prefer to ride out alone this morning."

"Mustafa's a good chap," Joss returned, ignoring her second objection. "She'll take to him soon enough. You can control the mare, can you not?"

"Of course!"

"Good, then," was all he said before, without a by-your-leave, he spanned Alex's waist with his hands and tossed her onto Clytie.

Joss's high-handedness igniting her temper, Alexandra said slowly, as if he were a simpleton, "I do not care to have company this morning."

Mounted now, he spared her a level but patient look. "In four years the proprieties cannot have changed so much that a young lady may now ride out upon the open highway without an escort, no matter if her destination is her own home."

He was right, but she was not pleased to admit it. "How do you know Beechfields is my destination?"

"I doubt that after a year you mean to visit Emerald Pond before Beechfields." Emerald Pond was the name Alexandra had given to Joss's favorite fishing hole. He'd taught her to fish there. Quietly, his eyes never leaving her, he added, "I'll go no farther than Granger's Hill, Alex. I've no wish to intrude upon your homecoming."

His understanding nearly undid her. Abruptly she spurred Clytie and tossed back over her shoulder, "Oh, very well, then! You may come along—brat."

At the sound of his highly amused laugh, some of the tension that knotted her shoulders whenever she thought of Beechfields eased, and she threw him a saucy look as he came alongside her.

Joss arched a wry eyebrow at her. "It would seem

fate has evened the score for you, brat-no-longer. Now it is I who must tag along on sufferance.''

''Hmmm,'' Alexandra agreed, though she knew their positions were not reversed at all. He had not waited for hours by the stables on the off-chance that she would saunter along and include him in her excursion—after an exhaustive amount of pleading. No, he had simply strolled out and insisted upon accompanying her, whether she wanted him or not.

And there was precious little chance she would not. Alexandra scowled. The thought was unwelcome. She could not afford to fall into old habits of feeling. Joss did not love her. Had he, he'd not have left her. Or, at least, he'd have promised to return for her. And he'd have written to remind her of his promise.

He had done none of those things. Nor, making the discussion of love moot, had he the funds to support her, though it did seem, she noted, eyeing the bottle-green riding coat that clung without a wrinkle to his wide shoulders, that he was able to support the services of the best tailors. Recalling his previous evening's engagement, she reasoned he'd won those funds at the tables, a source that would not yield enough to save Beechfields. Would she need Beechfields, if she had Joss?

The purely hypothetical question was not to be answered. Joss's voice interrupted her thoughts as they approached a path that led off into the woods. ''I'd like to take the Denby village road all the way, to see what's changed. If you like, we can return by the shortcut.''

Alexandra did not object. She had yearned fiercely to return to Beechfields from the moment she'd left, but now that the time had come, she was not so eager to confront the memories lying in wait there. Suddenly glad of the distraction he provided, she listened attentively as Joss rediscovered his favorite landmarks. The Widow Reynolds' cottage still stood on the left side of the road, and there was Squire Brodey's manor house upon the far rounded hill with its apple orchards, the object of a memorable lark, just out of sight. The "tunnel" also remained, though without their leaves the trees that arched across that section of the road between Penthurst and Beechfields did not create quite the same effect they would later in summer.

Then they were ascending the gentle slope of Granger's Hill, and Alexandra's chest began to constrict. At the top she would be able to look to the right and see Beechfields nestled in a deep flank of the hill's south side.

And there it was. Her heart pumped painfully. The rose-colored brick of her home and all its outbuildings looked as lovely as ever in the light of the early-morning sun. The neat white wooden fences surrounding the paddocks gleamed brightly, and almost, it was as if naught had changed. Only there was no stallion in the far field kicking up his heels in greeting to the day. He had been sold long since, of course, as had all the other horses.

"Will an hour be enough time, Alex?"

Her eyes on Beechfields, she could only nod before she started down the path that led at an angle to her home, the one she'd have to sell if Harry did not come up to scratch. . . .

Alexandra returned a half-hour later than she'd agreed. "I am sorry to be late," she said as she came even with Joss. "The time escaped me."

To Joss, she looked very brave just then with her chin as high as it would go, though there was the suspicion of moisture in her eyes.

"No harm done," he replied simply. "I occupied

myself finding you a snowdrop to wear.'' He was tall enough that he could reach up to tuck the tiny white bell-like flower in the buttonhole of her habit. ''There, now, you're wearing the promise of spring.''

Why, Alexandra could not be sure, but Joss's offering did what her reunion with Beechfields had not, quite. ''Now, look what you've done!'' she wailed. ''I am going to cry.''

''I did not intend that.'' Tears obscuring her vision, she did not see the gentle, regretful look he gave her. ''Here.''

With a sniff, she accepted the handkerchief he pressed into her hand. ''Everything appears well-kempt from here,'' Joss observed, looking away as Alexandra blotted her cheeks, to the quite lovely cluster of ivy-colored buildings that was Beechfields. ''Has the staff stayed on?''

''Some,'' she replied softly. ''Johnny Coates is still in charge of the farm. Do you remember him?''

''The greatest wizard with a horse there ever was?''

Through her tears, Alexandra smiled. ''I told him you had returned with a stallion to make his mouth water, and he's as eager as a boy to see Mustafa for himself.''

''He is still as wiry and leathery as ever, I imagine?''

''Yes, and dear. Beechfields seems almost under an enchantment, everything remains in such perfect order.''

Joss nodded. It only lacks its princess, he might have said, but did not. ''The shortcut or the road?'' he asked, mounting.

''The shortcut.''

When they came out of a stand of old elms at the bottom of Granger's Hill, they faced three wide fields that stretched away to the woods surrounding Penthurst's park. "I'll give you two lengths and still be the first to Cousin Charles's woods."

Their eyes met, and Alexandra's expression softened. "A distraction, Joss?" He did not reply, only shrugged offhandedly, but she smiled a little. "Thank you. As to a race, four lengths and you're on."

Joss had only to nod his head once before she was off, urging Clytie across the unplowed field as fast the mare could go. The fresh air in her face lifted her spirits, just as Joss had intended, and when he still had not overtaken her by the first hedgerow, Alexandra laughed aloud as she and the mare soared high above it. Halfway across the second field, she heard Mustafa's hoofbeats and leaned lower over Clytie's neck. "Faster, my sweet. Show him how we take stone walls in England."

The mare, seeming to understand, bunched her muscles to rise above the high stone fence that marked the outer edge of Lord Charles's property. Safely on the other side, Alexandra saw two riders emerge from the woods but did not allow herself to be distracted by them. She could see Mustafa's nose from the corner of her eye now.

Almost neck and neck, she and Joss thundered by the riders Alexandra realized distractedly were Harry and Miss Rutledge. "Faster, Clytie. Come on, now!"

Had the trees been even half a foot farther on, the day would have been Mustafa's, but they were not. "We won!" Alexandra cried, patting Clytie's neck as she slowed her to a walk. "We won!"

"And heroically, too," Joss conceded with a smile as pleased as hers. "It's a comfort to know you're as bruising a rider as ever, Alex."

"Alex!"

"Did you see, Harry?" Alexandra smiled triumphantly. "Clytie bested Mustafa—though it is true Joss spotted me four lengths."

"You could have broken your neck going over that wall!"

Alexandra's smile faded as she took in Harry's clenched jaw. "But, Harry . . ."

"You know Father forbade us to take it and that he'd good reason. And you too, Joss!" Harry swung around to glare at his cousin. "You were with Jim Brodey when he broke his arm there."

"Good day, Miss Rutledge." Joss, having pulled up beside the heiress, took the time to smile a greeting at her. "You look very well this morning."

"Joss!" Being kept waiting as if he were a pup of no standing rather than a titled gentleman of twenty-two had turned Harry a furious red. "I say you ought not to have encouraged Alexandra to such a rash act! She could have been hurt!"

Joss allowed a moment to elapse before he remarked in a level voice that quite contrasted with his cousin's outburst, "You are in a taking for nothing, Harry. In the first place, it was almost a decade ago that Uncle Charles forbade us to take that wall. We've grown a bit in the meantime. And in the second, even then, when she was only ten or so, Alex could have ridden James Brodey into the ground. I would not have put her to it, were she not capable of taking that wall."

Though she felt some satisfaction at Joss's defense of her riding abilities, Alexandra felt pity for Harry even more keenly. He had only lashed out in concern for her, and for his pains, he'd been made to look absurdly young before both her and Miss Rutledge. Seeing Harry's flush darken further, she spoke up.

"Harry, it was I chose to take the wall, and I knew I could manage it, because, to be truthful, I never heeded your father's injunction." When Joss gave a bark of laughter and Harry scowled more angrily, Alexandra realized she'd only made matters worse. "However," she went on quickly, "I do appreciate your concern. I can see it would be alarming to watch us"—she emphasized the plural pronoun—"attempt such an obstacle. In future, the gate will do for me."

As long as you are about, she added beneath her breath, but Harry, not hearing her condition, looked as if he'd been given the grail. "Oh, I say, Alex, that is the greatest relief! You don't know how alarmed I was."

Alexandra smiled, and not the least because Harry had allowed his horse to sidle closer to her and away from Miss Rutledge, who did look remarkably well that morning, if one considered having every hair in place a requirement for pleasing looks, which Alexandra supposed most people did, though no one could really ride and look so. At least she could not, but then, she'd chosen not to wear a little feathered hat perched at a jaunty angle on her carefully coiffed curls. Indeed, she'd left off all headgear but a ribbon that had come loose as she raced Joss. Now her hair tumbled untidily to her shoulders. Still, she had won the race, and Harry was smiling, so he must not be entirely displeased.

"I am surprised to find you so sensitive to another's concern for you, Alex." Joss's tone was casual enough, but the glint in his eyes caught and held Alexandra's attention, and though Harry's mount shook his head, snorting, as if his reins had been pulled tense suddenly, she did not notice. "I remember a time when you were positively infuriated by interest in your safety."

"You are referring to Blue Boy, I suppose?"

"Rather to how you chose to thank me for worrying over you."

"Well, you had no right to win him from Papa!" Alexandra protested, for though she was older and did see the argument they'd had in a more reasonable light, a certain vexation with what she had considered imperious behavior lingered.

"I had the right of concern," Joss replied, although not so sternly as he might have at the time, when she was twelve and he a lordly eighteen. "You had already broken one collarbone, and I did not then nor do I now believe I deserved a pail of icy water on my head for my efforts."

Miss Rutledge gasped, but Alexandra scarcely registered the sound. She was regarding Joss warily, for a sudden roguish smile had transformed his bland expression.

Her concern was not unfounded. "But, I'd my revenge, and I admit that even now I derive great pleasure recalling—"

"That will be enough!" Alexandra's cheeks were a deep, glorious, telling pink. "We are boring Miss Rutledge, and I think it is past time we returned home."

Joss laughed, his blue eyes dancing wickedly. "Oh, I very much imagine you misjudge that, my dear, but I'll give way. That blush is enough for me. As I said last night—"

For the second time in almost as many minutes, Alexandra cut him off. Harry was distraught enough. "I'm off," she declared, and was, before Joss could tell her again how indignation became her.

The others fell in behind her, but after only a little, Miss Rutledge cried out with excitement. If her intent was to have both gentlemen swarm to her side, she succeeded, for the two reined in to discover what she'd seen. Alexandra heard the word "thrush" said in reverent tones and went on.

She was frowning, but not, she told herself, because

it had occurred to her to wonder if a man—a grown man, not a young scamp—might prefer a perfectly turned-out miss to a flushed, tousled hoyden. No, certainly not.

She frowned because she was thinking of the half-wild ebony stallion, Blue Boy, that Joss had put from her reach.

He had tried to reason with her, she admitted, warning her the animal was too powerful for her. But, stubborn to a decided fault, she'd not listened to him, to her father, to Harry, or even to Johnny Coates, and had earned herself a broken collarbone. That very night Joss had engaged her father in a game of cards, with the result that in the morning Blue Boy had not been in his stall.

Oh, but she could still recall the vindication she'd felt when that ice-encrusted water had splashed down upon him! He'd had a friend with him too, John something, to see him sputter. Then . . . But Alexandra preferred not to think on the consequences of her act.

Her roguish grin fading, she admitted something she'd not acknowledged at the time. Joss's care for her had comforted her too. Her father had cared, of course, but he was wild himself, and proud, in all, of her determination, and poor Harry would never have thought to gainsay her.

Perhaps that was why she'd been so devastated when Joss had gone. She'd felt abandoned. He'd taught her half the things she could do: fish, race across the fields, laugh at Lady Sophy's imperious looks even; and always he'd looked out for her.

At first she had missed him so, she'd thought she would break in two. And he had never warned her he meant to leave! If she hadn't come walking home that chilly, blustery Valentine's Day, for it had been on his aunt's birthday he'd left, she might have missed him altogether. She thought he'd have looked for her to tell her good-bye, but she could not be certain. He had not seemed to have the least notion that his departure would crush her.

It was her father, coming out the door of Beech-fields, an arm around Joss's shoulder, who'd called out the news with one of his great laughs. "Alex! You're in time to bid Joss farewell. He's off to make his fortune in the world. Egad, but that wind's got a bite to it! You'll not mind if I take these older bones of mine indoors and leave Alex to do the honor of waving you off, will you, lad? Women are better at that sort of thing anyway. You know I'll miss you like the devil, though I think you're doin' the right thing. Can't be eating from Charles's, or, more accurately, Sophy's hand the rest of your life."

Alexandra had stared. "You . . . you are leaving for good?" she stammered, only to have Joss's responding grin cut her to the quick. He was breaking her heart with a smile.

And a quip. "Or ill! I've a notion to see the world and make a fortune or two. You'll wish me well, I hope, Alex?"

She must have replied appropriately, though she'd no notion then or later what she said, but she did recall watching him mount Blue Boy. The stallion had sidled restlessly until Joss brought him to order. Then, smiling, he'd leaned down, and before she'd any notion what he intended, he had tipped up her chin and kissed her on the lips. "Keep yourself well, my little brat. Who knows, but I'll come back and carry you off in style, when you've grown into those great green eyes of yours."

Something fell from his pocket as he straightened, and, her knees feeling like jelly, Alex sank rather than bent down to retrieve the delicately chased heart-shaped locket on a matching gold chain.

She held it up to him, but Joss closed her hand over it. "The heart's for you, Alex. Guard it carefully, for it's the only part of me that remains in England."

Inside, she had found the picture of Cupid floating on a fluffy cloud, and perhaps she had been tempting fate to take the god of love, his bow notched and primed, to her breast on the very day dedicated to lovers. Joss had had only to reappear before her in the conservatory for her attraction to him, hopeless though it was, to reawaken, rather as the earth comes back to life upon the return of spring.

"The fresh air feels good. Spring truly is coming!" Alexandra breathed deeply as Harry escorted her onto the balcony off Penthurst's ballroom, where large torches affixed to marble pillars revealed that a few other couples had also chosen to escape the closeness of the ballroom.

"For my part, I feel only winter in the air." Harry smiled. "But I shall endure the cold without complaint because I know I am the envy of every gentleman here for having you on my arm."

"Harry!" Alexandra laughed. "What a golden tongue you've developed!"

"It's the truth," he maintained with a gallant bow. "Everyone's beside himself to have you back among us. John Twickenham could not take his eyes off you. I noticed, if you did not, and your old dear friend Sarah Brodey is so giddy I accused her of enjoying more champagne than she ought."

"Lady Val does like to serve up greater quantities of champagne than any other hostess in the county," Alexandra replied rather obliquely as she looked off into the shadowy night. Harry would not like to hear the truth: that it was Joss, not champagne, that had left her friend dizzy with delight.

"I know he's not so handsome as Harry, but he has such an air about him, don't you think, Alex?" Sarah's eyes had been as bright as stars when she posed the purely rhetorical question. "My father used to say Joss was born able to attract the ladies, and now I understand why. I nearly swooned when he smiled that rakish smile! And the way he dances!"

Alexandra could not know how it would be to dance with Joss. She'd not had the pleasure. He had been far too busy greeting old friends and dancing with them.

She did enjoy the opportunity, however, as their paths had inevitably crossed even in so crowded a ballroom, to judge the accuracy of Squire Brodey's long-held opinion on Joss's attractions, and she had had to award the squire points for hidden talents of observation. Even the most elegant of the ladies Joss partnered, Lady Cecile Baldritch, had been reduced to deep blushes and fluttering lashes as they danced.

"Alex."

"Yes, Harry! I am sorry. I did not mean to be inattentive."

"Oh, no! I can imagine you needed a moment of quiet. You've been besieged all evening. But we are almost alone here." He glanced briefly to the nearest couple some little distance away and lowered his voice as he continued, "And I should like to take advantage of our privacy, as it may be the last we'll have. Mama's sisters came today, and tomorrow Father's side of the family arrives. Uncle Hugo ought to be here by luncheon, I believe." Alexandra smiled, for Harry's uncle was a great favorite with her, but she wondered, too, what it was Harry was having such difficulty getting around to saying.

"Now, I wish you will not take this in bad part,"

Harry begged, darting her an uncertain glance. "But, really, Alex, I believe I must warn you against . . . against following Joss's lead just as you used to do!" Feeling her stir, Harry went on quickly, his voice sharpening a shade, "He'll get you into difficulty! If you do not, I do remember that when he enticed you to join him in one of his escapades, it was you who ended up in the suds. You were the one your father birched after you and Joss sneaked off in the middle of the night to steal apples from Brodey's orchard, you'll remember."

"Oh, Harry! That was so very long ago! And Joss did try to convince Papa it was he who deserved the birching, only Papa took it into his head that I was old enough to know what I was about. Besides, to make up for my punishment, which between us I will admit was not so severe as it sounded, Joss brought me that setter, Puddles. What a dog! She wet everywhere."

"Alex!" Harry sounded exasperated, and glancing up, Alexandra could see his mouth had tightened. "You must be serious! Now we are older, our circumstances have changed, and the trouble Joss could bring you would be a great deal worse than a birching."

"Whatever do you mean, Harry?" she demanded, mystified. "I cannot imagine Joss will propose sneaking off to Squire Brodey's orchards again. It's not the season, for one thing."

"That is not what I mean, Alex!"

Alexandra stared. "Surely . . . surely you are not implying Joss would give me a slip on the shoulder?"

Harry looked away from her incredulous gaze to the shadowy lanes below. "Sometimes I think you've not the least notion how you look!" he muttered just loud enough for her to hear.

Alexandra did not take the compliment well. "Perhaps I do not, but I do know I am not such a henwit as to allow such a thing, nor is Joss such a rogue that he'd play me so false!''

"Now you are angry with me!" Harry cried, seizing her hand in his. "I am only concerned for you, Alex. You are such a beauty, any man would want you!''

But not Joss, she nearly said. He only mops up my tears and challenges me to ride recklessly across the fields. "Harry . . ."

"Say you are not angry!"

"I am not," she affirmed on a sigh. "I understand, at least I think I do, but I want to hear no more on the subject. In fact, I think I'm cool enough to brave the ballroom again.''

She essayed a smile, but Harry did not follow her lead. His gaze very solemn, he lifted her hand to his lips. "I am devoted to you, Alex.''

Alexandra felt oddly remote from Harry in that intimate moment when he placed a kiss upon her gloved hand. He professed devotion, but moments before he'd as good as proclaimed her a weak, silly girl who would be foolish enough to allow a man to have his way with her.

She managed to return the smile he gave her, but remained somewhat aloof as he led her back into the ballroom, where the musicians were enjoying a short intermission. Many of the guests were at the refreshment tables, but Alexandra had no difficulty noting that Lady Val still held court in the far corner, a dozen cupids she'd had painted on the ceiling years before floating above her head.

"Blast!" Harry's grasp tightened on her arm. "Mama seems to be having difficulty with Joss.''

Or he with her, Alexandra amended silently as she followed Harry's gaze. Lady Sophy was lecturing Joss emphatically while he listened with a faint, enigmatic smile.

"Come along, Alex," Harry directed, sweeping her off with him.

"Harry!" Lady Sophy seized her son's arm as if she needed physical support. "You must speak to Joss. He has arranged to have a waltz played!"

"A waltz! But it is scandalous!"

Joss arched his brow as Harry turned a horrified look upon him. "I cannot think a simple dance warrants such a look, Harry. It's not as if I am proposing an orgy, after all, though, given the origins of St. Valentine's Day, perhaps I should."

Alexandra could not fault Harry when he grimly declared Joss was only trying to be provoking. She suspected Harry was right, but, her curiosity piqued, she was not displeased when Joss shrugged off Harry's criticism. "It's entirely relevant to know the Romans, for centuries and centuries, held a feast in honor of young lovers on the day we celebrate as St. Valentine's Day. We Christians may have tacked on a martyr's name for appearances, but the spirit of the season is pagan. Thought of in that light, the waltz seems rather tame to me."

Joss's surprisingly knowledgeable dissertation only succeeded in bringing bright spots of color to Lady Sophy's cheeks, never a good sign. "It is unforgivable that you should speak of such things before ladies, Jocelyn Staunton! But I am not surprised. You've never had the least sense of what is fitting. I do, however, and if you do not tell the musicians you have reconsidered, I shall."

"Do so, Cousin Sophy, and you will disappoint Aunt Val, whose ball this is. She gave me her permission to have a waltz played."

Lady Sophy's spine went absolutely rigid. "You have

cozened her, as always, but never think you will take me in, sir! I know why you've come home! You think to wheedle an allowance from her to line your penniless pockets.''

Though Joss did not move a muscle, Alexandra saw a flame blaze to life at the very back of his eyes and did not wait to see if he could contain his temper. ''This is not the time for such a discussion, I think,'' she said quietly. Lady Sophy rounded upon her with a deadly glare, but Alexandra returned the look unmoved. ''Even now, ma'am, there are guests craning to see what is amiss, and I cannot believe you wish to provide grist for the gossip mill.''

At that moment the musicians struck up the first chords of the waltz Joss had requested. ''Well, it would seem the debate's decided.'' At the satisfaction in Joss's tone, or perhaps in response to the hated music, Lady Sophy drew herself up dangerously, but Joss, ignoring her, shifted his gaze to Alexandra. ''Will you do me the honor, Alex, of proving there is nothing unholy about the waltz?''

Alexandra registered the faint hiss that was Lady Sophy's reaction, and perhaps the hateful sound set her back up. Or perhaps she did not have it in her to capitulate to a woman who could speak so venomously and unjustly to another. Or perhaps she was moved by the headstrong, reckless streak she had, as she knew, inherited from her father. At any rate, her choice very clear, for Lady Sophy and Harry were arrayed on one side, tight-lipped and forbidding, while Joss, amused but watchful, too, stood on the other, Alexandra inclined her head.

''I would be delighted, Joss.''

As Joss led her out to the floor, she kept her head very high and ignored the uncomfortable feeling that Harry's eyes were drilling holes into her back.

"You do have some inkling how to waltz, I hope, Alex?" Joss inquired *sotto voce*. "I've little desire to trip with two hundred pairs of eyes upon us."

Made suddenly aware that they were quite alone on the dance floor, she confided beneath her breath, "An inkling only! Sarah Brodey taught me what she learned in London."

What Sarah had not made entirely clear was how very close she would be to her partner. And how her heart would pound almost painfully when he took her into his arms.

Afraid Joss must hear that pounding, she slanted him a glance from under her lashes and saw he was smiling his crooked smile. "Well, then, having had the best of instruction, you've only to relax, and we shall bring the thing off in fine order."

Made aware she was moving as stiffly as a knight in full armor, Alexandra concentrated upon putting everything from her mind but the lilting music. Joss's lead was firm and assured, and finally she began to feel rather as if she were floating. Having abandoned a careful count of her steps, she whispered on a sigh. "You are good at this, Joss."

He led her into another measured circle. "I've had practice."

"Were they very beautiful?"

"Did I miss something? Who?"

Alexandra did not glance up, though she could feel Joss's gaze touch the top of her head. "The women you danced with."

"Ah! Every one of them, to be sure."

Instantly her eyes flew up to meet his. His were dancing. "I don't believe you."

He laughed aloud, and tightened his hold on her waist. "You needn't worry, Alex," he whispered, his breath ruffling her hair as he spun her faster and faster so that she was obliged to fairly cling to him. "Not one could hold a candle to you." He was teasing her, she knew, but before she could decide with absolute certainty, Joss was adding, "But look! We're no longer the only scandalous pair in the neighborhood."

Effectively distracted, Alexandra glanced around to see that some five or six couples had decided to be daring. Harry was not among the gentlemen, however. Alexandra caught sight of him on the sidelines. He was still glaring at her. She tossed her head and determined to enjoy her waltz, whatever he thought. She might never again have the opportunity to float so dreamily around a ballroom. She'd either marry Harry and be forbidden the dance, or be exiled to Yorkshire, too poor to attend a ball even if one were held.

"That's it." Joss chuckled as if he were privy to her thoughts. "To the devil with small minds that condemn anything new. It's not a wicked dance, but a beautiful one, particularly when one is lucky enough to have a partner as staunch as she is lovely. Thank you for intervening before I said something I might regret to Sophy."

There was such tenderness in his smile, Alexandra's heart swelled almost painfully. "She was behaving—"

"No," Joss interrupted softly. "We'll not discuss Sophy during a lovers' dance at a lovers' ball. All Hallows' Eve is the time for her."

When Alexandra laughed with delight, Joss grinned conspiratorially, for he could not know, as she did, that her elation owed less to his admittedly good joke than to his likely quite idle remark that they danced a lovers' dance.

"Good morning, Alex! Do come and sit by me, dear child!"

Though she managed a smile as she slipped into the

vacant seat Lady Val indicated, Alexandra was keenly aware that Harry, by way of greeting, had thrown her a sullen, accusing look, while Lady Sophy had not so much as glanced up from her conversation with Mrs. Rutledge. Aside from Lady Val, only Miss Rutledge, in her customary polite way, had smiled a welcome.

As Alexandra was served a plate of eggs and toast points, Lady Val ruminated upon her ball, taking care to remark upon who among her guests had looked in decline. Then, allowing her voice to rise significantly, she came to the subject Alexandra suspected she had wished to address all along. "A rumor came to my ears suggesting I was almost denied the pleasure of watching you waltz, my dear, but I know little of the truth. Do you?"

Before Alexandra could frame a reply, Lady Sophy spoke with cold authority. "I objected to Jocelyn's scandalous whim, *chère* mama. I did not think pleasing him a sufficient reason to offend the sensibilities of our friends and neighbors."

"I do fear you were misinformed, Sophy!" Lady Val's smile was pleasant enough, but there was a martial glint in her old eyes. "It was not at Joss's request the waltz was played, but mine. You see, I wished to observe the infamous dance for myself, and too, I confess, I fancied the notion of having my ball talked of for months. Oh, and I got my wish!" She chortled gleefully in spite of, or perhaps because of, her daughter-in-law's taut expression. "Not many'll forget the sight of Alexandra and Joss. What a couple you made, my dear! He so tall and sure, you so lovely and graceful. Indeed I was a trifle surprised, Alex, that you knew the dance so well."

Alexandra met Lady Val's twinkling glance with a wry look. "Actually, Aunt Winifred and I were accustomed to practice almost daily."

"Minx!" Lady Val wiped her lips of the coffee she'd nearly choked on. "I should be astonished if your Aunt Winifred had even heard of the waltz. Which leaves the mystery: who did teach you?"

"If you must know, and I see you will have the secret from me—Sarah Brodey. She learned when she went up to London to visit her cousins summer before last."

"Sarah Brodey! Well, the chit has a trade to fall back upon if her papa should stick his spoon in the wall and leave her with naught."

"Grandmama!"

"Yes, Harry?" Lady Val inquired, all innocence. "Do you not agree Sarah must be a superb teacher, given how gloriously Alex danced last night?"

Alexandra was not surprised to see an unnatural amount of color surge into Harry's face. "I cannot say. I was procuring a refreshment for Mama."

"How sorry I am for you, Harry! You missed quite the high point of the evening. Did you dance the waltz last evening, Miss Rutledge? When Joss and Alex were joined by the others?"

Miss Rutledge looked understandably taken aback at being included in the perilous discussion. "Ah, no! No, my lady."

"And have you ever danced the waltz, my dear?" Lady Val persisted.

There was a moment's silence, during which Alexandra saw the heiress dart an anxious glance across the table at her mother. Alexandra could not see Mrs. Rutledge, but it seemed Miss Rutledge received permission to reply honestly, for she said, "Yes, Lady Valentine. I have been approved to dance the waltz at Almack's."

"So, they dance the infamous waltz at Almack's

now!'' Lady Val's exclamation contained as much satisfaction as it lacked surprise.

"The patronesses did allow the waltz to be danced at two assemblies last Season," Mrs. Rutledge leaned forward to explain; then, darting an anxious look at Lady Sophy, she hurried to add, "but there is still vast disagreement as to whether it is an appropriate dance for the young."

Lady Sophy elevated her chin to an uncomfortably high angle before proclaiming authoritatively, "I thought it entirely scandalous and far too intimate for unwed couples."

It was Lady Val, however, who had the final say in this particular round with her daughter-in-law. "I cannot believe we observed the same event, Sophy, for I thought it quite a lovely dance. And I did not see anyone ravished."

Alexandra lifted her cup of chocolate to hide the sudden warmth in her cheeks. She had not been ravished, certainly, but neither had sleep come easily to her after the ball. She had had only to close her eyes to feel Joss's strong arms about her again.

Suddenly restless, she glanced up to find Lady Sophy watching her, and for a moment she thought Harry's mother had read her thoughts, but even as another blush rose in her cheeks, she realized Lady Sophy was actually smiling, albeit thinly. When she glanced pointedly at her son, Alexandra saw she'd reason for her pleasure. Harry was attending most attentively to Miss Rutledge.

Alexandra excused herself soon after, giving the explanation that she was too weary to do further justice to her breakfast when Lady Val pointed out she had scarcely eaten a thing. Once in her room, however, Alexandra searched out her pelisse, for it was not rest she needed but a walk alone. Outside, she found the heavy garment necessary. The sky way overcast, and the wind was from the north.

Her thoughts as heavy as the dark clouds above her, she pulled her pelisse tight about her and ambled through the bare gardens, allowing her thoughts to wander as they would. She wished to go again to Beechfields. Perhaps she would take a lunch. No, Hugo Staunton was coming for luncheon. She would, therefore, sit with Harry and Lady Sophy again.

Was it possible she could set matters right with Harry? Did she wish to? Her mind skittered away from that question to Lady Sophy. Could she bear Lady Sophy for her mother-in-law? She thought of the cold, triumphant smile Harry's mother had given her and kicked out at a rock with her stout half-boot. *That* for Lady Sophy!

But she and Harry need not live at Penthurst, Alexandra reasoned after a moment. They could live at Beechfields, removed at least a little from Lady Sophy's imperious eye. Alexandra would have her own home, which was better, certainly, than losing it.

Which brought her back to Harry. His devotion had been short-lived. A mere dance seemed to have routed it. She kicked another rock. He'd behaved as if she were a leper at the breakfast table! Perhaps they were not so well-suited. A picture of the bleak moors of Yorkshire rose in her mind, and she kicked another rock so furiously it ricocheted off a tree and flew behind her.

"If I'd had the least notion you would throw rocks at me, I'd not have gone out of my way to find you." With a spurt of pleasure, of which she was entirely aware, Alexandra looked around to find Joss had ridden up behind her on a mare she did not recognize. "Kicking furiously at rocks is not the typical behavior of a young lady who has enjoyed a triumphant success at her hostess's ball the night before, Alex. Has something untoward occurred?''

Because she did not wish to discuss Lady Sophy or Harry with anyone, and particularly not with Joss, Alexandra shrugged lightly. "It is only morning-after-the-ball letdown, I think. But where is Mustafa?"

With an ease of movement she allowed herself to admire, Joss swung down from the mare. "At the squire's. Brodey invited me over for breakfast and a look at this mare he wishes to sell. I've ridden her out to see if she suits me."

Alexandra stroked the animal's glossy neck. "Does she?"

"She has a smooth gait, but I'm not so interested in riding her as in breeding her to Mustafa, which is why I'm here. I cannot remember her dam, but Brodey said you might recall her—a strong chestnut named Daisy."

"I do indeed! Father wished to buy her, but the squire wouldn't sell."

"So! Here you are."

"Harry!" Startled more by the intense bitterness in Harry's tone than by his sudden appearance, Alexandra shot to her tiptoes to look over the mare's neck. His hands on his hips, he looked very handsome in a sullen, brooding, Byronic way.

"I thought you were retiring to your room to rest."

Alexandra opened her mouth, but just in time mastered her temper. It would serve no good purpose, with Joss looking on, to inquire bitingly if Harry had been appointed her inquisitor. If their differences were to be resolved, it must be in private, when her temper, at least, had cooled.

"I decided the fresh air would revive me more quickly than sleep," she said, her voice level; then, in an effort at normalcy, she gestured to the mare.

"Come, look at this mount Joss is considering buying from the squire."

But Harry was not to be persuaded to take the olive branch so easily. "Two mounts, Joss?" he inquired with unveiled sarcasm. "That would seem a bit excessive for someone in your position."

"Would it, indeed? Now, I do wonder, Harry, what you deem my position to be."

Joss's silky drawl lifted the hairs on Alexandra's neck, and before the exchange between the two cousins could heat further, she said the first thing that came to mind. "What do you think of the mare as a mate for Mustafa, Harry? She's out of Daisy. You remember her?"

Harry's gaze whipped back to Alexandra. "I do, and I should say the mare will suit Joss admirably. Daisy was as undisciplined as she was unruly."

"But that is unfair!" Alexandra cried, ducking under the mare's head to confront Harry directly. "Daisy was spirited, not unruly, and she was a grand ride."

Harry turned very red, and, his hands clenching into fists, he demanded angrily, "Why ask for my opinion, Alex, if you intend to dispute whatever I say? But I did not come out to quibble over a mare Joss cannot afford anyway! I came to tell you Uncle Hugo has arrived and awaits you inside."

Frustrated beyond bearing, Alexandra watched Harry wheel about and stalk back toward the house. Now they could not even discuss a matter as neutral as a horse! Her future seeming to go up in smoke before her eyes; she lashed out at another rock, only to be reminded she was not alone when Joss laughed softly.

"I wonder how many pairs of boots it will take before you come to your senses and see he's not the man for you."

It was his laugh that acted as the final straw for Alexandra, though admittedly Joss's words did little to soothe her. He laughed though her future looked as bleak as the moors, and he never once thought to offer himself as the man for her!

"I am glad my predicament amuses you, Joss!" She whirled on him. "Forgive me if I do not share in your hilarity, however! To put it baldly, I've not twopence to rub together, and I do not believe I've either the knowledge or the temperament to be a governess or a companion. Ah!" She clapped her hands dramatically. "I have it! I shall be an actress, free as a bird as long as I give the audience a peek at my ankles."

"You *would* take the town by storm, I quite agree, but you'd not like the life, I fear. To live in any comfort at all, actresses must secure a patron, and you, Alex, pet, do not have it in you to play the role of conformable, clinging mistress."

He'd had an opportunity to say, "Come be my bride," but had chosen to mock her instead. Alexandra turned bright, mocking eyes upon him. "How helpful it is to have an authority's opinion. Joss! Thank you very much. And so I am left with one solution: marriage, if I am not to become a lonely creature like Aunt Winifred, buried alive on a godforsaken moor. And Harry will be as good a husband as any. No better! Because he is handsome, devoted, and I like him. The difficulties that have arisen between us are all your fault, you know. And I wish you had not come back!"

"Do you?"

"Yes!"

She had quite succeeded in wiping every vestige of good humor from Joss's expression. There was a light in his eyes, but it held no warmth. " 'Tis an easy wish to grant, Alex. I'll be on way, only allow me to wish you luck at finding pleasure in your marriage bed. I'd wager a deal that our oh-so-beautiful and oh-so-wealthy Harry will not care for lying with a spirited filly any more than he cares for riding them!''

"Beast!" she blazed back, so incensed he'd attacked her on ground where she had not a quarter, as he knew, of his knowledge, that she shook. "What does it matter to you who lies with me?"

A moment of thunderous pregnant silence followed. Then Joss demanded in a low, rough growl, "Do you really not know, Alex? Well, then, I'll show you."

As quickly as that, before she had any notion what was to come, Joss swept her up into his arms and kissed her. Unprepared for the surge of passion the feel of Joss's lips upon hers would unleash, Alexandra swayed helplessly toward him, grasping his shoulders for support.

She had loved Joss so very long! Giddy elation swept her. Did he love her? At the question, Alexandra tore her lips from his and, searching his eyes, saw they were so dark a blue as to be black.

No more. What message Joss's eyes held, if any, or even the significance of their deep color, she was not given the time to decide. Without the least warning, Joss suddenly thrust her from him. Dazed, Alexandra could scarcely comprehend his words when he announced evenly, "You'll be obliged to delay unleashing your temper on me, I'm afraid, Alex. Hugo has just appeared from around the corner of the house."

Alexandra turned about as in a dream. Hugo Staunton waved, and she tried to concentrate her whirling thoughts on him. He smiled at her. "Alex, my dear, you are, as ever, a pleasure to see!"

Seeing nothing but approval in his kind eyes, she allowed her shoulders to relax a fraction. "Thank you, Uncle Hugo. I am glad you've come."

"I trust your Aunt Winifred is well?"

Assured Alexandra's aunt was very well, Hugo, smiling eagerly, held out a hand to Joss. As it was the natural thing to do, Alexandra glanced at the man beside her as well, and was in time to see Joss's smile flash white and strong as he returned Hugo's greeting. Whereas her knees still felt so rubbery that she feared their trembling would be obvious, Joss stood easy and appeared as composed as if he'd done no more than break off a handshake with her moments before. No flush stained his cheeks, no suspicious brightness lit his eyes, and no emotion hurried his breathing.

Vaguely she heard Hugo declare he had imagined the natives would make mincemeat of Joss "somewhere east of Gibraltar." Joss replied, in a lazily amused voice, that if he'd not been minced, he had been fed minced lizard. As Hugo demanded to hear the particulars of the exotic meal, a wave of such resentment rose in Alexandra that she maintained her fragile composure only with the greatest effort.

That searing, earth-shattering kiss had been as nothing to him! Of course he was experienced. He'd likely kissed half a dozen ladies. No, probably more. Another kiss could mean little to him. She bit her lip as if to punish it for the warmth that made it tingle still.

Why had he kissed her, then? To tease her only? The thought made her want, quite suddenly, to fling something at him.

As she bit down more fiercely on her soft lip, another thought occurred. Joss's intent might have been more kindly. Perhaps he had thought to demonstrate to her how easily another man could supplant Harry in her thoughts. Only by clenching her hands tightly did she quell a desire to laugh. He'd put himself out for naught, if so! She'd long known one man in particular could put Harry in the shade. He always had.

"Well, Alex. What do you say? Would you care for a meal of minced lizard and boiled peacock eggs?"

"No!" Alexandra cursed herself, for the sharpness of her tone had caused Hugo to blink. She forced a smile. "I'm afraid I've never had much taste for exotic foods, actually. And, since I did promise Lady Val I would read to her this morning, I'll go along and leave you gentlemen to your discussion of them."

"If Mama has you now, then I claim you as my luncheon partner," Hugo told her with a fond smile.

"Until then." She inclined her head in the direction of both men and made to go.

"Alex."

Her step faltered. In the time it took to draw breath, she decided against ignoring Joss. "Yes?" She lifted her eyes as far as his starched neckcloth.

"I imagine this fell from your hair."

A hairpin lay in his tanned hand. Despite the heavy skies, it gleamed damningly there for all to see. Joss made no effort to hand the pin to her, merely held it out for her to retrieve herself.

She did, her fingers feeling suddenly clumsy as they came in contact with his warm skin. "Thank you."

Joss's hand began to curl as if he would capture hers, but she was quick. Pin in hand, she escaped without meeting dark blue eyes she knew would mock her.

"Alex! I must speak with you!"

Harry, seeming to have appeared from nowhere, swept open the library door. She'd not seen him or Joss since that morning, for Lady Val, deciding she was more fatigued by her own festivities than she'd realized, had invited only Alexandra and Hugo to join her in her rooms for luncheon. Alexandra inclined her head. "Yes, Harry. I agree it is time we talked."

"We should have some privacy here." He closed the door behind them. "Everyone is resting just now."

As everyone was not resting, only the ladies, Alexandra assumed Harry referred to his mother. "I think we'll be private enough. Harry. . . ."

"I want to apologize for this morning, Alex! I was . . . upset." When Harry raked his hand through his hair, she knew him to be truly distraught. He was normally painstakingly fastidious about his appearance. "Oh, Alex!" He'd not quite mastered a vexed, accusatory tone. "How could you have danced the waltz with Joss? Mama will never forget that you deliberately flouted her wishes."

"I saw nothing wrong with the dance, Harry. But I admit I went as well because Joss had my sympathy. I thought Lady Sophy said quite unforgivable things to him."

Harry's brow shot up. "Mama was only speaking the truth! Had Joss a feather to fly with, he'd have exclaimed it from the rooftops. How can he live without wheedling an allowance out of Grandmama?"

"He's not the sort to wheedle, Harry," Alexandra admonished almost wearily, then turned away before he could argue a point that had little to do with them. The French windows drew her. A dense, soaking mist had begun to fall from the dark clouds the wind had blown up. The terrace outside the window was visible, but she knew that only rolling lawns and an ornamental lake lay beyond, because the grounds at Penthurst had not changed since Capability Brown had laid them out in the last century.

Only the people changed at Penthurst. She looked back to Harry with a sigh.

"Do you know, Harry, I had forgotten the depth of the rivalry between you and Joss. It was always there between you, I know, but I suppose my own difficulties these past years obscured my recollection. Or perhaps''—she shrugged faintly—''perhaps I did not care to think on it overmuch, lest I be obliged to acknowledge things I'd rather have ignored.''

''Alex, I don't understand.''

Harry looked so genuinely bewildered, Alexandra gave him a smile that, for all it was frayed at the edges, was sincere. ''I apologize. I'm not making myself clear, I expect. What I mean to say is that when I was a child, I managed, in some way or other, to be loyal to you both. You were my oldest friend, after all, and though I admired Joss greatly, I did not wish to take sides between you. I blamed you both equally for the sour relations between you, but now I find I cannot be so impartial. I've been reminded since Joss's return that while he seldom spoke of you when you were not present, you were not so nice when he was absent, and often echoed your mother's disparaging sentiments, though why the two of you should resent him so greatly, having everything, as you do, I still do not understand.''

''Having everything!'' Harry's eyes bulged from their sockets, and for the first time in her life Alexandra thought him ugly. ''Joss is the one always had Grandmama's highest regard, though he is only her nephew and was ever up to some idiotic lark or other!''

''Larks you reported when you got the chance, didn't you, Harry?'' Alexandra's quiet voice held more sorrow than accusation, but Harry stiffened. ''After you mentioned that escapade in Squire Brodey's orchards, I remembered how it puzzled me that Papa should have chosen that particular night to look in on me in my bed, when it was not his custom to do such a thing. In the end I placed the blame on fate. I did not want, I suppose, to think anyone I considered a friend would betray me, even over so small a matter. I had told only one person what Joss and I planned for that night. I invited you to go along, but you told Papa instead, didn't you, Harry?''

"I?'' Harry's incredulity seemed genuine enough, but Alexandra remarked how he could not hold her gaze. "I . . .'' He flung away from her to pace the room. The fire drew him, and he kicked out at a log, sending a shower of sparks up the chimney. Then suddenly he swung back to face her where she stood before the French windows. "He was always taking you away from me! It wasn't fair!''

"You earned me a birching, Harry.''

His beautiful liquid brown eyes flared wide. "I never guessed your father would birch you, Alex! You must believe that. Joss was the one who deserved punishment! He's the one who lured you out into the night!''

When Alexandra did not reply at once, Harry rushed to her, grasping her shoulders tightly. "You do believe me, Alex?''

Alexandra could only stare at him and wonder how it was she had blinded herself to the truth. Harry, jealous of Joss from the first, had seized every opportunity he could find to get Joss into difficulty with Lady Sophy, Lady Val, or Alexandra. Even the incident with Lily Bailey had not been a mere misunderstanding between the cousins. Harry had chosen a time when she was present to announce Joss's interest in the girl by deriding her.

"I am releasing you from your pledge, Harry.''

"Releasing me? Releasing me? What do you mean?''

Alexandra shifted uncomfortably as his grip tightened. "I mean that we should not marry. Your mother and I will never—''

"It's not mother!'' He shook her violently. "It's him. You always preferred Joss to me. Always!''

"You are hurting me, Harry!" When his grip relaxed on the instant, Alexandra went on urgently, "This has naught to do with Joss! Truly, Harry. Perhaps I see matters more clearly because I've been apart from you for a time. I don't know. I only know I see now that you and I would never suit as husband and wife. I would drive you to distraction within—"

"You already drive me to distraction, Alex!" Harry cried, meaning another thing entirely. "Don't you understand? I've even defied Mama for you. She'd have had me write telling you not to come at all for this affair! But I would not do it, and I'll not let him have you!"

Seizing her to him, Harry mashed his lips down upon Alexandra's. Frightened, she struggled, pushing hard at his chest, and suddenly, reeling backward, she was free. Stunned by the unexpected attack and equally unexpected release, Alexandra stared dumbfounded at her old playmate, her hand on her mouth.

But he was not looking at her. He was looking over her head to the French window, and the triumph lighting his eyes gave Alexandra to suspect what she'd see when she turned.

And Joss was, indeed, standing in the door he had just opened, his hands on his hips, and his eyes, dark and cold as a midwinter midnight, on her. "Comparing responses, Alex?" His lip curled in derision. "Or merely mending fences? But don't mind me. You've work aplenty before you, if you intend to get Harry out from beneath his mother's skirts. I wish you luck and, of course, joy of all those pounds."

With a bow that mocked by its very grace, he turned on his heel and retraced his steps into the rain.

"The brute!" Harry muttered when Joss was, as Alexandra noted, out of earshot. "He's not worthy of you!" Harry fixed his gaze upon Alexandra and took a step toward her. "You must see that! And that there's no reason to break our pledge!"

Slowly Alexandra turned to Harry. For a long moment she regarded him in silence, taking in his high color and his eyes bright with supplication or, perhaps, victory over his cousin. And before she could think better of her intent, she dealt such a blow to his cheek that his head snapped back.

"That for our pledge, Harry, and for you! And for your contemptible stratagem!" Her silk skirts rustling furiously, Alexandra brushed by him, only to whirl back again. "And for your information, your forcing that kiss upon me when you saw him out the window was a complete waste of effort! Joss does not want me for his wife. I am a child to him!"

"There! My knight should be safe from you now, Alex."

A rueful smile curved Alexandra's mouth as she looked from the chessboard to Hugo Staunton. "I think you've forgotten my rook, sir."

"Blast! I've not played in so long, I'm no match for you, and that though you do seem a trifle distracted, my dear."

"Oh, no!" Alexandra met her opponent's kindly but searching gaze with some difficulty. "That is, I am a little weary still from all the dancing last evening. I apologize if I've been poor company."

"You could never be that, petite. I only spoke because I am accustomed to seeing your lovely eyes undimmed by shadow."

Alexandra hesitated. She'd have liked some impartial advice on her future, and though Hugo was Harry's uncle, he'd occasionally played avuncular confidant to her when she was younger. She weighed her words too long, however. As she parted her lips, the library door swung open, and for the second time that day Joss discovered her there in a *tête-à-tête* with a gentleman.

He flicked an inscrutable gaze over her, then addressed Hugo. "My apologies for interrupting so rudely. Moreton said everyone was in the music room."

Hugo rose. "Come in! Come in, Joss. You do not interrupt, but rescue. Alex is making a fool of me."

Alexandra make some sound of protest, but Hugo only shrugged it off as he crossed to the door where Joss still stood. "Come in," he repeated, going to the extent of taking Joss's arm. "Though Miss Rutledge is, indeed, entertaining in the music room, and quite nicely to be sure, Alex and I elected to enjoy a little solitude."

Joss could have extricated himself easily from Hugo's light hold, but only by behaving rudely to a man he liked, and so he'd little alternative but to allow himself to be led across the room toward Alexandra, whose head was bent over the chessboard as if she studied it intently.

"There." Hugo clapped him so firmly on the shoulder that Joss subsided into a chair before he realized it was Hugo's own.

"This is your seat, Hugo," he protested, half-rising.

"It was." Hugo laughed and waved Joss back into the disputed place. "Now you're here. I'll not play any more against Alex. She deserves an opponent up to her mettle."

Alexandra looked up then. Her eyes, set off by her thick auburn hair, were very green. A muscle in Joss's jaw tensed, and when he wrenched his gaze from hers, she believed he would quit her presence. He did not. He looked down to study the disposition of the chess pieces. Black was in considerable difficulty.

If Hugo thought it odd that Joss did not bid Alexandra good evening or that she did not inquire after the dinner he had enjoyed at Squire's Brodey's, he said nothing. Quite the contrary, smiling slightly, he went to fetch two glasses of brandy and a glass of ratafia from the sideboard, then settled himself upon a settee beside the chessboard.

As he had done with many things, Joss had taught Alexandra to play chess, and with his advent her fortunes suffered an immediate reversal, for he was the more experienced player. His grim expression unnerved her as well, shattering her concentration, and in only six moves Joss captured four of her pieces. The ruthlessness of his assault stung her to attention. Rallying, she captured his last bishop. Severely crippled, for he'd only one knight and two pawns to protect his king and queen, Joss studied the board.

He'd have had an easier time of his calculations but for Alexandra's gown. Of nile-green silk, the tiny beaded bodice was cut temptingly low. His mood, uncertain to begin with, was not improved each time his eyes strayed to the creamy swell of her breasts. How nice for Harry, he thought, and promptly lost one of his pawns.

Furious, he bent his thoughts to revenge and swooped down upon Alexandra's queen. Hugo whistled at the boldness of the move, then suddenly tipped his head.

"Now, who could that be?"

Because the library doors were open, the sounds of newcomers in the entrance hall below could be heard, though the voices were too distant to recognize.

"I don't think Mama is expecting more company, is she, Alex?"

Alexandra shook her head. "No, not that I know of."

"Well, I'll just go along and see who it is has stolen in upon us, while you stay and finish our game."

Tension thick enough to be cut with a knife filled the room even before Hugo closed the library doors behind him. Alexandra cursed beneath her breath as she reached to move her king to safety. Her hand was trembling

"Afraid of something, Alex?"

"No, of course not!" she retorted! Head high, Alexandra tried to meet Joss's regard calmly, but she had never seen his eyes glitter in such a way. "Have I reason to be fearful?"

"None that I know of. I merely remarked how you tremble. Can it be, if you are not fearful, that you tremble from eagerness for another embrace?"

Alexandra shot to her feet. "I certainly do not! And I'll not stay to be insulted."

"Insulted?" Surging up as as swiftly, Joss caught her arm before Alexandra could sweep by him. "I did not think to insult you, Alex, only to explain that I've no interest in competing with Harry for 'Best Embrace of the Valentine's Season.' "

Her eyes blazed. "That's just as well, Joss. You'd have lost!"

No sooner had she spoken than Alexandra regretted her words. They were the purest spite and entirely untrue. Angry with herself now as much as with Joss, she wrenched her arm free of his grasp. "I would go now," she muttered, passing him.

She had taken no more than two steps before she was arrested again, but this time it was his voice alone that drew her up short. "Am I to wish you happy, then, Alex?"

Biting her lip, she fought the desire to turn and fling herself into his arms. She would keep her dignity. "You may wish me happy anytime you like, Joss. I imagine I shall need all the good wishes I can garner."

Tears stinging her eyes, she hurried on, deaf to the sound of his footsteps. Before she was even aware Joss had followed after her, he was spinning her about.

"You are crying!" he said, his voice harsh as he stared into her shimmering eyes. "Why?"

"Oh, let go of me!" She jerked free of his hold. "I am tired. Nothing more." As Cupid must be from a long day of shooting his little arrows at all the wrong people: Miss Rutledge wants Harry; Harry wants me; I want Joss; and Joss . . . ?

"Alex!"

"What?" she snapped, her temper ignited by his warning tone. "Have you another Olympian pronouncement to make, Joss, or perhaps another perceptive observation on my character before you hie off for another four years, free as a bird? Don't allow me to delay you! Be gone, and good riddance to you and to all you blasted Stauntons!"

What she meant by that last inclusive pronouncement, Joss was not to know, though he did start after her. He was just reaching for her again, as Alexandra, brusquely wiping her cheeks free of tears, half-ran from him, when the library doors burst open and a crowd of people, headed by Hugo, surged into the room.

"Joss! Friends of yours have come to visit," Hugo exclaimed, indicating two women, both strangers to Alexandra, and a man who seemed vaguely familiar. Behind them were Lord Charles, Lady Sophy, her sisters, the Rutledges, Harry, and Lady Val.

Alexandra stepped back as Joss went to embrace the gentleman. "John! John Montague! Whatever are you doing here?" he demanded, clapping his friend upon the back.

John Montague beamed. "Lord Charles and Lady Sophy have graciously forgiven us for descending upon them in the middle of the night without the least warning, and I hope you will as well. I'd a letter from your brother, Richard, only yesterday, saying where you were, and as we'd plans to go up to town, we decided to start early and stop off to see you. Of course we thought to put up at the inn in the village, but for some reason or other there's not a room to be had."

"There's a mill over in Haughton Buxby tomorrow, and all the inns for miles around are booked, but I am delighted!"

"You remember Cecily, don't you?" John Montague stepped back to smile fondly upon the smaller of the two women with him. "We married the summer after you left."

"Of course I remember." Joss made an elegant bow over Cecily Montague's dainty hand. "How could I forget Cecily? She was the best dancer of her Season."

Pretty Mrs. Montague laughed delightedly. "And I see you are still the greatest flirt, Joss!"

"And here is Anne. I know you remember my sister."

Alexandra did not see much resemblance between John and Anne Montague. He was a solid, cheerful-looking man with unexceptional brown hair and nice brown eyes, while his sister was a curvaceous beauty with black hair and almond-shaped eyes more amber than merely brown.

"Anne." When Joss lifted the beauty's hand to his lips, she gave him a smile seductive enough to cause Alexandra's fingers to curl inward.

"I hope you've not forgotten me, Joss. I certainly have not forgotten you, though you have changed"— she gave a low, husky laugh as her eyes swept over him—"for the better, I should say."

Joss's laugh sounded very pleased to Alexandra's ears. "And I should say Beaufort showed remarkable foresight by snapping you up before you'd even had your come-out."

"Poor Beaufort!" Her eyes went very wide. "He was taken by a fever only two years ago."

Joss proclaimed his sorrow, and, Alexandra noted with a pain that made her wretched, remained beside the ripe widow.

"Come, seat yourselves!" Lady Val called out, having settled herself comfortably upon a settee. "I shall get a pain in my neck if I'm obliged to crane it so." With a gesture of the cane she carried more than used, she indicated Alexandra, who was hurrying to remove the chess set as the others seated themselves. "You've met everyone but Alexandra Talbot, here. I like to think of her as my granddaughter, though she's only my fairy goddaughter."

Despite the vicissitudes of the day, the remark made Alexandra smile as she turned, the box of chess pieces in her hand, to greet Joss's friends.

The ladies responded with varying degrees of politeness, but John Montague's jaw dropped. "I cannot believe you are the little hellion who, dressed in breeches, deluged Joss with icy water." Mr. Montague laughed. "I never saw him so angry. He spanked you, I believe, though the chase you forced on him was too fast for me, and I did not witness your punishment. I only caught up in time to see Joss wiping tears from your cheeks. Having believed he might murder you, I was astonished until I finally got a good look at your eyes. They were the largest, greenest eyes I'd ever seen. When I remarked on their power to Joss later, he said you'd been employing them to excellent effect since the cradle and would, when you'd grown into them, devastate the male half of England. I do believe, Miss Talbot, that time has come.''

The blinding smile John Montague received, and that though he had revealed to the assembled group the secret of Alexandra's humiliating spanking, was prompted only in part by his gallantry. Alexandra did thank him, but the vivid sparkle in her eyes was due, as she knew, to Joss's praise, stale and secondhand though it was. Almost, she glanced to Joss, but drawing on her will, Alexandra managed to avoid his eyes, busying herself instead with returning the chess set to its place in a Chinese lacquered cabinet. She'd not have him see her heart so clearly in her eyes.

When she returned, Moreton, having rolled in the tea cart, was assisting Lady Sophy to dispense refreshments. As Alexandra took a seat by Hugo, she saw that Harry was sitting very stiffly and silently by Miss Rutledge, while Joss, all conviviality, lounged upon the arm of John Montague's chair and chatted with both his friend and Mrs. Beaufort, whose smile reminded Alexandra of a cat that has just sighted a particularly delectable bowl of cream.

''Joss!'' At Lady Val's exclamation, all the quiet conversations that had been struck up as the tea was served fell silent. Alexandra, glancing around the imperfect circle, saw there was an air of expectancy on most of the faces turned, not to Lady Val, but to Joss. Even Harry, though his mouth drooped sullenly, looked watchful.

''Yes, Aunt Val?''

''I find it most tedious that I was obliged to learn a quite important fact about your travels from John, here, and not from you.''

''Oh?''

Joss sounded too innocent by half, and Alexandra

looked quickly to him. His expression was bland—unnaturally so.

"Yes! He had the remarkable news from Richard."

"Did he?"

"You are baiting me, boy! Out with it!"

Joss laughed. "A great deal happened to me in those four years, Aunt Val. I'm not certain to what in particular you refer."

"Perhaps I ought not to have said anything!" John broke in to exclaim. "But I never thought you'd have kept it a secret. After all, it's not every day a man arrives home a nabob, he's made such a fortune."

"Millions of pounds!" exclaimed someone, Alexandra never knew who. She heard nothing but "nabob," "fortune," "millions," "nabob" . . . over and over—only those few words that ought to have filled her with gladness that Joss had attained what he wanted.

But instead, they struck her like a fist in the belly. The hope—and it had endured all along, though unacknowledged for the most part—that the spark between them was not merely a figment of her girl's imagination died hard there in the library at Penthurst as she stared, sick at heart, at the swirling pattern of the Turkish carpet beneath her feet.

When he'd said, "Who knows but I'll come and carry you off in style," she had, God help her, in some secret recess of her heart changed the words to a promise. But he'd not even hinted at his riches! At the least, she'd thought them friends who would share good news, but they were not even that, it seemed. There could be only one explanation for his reticence. Apparently Joss had feared she would root after his wealth, and had been both disgusted and embarrassed by the thought.

She clenched her hands tightly, as if she might fall

apart if she did not. Joss despised her. It was all she could think.

"More tea, Miss Alex?"

Moreton's voice penetrated her fog. All her thought processes slowed, Alexandra looked up to shake her head, and found herself staring directly into Joss's eyes.

She'd not the resources just then to consider her own expression. She could only register the intensity of the look in his blue eyes. He seemed to wish to convey some silent message to her. What would it be? "Don't expect a penny!"—of course. "You've my locket, Cupid and his darts. Content yourself."

Mercifully, someone spoke to him, and Alexandra was released to return her attention to the rug, whose intricate pattern somehow helped her hold her increasingly disjointed thoughts at bay. But the following half-hour was an agony of waiting to seize the first opportunity possible to leave. Not even the sight of Lady Sophy stiffly avoiding Joss's eyes provided a distraction, and Alexandra thought she might scream if she had to listen to another of Mrs. Beaufort's low, throaty laughs or hear another exclamation about Joss's phenomenal wealth. When, at last, Lady Val declared herself ready for her bed, Alexandra leapt to assist her.

When they came even with Joss, Lady Val stamped her cane upon the floor. "I'll hear all the rest, particularly why it is you've been so reticent on this subject, tomorrow, my boy. You'll be obliged to tell all then, for it will be my birthday."

"Ah, yes, the day hearts are exchanged."

Alexandra kept her eyes upon Lady Val and raged at herself for imagining Joss had looked to her then. She watched Lady Val poke at him with the cane. "And birthday gifts. I'll expect a stunner, now I know you're rich as Croesus!"

"Take heart, dearest aunt. I've a notion I have just the gift you particularly desire."

"Ah! That would be fine indeed!" Lady Val exclaimed, seeming to understand the cryptic remark, whose meaning eluded Alexandra. "I confess I'd begun to fear you did not understand my summons, lad."

As she shifted away from the fat man encroaching upon her meager space, Alexandra wondered irritably if he had been asked to pay for two seats. He took up twice as much room as any other passenger on the mail coach she'd caught that morning at the Golden Bull. She hoped devoutly she would not be plagued by him for the entire two days to Yorkshire.

The journey south had taken no less time, but she had made it in a great deal more comfort. Lord Charles's coaches were all well-sprung. As if to emphasize the difference in her state, the mail hit a rut, and the fat man, tossing helplessly, crushed her against the door.

He righted himself immediately, apologizing profusely, and the desire to deal a punishing blow to his soft belly receded. Indeed, Alexandra even managed a smile and a mental apology when, to make amends, he offered her a hard candy. He was not, she conceded, the cause of her wretched mood.

She'd not slept at all the night before. Much of the time she'd paced her room, as if to keep ahead of the hurt that threatened to overwhelm her; but it had been before the fireplace, her knees drawn up to her chest, that she'd decided to take herself back to Yorkshire's moors. The very emptiness she'd so disliked appealed to her now.

She could lick her wounds there, as she could not at Penthurst, where Lady Val's birthday would be celebrated with smiles and cheers. And sultry laughs.

The thought of Mrs. Beaufort and Joss chuckling together turned her stomach and set her to packing a valise.

In an explanatory note to Lady Val, Alexandra had taken care not to mention Joss at all, citing, instead, the strained relations between her and Harry as the reason for her abrupt departure. The note and a small birthday gift, she'd left on her untouched bed.

The groom she had roused before the sun even topped the horizon had not questioned her request for a mount, she supposed because she was renowned among the servants at Penthurst for unorthodox behavior. Only when she stopped by Beechfields for one last look and encountered Johnny Coates, did she realize the stable boy might have been moved by sympathy for her pale, haggard face. Johnny had remarked upon it indirectly when he asked her gravely what tragedy had occurred.

She told him of her lesser loss. As she and Harry would not wed, she must put Beechfields on the block and return to Yorkshire. A man of few words, Johnny had said little in reply, except to object to her decision to travel alone, but short of pulling her from Clytie's back, he had not possessed the means to stop her. And so he'd accompanied Alexandra to the Golden Bull and waited with her. When it was time to board, she had kissed him on his leathery cheek and nearly broken down when she felt it wet.

"Hey, now, what's amiss!"

Starting at the fat man's cry, Alexandra realized the coach was slowing, though they were an hour from the next posting inn.

A broad, rawboned farmwoman across from Alexandra leaned her head out the window. "Ah, well," she reported to the others, " 'tis only a tardy passenger."

Her husband, or the farmer Alexandra took to be her husband, shook his head and muttered, "Odd, a mounted man catching the coach away out here!"

Alexandra pushed her knuckles hard against her mouth. The husband had spoken as the new passenger shouted something to the driver, and she'd heard just enough of the stranger's voice for her mind to play the cruel trick of insinuating he was Joss.

"Ah, there you are, Alex."

It was a measure of Alexandra's emotional state that she stared unblinking a full minute before she accepted that her mind had not conjured Joss, nor his blue eyes that were gleaming oddly, nor his smile. That strong smile hurt. Even if he'd no suspicion her heart ached, he knew they were at odds.

She lifted her chin. "You may tell Lady Val it was no use sending you to fetch me back, for I am determined to go to Yorkshire. Therefore, as there is no point in delaying these good people a moment longer, I bid you good day, Joss."

Alexandra sat back in her seat as if she expected the coach to lurch off on the instant. When it did not, she glanced mutinously at Joss. To her confusion, he was inclining his dark head toward her fellow passengers.

"My pardon for the delay, sirs and madam, but I beg you to be patient on this St. Valentine's Day."

Even before they'd heard him out, and though they suffered inconvenience, all three of her fellow passengers appeared more than patient when Alexandra turned in search of an ally. They appeared riveted. And little wonder. The man requesting nothing more than their patience sat a blooded ebony stallion, wore a grand greatcoat with half a dozen capes, sported Hessians polished to a mirrorlike finish, and beguiled them with a flashing white smile that might have charmed a partridge from its concealing thicket.

"You see," he continued as if they'd all the time in the world, "I've come to collect Miss Talbot, here, because she thought to escape me without so much as a farewell."

"This is absurd!" Alexandra ground her teeth together, wishing she might lash out at him for turning her private pain into a seven-day wonder for the amusement of strangers. Unable to deal such a blow, she contented herself with glaring stonily at a speck on the seat before her.

"She's a stubborn and headstrong chit," Joss observed, apparently unconcerned by either Alexandra's furious countenance or the fact that he blocked a public thoroughfare. "But I fear she does not deserve to bear all the responsibility for your inconvenience today. I admit to a measure of fault. I've been a fool, you see."

When the farmer's wife responded with a sympathetic clucking sound, Joss nodded solemnly. "It's true, I came back to England on her account, but idiotically, I refused to tell her. Jealousy, I am ashamed to admit, clouded my thinking." Because Alexandra could not credit that he was not gammoning her, she ruthlessly suppressed an almost overwhelming desire to gape mindlessly at Joss. He went on. "In my defense, I did find her, to all purposes, in the arms of another man, who is far handsomer than I."

"Oh, now!" The farmer's wife managed to convey in the mere two words absolute incredulity that any man could be handsomer.

"And has a title."

"Ah!" That from the more worldly fat man.

Joss nodded at his fascinated audience. "Now, I might have told her I was on an equal financial footing with my rival, but out of pride, I did not. I wished her to love me for myself, just as she had in the past."

That roused her. "You knew!" Alexandra accused, eyes flaming.

He met her angry look with a faint smile that held none of the humor threading his recital to the passengers. "How could I not, little Alex?" he asked without the least bravado. "From my first day at Penthurst, there was something between us. Do you remember? After Sophy swept her Harry from the hall as if I might contaminate him and left me behind uncertain of anything, you slipped your hand in mine, though you were only four, and assured me all would be well, for you'd a robin's nest to show me—only, you added, fixing those great eyes on me, I must help you reach it."

As from a distance, Alexandra heard the farmer and his wife chuckle. But she was lost in the soft gleam lighting Joss's eyes. "I cannot say, though, when it was precisely that I realized I loved you, Alex. Sometime between our disagreement over Blue Boy and before I left."

"But why did you not tell me?" she demanded, her voice roughened by the pain she'd felt when he had seemingly abandoned her.

Joss, hearing it, grimaced. "How could I speak of love and marriage, Alex? I'd not a penny in the world, nor any certainty I ever would have. I'd no choice but to seek my fortune and trust your father to keep you safe until I returned."

"Hey!" the driver, moved by some sense of schedule, called out. "You collectin' 'er or no?"

"Well, Alex?" His eyes were very, very blue. "Will you marry me?"

"Oh, my!" the farmer's wife exclaimed on a rapturous sigh.

But Alexandra was not in quite the same frame of mind as her fellow passenger. The farmer's wife had not been called, in so many words, both shallow and mercenary. "How do you know I love you now, if you did not before? Aren't you afraid I'll say yes merely to get my hands on your piles and piles of money?"

Joss's smile transformed his face. He looked a boy again, and Alexandra caught her breath. "I had it out with Harry this morning. I'd a suspicion all was not as I'd thought between you, and after some persuasion, he admitted you'd thrown him over before you had the least inkling of my fortune. And if that were not proof enough, the dagger looks you cast Anne Beaufort's way would have been." He laughed aloud when Alexandra, stiffening, opened her mouth to deny she'd even looked at the widow. "Don't deny what made me wish to kick up my heels, love! I savored each and every one of those deadly looks. Now, will you marry me?"

"You're not asking for me out of pity, are you, Joss?"

Joss looked over her head at their mesmerized audience to shake his head. "She fears I want her out of pity."

Alexandra felt as much as heard the fat man chuckle. The farmer, a more laconic sort, allowed his twinkling eyes to speak for him, while his wife sniffed audibly.

"I won't have you act coy, Alex," Joss remonstrated, though there was the tenderest of looks in his eyes. "You could easily vie for the title of the most beautiful woman in England, and you would walk off with the prize for bravest. No one else I know, even Aunt Val, can withstand Sophy as composedly as you. You, my sweet, are all the harem I need."

Alexandra smiled then, her face lighting with such radiance that the farmer's wife exclaimed in awe, "There, now! 'Tis truly the loveliest you are!"

All Alexandra could get out was, "Oh, Joss!"

Before the words had more than left her lips, Joss

had swung down from Mustafa and opened the coach door. "Shall we prove Aunt Val's the Cupid she's always fancied?"

"It was for me she summoned you home?"

"She wrote only that Jack's death had forced you to pledge yourself to Harry. She knew that would be enough to bring me back posthaste."

"Oh, Joss!" Alexandra did not even remark her pitifully limited efforts at expression. Her eyes swimming, her face illuminated by a tremulous smile, she held out her hand, but Joss ignored it and caught her down to him by the waist. The driver flung down her valise and almost in the same motion whipped his horses into action.

The coach passengers, however, were not to be denied the final scene of their enthralling, impromptu drama. Unashamedly craning their heads out the windows, they were to a person entirely gratified to see Joss draw Alexandra up against him and take her lips in a long, hard, and thorough kiss that she, it was very clear, returned measure for measure.

"Well!" sighed the farmer's wife when a bend in the road put the entwined couple from her sight. "If that was not a fine show for this St. Valentine's Day, I don't know what would be!"

It was a romantic sentiment with which the two men, though never vocally, heartily agreed.

Fathers and Daughters
by Patricia Rice

"I WOULD LIKE your permission to marry your daughter, sir." Lord Edward John Chatham stood nervously before the older man's desk. From his crisply immaculate white waterfall cravat to the elegantly tailored dove-gray pantaloons tucked correctly into a pair of gleaming Hessians, he was every inch the proper young gentleman. A thick head of burnished brown curls cut fashionably to fall forward over his forehead did not disguise the bleakness of his eyes as he watched the other man turn his back on him and walk away. The fact that he had been offered neither brandy nor a chair spoke ill for his hopes.

"I've been expecting this, Chatham." A small, slenderly built man, Henry Thorogood opened a drawer in a nearby cabinet and withdrew a sheaf of papers. As an astute businessman who had turned his family's dwindling estates into an extremely profitable and lucrative career, Thorogood was always prepared for every eventuality. The neat study in which they stood bespoke his natural methodicalness. He came forward and threw the papers on the desk. "Your vouchers, Chatham. Do you have any idea of the sum total of their worth?"

"Considerably more than you bought them for, I wager," Lord Jack replied wryly, acknowledging Thorogood's shrewdness in obtaining large discounts on practically worthless pieces of paper. Some of those vouchers had been so long outstanding that his creditors would gladly have taken a ha'penny on the pound.

"Enough to have you called before the court, in any case." The older man came to stand behind his desk again. The Thorogoods were an old and respectable family, but no title attached to their name, and Henry's immersion in trade had tainted their welcome in the highest echelons of society. Chatham, on the other hand, was the son of an earl and younger brother of an earl, the current holder of the title, in direct line to the succession, and an eminently eligible bachelor. Henry was well aware of these distinctions and refused to buckle under to the dictates of etiquette and society. He neither sat nor offered his noble guest a chair.

The young man paled slightly at the threat, but he remained steadfast, clenching his hands at his side. "I realize I have overspent my income for some time, but I have already given up my expensive habits and begun to pare down my debts. Except for repaying what you hold there, my allowance from my late father's estate is sufficient to keep Carolyn comfortably, if not quite in the style to which she is accustomed. She understands and has no objections to the modest life we must lead."

"You have already spoken to her? That was unwise. She is much too young to know her own mind. You should have known that of all the wealthy young girls available to buy you out of penury, my daughter was the least suitable. I have no intention of further financing your extravagance at my daughter's expense." Thorogood's voice was harsh and cold as he glared at the lordly young man before him. "You will stay away from Carolyn or I shall have you in debtors' prison so fast your family will not know where to find you."

Or even care, the young man acknowledged to himself. His elder brother had more debts than anyone could repay, but no one dared charge an earl with unpaid bills. He was on his own, as he had been since his father's death, when he was still a schoolboy. The present earl couldn't fish him out of prison any better than he could save himself from going. Lord Jack's jaw tightened at this new obstacle to his happiness.

"I love Carolyn, sir, and I have reason to believe she returns my affections. I will repay those debts in time. You need settle nothing on Carolyn. I will keep her on my income. We will be able to live comfortably in my mother's dower house in Dorset. She will come to no harm at my hands, I assure you." Although he spoke with confidence, Jack was beginning to relive the doubts that had plagued him ever since he had realized his idle pursuit of an heiress had become something much different and totally uncontrollable. He meant every word he said, but he couldn't help remembering Carolyn's youthful innocence. Did she have any idea what a modest life in Dorset meant? How long would it be before she grew restless and bored, deprived of the extravagances her wealthy father had led her to expect of life?

"She will come to no harm at your hands because I will not allow you to lay hands on her!" Thorogood shouted. He had expected the young lordling to crumple with his first shot. This obstinate refusal to acknowledge the facts gave Henry some admiration for the lord, but not enough to surrender his eldest daughter into the young fool's hands. If the man thought his title and family name fair trade for Carolyn's dowry, he would learn otherwise. Carolyn's happiness did not rest on titles, but on character. Chatham's profligate habits did not display the kind of character required for Carolyn's happiness. Resolutely Henry pressed his point. "I will call my daughter in here and you will

226 • *Patricia Rice*

tell her before my face that you will not see her again. In return, I will not call in your debts. Should you so much as show your face at my door, however, I will hand your vouchers over to the magistrate. Do you understand me?''

Jack heard and understood. Beneath his fashionably pale complexion he turned a shade grayer, but his eyes hardened and took on a light of their own. ''I understand you are destroying your daughter's life as well as my own. As you say, she is young and perhaps will recover. For myself, as long as you hold those vouchers, there is no hope for me. If you truly wish me to leave, I request a loan so that I may set about finding a means of repaying those debts.'' And of returning to Carolyn—but he did not say those words aloud; they held his last flickering hope of a life worth living.

The older man looked at the younger contemptuously, seeing the request as a bribe to ensure his silence. There were very few ways a gentleman could turn money into wealth without land and still remain a gentleman. The loan would be wagered at a card table in a mad attempt to win it all back and would never be seen again. If that was what it took, so be it. Henry nodded tersely. ''You will sign a voucher for the sum.''

Curling his fingers into his palms and feeling all his plans crumble to bitter ashes inside him, Jack waited for the servant to fetch Carolyn. They had known each other only a few brief months. Perhaps for her it had been a carefree lark, part of the experience of coming out into society. For him it was much more, but he had been careful not to let her see how deeply she affected him. He had never known such quiet, kind affection and cheerful joy as she had brought to him. It should be enough to treasure these few months of happiness they had shared. He tried to fix a careless expression on his face as he heard the unmistakable light patter of her small feet in the hall.

She floated into the room, a brilliant expectancy upon her face as she smiled into Jack's warm gray eyes. Her smile faltered somewhat as she met an unfamiliar cold barrier there, but she did not hesitate. All fragile grace clothed in pale green gauze and ribbons, her light brown hair piled artlessly above a slender throat and velvet eyes, she advanced bravely to kiss her father's cheek. In her hand she carried what appeared to be a red paper-and-lace heart. She turned and gave Jack another reassuring smile.

"Lord John has something he wishes to tell you, my dear." Henry rested a comforting hand on his eighteen-year-old daughter's shoulder. He had five daughters and no sons. Their mother had died giving birth to the youngest just two years ago. Carolyn had been his right hand and biggest comfort during those two years of grief and chaos. He would not surrender a gem such as this to a man who would not appreciate or care for the gift. The pain he was about to cause could in no way measure the misery of a lifetime of poverty and depravity. Someday she would understand that.

Carolyn turned the trusting blue of her gaze to Jack's irregular but handsome features. She knew the story behind the crook of his once-patrician nose, knew the tiny scar above one arched dark eyebrow had been earned during a childhood tantrum, knew he had inherited the Chatham pugnacious jaw and his mother's sharp Spanish cheekbones. She knew him with all her heart and soul and was ready to give the words that would allow her to share his life forever. The promise appeared in her smile as she waited for him to speak.

"Carolyn, I just wished to tell you that I am going away and won't be able to see you again."

She continued staring at him as if he hadn't spoken, waiting for the words that would surely follow. The light had left her eyes, so she had heard him, but she wasn't accepting what she heard. The red-and-white heart in her hand crumpled a little beneath the pressure of her fingers.

Steeling himself, telling himself it was for her own good, Jack tried again. "Your father has refused to give me your hand. I cannot keep you in the manner to which you are accustomed."

That, she understood, and the light quickly returned to her eyes as she turned to her father. "That does not matter, Papa! You must know that I have no care for silk gowns or balls or jewels. I should love to live in the country and will be quite content attending village affairs rather than London society. I know you mean well, Papa, but you must see that I love Jack too much to allow so small a thing as money to stand between us."

Henry turned a threatening look on the paralyzed young man. "Tell her, Jack. Do one decent, manly thing in your life."

Realizing he was being asked to cut his own throat, Jack threw the older man a murderous look, but as Carolyn turned questioningly to him, he ruthlessly whipped out the knife. "You don't understand, my dear. My debts are such that I would have to sell my home to pay them. Your father refuses to give you a dowry if you marry me. Without your dowry, we cannot marry. I must seek my fortune elsewhere."

Twin spots of color tinted Carolyn's cheeks as she absorbed this self-serving speech, and the blue of her eyes hardened to a more crystalline color similar to his own. "You are saying you courted me for my dowry? That you only meant to save yourself from debt and never meant any of those promises you made? That your pretty words were nothing but lies?''

Jack said nothing, but remained stoic as she wielded the knife he had given her. Carolyn could by turns be pensive and gay, serious and flirtatious, but never had he seen her in a temper. At his lack of reply, her anger seemed to boil and explode, heightening her color, making her eyes more vivid, but not once did it remove the ladylike melodiousness of her voice.

''They were all lies, weren't they? The courtly gestures, the sweet flattery? Did you go back to your friends and laugh at how easily I fell for them? Did they wager on how soon you would woo my wealth? All those promises . . .'' Her voice broke and her eyes glittered with unshed tears when he did not deny her charges. To compensate for her lack of words, she stalked across the room to stand in front of him and waved the fragile confection of red and lace before him. ''I don't even want to know how much my father had to pay you to do this. You must have realized I would have run off with you anywhere. I loved you. *Loved* you!'' Her voice cracked again, but temper had loosed her tongue and she could not stop now. ''Fool that I am, I believed your lies! I gave you my heart, and you had no idea what you possessed. You will never know now. No one will ever know. I'll not be such a fool ever again.''

Before his stony gaze she ripped the paper heart in half, then tore it again and again until it was in tattered pieces on the floor at his feet. She flung the last few bits at his snowy cravat. ''There's my heart. See what good it does you now.''

Carolyn stormed from the room, her large store of reserve severely depleted by the tantrum she had never indulged in to such extremes before. She slammed the door, rattling the precious Meissen vase on the hall table, and halted in the shadowed doorway to compose her face and hastily wipe away her tears.

Even as she stood there, she heard her father's low voice through the door. "I'll have the money for you on the morrow. I'll send my man around. I don't want to see your face here again."

Shuddering with dry sobs, she raced toward the stairs, no longer caring who saw her. It wasn't just a lovely valentine lying in torn pieces at the feet of the man behind her, but her heart. There would never be any repairing it.

Behind the closed door, the tall lord bent to pick up the flimsy pieces of paper heart that he had not deserved. He could see snatches of the fine penmanship of the child he had loved on the pieces as he gathered them. In his own heart, he knew they would never be whole again.

Grimly he pocketed the torn valentine, nodded curtly at his nemesis, and strode out, his long legs carrying him away as quickly as the laws of physics and nature allowed.

"I cannot get it to look lacy like the picture." Frustrated, Blanche threw down the tattered paper amongst the scraps already littering the library table. An unexpected ray of sun gleamed through the open curtains, catching her golden hair in a coronet of light that illuminated this dusky corner of the library as she bent over her task.

Smiling gently at the lovely picture the sight portrayed, the woman in the corner chair set aside her book and rose to see what task her younger sister had set herself now. Pale brown hair arranged unfashionably in an elegantly simple chignon, she moved with quiet grace and sureness as she came to stand beside her sister.

Blanche glanced up in relief as slender, competent fingers took up the misshapen piece of paper. "It is not at all like what you and Mama used to make. I thought I could follow the instructions in this magazine, but it is not the same. Show me how to make it lacy."

Carolyn held the tattered valentine, glanced at the magazine, and drawing on the strength she held in reserve for just such occasions, calmly sat down and picked up the scissors and a clean sheet of paper. "You have to cut the heart first, if I remember correctly."

Blanche watched in expectant silence as the plain square of paper shaped itself into a heart finely threaded with intricate designs and elegant scrollwork. Breathing a sigh of happiness, she eagerly took up the scissors when her sister laid them aside. "It is beyond everything, Lynley!" Her newly discovered grown-up manner disappeared briefly to let this childhood appellation escape. "Will you make one for George?"

Carolyn carelessly set the beautiful lace heart aside. "George would not know what to do with it. Whom are you making a valentine for?" Hoping to encourage her sister's confidences, she lingered to help fold the paper correctly and to pencil in cutting lines. Blanche had come out during the Little Season last fall, but she had shown no preference among the many suitors who swarmed around her.

"Why, for the first bachelor to appear at my door on St. Valentine's Day, just like the magazine says!" Laughing eyes lifted to meet her older sister's. "Why don't you make one too? Wouldn't fussy old George have a proper fit if you gave a card to someone else?"

"He is Lord Hampton to you, child. He would swallow a maggot if he ever heard you talk so. And one does not play childish tricks on her suitors. The marquess would have every right to be peeved should I start handing out love notes to someone else.''

Instead of being chastised, Blanche laughed gaily at her sister's admonitions. Five years her senior, Carolyn still managed to combine her motherly advice with just enough humor to keep the camaraderie of their sisterhood lively. ''I think you should have married when you were my age, Lynley. You have grown as crusty and dull as old Lord Hampton. You deserve each other. I can see the two of you on your wedding night. He will bow stiffly at the waist and offer you his arm to take you to bed, and you will make a deep curtsy and ask, 'Are you certain this is proper, my lord?' and the two of you will debate it until dawn.''

''Blanche!'' Equally mortified and amused at her eighteen-year-old sister's unruly imagination, Carolyn bit her tongue and began improving the lacy confection she had created earlier. ''You should not even be thinking such things. Besides, Lord Hampton and I are not even officially betrothed. If you are going to do that properly, you must learn to make smaller cuts.'' She pointed the tip of her pen at the offending design in her sister's hand.

Blanche shrugged and reached for a new sheet of paper. ''Everyone knows you will be as soon as his curmudgeon mother comes back from the Continent. And it's about time. You are twenty-three, Carolyn. Gossips will have you on the shelf. And just think what grand balls you can have when you are Lady Hampton! I think I shall have another Season just so I might meet all the noble gentlemen I have missed this year. Then, when I have found a duke or a marquess, we will both be able to bring out Alice and Jane. Why, with such high connections, we should find them princes, at least. Then they can introduce Penny to society, and she shall have to marry a king.''

Carolyn smiled at these high-flying flights of fancy. "I cannot think of a prince I would allow in the same room with Alice and Jane, and while I will admit not having consorted with many kings, I daresay they will all be a trifle derelict for Penny. At the tender age of seven, she may have difficulty finding a king who will play at patty-cake and hobbyhorse with her."

Blanche made a rude noise that one of her suitors would find quite startling from so demure and innocent a miss. "You didn't used to be so prim, Lynley. I remember when you first came out and you and that fellow with the broken nose made up the most horrendous tales to tell when you knew I was listening. Whatever happened to that gentleman? He was quite fun. Much more the thing than stuffy old George."

Proud of her hard-won self-control, Carolyn smiled and laid aside her pen and valentine. "We both grew up. Now, if you need no further—"

A gentle rap at the door signaled an intruder, and Carolyn swung around to greet the footman bearing a card.

"The gentleman's come to see Mr. Thorogood, Miss Carolyn." He held out the card for her inspection. "He asks that he be made known to the ladies while he waits."

When Carolyn's expected reply did not come, Blanche looked up in time to see her sister's face turn pale and her lips compress in a manner she had not seen in years as she stared at the card in her hand. Before Blanche could inquire as to their visitor's name, Carolyn regained her composure. "Tell the gentleman we are not at home," she announced firmly.

Blanche gave her sister an odd look. Carolyn very seldom stood on ceremony with their visitors. She was friendly to young and old alike. Who could this be that she would refuse him? Smitten with curiosity,

Blanche waited for Carolyn to return to her reading, then excused herself to disappear down the hallway after the footman.

Garbed in a heavy sable-lined cloak against the January cold, the gentleman waited in the salon doorway. As the servant repeated his message, the man bent his top-hatted head in acknowledgment and removed himself to the privacy of the salon until the master of the house could see him.

Curiosity thoroughly whetted now, Blanche slipped into the small family parlor behind the salon. The connecting door between the rooms had not been recently used and creaked slightly as she pulled it ajar, but a quick glance told her the stranger had not been disturbed from his pondering by the noise. He evidently did not mean to linger long, for he had not surrendered cloak or hat but held them on one arm as he stared at a porcelain figurine on the mantel. She could see by the dim light that his hair was sun-streaked and his complexion weathered, as if he were one of her father's ship's captains, but his richly tailored clothes were of the finest cut and not those of a poor seaman. The sable cloak alone bespoke his lack of commonplaceness. When he finally turned at the entrance of a servant, Blanche barely concealed her gasp of surprise. The man with the broken nose!

She had no opportunity to learn more. The man followed the servant out and up the stairs to the master's private study.

Five years older, Henry Thorogood still retained his slender build, although there was now a hint of a stoop to his shoulders and threads of gray in his dark hair. Lord Edward John Chatham observed these changes as he entered the book-lined study. Little else had changed in these last years, in this room, at least. He wondered at the refusal of the ladies of the house to see him, but his had been a whimsical gesture at best. Thorogood could have remarried by now; his new wife would not know his name. Carolyn's younger sisters were not likely to remember him. He could not expect to find Carolyn unmarried and still in her father's home after all these years. He had just been curious and tempted to find out what he could.

With the self-assurance of an older, more experienced man, Jack seated himself without his host's permission. He noted the older man's brief look of surprise and the trace of amusement in the slight lift of his brow, but he had only one purpose here and he was eager to get on with it. He waited for Thorogood to take a seat before he spoke.

"I have come to repay my debts, sir. I have brought the sum of the loan, plus interest. You will need to name me the amount due on the vouchers you bought."

Thorogood appraised the sun-darkened stranger seated across from him. In the ensuing years since their last encounter he had not forgotten the arrogant young lordling; in fact, he had had good reason to remember him. The changes wrought by the years were dramatic, but he would have recognized those stony gray eyes and that arrogance anywhere. Lord John had come into his own, it seemed. The question remained, had his character improved with time?

Ignoring his visitor's demands, Henry responded with coldness. "I will not accept tainted money. I have not heard of your brother's estates improving or of any of your family dying and leaving you a fortune. I would know from whence your payment comes."

Jack made an elegant sneer and withdrew a large purse. "Thank you for your confidence, but my money is honestly earned. You may speak with my superiors in the East India Company. It is not tainted, that is, unless you consider trade a taint. I don't believe you are in any position to quibble about that. Name me the sum I owe you.''

Thorogood weighed the bag of coins thoughtfully in his hand as he contemplated the young lord. He would be nearing thirty now, not young any longer, actually. Whatever he had been doing, it had taught him a new authority and assurance that the callow spendthrift had not possessed. He propped his fingers together in an arch and named a sum that would have made royalty flinch.

Jack gave him a look of disgust. ''That would more than cover the full sum of the original markers plus interest at a rate to make the shylocks cringe. If you think that is what I owe you for five years of my life, you are sadly mistaken. I will pay it, but I will have every marker I ever wrote in return. Should any more turn up at some future date, I will return them to you for payment.''

Henry concealed his surprise with a brief nod. ''I did not anticipate immediate payment. You may pay it as you are able.''

Chatham rose abruptly. ''I will give you a draft on my bank today if you can present the vouchers. I will not have your threats hanging over my head any longer than is necessary.''

Fully astounded, Henry hurried to the drawer where the markers had been kept all these years. Something in the way Lord Jack had phrased that sentence gave food for thought, but he would savor it later. He would step cautiously for now. He wondered if the careless name he had gone by in his youth still applied. ''Lord Jack'' no longer suited this imposing stranger.

The transaction completed, Jack threw the sheaf of papers in the fire and watched them burn before striding out without a polite word of courtesy to his host.

Five years of waiting for this moment had left him expecting an elation he could no longer feel. The deadness inside remained even with the burden of all those old debts lifted. He needed to seek some new stimulation now to keep his spirit from dying entirely.

Only recently arrived in London, he'd not had time to seek out old friends in familiar places. With his business accomplished, he felt ill-at-ease and restless. It was time to rejoin society and see how his reputation had fared over the cleansing solution of time.

Jack walked into White's and found little different in the decor other than a mellowing of additional age. Perhaps the faces behind the newspapers were slightly different or older, the youths behind the gaming tables seemed younger, he knew fewer than he had expected, but on the whole, the changes were slight. He moved easily toward the group in the corner of the back room, using his leisurely pace to identify vaguely familiar features. One of their number looked up and gave a whoop of recognition. Jack grinned at this irrepressible greeting. Peter's hair might have retreated slightly from his sloping forehead, his yellow waistcoat might be tighter over his paunch, but the cheerful beam of his round face remained unchanged.

"Chatham, as I live and breathe! Back from the dead, old boy? Have you come to haunt us in these dismal corridors?"

They drew him back into their circle without reproof, either glad of this diversion on a dull day or unaware of his fall into trade. Jack ordered drinks, joined in the genial jesting, and tested the waters carefully. Many of their former number were not evident in this gathering place. Some younger, newer faces watched this homecoming with disinterest or an eagerness to be amused, but he found no disdain. Yet.

Settling into a comfortably upholstered chair, Jack

turned the conversation away from himself and encouraged gossip about those faces among the missing. His companions eagerly grasped the opportunity. In this time-honored fashion he learned how little things had changed beyond the names and the faces.

"And Beecham? Has his father stuck his spoon in the wall and left him all those barrels of gold yet?"

The slender young toff with the diamond stickpin, sitting beside Peter, waved his hand lazily. "The old Judas will never die. Last I heard, he was swearing to leave everything but the entailment to some young niece. Beecham's out courting her right now. She's a Friday-faced female if ever I saw one, not even been presented yet."

"The last lot of lovelies seem sadly lacking compared to those when we first came down, don't they, Harrison? They're all so demmed . . . green, somehow," Peter completed his sentence weakly.

General laughter ensued at this assessment, but it gave Jack an opening to the topic closest to his well-concealed heart. "And the Incomparables of all these years past? Where are they now? What of our number have shackled their legs for beauty?"

This regenerated the conversation as they sought to remember the reigning toasts of other years and who had carried them away into marital bliss or discord as the case might be.

Peter summed it up best after a fevered discussion. "They're all married and surrounded by whining brats is what they're doing. Seems a demmed shame to waste all that loveliness."

The gentleman with the stickpin shook his head in disagreement. "Not all. The Tremayne wench married some ancient baronet with a pot of gold, who popped off a few months later. She's sitting in splendor over on St. James's now, entertaining lavishly. I hear Bulfinch has been dipping his pen there.''

Peter brightened at a renewed memory. ''And the Thorogood eldest, what was her name, Jack? You used to be smitten with her. She's leading her young sister around this Season. She ain't never been wed that I know of. I'm surprised she ain't wearing caps by now, though she's still a lovely lass.''

Before Jack could respond or even untie his tongue and allow his heart to drop from his throat after the shock of this news, Harrison made a deprecating gesture. ''Hampton has her claimed. She's a smart one. She hung around for a title to remove the stench of trade. Wait and see, she'll have that brood of her father's married off to the cream of the crop as they come along. Watch your legs, men, they'll be in her trap before you know you're caught.''

Jack peeled his fingers from the arm of the chair and reached for his glass. ''George still unwed? He's older than any of us. How did the little Thorogood snare him?''

''He ain't snared yet. There's been no announcement. I wager it waits on his mama's approval, but if he don't come up to snuff soon, the chit will have her comeuppance. The ladies are raising eyebrows at his marked attentions without a ring on her finger. I daresay that devilish father will force the matter soon enough. Hampton was a fool to dabble in those waters. Thorogood's a shark.''

Jack heard the stem of the glass crack beneath the pressure of his fingers. Forcing himself to relax and look bored, he rose and prepared to depart. ''Maybe someone ought to warn Hampton what he's getting into. Good night, gentlemen. It's been entertaining, but there's a certain little lady who's expecting me.''

He walked off and was gone before they realized he

never had said where he'd been or what he'd been doing these past years.

"No, don't add the gold pins, Blanche! They are very lovely, but you will have to save them until you're older. The pearls will do just fine. You will be prettier than any other girl there."

"Fustian!" Blanche glared in the mirror at her reflection. "I shall look a simpering idiot like all the rest. Why can I not wear cloth of gold like yours? You look like an angel just down from heaven. I look like a frumpy mushroom."

Carolyn smiled gently at her sister's nervous starts. Admittedly, virginal white tended to be tedious, but the extravagant gauze and lace of Blanche's ball gown were not exactly the common touch, and the lavender sash and embroidery enhanced her slender charms daringly enough. She would be a sensation, as usual, but she would not be persuaded.

"I don't have wings and you're not edible. You already have more suitors than you need. I don't know what you're worried about. Is there someone special you wish to impress?"

Carolyn's practicality always put a damper on her nervous hopes. Swinging around to observe her sister's elegantly draped gown, Blanche offered a reluctant smile. "No. I just thought it might be a pleasant change if I could be as beautiful as you. Your suitors are so much more interesting than mine."

Carolyn laughed. She had not spent half the attention on her own preparations as she had on Blanche's. She had bidden her maid merely to loop gold twine through her smoothly arranged upsweep, added a chain of silver and gold to her throat, and, wearing a gown she had worn the year before, called herself ready. Admittedly, her maid had teased a few loose tendrils into curling about her ears and shoulders, but they did that normally enough before the evening ended. She had no illusions about the men she would meet tonight. They had been attending her over five years now, and she was as heartily bored with them as they were with her. At one time or another, as fortunes waxed and waned, one or another of them would grow amorous and make an offer, but she had learned how to let them down lightly. Among the older set, it had become a game of nothing ventured, nothing gained. Wagers had been won or lost in earlier years. Lately, there were few takers on a sure thing. The eldest Thorogood girl had set herself firmly on the shelf. Few had any interest in being rejected in an attempt to remove her.

That was why Hampton's suit had caught everyone concerned by surprise. He had been an eligible *parti* on the Marriage Mart for a decade but had never shown any interest in indulging in the favors waved before his nose in attempts to catch his jaded interest. Wealthy, titled, and young enough to be considered well-looking, he made many a young girl weep with envy when he escorted one of society's more mature widows onto the floor. The gossip about his misalliances with these more worldly women was discreet. He never gained the epithet of rake, for he seldom spared a second glance to the innocent.

His studious courtship of Carolyn Thorogood had the *haut ton* all agog. She was neither worldly nor a widow. Not a hint of scandal attached to their relationship except in the fact that the courtship had lasted a good six months now without an announcement. That in itself was a record of sorts. Hampton had never assiduously courted any woman, young or old, for that length of time, and Carolyn had never allowed any courtship to go on so long without a firm rejection.

Wagers once more were rife over whether the elusive toast would finally be snared.

Well aware of the tongues flapping behind her back, Carolyn did nothing to encourage them in either direction. She concentrated on bringing out her younger sister and seeing that Blanche was properly attended. George Hampton's suit did not interfere with her goals, and aided it in many ways, so there was no reason to discourage him. She was well aware he had finally decided he needed an heir and had settled on her as older and more mature than the fresh crop of young innocents on the Mart. His less-than-romantic courtship caused her no pain. If she finally agreed to his proposal, it would be because she had finally decided she wished a family of her own too, and he was wealthy enough for her not to fear he wanted her for her dowry. It seemed a good, stable way of venturing into the treacherous waters of matrimony.

But Blanche was still filled with romantic illusions and Carolyn had no desire to remove the misty film of fantasy from her eyes yet. The time would come soon enough when the more objectionable suitors were weeded out and Blanche began to realize that marriage was a financial proposition and not a romantic one. For now, let her believe in love. It might happen. Even fairy tales came true upon occasion.

Blanche and Carolyn entered the ballroom that night on their father's arms. As a wealthy widower, Henry Thorogood was much sought after himself, and he had no difficulty in amusing himself while keeping an eye on his two beautiful daughters. Still, it was on Carolyn that he relied to act as chaperone for Blanche's high spirits. He seldom need interfere himself. Carolyn was immensely capable in dealing with overardent young gentlemen and advising her sister on propriety. Thorogood watched her though half-lowered lids as she smilingly refused one notorious rake and deflected a debt-ridden young lord with a request for some punch. Carolyn had learned propriety too well. Her natural happiness had become something much less animated, an artificial facade of smiles and gentle words that fooled the rest of the world but not her father.

Sipping his drink, he watched Carolyn's smile fade in weariness as she was momentarily left alone. The daughter he had known from infancy had been exuberant in her joy, passionate in her beliefs, dramatic in her sorrows. She had wept and laughed and infuriated alternately, until her eighteenth year. That was the year she had grown up, and he had not seen that girl again. As dutiful and pleasant as this new woman was, he rather missed the tempestuous girl. His eyes narrowed thoughtfully as he observed the two young men approaching her now.

Instantly aware that she was being watched, Carolyn raised her head with a renewed smile and sought George Hampton's properly attired figure bearing down on her. Garbed in sober black tailcoat and pantaloons, his immaculate cravat a masterpiece in simplicity, his stride one of noble arrogance and authority, he looked the part of wealthy aristocrat without need of the hauteur marring the faces of many of the nobility with whom she was acquainted. He seldom smiled, but she sensed a pleased look on his face now as he caught her eye.

In idle curiosity, Carolyn turned her gaze to the man at the marquess's side. She knew George frequented White's and several other of the gentlemen's clubs, but he seldom introduced her to his male friends. She wondered occasionally if it was out of embarrassment because he had attached himself to a female without title whose wealth came from trade, but she did not let the question concern her much. He made a pleasant companion and they got along well enough. Still, she couldn't help wondering about the stranger he evidently meant to introduce to her.

At this distance Carolyn could tell only that the stranger was unfashionably weathered in a startlingly attractive manner. His rather longish brown hair had light streaks from the sun, and his eyes seemed much lighter than the rest of his bronzed face. His gray swallow-tailed coat fit comfortably to unfashionably muscular shoulders, and his impeccably tailored matching trousers did not hinder his long, eager stride. Dressed for comfort more than style, he exuded a self-assurance she found instantly compelling. Unnerved by this sudden unexpected attraction to a stranger, she raised her gaze to search his face as they came closer. Shock brought her hand to her middle as if suddenly assaulted by a hideous pain, and her face paled a shade whiter.

Her plight did not go unnoticed by the newcomer. Cold gray eyes swept over her without demonstrating any emotion, finally lifting in dark acknowledgment at judging himself to be the cause of her distress. At his side, Hampton seemed oblivious of her lack of response as he introduced his companion.

"Do you remember Chatham, Carolyn? I daresay he was before your time. He's been in India practically since you were in short skirts."

Carolyn managed a weak smile and extended her hand. "I am not so young as that, my lord. I remember Lord John from my first Season." As his callused brown hand closed around hers, she wanted to jerk away, but that would be demonstrating a childish emotion she no longer felt. She forced a more pleasant expression to her lips.

"He's a bit out of touch with the current crop of lovelies. I told him you would be happy to surrender a dance or two and introduce him to a few suitable misses. That sister of yours might be just in his style.''

Carolyn's aghast expression went unnoticed by the nobleman pleased with his helpfulness to both friend and would-be fiancée. Jack read her dismay without compunction and refused to release her hand.

"I believe the musicians are beginning a waltz, Miss Thorogood. You were reluctant to try it when last we met. Shall we?''

With her intended standing by affectionately rewarding her with his smile for her compliance, Carolyn had little choice but to follow Jack onto the dance floor. She remembered a time when she had stubbornly refused to indulge in the decadent dance sweeping the fast set, even when the man she loved offered to teach her. After he left, it seemed scarcely a point worth defending. She had been waltzing for years, but that same defiance returned with just the touch of Jack's hand. She wanted to stomp her foot and slap him and tell him to behave. It would have been apropos back then when he had been whispering sweet nothings in her ear all night. Such behavior now would be singularly inappropriate.

"You cannot kill me with looks, Carolyn. Smile and put a pleasant face on it before someone remembers old gossip and reminds George.'' Jack slid his arm around her slender waist with the possessiveness of familiarity, swinging her effortlessly into the steps of the dance as he spoke. "You're more beautiful than I remember,'' he added thoughtfully, searching her face when she did not respond.

"And you're more arrogant,'' she retorted heatedly. Under the intensity of his scrutiny, she felt a flush staining her cheeks for the first time in years. Her fingers itched to smack him, but his long masculine physique held her firmly, and the familiar sensations of years ago swarmed alive and well through her rebellious body. He could hold her like this for the rest of the night, and not a muscle would stir in protest.

"I see your temper has not cooled with the passage of time. I suppose you are the one who refused to see me yesterday. I did not expect to find you still in your father's house. I thought you would be married by now."

She hated the speculation in his eyes. The arrogant fool was wondering if she had waited for him. She would disabuse him of that notion immediately, if only she could find her tongue. "I have grown choosier with age," she finally gritted out between clenched teeth. She could feel the heat of his hand even through his glove and her gown. She hated him for reminding her of sensations better forgotten.

"So it seems. George is quite a catch. You cannot fear he is a fortune-hunter. When do you set the date?"

He asked that agreeably enough, and Carolyn glared up at him with suspicion. He seemed taller than she remembered, but then, George was nearly her height and she was accustomed to dancing with him. The white flash of Jack's teeth against his sunburned face irritated her, and she answered with as much aloofness as she could muster, "We have an understanding that suits us both, my lord."

"An understanding? How formal that sounds. Has he kissed you, Carolyn, or is that not part of the agreement? It would be damned hard to court you for long without stealing a few kisses, particularly for a man of George's inclinations. How much longer before that understanding leads to something else, Carolyn? I'd like to lay my wagers on the winning side."

Rage rose in her, a blinding rage that made Carolyn want to scream and shout and kick and cause a scene right here in the middle of this elegant dance floor.

Jack had always been able to rouse her ire with a word or a wink, but he had always appeased her quickly afterward. The memory of those tender scenes added fuel to the fires of anger. His insults this time would get no response from her.

"You have become an insufferable boor, Jack. It is lucky for us that my father intervened in time."

Carolyn's haughty disdain made Jack furious, and at the same time, her words pierced him like shards of hell. Five years he had worked and waited, abstaining from society, from the luxuries of civilization, from everything he had ever known, just so he might come back and look her in the eye once more. He had been prepared to find her happily married with babes around her feet. She deserved that. He would never have wished her unhappy. But he had never imagined her like this, cold and bitter and haughtier than any princess. Something wasn't right here, and he'd be damned if he would let her slip through his fingers again without knowing why.

He deliberately ignored her harsh words. "When George spent hours raving about your pleasantness and agreeableness, I thought he'd got the wrong sister. Agreeableness is not what I remember most about you. I can see you haven't changed, so who is this Carolyn that George is talking about?"

His spiteful remark deserved no reply, and as the dance ended, Carolyn dropped his hand like a hot coal. She turned stiffly in search of George and grew tense at the sight of Blanche waiting with curiosity at his side, watching her and Jack. When Jack attempted to take her elbow to lead her back, she shook him off.

"Stay away from Blanche, Jack. I'll not have you spoiling her life." She could have added, "as you spoiled mine," but she would never admit that out loud.

He sent her a swift look, as if he heard the unspoken end to that sentence, but her lovely blue eyes had grown cold and stony and he found no evidence that he had heard aright. He turned his gaze to the young blond beauty waiting beside Hampton and shook his head. "By Jove, it's hard to believe we were ever that young. Are you certain she ought to be out of the schoolroom?"

Carolyn flashed him a look of irritation. "She's eighteen." Just as she had been when she had fallen head over heels for this unscrupulous rake, but again, she left the words unsaid. He knew them as well as she.

Had she turned to see Jack's face, she would have seen the fleeting look of pain in his eyes, but she was hurrying across the floor, eager for escape and heedless of the pain she left behind. She had once been as young and innocent as that vision in white. The similarities between that young girl there and the woman running toward her were so strong as to shake Jack to the core. Once Carolyn had looked at him with that wide-eyed dewy look that made his heart pound and his palms sweat. The palpitations now weren't for the young girl, though, but for the memory of the girl he had known. Blanche's glorious smile was nearly the same as Carolyn's had been, but the eyes were more cautious. She distrusted him much sooner than the young Carolyn ever had. Jack wondered what she knew of him, but suspected it was only curiosity that kept her gaze in his direction.

He felt Carolyn's tension as the introductions were made, and even George was looking at her with curiosity when she made no pleasantries but immediately insisted that she and Blanche must repair to the powder room. The stunningly demure woman Jack had observed from across the dance floor earlier had lost her composure, and the war of emotions in her eyes was plain to see for all who looked. Fortunately for her, George was blind to the nuances of female expressions. Politely Jack made his excuses and departed before he could drag Carolyn off to a corner and shake her until he received some explanations. If he needed time to gather his scattered wits, so must she.

Carolyn watched with a cry in her throat as Lord John's proudly straight back retreated. How could he be even more incredibly handsome and wicked than she remembered? She had never known him for the devil that he was until that last night, but she had just seen him looking at Blanche in that same way he had once looked at her. He wouldn't! Heaven help her, but she would kill him with her bare hands if he so much as held Blanche's little finger. Surely he was not so beastly arrogant as to believe he could win this second round by using her sister?

By the time she got home that night, Carolyn's head pounded with the thunder of her memories and fears. For nearly five years she had maintained her composure, playing the part of doting older sister, loving daughter, and society maiden. For five years she had refused to think of Lord Edward John Chatham. Just as she had thought herself fully recovered and prepared to consider marriage from a more sensible viewpoint, he'd reappeared like some demon straight from hell. What was wrong with her that he could still make her feel like this after all these years? She *hated* him. How could he stir her into this writhing agony of need and chaos and uncertainty after all he had done?

It wouldn't do to ponder the thought too long. Soon George's mother would return from the Continent and they would obtain her approval and Carolyn would be wedded and safe. With both her father and George to protect her, Blanche would be out of Jack's reach.

There were too many other girls on the market for Jack to try his hand at another Thorogood.

Still, as she drifted off to sleep, Carolyn could not keep from dreaming of warm gray eyes and long legs striding eagerly toward her. So light those eyes had been, almost as if illuminated from within when they gazed on her. She felt them even in her sleep, warming her to the marrow.

When the enormous bouquet of impossible roses arrived early the next day, Carolyn nearly refused to accept them. Jack had ever been given to such extravagances, even when he hadn't a ha'penny for food. She knew they had to be from him, but telling herself that there was some chance that George might have grown sentimental, she read the card. The words "I need to see you" had scarcely grazed her mind when she heard Jack's voice in the doorway.

"I told the servant not to announce me. I didn't want to be turned away again." His wide shoulders filled the narrow space of the salon door. The expensive tailoring of his deep blue frock coat emphasized the breadth of his chest and the narrowness of his hips in their tight pantaloons, and Carolyn had to force her gaze to his sun-bronzed features. That was no relief, for the dizzying lightness of his eyes made her throat go dry, and her fingers longed to caress the blond streaks in his burnished curls.

The footman hastily disappeared, leaving Carolyn clinging to the roses. Jack properly left the door open, but they both knew there was no one but the servants to hear them, and they would not interfere. She tried to pry her tongue from the roof of her mouth as she measured the astonishing knowledge that he was here, in her house, in the same room with her after all these years, but she couldn't shake her disbelief. She felt as if she were still dreaming.

Dressed in a frail muslin of sprigged lavender, her hair carelessly tied in loose curls at the crown of her head, she had the grace and the startled velvet eyes of a gazelle. A hint of lavender scented the air around her, speaking of springtime and wildflowers and the beauty of an English rose. Jack could not take his eyes away, and all his carefully prepared speeches disappeared in a misty haze of yearning. For five years he had dreamed of this. He still could not believe he was so blessed as to find her unmarried. His hands actually shook as he reached to set the roses aside.

"We need to talk, Carolyn. I have so much I want to say to you, I don't know where to begin. I caught you by surprise last night. I'm sorry. I didn't mean those things I said. I had been listening to George sing your praises until I wanted to plant him a facer. That's why we have to talk. I want another chance, Carolyn. Will you listen?"

She flushed hot and cold hearing that deep, seductive voice again, feeling it wash over her with lingering promises of passion. She hated him for doing this to her again. She was old enough to know better. He had no right to come here and disturb her life all over. She wouldn't let him. She steeled herself against the impassioned plea of his voice, refused to see the pain and hope in his eyes. He deserved to suffer for what he had done. It was her turn to hand out pain.

"Get out, Jack," she told him coldly, meeting his eyes without flinching. "If I never see you again, it will be too soon. If you ever dare perpetrate this underhand trick again, I will have the servants bounce you out on your ear. You may take your vulgar flowers with you when you go. Try them on some poor cit who is desperate for a title. Don't ever try them on me again."

She swung around and started for the far door to the

parlor. Stunned, Jack could utter no word of protest. In all these years of envisioning this scene, he had never imagined the coldness of her reception. The iciness penetrated his lungs, making it difficult to breathe. Too many hot summers, he thought wryly and erratically to himself as he felt the chill of the unheated room begin to take over and shudder through him. He heard the door close after her and still he could not move. He kept waiting for the blessed numbness that came with time, but it eluded him. He shook as if with fever.

He had expected anger at worst. Carolyn could be docile and patient and loving and eagerly understanding, but when she felt threatened, she retaliated with a temper that left scars long after. He could still feel the sting of her words from that night they had parted. They had lingered under his skin like some insidious poison for years. Those torn pieces of heart she had thrown at him had bruised as if they were stone, but her words had caused permanent damage. He had feared she would never forgive or forget, but never had he thought it would be like this. She had meant it when she said he would never know her heart again. The woman who had just left this room had no heart. That was what he had sensed missing last night. All that loving, trusting innocence he had once known had disappeared, bricked up behind a brittle facade of composure and disinterest. The Carolyn he had known had ceased to exist.

Aching as if with cold, Jack turned and slowly retraced his steps to the front door. The roses lay, forgotten, in the icy salon.

Blanche watched covertly as her sister paced the library, ostensibly in search of some volume of verse appropriate for the valentine they were making. It had been days since the ball where the man with the broken nose had made his appearance, but Carolyn's complaint of the headache had kept them confined indoors ever since. Blanche had little reason to object, since her suitors were overflowing the salons with their flattering lies of missing her, and flowers spilled over the furniture as reminders of their attentions in her absence. The social whirl was amusing, but she had spent most of her life in her father's country home and knew well how to entertain herself without need of constant attention. Her concern was more for Carolyn.

Blanche had learned nothing about Lord Edward John Chatham from discreet inquiries of her callers, but she had found his abandoned flowers and note in the salon the day after the ball. The fact that Carolyn had refused to appear in public ever since was serious cause for concern. She had never seen Carolyn troubled or discomposed. The time Alice had fallen from the tree and broken her arm had thrown the entire household in an uproar, but not Carolyn. She had directed servants, comforted Alice, and had everything calm before the physician arrived. Even their mother's death had not caused this withdrawal from family and friends. Carolyn had grieved terribly, but she had been the mainstay of the family throughout that tragic period. She had not bolted herself behind closed doors and refused to come out.

"Perhaps I shall write a poem of my own," Blanche suggested to divert her sister's attention from pacing. "Am I allowed to make personal allusions in poetry?"

Carolyn clamped her fingers into her palms and pulled together her distraught nerves as she turned back to her sister. She was being ridiculous. After what she had said, Jack would never cross their portals again. There really was no cause for concern. Blanche was a sensible girl beneath her frivolous romantic fantasies. She would listen to reason should the opportunity be needed. Mouthing these platitudes to herself, she forced a serene smile to her face.

"What personal allusions can you make when you don't know whom the card will go to? An 'Ode to His Shining Eyes'?"

Blanche grinned in appreciation of this sign of Carolyn's returning humor. "I can refuse to come down until someone meeting the description arrives. It's only the first man I see that day that counts. I shan't have to see anyone if I don't wish."

"Horrible child, that takes all the fun out of it. What if we had no servants? You would have to answer the door and accept the first man who came in."

"I should sneak around and see who it was before I answered. If it was someone unacceptable, I should just pretend I was not at home. I'll not give my favors for a year to a man with no wit to appreciate them."

"You are spoiled beyond redemption." Carolyn inspected the lacy creation of ribbons and paper that Blanche had painstakingly put together. "It is quite good without a poem. Do not give them any ideas." She set the heart down and squared her shoulders decisively. "It is quite pleasant out. Would you care to accompany me for a stroll in the park?"

Blanche shuddered at the thought. Carolyn's idea of pleasant weather was a day without rain. Never mind that icicles still hung from the eaves. And "stroll" translated as a fast gallop on foot through deserted lanes at a hideously early hour, when there was no one to attend them. It did not strike Blanche as a particularly elegant way to spend the morning.

At Blanche's blunt refusal, Carolyn shrugged and went in search of her wraps. She had been confined inside for too long. She needed exercise to disperse these nervous fits and restless urges. A bruising horse ride would be more suitable, but that was not permitted in the crowded city parks and streets. A brisk walk would be just as beneficial.

Fetching her resigned maid to accompany her, Carolyn wrapped herself in a blue velvet pelisse lined with a fur that nearly matched the color of her own rich tresses, had she been vain enough to notice. Instead, her thoughts were far removed from her own looks as she set out to circumambulate the park.

A thaw had set in and the last patches of snow were disappearing into the grass and the icicles were dripping rivulets from bare tree limbs. The Serpentine still held patches of ice glinting in the sunlight, and Carolyn turned her mind to the beauty of the day. It felt good to stretch her muscles and breathe fresh air again. She had been quite childish in hiding from the ghost of her imagination.

A bright red ball bounced across her feet, nearly causing her to trip, but she was adept at eluding such objects. With four younger siblings underfoot at various times of the year, she had learned to keep a tremendous store of patience. With a smile at this simple pleasure, she turned to find the runaway ball and return it to its owner.

With the object firmly in her gloved hand, she sought the youngster who had thrown it. To the side of the road and down a slight embankment stood a tiny figure garbed head to foot in warm furs and velvet, her pitch-black hair streaming out from a fur cap framing a strangely tawny face. She held back shyly, not willing to come forward to retrieve her toy from the grand lady.

"Shall I throw it to you?" Carolyn offered, quite content to be playing at simple childhood games for a time.

When the girl made no move but a timid nod, Carolyn gently heaved the ball toward her mittened hands. They sprang up instantly to catch the gently thrown ball, an adeptness that signaled someone had played this game with her with frequency.

As the child smiled shyly and clasped her ball, a dark figure unfolded from its relaxed position against a tree trunk and came forward. "Thank the lady, Amy."

The voice smote her with the swiftness of a rapier, and Carolyn stepped backward instinctively. "Jack!"

Only then did the top-hatted head lift to peruse the elegantly feminine figure on the path. Gray eyes shuttered cautiously, and a leather-clad hand protectively reached for the small shoulder of the child. "Carolyn." He nodded warily.

An awkward silence fell, of which the child showed no awareness as she held out the ball. "T'ank you, m'lady," she lisped carefully. "Will you play?"

As shaken by Jack's presence as by the dilemma of the child's accompaniment, Carolyn could make no reply. Dazedly she tried to orient herself, to find some perspective to approach the situation, but she could not. She only waited in bewilderment for Jack to rescue her.

Caught unaware, Jack, too, had difficulty surmounting a meeting that he had never anticipated. He had never intended to keep Amy a secret, but there had been no opportunity to mention her. His fingers squeezed his daughter's shoulder reassuringly as his tongue summoned some form of polite introduction.

"This is my daughter, Amy. Amy, say hello to Miss Thorogood."

As the two exchanged shy greetings, Jack regained some of his assurance, and he glanced expectantly around. "Are you with someone, Carolyn? Surely you did not come out here alone?"

Briefly puzzled by this return to the mundane, Carolyn glanced around for some sign of her maid. "Florrie was right behind me. I do not know where she is got to."

Knowing Carolyn's galloping idea of a walk from old times, Jack shifted his daughter to his shoulder and climbed up the small embankment to the path. "There are still some dangerous patches of ice. We'd better look for her."

Somehow, it seemed perfectly natural to be walking along at Jack's side, his shoulder marching at the same height as her eyes, blocking half the view, but without disabling her in the least. She knew his sharp eyes would find Florrie first, and she need only concentrate on watching her step, since his arm was occupied keeping his daughter in place.

His daughter. How peculiar to think of Jack with a daughter. He must have married soon after he left London, to judge by the age of the child. Perhaps he had had someone else with a wealthy dowry waiting behind stage in case his first offer fell through. It pained her still to think these unkind thoughts of Jack, but she had to face reality. She had known he was in debt and would have to leave London. Now he was back and seemingly in funds again. There simply was no other explanation.

"That must be Florrie over there on the bench." Jack pointed out a woebegone figure in heavy wool and bedraggled bonnet. The figure looked up at the same time that he spoke, but she made no move to rise, and her expression became even more pitiful.

Carolyn broke into a quick stride. "Florrie! What has happened? I only just missed you. Why did you not cry out?"

By the time Jack trotted up, Carolyn was already kneeling in the mud, ruining her pelisse and velvet walking gown as she examined the maid's outstretched ankle. She glanced up as Jack set his daughter down and crouched beside her.

"She has twisted her ankle pretty severely. It's beginning to swell. I must get her home."

"My carriage isn't far. Will you be all right waiting here? You won't be too cold?"

His concern did not seem in the least feigned. Perhaps that was why she had believed in him so thoroughly. He should have been on the stage. Carolyn quelled the haughty words that came to her tongue. Florrie needed help. She had no right to question from whence it came.

"I'll be fine. Why don't you leave Amy with us? You could fetch the carriage more quickly that way."

Jack helped her to rise and glanced uncertainly from Carolyn's open expression to his daughter's childishly trusting gaze. She was right that he could move more swiftly without the necessity of carrying this small burden, but he had never left Amy with strangers before. He and her ayah and Mrs. Higginbotham were all he had trusted with the child. But this was Carolyn. He nodded quickly in agreement.

"I'll be back shortly. You'll take cold if you don't have a dry gown soon."

He strode off, leaving Carolyn to stare after his elegantly clad back with perplexity. Why should he be worried if she caught cold? She turned her straying thoughts back to her injured maid and the curious child. She had no business trying to read Jack's mind.

By the time Jack returned with the carriage, Carolyn and Amy were laughing gaily, and even the maid smiled at their antics. In her love for pretty and exotic objects, Amy had obviously charmed Carolyn out of the long, arched feather that had adorned her bonnet, and it now stuck absurdly from Amy's furred cap. They both looked like naughty children when Jack jumped down, and he couldn't help but laugh at their expressions.

"Had I dallied any longer, she would be parading around in your slippers with your pelisse flung over her shoulders and dragging in the mud behind her." He pretended to pinch Amy's nose, and the child laughed with the trill of a little bird. "She is dreadfully spoiled. Now, thank Miss Thorogood for playing with you and let me help Miss Florrie into the carriage, there's a good girl."

The pride and love on his face were plain to see and could scarcely be part of his theatrics. Carolyn felt a tug inside that she dared not recognize, and she turned away from Jack's uneven features to help Florrie to her feet. Had it not been for her father, that little girl could be her own, and Jack would be looking at their child like that. It would not do to think along such lines. It was over and done and best forgotten.

Jack discreetly held Carolyn's hand no longer than it took to help her into the carriage. He kept the conversation general as they drove the short distance to the Thorogood residence. Never once did he give any indication of the severed relationship between them. Carolyn was grateful for his discretion but left uneasy by it. He behaved the perfect gentleman. Could his disguise be so thorough?

He handed Florrie over into the care of one of the footmen who ran down the stairs to open the carriage door. He bowed politely over Carolyn's hand in parting, and he made no attempt to cross the portal from whence he had been barred. Carolyn stared after his departing carriage in something closely akin to shock. She had spent these last days thinking of him in terms of a devil in tailcoats. She could not easily twist her thoughts to consider him as a knight-errant.

The next day, however, she gladly accepted the call of a Mrs. Higginbotham and one miss Amy Chatham.

The child was primly garbed in layers of velvet and fur, as she had been the day before. Her hair had been pulled back in a coronet of braids and her hat no longer bore the swooping feather that had adorned it on parting yesterday. Mrs. Higginbotham held grimly to her hand as she plowed into the salon, and Carolyn held her breath anxiously, as she expected the powerfully built matron to sit on the tiny child as they both attempted to occupy the same love seat.

"Good morning, Amy. Did you find a better hat to fit your feather on?" Carolyn offered the stiffly shy child a smile.

"That is the reason we are here, Miss Thorogood." The jarring accents boomed from the matron's massively built chest, vibrating several delicate figurines on the table. Carolyn tilted her head in curiosity to better observe this natural phenomenon. Satisfied she had her hostess's attention, the woman continued, "His lordship insisted that his daughter thank you for the gift of the feather. She is much inclined to take things she admires, and he hopes she has offered no harm to your apparel."

Carolyn heard this with mild astonishment. Too well-bred to show her amusement at the woman's artificial attempts at elegance, she nodded politely and turned her attention to the child. "I thought the feather much more becoming on you than on me, Miss Amy. I used to have a doll that liked to wear hats. Do you have one like that?"

Dark eyes immediately lit with delight, and she nodded with a shy smile. Before she could say a word, her companion intruded. "The child has far too many dolls, in my opinion. Her father spoils her, and she does not know her place. I've not had much time to take the matter in hand, but I assure you, it will be accomplished in time.''

The woman's encroaching self-importance was a source of amazement, but Carolyn had met her sort before. It was interesting how people with no claim to name or fortune or accomplishment could adopt an immense snobbery when come in contact with people who had any. Perhaps it was a means of hiding a feeling of inferiority, but in this case, the child was suffering for it. Carolyn permitted herself a small frown.

''Miss Chatham seems singularly well-behaved to me, Mrs. Higginbotham. I have four younger sisters myself, and not one of them ever behaved so properly on a formal call at her age.'' With this mild reproof, she returned her attention to the child, who had instantly withdrawn her smile at the sounds of discord. ''I would be pleased to have you to tea one day, Miss Chatham. I rather miss my younger sisters, and I should enjoy having your company. Would you like that?''

Again the dancing lights returned to the little girl's huge velvet eyes, and a smile illuminated her small brown face. Before she could utter the smallest word, Mrs. Higginbotham rose in a grand flutter of shawls and lace.

''You are too kind, Miss Thorogood, but I cannot let her be foisted off on respectable company. I came only at her father's insistence. We would not think of intruding again. Good day to you.'' She sailed from the room with Amy in tow.

Visibly annoyed by now, Carolyn held her temper in check until her guests had departed, then contemplated sitting down and sending Jack a scathing note on the unsuitability of his choice of governess, if governess she were. By the time she reached her desk, however, common sense prevailed, and she set the pen aside. She had given up any right of interference in Jack's life the day she had thrown him out of the house. He would only ridicule and ignore any message from her.

Still, the memory of her anger at the encroaching Mrs. Higginbotham and her concern for the timid child returned swiftly when next Carolyn saw Jack. It was inevitable that she see him again. She could ban him from her own home, but not from every house in the *haut ton*. A seemingly wealthy, eligible bachelor was welcome anywhere he went. That he would attend many of the same events as she was a foregone conclusion. Her decision to avoid him wavered under the burden of her anger and concern.

She looked absurdly sophisticated, Jack observed as Carolyn drifted across the music room, regally exchanging pleasantries with half the *ton* in her path. He could remember when she was just a charming girl with a delightful smile to single her out from the legions of young lovelies. It was hard to acquaint that young girl with this elegant young woman with her head held high and a polished smile affixed to her face, but he had seen glimpses of the girl the other day in the park. He pondered that anomaly as he realized he was actually Carolyn's goal in crossing the room.

"It's good to see you again, Miss Thorogood," he intoned formally as he bowed over her hand.

Concentrating on her purpose, Carolyn ignored the fact that Jack managed to make himself look thoroughly at home in any environment. Gold and jewels glittered at throats and wrists all around them. Diamond stickpins, gold watch fobs, and pearl shirt studs adorned the formal attire of all the gentlemen. In simple black with nothing more glittering than his pristine cravat and intelligent eyes, Jack still appeared the part of arrogant nobility.

"I'd like a word with you about your daughter, my lord," she said boldly. When his dark brow rose a fraction, she refused to retreat. "I know it is not my place to interfere, but you must admit that I have some experience with young girls, and you do not."

He nodded politely in acknowledgment of that fact. In truth, he could do little more. That faint scent of lavender and wildflowers enveloped him, and he had to focus his concentration on keeping his hands at his sides and his eyes on her face, when it seemed much more natural to encompass her graceful waist with his arm and feel her soft breasts pressed into his side. Even concentrating on her face wasn't helpful. He had reason to remember the passion and promise of those rose-pink lips. Unlike calculating young maidens, once Carolyn had given her heart, she was lavish with her affection despite the fact that there was no formal engagement. She had trusted him.

When Jack made no further effort to encourage or reject her observations, Carolyn cautiously phrased her complaint. "This Mrs. Higginbotham seems somewhat overbearing for a child as timid as Amy. In fact, I wouldn't be surprised if Mrs. Higginbotham isn't the cause of her timidity."

That elevated his attentions to a more respectable level. Jack straightened from his casual position against the newel post to take Carolyn's arm and lead her toward a quiet alcove. When he had settled her on a backless velvet-upholstered settee, he frowned down at her anxious expression.

"I could not bring Amy's ayah out of India. Mrs. Higginbotham had only just lost her husband, and she offered to accompany me and care for Amy on the journey home. She has been quite indispensable. What rackety notions have you got in your head now about that proper lady?''

His harsh words brought a caustic reply. ''She is no lady. She's an encroaching mushroom intent on crushing your daughter into a nonentity for some obscure reason unknown to me. I cannot know anything about your household, but Mrs. Higginbotham seems prepared to rule it. She as much as said that you spoil Amy and she will not allow it to continue.''

To Carolyn's surprise, Jack's expression grew weary and unhappy instead of angry at this declaration. Rocking back on his heels, he stared at the garish painting over her head before replying. Aware that a room full of people could watch their every action, he kept his words curt.

''Amy is not legally my daughter. I daresay Mrs. Higginbotham has taken it upon herself to protect society from such scandal. I will have to speak with her.'' He held out his hand and gestured to the room behind them. ''I can feel your father's eyes burning a hole in my back. Perhaps we should join the others?''

Carolyn reluctantly placed her gloved hand in his and stood beside him. He smelled faintly of sandalwood and some musky scent that was all his own, and again that feeling of comforting familiarity at his size and strength swept over her. Other men tended to make her nervous and uncomfortable when they stood this close. Not Jack. Never Jack. He fitted beside her as neatly as her glove fitted her hand. It was a most depressing thought.

''I did not mean to cause anyone trouble,'' she murmured as they stood there, unwilling to return to the milling crowd. ''But Amy seemed to be such a sweet, eager child. When we are in town, I miss young Penny. I thought it would be fun for Amy as well as Blanche and me if she came to visit. Mrs. Higginbotham informed me in no uncertain terms that that wouldn't be permitted. If those were your orders, I shall understand, but Amy seemed dreadfully disappointed and intimidated. I hate to see a child unhappy.''

Jack sighed and squeezed her hand before he realized he should no longer be holding it. He released her but made no effort to lead her back to her father. ''Perhaps Mrs. Higginbotham is right. I cannot believe your family would approve of your associating with a half-Indian child from the wrong side of the blanket. It isn't done. I'll have to move her to Dorset, but she has been so frightened by all these changes in her world, I couldn't bear to send her away just yet.''

Heat flared in Carolyn's cheeks as she realized the intimate admission Jack had just made. No gentleman ought to admit to illegitimate children or mistresses before a lady. Carolyn would have been shocked if any other man had said it. The shock she felt now had little to do with his scandalous admission and more to do with imagining Jack going from her arms to some stranger's and the intimacy involved in producing this child. She couldn't find her tongue to reply, and he glanced down at her with curiosity.

''Have I offended you? I thought you were already so furious with me that nothing further I did could offend you more. I apologize if I spoke out of turn.''

Carolyn forced her tumultuous emotions into control and offered a brittle smile. ''I'm not offended. Perhaps my pride is. You did not lose much time finding a mistress, if I'm any judge of a child's age. I shouldn't be so surprised, but even after all these years of knowing what you are, I find I am. But I do not blame the child for the father's faults, and neither will my family. She is welcome in our home at any time.''

The smallest inkling of hope gnawed hungrily at his insides as Jack gazed down into Carolyn's flushed and averted face. She spoke with more sophistication than the young girl he had once known, but the raw emotions couldn't be entirely concealed by her poise. The frozen tundra he had met with earlier wasn't quite so thick as he had believed. Amy had warmed a hole through it in a single meeting. What would it take to melt the whole and discover the truth beneath?

If he wanted truth, he had to offer honesty. This wasn't the place or time, but he might have no other. Touching her elbow, Jack guided her toward the refreshment table, easily skirting the crowd. He kept his voice low, bending his head closer to her ear. For all anyone knew, he could be speaking sweet flattery.

"Carolyn, I have never been more than a man, never claimed to be. Perhaps I cannot fit the perfect ideal you have made of your father, but he has only somehow been more discreet than I am. Until you give me permission to speak as a lover, I cannot defend myself further. Should that time ever come, I will tell you all you wish to know of Amy. In the meantime, I can only thank you for your concern for her welfare. I am glaringly aware of my faults, and I doubt that forgiveness is possible, but I would cry friends, if only for Amy's sake."

She had forgotten how smoothly Jack could erase all transgressions with his words. In the same few sentences he could raise her ire and soothe her ruffled feathers. He was quite right, actually. He should not be talking to her of Amy's origins, but to suggest there might be a future time when he had that right was above and beyond all else. She ought to slap him right here in view of everyone, but his mention of Amy's need for friends diverted all anger. Obviously, if he loved no one else, he loved his child. For Amy's sake, he said these things.

For Amy's sake, she might possibly agree to them.

He knew that. Carolyn looked up at Jack with suspicion, but there was no triumph in those gray eyes. They glowed with a strange intensity as he awaited her reply, but there was no indication that he knew it in advance. His anxiety was only for Amy.

She nodded slowly. "If you can tame the dragon lady, I would have Amy come for tea. I know she is much too young, but little girls like to play at being grown-up. She will learn to get on in society that way."

Jack halted and caught her elbow to swing her around to face him. "I thank you, Carolyn, but she is not likely to be part of society. Surely you must see that."

She met his eyes coolly. "If you legally adopted her, she would be accepted, but that is your decision. All I can do is entertain her for a few hours a day."

Jack stared down into Carolyn's porcelain face, willing himself to see there what he wanted to see. Amy needed a mother. How many women would accept him knowing they would have to accept his bastard daughter too? He had thought briefly of finding her a loving family willing to raise her as their own, but he had not been able to bring himself even to look for one. Now here was Carolyn telling him to adopt her. Surely she knew that would be condemning him to a life without a wife, Amy to living without a mother?

He dared not think further than that, although all his heart yearned to do so. He made a slight bow of acceptance to the truth of her words. "Send around a note as to a convenient time for you. I will make certain that she is there."

Amy arrived promptly at the time designated, the feather perched archly over her tiny nose from a bonnet otherwise decorated in roses. Her guardian dragon sniffed loudly as Carolyn greeted the child.

"His lordship said I might leave her here briefly while I do some shopping." The disapproval on her face was more than apparent.

Carolyn dismissed her without a glance. "She will do quite nicely with us. Thank you, Mrs. Higginbotham."

Without a backward look, she led Amy to the library, where Blanche waited impatiently.

At the sight of Jack's small daughter, Blanche exclaimed in surprise, threw Carolyn a swift look, then knelt to remove her bonnet and cloak. The little girl gazed at Blanche's blond curls with awe and obediently stood still under her ministrations.

"It is a pity our Penny is not here to play with you. I'm certain you would get on tremendously." As protective as Carolyn of her younger sisters, Blanche easily accepted this new arrival. Carolyn had only mentioned that the child seemed exceptionally timid and perhaps a little frightened by her new surroundings. Blanche had been curious and willing to satisfy her curiosity, but it was more thoroughly stirred than before at the sight of the child's brown features.

Once freed of her outer garments, Amy wandered to the table where Blanche had been working. Scattered bits of paper and pens and scissors covered the leather working surface, and her velvet gaze fastened on the elaborate valentine. "What's that?"

Carolyn laughed. Jack had mentioned that she had a penchant for lovely and exotic objects. To a child's eyes, that lacy red-and-white confection would seem quite exotic. She helped Amy into a chair at the table. "That's a valentine. It's a gift to someone you love on St. Valentine's Day. Would you like to make one?"

To Blanche's amusement, her prim-and-proper older

sister sat down at the library table and proceeded to instruct a four-year-old in the intricacies of valentine making. She had not seen Carolyn so animated in years. Whatever was going on here, it was good for her. Blanche rang for tea to be brought in the library. If she remembered correctly, four-year-olds preferred sweets with their instructions.

Over the next few weeks, Amy came to visit on a number of occasions. Sometimes they persuaded her to listen to a story or go for a carriage ride in the park, but mostly her fascination led to the glorious array of ribbons and pretty papers scattered across the library table. Dissatisfied with her first attempts, Blanche continued to make more and more elaborate cards, and Amy's awe at their extravagance did not cease. Under Carolyn's tutelage, she painstakingly constructed one of her own. In showing the child what to do, Carolyn created a card for the first time since she was a child of Blanche's age.

Jack sometimes accompanied his daughter to the door, but conscious of Carolyn's earlier threats, he politely declined to enter until he had been specifically invited. Carolyn stubbornly refused any such invitation, although when they met at social affairs, she willingly spoke with him of his daughter's progress. Since often this was in the company of Lord Hampton, Jack could not put any favorable construction on their new relationship. She kept him firmly in his place, but he could not resign himself to believing he had arrived to find her still unattached, only to watch her marry another. He consoled himself into thinking it was only a matter of biding his time.

Time rapidly ran out one frosty February day, however. The unsettling news that George's mother was actually on her way home from the Continent was quickly superseded by a more immediate calamity. Jack came home to a household in an uproar and two physicians in the nursery. In near-hysterics, Mrs. Higginbotham cowered in a corner, exhorting the physicians alternately to take care and to do something.

In a trice, Jack was pushing between the maids and doctors around the tiny bed to find his daughter lying limp and pale against the sheets. Hiding his terror, he knelt beside the bed and touched his hand to her smooth forehead. It burned with fever.

With a stricken look, he turned to the elder of the two physicians hovering respectfully in the background. Jack could not speak, but the medical man replied to his expression without need of questions.

"The child was overexposed to the cold, and I suspect she has eaten something while outside that does not agree with her system. She has been vomiting steadily until now."

A murderous anger began to build as Jack turned his icy gaze to Mrs. Higginbotham and the two nursemaids he employed to look after one small child. The nursemaids chattered in tandem, making it impossible to decipher a word. He focused his ire on the massive woman cowering in the corner.

Realizing it was a matter of self-preservation, Mrs. Higginbotham drew herself up to her full height and presented the woeful tale in the best light she could.

"She took my sewing scissors and cut up the frontispiece of one of your books in the library, mangled it dreadfully, she did. I caught her when she was cutting the fine lace off one of her gowns. She's badly spoiled, m'lord, if you'll forgive my saying so. I thought to teach her a lesson, so I sent her to an empty garret to reflect on her bad behavior. She weren't there no more than an hour or so."

Her composure was slipping badly, and with it, the

artificial elegance of her speech. Jack continued to stare at her grimly, determined to have the whole tale before he ripped the nursery and everyone in it to tiny pieces.

At his silence, the woman took a deep breath and continued, ''When Maisie went up to fetch her for her tea, she wasn't there. We looked everywhere, we did. There's not a bit of furniture in that room. She couldn't of hid. She just up and disappeared.''

Since the garret she referred to was icy cold and accessible only by the back stairs, Jack found nothing mysterious in this. He was not blind to Amy's less-than-obedient nature. She wouldn't have stayed in that dull, cold room for long, and he doubted that there was a key to be found to fit the lock. Given the opportunity, she would have slipped back down the stairs. Where she had gone from there was anybody's guess.

''Where did you find her?'' he demanded curtly when it became apparent the woman would not willingly volunteer any more information.

''Begging your pardon, m'lord,'' one of the maids interrupted when Mrs. Higginbotham seemed unable to reply. ''Timmy followed her footsteps in the snow. They got kind of confused in the park, he said, and he came back to get some others to help him. They said they found her by the far gate. She didn't have no coat nor nothin' on—just her wet dress,'' she amended at the furious blaze in Jack's eyes.

The fury was as much for himself as for the servants. He had brought the child to a strange climate that her small body could not easily endure and that her mind had not learned to fear. He had left his only daughter in the care of thoughtless servants and a woman he had been warned did not approve of or even like her. He had selfishly not even made any attempt to find Amy a better situation, not wanting to admit that he couldn't care for her by himself, not wanting to be parted from the one creature on God's earth who loved him for himself. And this was what he had brought to her.

With a strangled cry, Jack gathered Amy into his arms and ordered everyone else out. She would be well again, if he had to pour his own life's blood into her.

When Amy didn't appear at her appointed time the next day, Carolyn was curious and disappointed. She had grown fond of the child and enjoyed watching her blossoming with care and attention. Oddly enough, the news that George's mother would arrive in London next week did not excite her so much as watching Amy master the scissors and paper to cut an almost perfect heart. Reporting this progress to Jack seemed more consequential than speculating as to whether the dowager marchioness would consider an insignificant but wealthy chit as wife material for her son.

Unable to curb her curiosity and concern, Carolyn sent a maid around to inquire as to the reason for Amy's absence. When the maid returned with the news, Carolyn picked up her skirts and headed for the stairs.

"Send word to Nanny that I have need of her fever medicine, the recipe for the cold posset, some of those dried herbs we picked last summer for steaming, and perhaps the purgatives. Just tell her what you have told me. She will know what to do." The instructions streamed behind her as she hurried down the stairs.

At the last sentence, Florrie nodded in relief. Even if she forgot part of these hurried orders, Nanny would know what was needed. She watched in concern as Miss Carolyn called for her cloak and a carriage.

Surely she could not be thinking of going to a gentleman's house unescorted.

Carolyn wasn't looking at her flight in precisely that light. She had nursed her four sisters through all manner of childhood illnesses. She knew what Amy needed. Since Blanche was from home at the moment and her maid had to get word to Nanny, it seemed expedient to go alone. The only consequence she had in mind was seeing Amy back to health.

Finding herself suddenly confronted with the door to the town house Jack had taken for the Season, Carolyn experienced a momentary qualm, but when the door opened to reveal a frightened Mrs. Higginbotham standing in the hallway beyond the doorman, her resolution firmed. She announced herself and stepped across the portal without giving the servant time to refuse her entrance.

"Where is Amy?" she demanded firmly of the startled matron. The woman in all rights belonged in the nursery with her charge. Such scandalous breach of duty ought to be reprimanded. Jack certainly ran a loose household.

"She is ill in bed." Mrs. Higginbotham drew herself up defensively, prepared to fight on more even terms with this interfering female than she could with his lordship.

"I wish to see her." Ignoring the challenge in the woman's eyes, Carolyn started for the stairs. The nursery would have to be upstairs. She would find it for herself if necessary.

"You can't go up there!" Scandalized, Mrs. Higginbotham lurched after her.

Carolyn blithely sailed upward. "Just tell me which room. I'll find my way. You needn't concern yourself further."

"You can't go in there!" the woman repeated with slight variation. "His lordship's in there!"

It had truly never occurred to her that Jack would be in the nursery with his ill child. Her own father had probably never seen inside the nursery doors, but he'd had a wife and daughters to see to the care of his younger children. There hadn't been any necessity for involving himself personally in childhood illnesses. Still, the thought of Jack sitting at his daughter's bedside sent Carolyn's heart pounding, and she experienced a momentary hesitation about entering.

A door at the end of the hall opened and a nursemaid came out carrying soiled linen. Without another thought, Carolyn hurried in that direction. Mrs. Higginbotham beat a hasty retreat.

Carolyn halted in the doorway to get her bearings. The room was lavishly decorated in flowered wallpaper and sprigged-muslin curtains and a narrow canopy bed in blue velvet. Toys stood on shelves everywhere, and an alcove to the side was obviously intended for the maid's cot. It looked undisturbed at the moment. The only signs of life were near the bed.

Her gaze fell on Jack's haggard face first. He had drawn a rocking chair from the fireplace to the bedside and rested with eyes closed and his head against the high back. Lines of weariness etched his handsome face, and his rumpled clothes bore the certain signs of having been slept in. He retained none of the self-assured, polished demeanor with which he met the world. His dark curls stood on end as if he had been raking his fingers through them. His immaculate cravat had been pulled loose and flung aside, and a day's growth of beard bristled along his darkened cheeks. Carolyn bit her lip against a sudden surge of longing and turned her gaze to the bed.

She caught her breath at sight of the pale, motionless figure beneath the covers. She looked so tiny and defenseless, and only the spots of fevered color on her round cheeks gave any indication of life.

Her gasp brought Jack's eyes open, and he stared in disbelief at Carolyn's elegant figure posed in the doorway. She had not disposed of her pelisse or muff, and her cheeks still bore the fresh color of the cold outside. He fixed his gaze on her terrified eyes, and denying himself the relief flooding through him, said, "Carolyn, you have no business here. You must leave, at once."

She ignored his words. Unfastening the frog at her throat, she laid her pelisse and muff on a nearby chair. It was easier if she kept her gaze on the child in the bed and not the haunted man at her side. "You need some rest. Go get something to eat and lie down for a while. I'll sit with her."

Jack rose and clasped her arms before she could go closer. "For God's sake, Carolyn, go home before someone finds you here."

Carolyn's gaze finally swerved to meet his, and the heat flooding through her from the love and anguish she found there melted her insides. She had never experienced anything quite like this before, and she resisted the desire to fall into Jack's arms and hang on for dear life. She was disappearing into his eyes, and the feeling terrified and thrilled her. Nervously she looked away again, and recovered her strength as she remembered her purpose.

"I've sent to Nanny for her basket of nostrums. They seem to be more effective than most of the medicines the physicians use. We've certainly tested their efficacy often enough. Go rest, Jack. I'll come to no harm sitting here. And I do have considerable experience at nursing children."

Jack clung to her arms, staring down at her bare

head with soaring despair and hope. She had no right to be here, but he needed her desperately. Just her presence had brought a return of hope. He felt the strength of her resolve, knew the magnitude of the character behind it, and knew beyond any doubt that if anyone could nurse Amy to life, it would be this woman in his hands. But in allowing her to do so, he would almost certainly be destroying her life. Unless . . .

He let the possibility of that one exception wash through him like a soothing balm. If she still cared, if she could possibly choose . . . He daren't let his thoughts wander to the borders of the impossible. He hadn't had any sleep in thirty-six hours. He was merely dreaming with his eyes open.

"I'll have Mrs. Higginbotham come up. Then I'll send for your carriage. You can't stay."

Carolyn gave him a brisk look, pulled from his grasp, and began removing her gloves, all traces of wavering gone. "You would do better to send that woman packing. If it eases your conscience, send one of the nursemaids up. We'll need a constant supply of fresh water. Has the cold settled in her lungs?"

Jack was too weary to fight both Carolyn and himself. He felt singularly helpless staring at the lifeless features of his daughter night and day. He had no notion of how to go on. Carolyn did. He grasped desperately at the offer.

Within minutes he had explained what happened, what the physicians recommended, and the results, or lack of them. Carolyn sat beside the bed as he spoke, touching gentle fingers to heated cheeks, avoiding looking too closely at the man behind her. He had been right when he had said he was just a man. Seeing him like this brought all her foolish fancies home. He was suffering in a way she had never experienced. The lordly rake she had condemned, the gentle lover she had worshiped—both were only small facets of his character. Men weren't so simply defined with a word or two. She had a lot yet to learn. Perhaps her father had protected her too well.

She felt him hovering uncertainly behind her, fearful of what would happen should he leave his daughter unguarded for even a moment. She turned and touched a hand to his sleeve, daring to meet his eyes just this once. "Go, Jack. You have done everything humanly possible. The matter is in God's hands now."

He needed to be reminded of that. Nodding, he pressed her fingers. Not daring to say more, he left hastily in search of a maid.

Telling himself he would nap only a few hours, Jack collapsed, still dressed, on a guest bed near the nursery. When he had fully recovered his faculties, he would decide what to do with the obstinate Miss Thorogood. She would certainly be missed by dinner. He had no illusions that she had told anyone where she was going, or she would have been prevented. Somehow, he would have to find a way to spirit her back into the safety of her own home. When he woke.

It was nearly midnight before he opened his eyes again. It took a minute to recollect why he slept in a strange bed with all his clothes on. He hadn't been that drunk in years. When the memory came, it was with a rush of pain and fear, and he hastily swung his legs to the floor.

Amy's room was lit by a branch of candles. In their flickering light he watched Carolyn wring out a cloth in a washbowl and gently place it over his daughter's forehead. A worried frown lined Carolyn's brow as she worked, and he could see that she was biting her lip. In fear, he turned to observe Amy more closely. She was tossing restlessly. As he came closer, he could see the fine sheen of perspiration on her small face. Even as he watched, he heard her low moan, and the bottom seemed to fall out of his stomach.

"What is wrong? What can I do?" he whispered hoarsely, coming to stand beside the bed.

Carolyn glanced up at him in relief. "Her fever is rising rapidly. We must keep it down. Call some of the servants and have them bring up snow to add to the washbasin."

Jack looked at the empty cot where the maid should be and shook his head in disbelief. Where in hell were his servants? Furiously he went in search of a maid. His daughter could be dying, and they all lay cozy in their beds. He would fire the lot of them on the morrow.

He forgot his temper a little while later as he cuddled his unconscious daughter on his lap while Carolyn applied the cold compresses to her brow. Amy seemed to lie quieter in his arms, and he felt better holding her close. She was so damned small and helpless. She needed him to protect her, and he hadn't done a very good job of it. Perhaps this was God's way of telling him he didn't deserve love. He'd certainly failed the child's mother. And Carolyn. He looked up to watch the grim lines of worry on her lovely face.

"I meant to send you home hours ago," he murmured more to himself than to her.

"I wouldn't have gone." Carolyn carefully packed the latest bowl of snow into a cloth. "You needed sleep, and Mrs. Higginbotham is useless. I'm afraid I yelled at her."

The idea of yelling at that redoubtable matron had never occurred to Jack. He lifted a surprised brow at this delicate lady beside the bed, gently applying compresses, and wondered what other secrets she hid. How much did he really know of her, after all?

"Did you yell at the maids too? I thought I specifically assigned them to helping you while I slept."

"They're sweet, but they haven't a brain between them. Mrs. Higginbotham dismissed the one who spoke up earlier, and she told the other to go on to bed. Then she went off to bed herself." Carolyn offered a small grin. "I gave her her marching orders, but she didn't seem to think they were final."

"Did you, now?" Jack leaned back against the wooden headboard and made Amy more comfortable in his arms. Carolyn's proximity and the faint scent of wildflowers soothed him. Under other circumstances, they would have aroused him, but not when his daughter lay ill in his arms. He just needed Carolyn's reassuring presence close at hand to let him know all would be well in a little while. "You're developing quite a nasty temper, my love."

Carolyn didn't even give him a second glance at this endearment. She'd heard his honeyed words before. She had yet to see proof of them. "I've always had a nasty temper. You just never came across it before."

"I think I've encountered it once or twice of late, and I remember a particularly brilliant tantrum that haunted my worst nightmares for years. Had you shown Mrs. Higginbotham that, she would be out of the house by now."

That caused Carolyn to meet his gaze. In this light, she could discern little of Jack's expression, but what she saw made her vaguely uneasy. His light words had a peculiar intensity. Ignoring his reference to another time, she kept to a safer subject. "I'm sorry I did not let my tongue fly, then. She is your servant, so I held back."

Amy stirred in his arms, and Jack returned his gaze

there, brushing a strand of ebony hair from her dark complexion. "She will have to go. I just didn't know how to go about interviewing governesses or nannies. I don't know very much about children, I suppose."

Carolyn sat in the rocker and replied softly, "You know how to love them. That is what counts most."

At the gentleness of her voice, Jack relaxed slightly, and closing his eyes, leaned back against the bed. "I don't know what I would have done these last years without her. She is the only softness, gentleness, that I know. I hold her, and she smiles at me with all the love and trust in the world. I needed her faith to keep from losing mine."

Tears came to her eyes, and Carolyn had to look away from the man on the bed. He was so large sprawled across the child's narrow mattress, but he looked perfectly natural like that. She wondered how many nights he had sat just like that, rocking his infant daughter to sleep. "Her mother?" she heard herself asking.

Jack didn't look up. His mouth tightened into an ironic curve. "If you wish more evidence to cast me aside, that tale ought to do it." When she made no reply, he shrugged lightly and continued. "The poverty in India is excruciating. Many times worse than you see on a London street. Servants can be had for the offer of a roof over their heads and food in their bellies. I was saving every brass farthing I could put a hand to, so I led a very simple life, two rooms and one old ayah to look after me."

He felt Carolyn rise to change the soaking compress, but he didn't open his eyes. He would have this story told and done with. There would be no more illusions between them. "With nothing better to do in the evenings, I was drinking heavily. I won't go into details of what life is like down there, but drink kills a lot of us. I suppose my ayah feared losing her lucrative position, or perhaps she sought a second income or a measure of comfort for another. Whatever her inscrutable reasoning, she brought a young girl to me one night when I was half out of my mind.''

Jack opened his eyes then to watch Carolyn's expression at this revelation. He was going far beyond the bounds of propriety to speak these things, but he wanted Carolyn to know all that he was. He had fooled her when she was younger, filling her head with romantic fantasies while concealing the harsher side of his life. It had been an act of desperation at the time, just as the truth was now. Perhaps he was older but no wiser. Carolyn's expression told him nothing, and he took that as permission to go on, though he felt as if he were cutting his own throat once again.

''She became my mistress. There is no polite way to state it. I had no intention of marrying her. She filled a place in my life that was empty, but we scarcely spoke the same language. She was young and ignorant and became pregnant immediately. It made her happy, so I suppose that was what she wanted. She knew it would give her a position of comfort for the rest of her life in my household. That's the way things are done down there.''

Carolyn made a small noise that sounded almost like a sob, but he couldn't stop now. It all had to be said. ''She died shortly after giving birth to Amy. It was only then that I learned my mistress was also my ayah's daughter.''

A soft exclamation indicated Carolyn heard and understood, but she made no other reply to this tale of Amy's origins. It was a tawdry tale, at best. He could have done as so many others had and left the child behind, but just as he had been unable to send the old woman and babe away at birth, he could not do it four years later. With a sigh, Jack snuggled his daughter closer, clinging to her warmth.

"I'm glad you told me," Carolyn offered once she recovered her composure. She hoped he couldn't see the tracks of her tears down her cheeks. The thought of his loneliness in that horrible place of exile and the mother willing to sacrifice her child to a life of infamy rather than allow her to starve tore at her heart. She was glad he had saved Amy from such a life. "Will you adopt her?"

Jack looked up and caught her eye. "I think that depends on several things," he answered slowly. The telltale blush did not rise to her cheeks and he saw only curiosity in her eyes. His hopes plummeted, but he clung fiercely to their remains. "Yes, I will probably adopt her," he answered shortly.

Carolyn did not understand the sharpness of his words, but she was not given time to consider it. Amy began to shake and moan, and perspiration poured freely from every pore, drenching her tiny night shift. There wasn't time to do anything but act.

Afraid to expose her to the chilly night air, they wrapped her in blankets until she lay still once more. Then, hastily removing wet garments and finding dry ones, they returned to the previous routine of applying compresses. Within the half-hour she was shaking again. Steadily they worked throughout the night.

Shortly after dawn the kitchen sent up tea and toast, and Jack sent for the nursery maid and Mrs. Higginbotham. The maid arrived hurriedly and applied herself to changing the linen, giving the master and the lady surreptitious looks in the process. Both looked haggard but vaguely triumphant. The little girl seemed to be breathing easier.

Mrs. Higginbotham didn't arrive until an hour later. She gave Carolyn a small smirk and turned her full attention on Jack. His rumpled clothes of two days before set her slightly aback, but the snarl on his face made her visibly quail. She turned immediately to the offensive. "I beg your pardon, my lord, but I was told in no uncertain terms that my services weren't required. I will be more than happy to sit with the child while you get your rest. You shouldn't have the burden of nursing an ill child. I'm certain you have much more important things to do. Shall I ring for your bath to be sent up?"

Jack's lips tightened, but he held his temper with remarkable aplomb. Carolyn admired his performance. She would have scratched the woman's eyes out. More important things to do, indeed!

"We'll no longer be requiring your services, Mrs. Higginbotham. I will speak with my secretary when he arrives, and he will advance you six months' salary. I would like you to remove from the household before day's end."

The woman stared at him in astonishment. "On what grounds, my lord? Have I not cared for the wee one like one of my own, dressing her in all that is fine and seeing that she is properly instructed in conduct? I cannot be blamed that her kind cannot learn simple obedience. I have done my utmost to teach her."

Jack rose to his full threatening height and the woman stepped backward. "Out, Mrs. Higginbotham, before I lose my patience. I recommend that you do not seek any other position requiring understanding or compassion, for you have none. Leave us, at once!"

He practically roared this last, and the woman gave a squeak of alarm and rushed to the door, throwing Carolyn a malevolent look in parting.

Jack collapsed into himself, but a sound from the bed quickly returned his attention there. Amy sneezed, then opened her eyes. "Papa?" she inquired weakly as he scooped her into his arms.

Jack's shining eyes and radiant smile brought tears to Carolyn's eyes as she met his gaze. Touching her hand to the child's cheek and ascertaining that it was considerably cooler than before, she felt relief flood through her and felt the same in him. They needed no words of understanding.

"Nanny's basket will have arrived by now, she murmured. "I will go home and fetch it."

Jack's smiled faded. "Not yet, Carolyn. Wait until I can come with you. I would not have you face the consequences alone."

She had not given much thought to consequences. She had possessed the freedom to come and go at will for some years now. Her father trusted her to do the proper thing. In all probability, he did not even know she wasn't at home. She offered Jack an uneasy smile. "That isn't necessary. My maid is the only one who knows, and she won't talk. You needn't worry."

Amy's fit of sneezing, followed by her hungry complaints, distracted them both for some while. Jack became frantic when she cried and spit up her toast. Carolyn soothed him and the child, offering apple juice and tea laced with honey and slicing the toast up into soft, buttery strips dotted with cinnamon. Between Jack shouting orders at an army of servants racing up and down the stairs and Carolyn patiently doctoring the food brought to suit an invalid, they succeeded in getting the first decent meal into Amy that she'd had in days.

Their triumph did not last long. Just as they got Amy into another clean gown and asleep, a roar in the lower hall warned that still another hurdle awaited. They exchanged glances at the familiar cadence of furious words. Carolyn's father had discovered her whereabouts.

She paled slightly at the unexpectedness of this visitation, but held her head high as she heard his angry strides outside the door. Not daring to compromise her further by touching her, Jack kept a respectful distance as the door burst open.

Henry Thorogood quickly took in his daughter's wrinkled walking gown and weary expression, Jack's rumpled clothes and defiantly protective air, and the tiny child lying curled beneath the covers. The vulgar message that had brought him flying here had no basis in fact; he knew his daughter too well to see anything else in this scene but what it was. He concealed his sigh of relief and turned his furious gaze on the young man who had so successfully turned his comfortable world inside-out.

"I will see you in my study in one hour, Chatham. Come, Carolyn, we will go home."

Stiffly Carolyn looked from one man to the other. Had they been tomcats, they would have their backs arched, their hair on end, and they would be spitting. That was an odd way to picture Jack, and she threw him a second look. His fingers were curled around the chair back while he engaged her father in a duel of glares. The tension mounting between them was too electric to bear. Silently she picked up the pelisse and muff she had thrown over the chair the day before and walked out of the room.

Angry shouts echoed up and down the hallways, vibrating the normally quiet air of the sedate Thorogood household. Blanche sent her sister a speculative look as she sat reading in the far corner of the library. Carolyn's air of indifference didn't fool her this time. She looked like one who hadn't slept in weeks, and the book she held was upside-down. Something was going on, but no one had given thought to informing Blanche.

Carolyn didn't seem surprised when the footman came to fetch her. She shook out the warm yellow skirts of the fine wool gown she had hastily donned, wasted no time tidying her loose arrangement of curls, and proceeded out, as if walking to her execution.

Her father at least had the decency to leave them alone for this interview, she observed as she entered the study to find only Jack waiting there. He had that haunted look on his face again, but his eyes were warm as they took in her appearance. He made no attempt at an improper embrace, as he might have in earlier years, but Carolyn felt his desire to do so. She was grateful for his restraint.

"How is Amy?" Although she had left the child little more than an hour ago, it seemed much longer. She would hear this news before the argument to come.

"Sleeping when I left her. Your maid brought the basket of remedies. I thank you for your concern."

His formality indicated uneasiness. Carolyn could understand that. Her father could have that effect on heads of state. Nervously she took a seat and clasped her hands in her lap. "You needn't look like that, Jack. He doesn't bite."

Jack made a wry smile. "I wouldn't swear to that. He's in the right of it, though. I have compromised you beyond repair. I'm obliged to offer for you."

She had hoped he would phrase it a little less bluntly. It would be soothing to her injured feelings to hear him mouth a few of the pretty phrases he was so good at saying. Just for a little while she would like to cling to the illusion of those long-ago years.

Her smile matched his as she replied, "I am obliged to refuse."

Jack's shoulders slumped imperceptibly and he turned to play with the candlesticks on the mantel rather than reveal his expression. "You cannot, Carolyn. That Higginbotham woman is spreading word far and wide. I could slit her throat, but the damage will already be done."

She had not expected that. Wildly, Carolyn contemplated her alternatives, but her ability to think straight had flown out the door when Jack entered it. She shook her head in hopes of freeing it from cobwebs. "We can deny everything. I'll not be forced into marriage."

"I knew you would say that." Bleakly he turned back to face her. "Can you not even consider it, Carolyn? Would it be so horrible a fate? I'm quite wealthy now, you know. I can support you in any manner that you choose."

Carolyn rose and gave him a cold glare at this insult. "What does wealth have to do with it? I would have married you when you were penniless, but you preferred gold to me. Go wed your gold, Jack. I'll not have any part of your lies."

She swung to leave the room, but he stepped forward and caught her wrist, his face a mixture of despair and desperation. "Is it George? Do you love him? I will go speak to him today and explain all that has happened. If you love each other, this misunderstanding can't come between you."

Carolyn gave him an icy look and refused to reply until he dropped her wrist. "Explain what you wish to whomever you wish if it eases your conscience. Good day, Jack."

She swept out in a trail of lavender and wildflowers, leaving him bereft. The fury in Thorogood's expression when he returned did not ease Jack's pain. He had lost her. The terrible emptiness that followed this realization could only be filled with silent screams of anguish.

Despite her lack of sleep, Carolyn did not find rest easy that night. She couldn't erase the look in Jack's eyes when she refused him. Surely he had not expected her to agree after what he had done to her? What did he stand to gain by offering now?

Amy. That thought came instantly to mind. He needed a mother for Amy. That much was obvious. She must have filled him with confidence when she had so foolishly taken the child under her wing. Instead of pretty words, he meant to woo her with his daughter.

Why did that notion not ring true? She was quite old enough and experienced enough by now to know when she was being manipulated. She had no more romantic illusions. George, at least, had the sense to treat her as an intelligent human being capable of making decisions without having to be wooed and won with silly words and gestures. Would Jack ever consider her in such a light?

That thought made her even more restless, and she got up to put on her robe and pace the room. George's polite note had only said that Jack had been to see him and that he understood all. What did he understand? Did he understand that she needed the reassurance of his presence, of hearing his voice say the words? Obviously not. Jack had, or he wouldn't have been so quick to go to George to explain it. Had it been Jack she had been considering instead of George, he would have been at her door within the time it took to receive the message. Jack had never stinted her in his attentions.

Nor did he now. There was another bouquet on her dressing table with a note telling her how Amy fared. She had nearly cried when she had seen it. All day she had felt isolated. Her father wasn't speaking to her.

George's stilted message hadn't helped. And no one had come to call. Only Jack's thoughtful note bringing news of his concern for her had come to break her loneliness.

She was mad to be thinking like this. In a few days George would be escorting her to the usual social functions, the gossip would subside, and everything would be back to normal. Why should she place any consequence on a few flowers and kind words? Jack had always been lavish in his attentions. That was just his way. It didn't mean anything.

But, may the heavens preserve her, she wanted it to mean something. She wanted to know that bouquet meant he cared for her. She wanted to know he offered for her because he loved her and didn't wish to be parted from her again. She wanted to believe that he had come to her that day after the ball to explain his undying love and the misery he had suffered in those years apart, the same misery she had suffered and was suffering still.

Flinging herself weeping on the bed, Carolyn finally found comfort in repose. Only in her dreams could she believe that the warmth in gray eyes and the eager caress of browned hands meant something more than selfishness.

The days slipped away like the steady drip of the icicles outside the windows. Carolyn retreated inside herself just as Blanche remembered her doing those years ago during her first Season. Back then, she had at least continued to attend social functions, although with an icy brittleness that displayed little pleasure. This time, she refused to go out at all, putting a severe damper on Blanche's own social life. Something drastic had to be done, and swiftly.

The litter of paper and scissors and a crudely cut heart on the library table made Blanche smile in anticipation. Glancing surreptitiously around the room to be certain Carolyn was nowhere to be seen, she carefully completed the larger card with a few pen strokes, added the one Amy had made, wrapped both in a length of vellum with a scribbled note, and summoned a footman. St. Valentine's Day was for lovers. The gentlemen who had appeared at their door earlier this day weren't lovers, just men playing at games. Her romantic heart hoped she had made the correct surmise in sending this particular valentine.

Jack opened the slender package in his study, where he was working over long-neglected correspondence. The sight of the two lavishly decorated cards brought back such a painful memory that he nearly threw them aside as someone's idea of a malicious joke. But the crudity of the one card caught his interest, and he cautiously picked up the message accompanying it.

After reading the brief note, he more carefully studied the two hearts. Both were made with loving hands, one pair childish and uncoordinated, the other talented and gentle. He remembered well the poem inscribed inside the larger heart. He remembered the occasion when he had last quoted it. His hands shook and tears sprang to his eyes as he read it again. Surely, after all these years, she would have forgotten so silly a verse had it not meant something to her? Why, then, would she not say the words to his face?

Pondering this peculiarity, Jack took the smaller heart in his hand and went up the stairs to where a rapidly recovering child was wreaking havoc with her impatience to be out of bed. At the sight of him, Amy leapt from beneath the covers to hold her arms out and bounce upon the bed.

Her joyful cry of ''Papa'' brought a smile to his weary face, and Jack caught her up in a hug, careful not to crumple the paper in his hand. When he set her down, he presented the childishly beautiful card with a flourish.

"Do you remember this?"

Dark eyes lit with excitement. "Lynley helped me! It's for you."

"Lynley?" Jack sat on the edge of the bed and smiled at the childish name for so gracious and lovely a woman as Carolyn Thorogood. As Amy pointed out the card's many and varied features, he could hear Carolyn speaking in the voice of his daughter. Loneliness and a desperate need for her company welled up inside of him. He could not keep on living this half-life. Something had to be done, but he had run out of ideas. How did one go about wooing someone he had courted once, only to slam a door in her face? What he had done was unforgivable. How could they ever go back to that time again?

Something Amy was chirping caught his ear, and he turned his attention back to her. "What was that, love? Lynley said what?"

"Don't break it, she said," Amy gave him a look of disdain at his lack of attention. "You got to keep it forever and ever and ever," she admonished in a tone that reflected the adult she mimicked.

Don't break it. Jack thought of the torn pieces stored all these years in an ivory music box of his mother's. He had carried that broken heart halfway around the world with him as a reminder of how low he had fallen. If only he could put those torn pieces back together again and start all over.

The vague stirrings of an impossible idea came to mind, but nothing was too impossible to try in this desperate gamble for a love he had lost and wished to win back again. Giving Amy a kiss and thanking her with a hug for his beautiful valentine, he rose and went in search of the music box.

Many tedious hours later he had pasted and pieced dozens of torn bits of lacy paper on a large sheet of vellum. Giving the ragged result a wry look, Jack admitted to himself that his chance of winning this gamble with such feeble backing was slim, but it was all he had.

Forgetting cloak and hat, he set out into the fast-growing darkness of the winter streets, gripping the forlorn fragments of an old valentine. He carried no roses or candy or trinkets as a proper valentine lover should. Instead, he carried his heart in his hand.

When notified she had a visitor, Carolyn refused to see him, as she had refused all visitors this day. She didn't have the heart to exchange witty sallies with friends or suitors on the state of her love life on this day for lovers. Tomorrow, maybe she would venture out again. George had been remarkably silent this past week, but the combination of the scandal and his mother's arrival would explain that. He had sent another reassuring note, but it hadn't reassured. She hadn't even finished reading it.

The footman returned some minutes later with a large bit of paper on his salver. Carolyn gave him a look of irritation for thus interrupting her morose thoughts again, but she took the awkwardly large message he offered. Her eyes widened in surprise and she rose to carry it to a brighter lamp to better peruse what she wouldn't believe she was seeing.

Carefully pieced and pasted back together was the valentine she had created five years ago for the man she had meant to marry. The faded ink still bore the words of the poem Jack had written for her when he had asked if she would marry him, the same poem she had written on the valentine she had left downstairs in the library, writing the words as if it had been only yesterday when last she heard them.

Tears poured down Carolyn's cheeks as the feelings of that long-ago time flooded through her, unlocked by this tattered heart that Jack had so painstakingly recreated. He had kept it all those years. Why?

Without a word to the waiting servant, Carolyn swept out of the room and half-ran to the front salon, where visitors waited, the tattered valentine clutched possessively in her hand. She had to see him face-to-face, to hear his reply. She had to know why he had kept this shattered heart for all these years. And why he had put it back together now.

Jack glanced up as she ran into the room. His weathered face had a lined and harried look to it, and there was a wariness in his eyes at her abrupt entrance, but he moved toward her as steel draws toward a magnet.

"Why?" She waved the forlorn heart beneath his nose.

He didn't need to understand the question. The answer was in his heart. "Because I love you. Because I've always loved you. Throw it back in my face if you will. I deserved it then. I've worked hard not to deserve it now, but that's for you to decide. I can't bear this loneliness any longer, Carolyn. I've worked and waited these five years in hopes of winning at least your respect, but what I want is your love. Can you ever forgive me and start anew?" He was not too proud to beg, but he desperately wished he dared take her in his arms while doing so. The cold air between them chilled his heart.

Carolyn stared at him in disbelief, not daring to believe the words. He had destroyed her with just such words before. She couldn't let him do it again. Her gaze faltered at the smoky gray intensity of his eyes, and she dropped it to the valentine in her hand. Her fingers instinctively smoothed the crumpled paper.

"I can't. How can I?" she murmured, almost to herself. "You sold my love for money. It's gone. There can be no love where there is no trust."

His heart ached, and he finally gave in and reached for her. Whether he hoped to prevent her escape or pour his love into her, he couldn't say, but the contact was electric. They both jerked with the jolt, and Jack couldn't have moved away if his life depended on it.

Holding her arms, he poured out his feverish response. "I paid him back, Carolyn. I paid your father back every cent I ever took from him. He was right. I had no right to ask you to share a life of penury with a careless spendthrift. I do not condone his methods, but he did what he had to to protect you. I didn't take his money in exchange for your love. I never wanted his money. He gave me no choice. Please understand that, Carolyn. Turn me away if you will, but not without understanding that I have never stopped loving you, that everything I have done has been for love of you."

Carolyn wanted desperately to be enfolded in Jack's embrace, to accept his words unquestioningly, to feel his strong arms around her and hear his heart beat beneath her ear, but she had learned her lesson at his hands too well. She shook her head blindly, refusing to meet his eyes.

"I heard you that night. Father paid you to turn me away. Don't lie to me anymore, Jack. I can't bear it."

Jack felt anger for the father who had allowed her to continue to think these things all these years, even after the debt was repaid. But the plea in Carolyn's voice called to him, and he gently pulled her into his arms. He rejoiced when she made no effort to fight him. The scent of lavender wafted around him, and he inhaled deeply. He could easily spend the rest of his life drowning in that fragrance.

"I've never lied to you, my love. Please believe me. Every word I've said is true, although I once put them cruelly to drive you away. I didn't want you wedded to a man lounging in debtor's prison. I didn't deserve you then, and I knew it. Your father's ultimatum only made it clear to me. I hated him for making me face the facts, but he gave me the opportunity to redeem myself, and I took it in hopes of one day being able to look you in the eye again. The money he offered was a loan, my love. I repaid it with interest. You may ask him if you have doubts."

Carolyn tried to make order of her swirling thoughts, but enveloped in Jack's arms, she could only drink in the radiant heat of his body and the ecstasy of his hard strength beneath her hands. She didn't wish to think of anything else.

She didn't need to think of anything else. A door slammed, and a harsh voice exclaimed, "What is the meaning of this? Damn you, Chatham, haven't you caused enough scandal—must you create more?"

Carolyn jerked and would have fled Jack's arms, but he held her firmly, entrapping her in his protective hold as they both faced her father together.

"If you'll excuse me, sir, I am asking your daughter to marry me. I do not believe I need your permission anymore."

"You do not need my money anymore, is what you mean! She refused you, Chatham. I'll not see her made unhappy. Get out of here before I call the constabulary."

Carolyn straightened at this threat, and without a second thought to her words, she answered her father's furious glare steadily. "Jack will leave when I want him to. If you throw him out, I go with him. You tore us apart once before, but I'm older now and know you are not infallible. Had you but trusted my judgment then, we neither of us would have had to suffer all these years. This time, the choice is mine. You cannot force it." She felt Jack's arm tighten around her, and this time she allowed herself to lean into his embrace.

"Shhh, Lynley," Jack whispered placatingly in her ear as her father's face grew suddenly ashen. "Save your temper for another time. I'm a father now too, and I know what it is like to protect a daughter. It is easy to think the safe thing is the right thing. No one wants to take chances with the ones they love."

Carolyn turned eyes brimming with love up to Jack's face, and her smile was one of joy and acceptance. Her words, however, had the ring of a woman who had set aside childish fancies. "You are not my father, John Chatham. If it's marriage you want, you had better learn I am no longer a gullible child to be swept away by your facile tongue. I can fight my own battles, thank you."

The warm chuckle in her ear made her heart quake. "Anyone who can simultaneously rout Mrs. Higginbotham and capture my daughter has my full respect, my love. I do not doubt your abilities. It is your temper I fear."

Henry Thorogood watched this display with bemusement but had the sense to hold his tongue. The young lord had a quick way with words, but perhaps that was what Carolyn needed. He certainly couldn't fault the loving attention the young man showered upon her, although he certainly could fault his methods. With a loud throat-clearing to remind them he was in the room, he interrupted what could easily have become a rather intimate exchange. "I cannot leave the room unless I know a formal betrothal has been formed."

Carolyn turned her smile from Jack's loving gaze to her father's stiff figure. "Leave the room, Papa. Jack may talk with you later."

She felt the joy rocketing through the man holding her as her father glared and stomped from the room. She wasn't certain what she had done, but in her heart, it felt right. She turned her gaze expectantly back to Jack.

"I love you, even if you are as spoiled and obstinate as Amy." Jack's mouth curved lightly as she moved more fully into his embrace.

"Don't forget bad-tempered and willful," she reminded him, standing on tiptoes to reach his lips with hers.

"And mine." Firmly and resolutely, Jack covered her mouth with his, drawing her possessively into his hold so she could have no uncertainty as to what he meant.

"I never said yes," Carolyn gasped some minutes later when he gave her time to gulp for air.

"Yes you did, five years ago. It's been a long betrothal, my love. Shall we make it a hasty wedding?" Jack held her eyes with desperate intensity.

"Will you explain to George?" Carolyn asked, postponing her acceptance of this joy Jack offered her with open hand. She still could not quite believe it. She needed time.

Jack smiled. "I've already explained to George. He's a very understanding man. He's willing to let you choose."

"He'd give me up without a fight?" she asked in mock incredulity.

"He knows I'll put him six feet under if he stands in my way. Give me a date, my love."

"Christmas," she said firmly.

Jack bent his head closer and spoke inches from her lips "Try again."

"Easter," she murmured, rising to the temptation.

And as that holiday was little more than a month away, Jack said, "Done," and closed the compact with a kiss.

Although the sun shone and the guests wore their spring pastels for the occasion, the ebony-haired flower girl wore red velvet and the blond bridesmaids wore white lace and carried valentine roses when the bride walked down the aisle that balmy Easter Day.

When the ceremony ended and the groom's sun-darkened face bent to take the kiss he had earned from his shining bride, he gave no sign of surprise as their audience broke into gales of laughter rather than happy tears.

There at the foot of the altar two dancing cherubs in white and red cavorted to the sweeping swells of organ music, heedless of the solemnity of the occasion. The bride smiled softly into the groom's eyes, and the look they exchanged bespoke the distinct possibility that another cherub would be on the way before year's end.

The Antagonists
by Joan Wolf

ONE OF THE greatest misfortunes that can befall a young man in his formative years is for him to become an earl. Perhaps there are some tempers that would not be spoiled by such an experience, but when the young man is a top-lofty boor to begin with, the addition of an earldom can be fatal.

This is what happened to Hugh Lesley St. John Lydin, sixth Viscount Coleford and fifth Earl of Thornton. I shall tell you about it.

When his heir was but sixteen, the fourth Earl of Thornton was killed in a hunting accident. The earl's death left his son, then Viscount Coleford, and his daughter, Caroline, as the sole family inhabitants of Thornton Manor, the Lydin estate in Derby. The death of his father also transformed Hugh from Viscount Coleford into the fifth Earl of Thornton.

Shortly after the fourth earl's death, the entire Lydin family held a meeting in order to decide what was to be done about the orphans, as the countess, unfortunately, had died at Caroline's birth. My mother was one of those summoned to attend this meeting, and before she left she explained to me that the official guardian and trustee for the new earl and Caroline was their uncle, the Honorable George Lydin. My mother further explained that although the Honorable George was willing to see to the business aspects of the Thornton fortune and property, he did not desire to move his trunks to Derby. It seems that George Lydin was accustomed to spending most of his time in London, where he was a member of the government.

The purpose of the family meeting was to find someone to live at Thornton and be a mother to Caroline. The family was not so concerned about the new earl, my mother said. He was away at school for most of the year. It was Caroline who needed a mother, and the mother the family eventually came up with was mine.

Mother, unfortunately, is a widow. Also unfortunately, she is not very plump in the pocket. The opportunity to live at one of the country's greatest estates was too tempting for her to resist, and almost before I knew what was happening, I found myself being driven up a seemingly endless graveled drive on my way to meet the cousin my mother insisted on referring to as "darling Caroline."

It seems that "darling Caroline" was just my age, eleven, and, owing to this stupid coincidence, the entire family had assumed that the two of us were bound to become bosom friends. Which just goes to show you how amazingly idiotic adults can sometimes be.

Though I would have died before admitting it out loud, I was very impressed by my first view of Thornton Manor. The house is *enormous*. Mother and I had been living in a small cottage in Wiltshire, and the sight of the great stone mansion, with all its hundreds of windows sparkling in the sun, did truly inspire awe.

I suppose I ought to say here, in case you are interested in that sort of thing, that Thornton Manor is a relatively new house, built by the present earl's grandfather in what my governess, Miss Lacy, calls the Palladian style of architecture. Also according to my governess, "It is classically proportioned, with a central part that is three stories high flanked by matching wings at either end. The rows of identical windows are punctuated by a pattern of pillars and pilasters, which stand in graceful contrast to the smooth pale stone of the building.''

Such a mouthful of words to say that it is an excessively lovely house!

''Are we actually going to live there?'' I breathed, staring out the window of the coach. The coach, I might add, belonged to the earl, had been sent to transport us in comfort and style, and was exceedingly elegant. I had been afraid to put my feet up on the squabs the whole day.

''Yes, Dinah, we are.'' Even my mother's voice sounded hushed. We are not noble folk ourselves, and are not accustomed to such grandeur. Mother always said that her cousin, the one who had married the fourth earl and had so inconveniently died when Caroline was born, had stepped considerably above herself with the match. My own father had been a simple army officer, of good though not noble birth. I had always thought Papa was noble in every other way, however. And he was brave. He had been killed in the Peninsula two years before, and I still missed him.

As the carriage pulled up before the steps of the house, the great door opened and a liveried servant, of scary-looking dignity, descended the stairs. Lackeys scurried to open the coach door and put up the wooden stairs. Mother and I got out.

My mother is rarely frightened by this sort of thing. She was not nobly born, true, but she has gone through life with one very useful advantage. She is beautiful.

''Mrs. Stratton,'' the majordomo said deeply. He bowed. ''Welcome to Thornton Manor.''

My mother smiled. ''Thank you, Edwards.''

I stared at her in surprise. How had she known the man's name was Edwards?

My mother returned my look and frowned slightly. "This is Miss Dinah," she said.

The powdered head inclined my way. I almost curtsied, he was so dignified. Then I had to suppress a grin at the thought of what kind of an impression that would have made!

We proceeded up the stairs and into the front hall. Coming down the stairs as we entered was a young girl who looked to be about my age. She had long blond hair and large blue eyes and was dressed in an immaculate pink frock.

Caroline, I thought. Darling Caroline.

"How do you do, Aunt Cecelia," a softly pretty voice was saying. "I am so happy you have come to live with me."

"Darling Caroline," my mother said. "My dearest child. How good it is to see you again."

Mother and Caroline had met before, though this was my first introduction to my new little friend.

"See whom I have brought," Mother was going on. She was using her warmest voice. I thought she sounded like a pigeon cooing. "A new friend for you. My daughter, Dinah."

Dutifully I stepped forward. Politely I murmured, "How do you do."

"I am so happy you have come," Caroline said, and smiled as if she meant it.

I gave her a half-grin in return. Then, getting right to the heart of things, I asked, "Do you like dogs?"

"Yes," Caroline said.

I turned to my mother. "Then we can send for Sergeant, Mother. I *told* you Caroline was sure to like dogs."

"Is Sergeant your dog?" Caroline asked. "Of

course you must send for him. You must miss him terribly.''

As I had been parted from him for only a day, I had scarcely had time to miss him terribly. But I appreciated the thought and allowed my grin to widen a little. ''He's a wonderful ratter,'' I volunteered.

Caroline's celestial-blue eyes widened.

''That is quite enough about that wretched animal, Dinah,'' my mother said briskly. ''Darling Caroline, would you be kind enough to show us to our rooms?''

I am happy to be able to report that none of my worst fears about the move to Thornton Manor came true. Caroline turned out to be a very pleasant girl, and I did not at all mind sharing my time or my mother with her. We had a governess whom we had lessons with every morning. The lessons were very dull. At home I had studied with our old rector, who was much cheaper than a governess, and he had given me books you could actually think about. Miss Lacy liked to skim over the surface of things, and every time I asked her *why*, she got flustered and told me to look it up.

I discovered that there was a splendid library at Thornton, and I soon got into the way of bringing my own books to our lessons. I think Miss Lacy was relieved not to have me asking questions anymore.

But by far the best thing of all about Thornton was the stables. The last earl had been a keen hunter, and the stables were filled with beautiful, well-conditioned horses. I had adored horses all my life, and when Papa was alive he had always made certain I had a pony. He was a great horseman himself, even though he was not in the cavalry. It costs a great deal of money to be in the cavalry, you see, and so unfortunately Papa had been forced to settle for the infantry. But he had taught me to ride when I was three years old, and I had had my own pony until Papa died. Mother could not afford to keep a pony for me on her widow's pittance, and I had been horseless for the last two years.

Caroline had two lovely ponies, and she let me ride one. The only drawback to this otherwise splendid arrangement was that I had to go out riding with Caroline, whose speed in going cross-country was far slower than what I liked. I soon found a remedy for that particular problem, however. I got up at five in the morning and rode out with the stable lads, who were exercising the earl's big hunters. Lucky, my pony, loved it, and would tear along on his sturdy little legs beside the big horses, blowing through his nose in sheer delight.

I think I was happy for the first time since my Papa died. And then summer came, and the new earl came home from Eton.

For as long as I live I shall remember my first view of the fifth Earl of Thornton. The entire staff had lined up on the front steps to greet the new master. I thought privately that it was a silly way to greet a sixteen-year-old, no matter what his title, but I kept my thoughts to myself. Mother, Caroline, and I were poised by the front door, waiting to offer our own welcome. News had come to the house five minutes before that the earl's coach had been sighted on the main road, and the notice had given us time to get into position.

We waited. Finally, through the trees on the lower half of the drive, I could see the horses. Then the coach was out onto the open drive, and in a minute it had come to rest before the front stair. Edwards descended to greet his master. The door to the coach opened, the wooden coach stairs were set, and finally the earl came out.

The first thing I noticed about him, the first thing I think anyone would notice about him, was the fairness of his hair. It was purely flaxen, a color rarely seen on anyone older than six or seven years old. He was tall and slim, and the smile he turned upon Edwards was just beautiful.

I thought he looked like an angel.

Which only goes to show that appearances are not to be trusted.

A husky brown-haired boy was getting out of the coach next. The earl had written to my mother that he would be bringing a friend home with him for part of the summer holiday, and this, obviously, was the friend. The two boys started up the stairs.

The servants were all bobbing curtsies and bows and the earl grinned and tossed a word here and there to faces he recognized. Then he was standing before us.

"Aunt Cecelia. How lovely to see you." And he gave Mother that beautiful smile. His eyes were a very clear, very brilliant blue.

Mother smiled back. "Thank you, Thornton," she said in her prettiest voice.

Caroline pushed forward and reached up her arms. He stooped to give her a brisk, businesslike hug. He said something into her ear that made her laugh. Then he looked at me.

The blue eyes widened as he took in my hair. "What a fiery head!" he said. Then, "You must be little Dinah." And he gave me the most top-lofty, the most patronizing smile I had ever received in all my life.

I stared up into his face. My palm itched to smash across one of its hard cheekbones. I *hate* to be teased about the color of my hair. Nor do I appreciate being called "little."

"I am Dinah," I said. "And I am not little. I am just the right size for my age. And it's rude to comment on the color of a person's hair."

"Dinah!" My mother was appalled. "Apologize to Thornton at once."

I gritted my teeth.

"It's quite all right, Aunt," said that top-lofty voice. "Perhaps she will learn some manners by the time she turns twelve."

You didn't. But I kept the thought to myself.

"Dinah is very sensitive about her hair, Cole," Caroline said. Then, in confusion, "Oh, dear, I suppose I can't call you Cole anymore."

"No, he is 'Thorn' now, Lady Caroline," said the earl's friend, whom he had introduced to my mother as Mr. Robert Merrow. "It took us a few weeks to grow accustomed to it at school, but it seems quite natural now."

Caroline said, in a puzzled voice, "No one ever called Papa 'Thorn.' "

A strange look came across her brother's face. "No one ever called Papa anything other than 'my lord.' "

"That is true," my mother said. "He was a most aristocratic man. Shall we go into the house, Thornton? You will like to show Mr. Merrow where he is to stay."

I arrived at the stables early the following morning, ready to ride out with the hunters as usual. I was surprised, and not pleased, to find Thornton there before me.

"Dinah!" he said, staring at me in surprise. "What are you doing here?"

"I come every morning to ride exercise with the stable lads," I answered. I took care to speak politely. I was rather afraid that I had been rude the day before, and I was determined not to put myself in the wrong again.

"You?"

That top-lofty look was back on his face. My palm itched.

"Yes, I," I replied with great dignity. Imitating Edwards, I raised my chin and gazed off into the distance. "The lads don't mind, and it is good for Lucky to stretch his legs. We don't go above a slow canter when I ride with your sister."

"Caroline is chickenhearted," her brother agreed. "She took a bad fall a few years ago and was laid up in bed for three months. She's been afraid to ride ever since."

"Considering that your father was killed by a fall from a horse, perhaps she has cause for her fear," I snapped.

His eyes widened with surprise. I had a sudden suspicion that very few people ever snapped at Thornton.

I resumed my gaze off into the distance. He said, "That expression you're wearing makes you look just like Edwards."

I could feel myself flushing with annoyance. My skin is very pale and has an irritating habit of revealing feelings I would much prefer to keep hidden. I glared at him and caught him staring at my legs. "What," he asked with greatly exaggerated astonishment, "is that suit you're wearing?"

To my fury, I could feel the blood rush once more to my cheeks. "It is not a suit!" I gritted through my teeth. "It is a riding costume." I followed his eyes and looked down at my person. I was wearing boy's breeches, actually. My mother would have swooned if she knew. When I rode with Caroline I wore the habit my mother had had made for me when we came to live at Thornton Manor.

"Good God," Thorn said, his eyes swinging next to a spot beyond my shoulder. "What is that?"

It was Sergeant, who had been visiting in the paddock and had now come to join me for our morning ride.

Sergeant was a large dog. In fact, he was not a great deal smaller than Lucky. And, to be truthful, I suppose he was rather homely. *I* thought he was beautiful, but I loved him. Upon first glance, I had to admit that he was not . . . ah, taking.

"This is my dog," I told the earl. I fondled the too-large brown ears. "His name is Sergeant."

"What a dreadful-looking creature," Thorn said, and snapped his fingers. Sergeant, the fool, went immediately to have his ears scratched.

The head groom came up to us. "The horses are ready, my lord," he said. "And Lucky is ready for you, Miss Dinah."

"Does this baby really ride out with the hunters?" Thorn asked insultingly.

"Every morning, my lord." The head groom's name was John, and he was one of my particular friends. "She's a neck-or-nothing rider, my lord. Just like you was at that age, if I may say so."

My cousin and I looked at each other, equally revolted by the comparison. "She's a girl," Thorn said, curling his lip.

"I can ride every bit as well as you can," I shot back. "Even if you are five years older."

"Ha." We eyed each other. "We shall see about that," Thorn said.

"Now, my lord," John said placatingly. "Let's not have any accidents."

"Accidents?" Thorn raised fine golden eyebrows. "How could we possibly have an accident? Miss Dinah rides like a centaur. She just told me so herself. And you agreed."

My papa had told me about centaurs. "I ride better than a centaur," I said.

We glared at each other. Then he gave me a very nasty grin. "Come along, Red," he said, "and we shall see."

I followed his back toward the paddock, inwardly vowing to show him even if it killed me.

It almost did. In my zeal to show off my horsemanship, I put Lucky at a fence that was too high for him. As was to be expected under the circumstances, we came to grief. I collected some notable bruises and sprained my ankle. Lucky, thank God, was all right.

The only bright light in the morning was that Thorn got into trouble with John, who told the earl he had "provoked" me into it. He had, of course, and the reprimand was fully justified. Thorn was absolutely furious at being in the wrong. Typically, however, he was not furious with himself, but with me. Over the years, one thing I was to learn about Thorn: he never, ever thought he was in the wrong. And he usually was, even though he always tried to put the blame on me.

The years went by. Thorn left Eton and went to Cambridge, where he did odiously well. During the holidays he would return to Thornton Manor and let my mother and Caroline feast upon his meretricious charm. Very often he would bring a friend with him. His friends were usually quite nice, although they all had an unfortunate tendency to fawn upon Thorn. Of course, he was an earl, and, according to my mother, very rich.

To give his friends their due, however, I don't think it was entirely Thorn's title or his wealth that impressed them and made them worship him in the most odious way. Thorn never suffered from any of the usual trials that beset adolescent boys. His complexion was never marred by a spot; he grew evenly and gracefully, with none of the awkwardness that marked so many other boys; he could ride and shoot and wrestle better than anyone else at school. All these things impressed his friends, and they deferred to him in the most revolting manner.

The fact of the matter is, everyone around Thorn spoiled him to death. He was so accustomed to being toad-eaten that when he met up with someone who was not inclined to worship at his shrine, he became insufferable.

I hated to argue with him. He had an unfair advantage, having been to Eton and Cambridge and having learned all sorts of things I knew nothing of. It made me livid to have him quote Latin at me. He knew that, of course, and used to quote it at me all the time.

And he called me Red.

Let us get one thing perfectly clear. My hair is not red. It is strawberry blond. When I was little, Papa would call it red-gold, but when I grew older he was forced to admit that it was really strawberry blond. My mother said it was strawberry blond. Caroline said it was strawberry blond. Only Thorn insisted that it was red, and he did it simply because he knew it annoyed me.

Despite Thorn's holiday visits, however, I found the years I spent at Thornton Manor exceedingly pleasant. Caroline and I had scarcely a thought in common, and yet, despite our differences, we liked each other very well. Perhaps it was our very differences that kept us such good friends. We did not tread on each other's toes.

Caroline was talented musically, and she also had a gift for drawing. Neither of these subjects interested me in the slightest. I did like learning a new language, however, and it was not long before I could speak French and Italian as well as Miss Lacy. I was certain that I could learn to speak both languages even better than she, but there was no one to teach me. Until, that is, Mother brought in the Italian dancing master.

His name was Signore Montelli. He came in the autumn of the year that Caroline and I were to make our come-outs. The come-out was actually to be in the spring, but Mother wanted us to attend some local parties over the winter—to acquire some "polish," she said. And so the dancing master came to Thornton Manor.

That was the same year that Thorn came down from Cambridge, the year that he turned twenty-one and officially entered into his inheritance. No longer would Uncle George have to approve anything Thorn might wish to do. He was his own master now, Mother said. She also said that I ought to be nicer to Thorn, that he could turn me out of the house if ever he decided he wanted to be rid of me. And turn her out too!

The scene she painted was quite pitiful. Where would we go? How would we live? My beautiful come-out (which Thorn was going to pay for) would be lost. No more horses. I should have to become a governess like Miss Lacy, and Mother would probably end up in the workhouse.

I didn't believe a word of it. Thorn would never put himself so far in the wrong as to turn a widow and her child out of his house. I knew him too well. Such a gesture would not accord at all with his sublime picture of his own nobility. Mother was perfectly safe.

When I explained all this to her, all she did was give me an exasperated look and totter off to pour out her troubles to the housekeeper.

To return to the Italian dancing master. He arrived at Thornton Manor in September to teach Caroline and me the intricacies of the various dances we would be expected to know when we went to parties. Mother was most particular that we must learn to waltz. It would be utterly mortifying, she said, to be asked to waltz and to disgrace ourselves, and her, by clumsiness. The other dances did not present such a challenge, but one was held so closely against a gentleman in the waltz that Mother was certain it would be quite difficult to keep from treading on one's partner's toes.

Signore Montelli had flashing white teeth and was quite nice. He was particularly nice to me. He talked Italian to me, and it was extraordinary the progress I made in the language when I had the stimulus of actual conversation.

Needless to say, neither Caroline nor I was ever left alone with Signore Montelli. Either my mother or some other chaperone was always present, so it was not until the wily Italian caught me unawares in the library one day that I realized his dastardly intentions.

He kissed me. He grabbed me by the shoulders, pushed me up against a wall of books, and pressed his drippy wet mouth over mine. I was so astonished I could hardly move.

The man, after all, was *old*. He had to be thirty, at least. Far too old for this sort of thing, I thought.

"My little Titian beauty . . ." he was mumbling. He actually began to kiss my neck. "Such hair . . . such skin . . . such magnificent eyes . . ."

He raised his head and looked down into my face. "You like me, yes?" he said. "You press yourself against me in the waltz . . ."

I had thought that was what you were supposed to do in the waltz. He had told me that was what you were supposed to do in the waltz.

"No." I said. "I do not like you. And if you kiss me again I shall tell my cousin Thornton. He is the best shot in the country and he will kill you."

The warm Italian skin turned pale. He was so close I could see where the beard was beginning to grow under his skin. He stared at me, his mouth a little open. He looked so like a fish that I almost laughed.

"You would not do that," he said.

"Not if you give me your word never to touch me again," I said. "Or," I amended, "at least not to kiss me. I suppose you have to touch me if you are going to dance with me."

"My perfect little Titian," he breathed and, leaning closer, he touched my cheek. "You would not tell your cousin."

"Who the devil is this Titian?" I demanded, slapping his hand away. "And I most certainly will tell him."

He stared at me as if I were a barbarian. "Titian is a painter," he said. "A very great painter. He is famous for painting ladies with red hair."

"My hair is not red. It is strawberry blond."

"No, *cara,*" he said. He smiled at me almost tenderly. "It is red. Red like copper, red like firelight, red like—"

"That is quite enough, *signore*. Do I have your word, or do I tell my cousin?"

Well, after a bit more discussion, he gave me his word. He kept it, too. Thorn actually did have a reputation as a marksman, although it was highly inflated. He had won some sort of silly wager at one of the London clubs. We had heard about it all the way up in Derby. It sounded to me as if Thorn were utterly wasting his time in London, but I forbore to say a word. In my opinion, anything that kept him away from Thornton Manor, and hence out of my way, was all to the good.

Mother spent the entire winter preparing Caroline and me for our come-out in society. For those of you who are not familiar with what a come-out entails, I will describe it.

First and foremost, the purpose of a come-out is for a girl to find a husband. Girls, you see, must have husbands. If a girl does not have a husband, she must: a. become a governess (if she is poor); b. go and live with a relation and become a drudge (also if she is poor); or c. set up her own establishment and scandalize everyone (if she is rich).

I was poor, otherwise the last option might perhaps have interested me. I was most emphatically *not* interested in becoming a governess or a drudge, and so it clearly behooved me to find a husband. Thus, the come-out.

There were, however, two great drawbacks to success in my quest. The first, and by far the more important, was the fact that I was poor. In general, men do not like to marry poor wives. They like to marry wives with money. But Papa had been only an infantry officer, and Mother had only a small portion of her own, so neither of my parents had been able to provide me with the all-important marriage portion or dowry.

This was a distinct problem. Mother kept telling me stories about these poor girls she had heard of who had made brilliant marriages, but I had a healthy skepticism about these stories. The thing Mother didn't seem to notice about all her fairy tales was a very important point: all of these brilliantly married heroines had been beautiful.

The problem of the dowry was actually solved the month before we left for London. And it was solved by, of all people, Thorn. He offered to provide me with a dowry.

Mother was speechless with gratitude. "It is just enough, Dinah," she told me breathlessly. "Enough to make you respectable, enough to make you acceptable. Oh, bless the boy!'' A repressive look at me. ''Considering how rude you always are to him, Dinah, I think it is absolutely princely of him to do anything for you at all.''

''Nonsense,'' I said. ''There is nothing in the least princely about it. Thorn is simply terrified that he will have me on his hands for life if I can't find a husband. This dowry is purely in his own self-interest, Mother. Don't be fooled.''

So was solved problem number one, the matter of the dowry. Problem number two was a trifle more difficult. It had to do with my hair.

In our world, red hair is not considered attractive. Not that I have red hair, mind you. It is strawberry blond. But I am forced to admit that to some people it might appear red.

The color is bad enough. It is also very, very fine, and very, very curly. In fact, it is so fine and curly that it is impossible to confine it into any semblance of order. It just sort of floats around my face and shoulders in a cloud of rosy ringlets.

I hate it. I cut it all off once, when I was fourteen, but it looked worse. It was grown in now, to touch my shoulders, and it did what it wanted to.

Caroline had beautiful hair, smooth and straight and properly blond. Caroline also had beautiful big blue eyes. My eyes are gray-green in color. They are all right. Not beautiful, like Caroline's, but acceptable. I will never have my mother's beauty, but as I have grown older I have begun to look more like her. I am not unpleasing. Except for the hair. And the hair, unfortunately, is not something that one can easily overlook.

It was probably a very good thing that Thorn had come up with a dowry, otherwise he might very well have been stuck with me for life!

To continue about the come-out: one comes out during the Season. The Season traditionally begins with the opening assembly at Almack's, which event usually takes place on the Wednesday following Easter Sunday. The Season then continues until the summer, at which time the *ton*, that is, the fashionable set, deserts London for the country or for Brighton.

In the fall the *real* hunting season begins, when one goes out on horseback after foxes. During the social season in the spring, the hunting is aimed at finding a mate. Young girls look for husbands, bachelors look for wives, married people look for lovers . . . you see the picture I am painting.

A great deal of the hunting—at least the husband-hunting—takes place at Almack's. This is a social club that holds assemblies every week and attracts only the *crème de la crème* of the *ton*. You must be given a voucher by one of the patronesses of the club in order to attend an assembly. Almack's is very exclusive. According to my mother, it is also known as the Marriage Mart, so you can see what its function in society is.

Caroline and I, of course, had vouchers to Almack's. The sister and the cousin of the Earl of Thornton would be acceptable anywhere, so my mother informed us grandly. Before we went to Almack's, however, there was to be a great ball held in London at Thornton House in Grosvenor Square. The purpose of this ball was to "present" us to society. My mother had schemed to make this ball the grandest, most-talked-about event of the Season, and Caroline and I were beginning to be sick of the very subject when the time finally came for us to depart for London and our fates.

Thornton House was the town house of the earls of Thornton. It had been built by Thorn's grandfather, the same earl who had built Thornton Manor in Derby.

Thornton House was generally referred to as the "town house" or "Grosvenor Square," as it became too confusing to speak of both Thornton House and Thornton Manor. The town house had actually been closed up since the death of Thorn's father, but it was opened up for Mother and her charges, and on the day of our arrival it looked very grand indeed. Mother had explained that previous to our arrival, Thorn had lived in just a few of the rooms during his sojourns in London. Apparently he had eaten and been entertained elsewhere. However, now that there would be more than just himself in residence, the town house had been fully staffed and cleaned and stocked and Thorn himself would join us when he returned to London from Scotland, where he was visiting a friend.

My bedroom was very pretty, with freshly polished furniture, fresh flowers, and old chinz coverings. I liked it immediately, and helped Liza, the maid who came to unpack for me, fold my clothes into the enormous wardrobe that took up almost an entire flower-papered wall. Actually, I had not brought too many clothes. Mother planned to buy new wardrobes for both Caroline and me, with Thorn once more putting out the blunt—he was certainly anxious to be rid of me—and so we had left home with only the bare necessities. Our old clothes, according to Mother, were all right for the country, but would not *do* for London.

I was not overly concerned about my clothes. I was concerned about my horses. It's not that I doubted that the Thornton House stables were anything less than first-rate. The house had been closed up, but Thorn had opened the stables the first time he had come to London. Thorn might be a pain in the neck in most ways, but one can always count on him to see to the welfare of his cattle. No, it was not that I doubted the excellence of the stables, but, like myself, my horses had never been away from home before and I hoped they were not feeling too strange. They had been sent on a day ahead of us, and I was concerned about them. As soon as I decently could, I made my way to the stables.

The first person I saw when I got to the stables was Kevin. Kevin was one of the grooms from Thornton Manor who had accompanied the horses to London; he was about my own age and was a particular friend of mine. He grinned when he saw me.

"Do you not be fretting, Miss Dinah. The horses are grand."

I heaved a sigh of relief. "No problems on the road, Kevin?"

"None at all." His grin widened. "Well, almost none. Sebastian was after making a bit of a scene flirting with a good-looking black mare at one of the inns we stopped by, but otherwise all went fine."

I sighed again. "I wonder when Sebastian is finally going to realize that he's a gelding and not a stallion?"

"Some of them never realize it," Kevin said. "Particularly those that are gelded late. Truth to say, from the looks of her, the mare didn't know the difference either." Kevin grinned wickedly, and I grinned back. My mother would have had heart palpitations if she had been able to hear our conversation. She has a very odd notion of what is "suitable" for a young girl to know. If I hadn't spent half my life hanging about the stables, I would have been appallingly ignorant about the entire business of reproduction.

As you may have guessed, Sebastian is my horse. He is an extremely handsome chestnut thoroughbred, just under sixteen hands in height, and not of a placid disposition. If he had not been gelded, he would have been completely unmanageable. I really should not have brought him to London, but I would have missed him dreadfully if I had left him home. A horse that could learn not to kick a hound could learn not to spook at city traffic; or so I reasoned.

"And how is Max?" I asked next, referring to Caroline's horse. Max is an enormous bay gelding that had had a long and illustrious career before moving into scmiretirement as my cousin's mount. Max had done it all: he had raced and won, and he had hunted for years with the best hounds in the country. Now, at the age of sixteen, he lived off the fat of the land at Thornton Manor, and carried Caroline with grace and safety wherever she might wish to go. He was a marvelous old campaigner and I adored him. It was I, in fact, who kept him in condition. The amount of riding Caroline did would not have begun to exercise him properly. If the truth were known, I always thought of Max as my horse too.

I produced a bunch of carrots. "I brought some treats," I said.

"Come along," Kevin said, "and I'll show you over the place."

I spent a very pleasant two hours chatting in the stables with Kevin and the other grooms and helping to hay the horses, and then I made my way back to the house. Unluckily, the first person I met as I came in the side door under the stairs was my mother.

She glared at the pieces of hay that were sticking to my green traveling dress. "We will be dining in less than half an hour, Dinah," she said. "Get dressed."

"Yes, ma'am," I said. I have ever found that the best way to handle my mother is to agree with everything she says. It makes life much easier, and once her back is turned, I can do as I please.

I was hungry, however, and so this time I did as I was told.

We spent the next two weeks shopping. At first it was fun. I like a pretty dress as well as anyone else, but after one week of it I thought that enough was enough. In fairness, I suppose I must say that my mother and Caroline did not get bored; but I most certainly did. Such a fuss about clothing!

"Well, Dinah," my mother said when I commented upon her obsession with our wardrobes, "you are just as boring when you begin to prose on about horse feeds."

I must confess she had a point. I find the subject of horse feeds utterly fascinating; I suppose Mother feels the same way about clothes.

Two days before the great day of our come-out ball, Thorn finally put in an appearance at Grosvenor Square. Mother was furious with him for not having arrived earlier. I cannot imagine what she expected him to do that she should have wished for an earlier arrival. I could quite understand that it was important for him to be there on the night of the ball, but he was only bound to be a nuisance in every other way. I was rather hoping he wouldn't show up until the afternoon of the ball itself. I had a feeling he would not be pleased that I had brought Sebastian to London.

Sure enough, the first thing he did when he arrived was to go check the stables.

"Dinah!" he shouted, charging into the hallway after he had been gone only fifteen minutes. "What the devil do you mean by bringing Sebastian to London? I told you to bring Anicet. Sebastian is much too hot to trust in the streets of a large city."

He *had* told me to bring Anicet, and I might even have indicated to him that I would bring Anicet. But even though Anicet is a very nice mare, I just had not been able to bring myself to leave Sebastian behind.

I said airily, "He is doing just fine, Thorn. There is

no cause for worry, I promise you. I take him to the park very early for a nice long gallop, and that shakes the fidgets out of him. He has been very mannerly, I assure you.''

"So mannerly that Kevin tells me he almost put you under the wheels of a coach yesterday,'' returned my cousin.

Blast Kevin, I thought. "The stupid coachman blew his horn almost into Sebastian's ear!'' I said. "I jumped myself.'' I tried an ingratiating smile. Thorn's eyes had grown very blue and he had that look he gets on his face when he is contemplating a particularly unpleasant course of action. I would die if he ordered me to send Sebastian home. "If I get killed, think of the money it will save you,'' I said.

"Dinah!" That was my mother's horrified voice.

"Don't talk like that." That was Caroline's soft-hearted protest.

Thorn grinned. "You have a point,'' he said, and I knew that I had won. Sebastian wouldn't be sent home—at least, not immediately.

Thorn had arrived in London accompanied by the Scottish friend he had gone to visit. The friend's name was Douglas MacLeod, he lived on an island called the Isle of Skye, and he was very nice. Thorn had met him only a few months before, at some party or other they had both attended. Douglas—he told me to call him Douglas—was a few years older than Thorn, but Thorn often fools people with the fake maturity he can assume. A number of his friends were older than he.

The two of them went out after dinner to some club or other, but before they left, Thorn said to me, "I will accompany you to the park tomorrow morning, Red. Do not leave without me.'' This statement was accompanied by the chilling look that he always hopes will cow me. Actually, I do not much like it when

Thorn looks like that, but I would die before I let him see that he had intimidated me.

I gave him a sunny smile. "Are you really prepared to arise at six in the morning?"

His lips tightened. "Yes," he said baldly, gave me that look again, and left.

"Oh, dear," said my mother, "I knew Thornton would not approve of your bringing that horse"—Mother always referred to Sebastian as "that horse"—"to London. Now he is angry. Really, Dinah, *why* must you always be at loggerheads with him?"

You can imagine my indignation. *"I?* I am not the one at loggerheads, Mother. All I have done is to bring my own horse to London. I cannot understand why Thorn is behaving as if I have stolen him!"

"It is just that he fears for you, Dinah." It was Caroline's soft voice. She gave me a rueful smile. "Someone has to fear for you. You certainly have no fear for yourself."

"I have fear when it is sensible to have fear. There is nothing to fear in Sebastian. As Thorn will see for himself tomorrow morning. *If,* that is, he can rise with the dawn after having been on the town all night."

On this parting shot I adjourned to my own room to send a quick note to the stables telling Kevin to cut back on Sebastian's grain so that he would not have too sharp an edge on him in the morning. I had no real doubt that Thorn would miss our appointment. He had never needed very much sleep.

The early-April morning was soft with pale post-dawn light when I met Thorn in the stableyard the following day. He was dressed as he would have dressed for an afternoon outing on Rotten Row: blue riding coat with brass buttons, leather breeches, polished top boots, and a crisp, perfectly tied cravat. His uncovered head reflected the light of the morning. He tapped the rim of my riding hat with his crop and said lightly, "You've hidden all your hair. Good. If you make a cake of yourself, no one will know who it is."

I glared at him. "I will not make a cake of myself."

There was the sound of iron-shod hooves on cobblestones, and our two horses, fully tacked, were brought into the stableyard. Sebastian looked to be on his best behavior, thank God. The only other horse he liked was Thorn's big gray gelding, and he seemed pleased to be with Gambler again.

Thorn had a stableful of horses at home, but Gambler was his favorite, one of the horses he usually took when he went to hunt with friends. Gambler was nearly seventeen hands of pure power, but his disposition was amiable. This is not to say he was an easy horse to ride. In fact, in his own way Gambler could be as big a problem as Sebastian. He didn't explode into fireworks, à la Sebastian; Gambler was more subtle. When he didn't like his rider, he simply dropped all his considerable weight onto his forehand and lumbered like an elephant. When Thorn rode him, Gambler strode forward from his hindquarters and looked marvelous, but put a less competent rider on his back and he died. Spectacularly. Thorn liked him because he had wonderful spirit, and would jump anything. He would jump anything for Thorn, that is. I have been a witness at what he would do for someone else. It was not an edifying spectacle.

Spookiness was not one of Gambler's problems, however, and his big, calm presence was a decided help to Sebastian. Someone from home was out on this terrifying, strange street with him, and it made him feel much more confident. He jumped and bucked only a half-dozen times before we were in the park.

We opened up the horses almost immediately and let them stretch out into a full run. As usual, Gambler went just slightly ahead, and Sebastian hung very comfortably at his big gray shoulder. The chill April wind brought tears stinging to my eyes, and I laughed out loud in pure delight. At the sound of my voice, Thorn turned his head. I saw the white flash of his teeth. Probably the only time we two were in accord was when we were out together on horseback.

Finally the path began to wind into the woods, and Thorn sat down in his saddle. The horses slowed, first to a canter, then to a trot, and finally to a walk. The birds were calling in the trees, the sky was a brilliant clear blue, the exact color of Thorn's eyes, and Sebastian snorted loudly with the sheer pleasure of the day. I heaved a hearty sigh myself, counterpoint to Sebastian's snort. Thorn chuckled.

"Every time I want to strangle you, Red, I force myself to remember that you are probably the best rider that I know. It almost makes up for all your other failings."

Fierce pleasure scalded my heart. Thorn never complimented me. "Better than you?" I asked.

"Of course not." A small, superior smile curled the corners of his mouth.

Prudently I refrained from the comment that hovered on my lips, and said instead, "Then I may keep Sebastian in London?"

"Small chance I ever had of getting you to send him home," my cousin retorted.

"Well . . ." I murmured. I couldn't suppress a grin. "True."

"How are things going for the ball tonight?" he asked after we had ridden in silence for several minutes.

"Thank God this wretched ball is finally going to happen, Thorn!" I exclaimed. "Mother is a madwoman on the subject. She has talked of nothing else

for the past month, at least. If I don't attach at least
three eligible suitors who will propose to me within
the week, I shall feel as if I've been a failure as a
daughter.''

He gave me a sideways flash of blue. "You don't
have to pick out a husband within a week, Red. Take
a month, at least.''

I sighed. "Perhaps there will be an eligible gentleman in London who is blind to colors,'' I said gloom-
ily.

"Why should you say that?'' He sounded surprised.

"Well . . .'' I certainly didn't think I would have to
point out my defect to Thorn of all people. He was the
one who insisted on calling me "Red" all the time.
"Don't be dense, Thorn,'' I said crossly. "You know
what I mean.''

He halted Gambler, and Sebastian, the adoring fol-
lower, stopped also. Thorn reached over and put a
hand on my arm. "No,'' he said, "I don't know. Tell
me.''

I scowled at him. "My hair, stupid. Who will want
to marry a girl with hair the color of a sunset?''

I looked away from the astonished expression on his
face. I could feel that my cheeks were the color of the
sunset also. I hated Thorn for making me say my most
secret fear out loud, and I pulled my arm away and
nudged Sebastian with my leg to make him go forward. I suppose I nudged him too hard, for he bucked
and then bolted. It took a few minutes to get him back
to order again.

Thorn said to me, as our horses walked side by side
back toward the gate, "Dinah, I had no idea you felt
this way about your hair.''

"Mphh,'' I said.

"I hate to have to say this.'' His voice had an odd,

rueful note to it. "I must confess that I have enjoyed teasing you about your hair for years."

"I noticed," I said in a muffled voice. To my absolute horror, I was feeling a little teary. I really was dreading this night, when I would have to stand in front of half of London in all my flaming glory.

"Dinah," Thorn said, "your hair is beautiful."

"Mphh," I said again.

"Listen to me, you little witch." He reached out and took hold of my arm again, and both the horses stopped once more. Reluctantly I looked at him. He was the one with the beautiful hair, I thought, watching it shine, thick and flaxen in the sunlight. If only I had hair like that.

"Listen to me," he said again. "Your hair is beautiful. In fact, it is the most beautiful hair I have ever seen in my life. The men will be lining up to dance with you."

I suppose my face conveyed my skepticism, for his fingers tightened on my sleeve. "Do you know that there is a great Italian artist who is famous for painting ladies with hair not half as beautiful as yours?"

"I know," I said, nodding wisely. I was so pleased for once to be able to show him I was not an imbecile. "Titian. Signore Montelli told me about him."

"Who is Signore Montelli?" Thorn asked.

"The Italian dance instructor Mother engaged," I replied. "He kissed me in the library and called me a little Titian."

"He *what?*"

Too late, I realized my mistake. "It was just a little kiss, Thorn. He caught me unawares. I told him he had better not do it again or you would shoot him. He never did."

Thorn rolled his eyes upward toward the heavens. It is a particularly irritating mannerism of his, supposed to indicate that I have said or done something outrageous.

"He surprised me," I repeated. "He was really quite old." I thought back upon that moment in the library. "And his mouth was wet," I added in disgust.

Thorn snorted. "How old?"

"He must have been thirty, at least."

"Good God. Dinah, you are impossible. Thirty is not old!"

"It is old to me," I replied with unimpeachable logic. "I have yet to turn eighteen."

Thorn took his hand off my sleeve, straightened up, and began to walk his horse forward. "Well," he said, "this Italian dancer may have been old and wet-mouthed, but he certainly wasn't put off by your hair. Have you ever thought of that? Did he try to kiss Caroline?"

I could feel my eyes widen. "No," I said.

"There you are," he said.

I thought for a few minutes. "Perhaps I shall have to look for an Italian gentleman," I said at last. "They seem to have a penchant for red hair."

"I think you will find that a number of English gentlemen will have a penchant for red hair as well," Thorn said.

"Do you really think so?"

"Yes."

We continued along the path in silence. I was feeling considerably better. Of course, my mother and Caroline had been telling me for years that my hair was not so bad, but I hadn't believed them. Thorn was a different story. He would die under torture before he flattered me. If he said my hair was all right, then it was.

I turned to look at him. He was watching the path before us, his tall body erect and easy in his saddle, his rein long enough to allow Gambler to stretch his neck. Thorn was twenty-two. That was the age man I should be looking for, I thought.

He must have felt my eyes, for he turned his head. I was feeling unusually kindly toward him, and I gave him a big smile. He blinked. "What was that for?"

"You made me feel better about my hair," I said. "Thank you."

He blinked again. "I am going to write this down in my appointment book when I get home: 'TODAY DINAH SAID THANK YOU.' "

"Why should I even try to be nice to you?" I demanded. "Every time I make an effort to be civil, you make fun of me."

He surprised me. "Sorry, Red," he said. Then, with the ghost of a grin, "It was the shock of it, you see."

I stuck my nose in the air and refused to talk to him for the rest of the ride home.

I shall tell you about the come-out ball.

It began with a dinner party for what my mother called "a few select persons."

These persons numbered twenty-six.

Chief among the dinner guests were Uncle George and Aunt Harriet. The Honorable George Lydin was not actually my uncle, though he had graciously given me permission to call him thus shortly after I had come to stay at Thornton Manor. He was the younger brother of Thorn and Caroline's father, was a minister of some kind in the government, and had been the administrator of Thorn's fortune until Thorn had turned twenty-one.

He was rather stuffy. Thorn said he was a quintessential Tory (Thorn being a Whig). However, he had always tried to be kind to me. He had once even brought me a doll. I never played with dolls, and would much rather have had a new bridle, but I never told him that. I had given the doll to Caroline to add to her considerable collection, and Caroline had given me a new bridle for my next birthday.

Filling out Mother's table in addition to Uncle George and Aunt Harriet was an assortment of their friends. Mother, you see, knew no one in London and had had to rely heavily upon the Lydin family connections in the matter of establishing herself in society. The biggest coup of the evening, according to Mother, was the presence of Lady Jersey, who was a friend of Aunt Harriet's. Lady Jersey was the patroness who had procured us vouchers for Almack's, and her sponsorship was evidently a very desirable thing.

The dinner was excruciatingly dull. Thorn sat at one end of the table, and Mother sat at the other. Caroline and I were squashed in the middle of the highly polished mahogany board, but, needless to say, not next to each other. I was placed between a red-nosed old earl and a young man who kept telling me about some bet he had placed at White's. I was utterly uninterested in this silly bet, but I did my best to be polite, and smiled and nodded as if I were listening to him the whole time he was prosing on. I fared better with the red-nosed earl, who turned out to be a fanatic huntsman. We exchanged hunting stories for the remainder of the dinner, both of us enjoying ourselves more than we had expected to.

After dinner we all went up the staircase to position ourselves in the small anteroom before the ballroom to greet the guests.

Mother had done wonders with the ballroom. It was decked with fresh flowers and smelled perfectly lovely. The polished wooden floor shone like glass. There were mirrors on some of the walls, and the mirrors reflected the crystal of the chandeliers and the points

of light that were the candles in the crystal wall
sconces. It truly did look lovely. And so, I must confess, did Caroline and I.

Caroline was always a beautiful girl, but tonight she
looked breathtaking. Her gown was the traditional
white, laced with blue ribbons the exact color of her
eyes. The high-waisted cut of her dress accented her
tall slenderness. I had always begrudged Caroline
those two extra inches she had on me. Her blond hair
had been cut to lie in light feathery curls around her
face, and then was swept up in a sleek and stylish
arrangement at the back of her elegant head. I grinned
at her as we were taking our places, and she reached
out to squeeze my hand.

"You look beautiful," she whispered to me.

Caroline is a very generous girl. "So do you," I
whispered back. We assumed our places between my
mother and Thorn, and as we waited for the first guest
to be announced, I looked down at my own person.

My gown was white over a pale green underdress
and it was quite the prettiest dress I had ever owned.
The London hairdresser who had done my hair as well
as Caroline's had caught it back behind my ears with
pearl-encrusted combs and cut it so that it looked more
like a cascade of curls and less like a wild bush. I had
a string of pearls around my throat, and small pearl
earrings in my ears, and though I would never be a
beauty like Caroline, I thought I looked very well.

In fact, I was feeling better about this come-out than
I had ever thought I could. Thorn had told me before
dinner that all of his friends had promised to dance
with me, so I was certain of spending at least part of
the evening on the floor. This was an enormous relief;
I had spent a few sleepless nights imagining my mother's disappointment if I were not asked to dance at all.

"Viscount Eddington," the majordomo intoned, and

a young man who turned out to be one of Thorn's friends came down our line.

"Lord and Lady Rivers," the majordomo said next, and two more people started down the line.

At the height of the arrival period, the staircase was jammed with people waiting to be announced, and the entrance hall inside the front door was filled to capacity. They were even queuing up in the street! Mother was in heaven. The ball was already being labeled a "sad crush," which is apparently the highest accolade any hostess can achieve.

The worst part of the ball for me came when Caroline and I had to open the dancing. It was very frightening, having to go out on the floor in front of all those strange people and dance under the scrutiny of so many critical eyes. I would far rather have faced a six-foot gate on Sebastian than have ventured out onto that floor! Thorn danced with Caroline, and Uncle George danced with me. Thank heaven our solitary demonstration did not last long; after about a minute, at the orchestra leader's urging, the floor began to fill with other couples.

Uncle George saw the look of relief on my face and smiled. "You dance very well, Dinah," he said kindly. "And you are in particularly good looks tonight. I have always thought you to be a very pretty girl."

"Thank you, Uncle George," I said.

"And how are you enjoying London?" he asked.

The dance was soon over, and then I was surprised to see Thorn bowing before me. "Your turn," he said when I just stared at him.

"Oh," I said. "Are you going to dance with me now?"

"No," he answered with awful sarcasm. "I am going to dance with the Queen of Sheba. Come along, Red, and stop being so stupid."

He took me by the hand and towed me out to the floor to join a set. I glared at him, but we were too close to other people for me to give him the set-down he deserved. He placed his hands upon my waist and I lowered my glare to his cravat.

It has always annoyed me that he is a full head taller than I.

The music started, our feet moved in rhythm, and we danced.

Neither Caroline nor I was allowed to waltz at our come-out ball. This is a very strict, and I think very silly rule of the patronesses of Almack's. It seems they have decreed that one of them must formally give her permission before a young girl is allowed to perform the waltz.

So I did not dance any of the waltzes at my own ball, but to my utter astonishment, I danced every other dance of the evening. My card was filled in the first ten minutes of the ball! Nor was it only filled by Thorn's friends, who rallied round with great loyalty. A great number of other gentlemen, some of whom Thorn did not even know, asked to dance with me.

It was a great relief. Caroline danced every dance also, but that was not a surprise. My mother was beaming. I was so pleased for her. She had worked so hard, poor thing. It would have been dreadful if I had had to spend the night sitting with the chaperones.

We did not get to our beds until three in the morning, and I must admit that I did not arise the following morning to take Sebastian for his daily gallop in the park. When I finally opened my eyes, the bright sun streaming in my window told me it was much later in the day than my usual six-o'clock awakening time.

"Why did you not wake me?" I demanded of Liza, who was the housemaid who brought me my morning tea. "I *never* sleep this late."

"His lordship said to let you sleep, miss. He said you were not accustomed to going to bed as late as you did last night."

"Blast Thorn," I muttered under my breath. Sebastian would probably be kicking his stall down by now. There were no pastures for turn-out in London, and he was not accustomed to standing in a stall for such long periods of time. Much as I hated to admit that Thorn was right about anything, I was beginning to think he had been right about bringing Sebastian to London. It was not fair to the horse to confine him the way he was necessarily confined in the Grosvenor Square stables. The grooms hand-walked him around the stableyard for a few hours every day, but it was not the life he was accustomed to.

In my own defense, I must point out that I had not realized how much time Sebastian would have to spend in his stall.

I finished my tea and got out of bed. "Put out my habit, please," I said to Liza, who was now standing in front of my wardrobe.

"Your riding habit, Miss Dinah?"

"Yes."

"But it will be the calling hour shortly," the maid said. "Surely you will want to be home to receive any gentlemen who may call?"

"What I want to do," I said evenly, "is exercise my horse. Put out my riding habit, please."

I had finished washing my face and hands and was about to get dressed when a very young maid came in with a note for me. It was from his lordship, she said shyly. It contained one sentence: "I rode Sebastian for you this morning. Thorn."

Well, part of me was grateful to him, of course. I really was worried about Sebastian. And part of me was furious with him. It was owing entirely to his orders that I had not been awakened at my usual time so I could exercise my horse myself.

On the other hand, I still felt tired. I could imagine how I would have felt if I had arisen four hours earlier.

I decided I would ignore the whole situation unless he brought it up first. If I thanked him, it would appear as if I had been glad of the extra sleep, and if I upbraided him, I would appear churlish. How typical of Thorn, I thought with exasperation as I told Liza to put out one of my new day dresses. He always managed to put me in the wrong!

Liza had not been mistaken about the calling hour. At least a dozen gentlemen called to see Caroline and me during the course of the morning. Before I had quite realized what was happening, I had promised to ride with Viscount Eddington in the park that afternoon, and to go see the wild animals at the Tower with Mr. Richardson the following morning.

April passed in a whirl of this kind of activity. There were dances, assemblies, routs, theater parties, opera parties, Venetian breakfasts, musicales, rides in the park, and drives in the park. Mother had been right about our clothing. One needed an enormous wardrobe in order to keep up with the endless chain of social engagements one seemed to have in London.

I am also pleased to report that I even collected some potential suitors. There were three of them whom Caroline and I labeled as definite "possibles."

One was Thorn's friend Viscount Eddington. He was a good-looking, good-humored young man of twenty-four. He had a nice smile, some fairly decent property, although not in a county notable for its hunting, and apparently was comfortably rich.

Then there was Douglas MacLeod, who had been staying with us at the Grosvenor Square house until he removed to a cousin's. I liked Douglas very well, even though he was a trifle too serious-minded to make for easy company. He was a second son, which had kept him off our original list since I was aiming for a husband with a nice estate and horses, but according to Mother, who had had Uncle George check his credentials, Douglas had an independent fortune from his maternal grandfather. Caroline and I then put him down as a distinct possibility.

Last, but certainly not least, was Lord Livingston. Lord Livingston was certainly older than the husband I had envisioned. In fact, he was almost as old as the dastardly Montelli, but he was excessively handsome and excessively rich. He was a prime "catch" on the Marriage Mart, and it was a definite feather in my bonnet that he appeared to be interested in me.

I might mention here that *the* biggest catch on the Marriage Mart had turned out to be none other than Thorn!

Caroline also had a flock of admirers, but we never bothered to make a list of "possibles" for her. She had known whom she wanted from the first week of our stay in London. The moment she and Lord Robert Dalviney had laid eyes upon each other, it had been decided. I had never believed in love at first sight, but the fact of the matter is, it happened to Caroline. I saw it. Everyone saw it. And everyone knew it was merely a matter of time until their engagement would be made official.

With Caroline settled, the attention of the family naturally turned to me. I quite understood that, considering the amount of money that Thorn was expending, I was expected to catch a husband. I can assure you that I did my best.

I went driving with Lord Livingston, riding with Douglas MacLeod, and to Gunther's for an ice with Viscount Eddington. I danced with them all at every ball and rout and assembly I attended. I tried very hard to notice only their good points.

They all had distinct drawbacks, of course.

Viscount Eddington was an unimpressive rider, and if the horse he rode in London was any indication, he was no judge of horseflesh either. Of course, this could prove to be a positive factor. With such a husband I should probably have a pretty free hand in the stables. On the other hand, it would be nice to be married to a man one could ride out with for a morning's gallop without fearing that he would fall off and have to be carried home on a hurdle.

Douglas MacLeod was a decent horseman, but he was terribly intense. He took everything I said so seriously! You may not have noticed, but I have a tendency to exaggerate. With Douglas I was always watching my tongue so as not to alarm him unduly or hurt his feelings. I was beginning to fear that a lifetime of watching one's tongue could prove to be a trifle tedious. It would be nice to be married to a man to whom one could speak one's mind without fear of his brooding upon your words for half the afternoon.

Then there was Lord Livingston. He was probably the best of the lot, but I wasn't certain if I could bring him up to scratch. According to my mother, he had a reputation for breaking hearts. I could quite understand how that might happen; he was a terribly attractive man and a dreadful flirt. He certainly flirted with me, but I didn't know if he meant anything beyond the flirting. Livingston was a man of the world, and men of the world were utterly beyond my experience. To tell the truth, he sometimes made me a little uncomfortable. One never knew what he was thinking. I like to know where I stand with people, and I was beginning to think it might be uncomfortable to find oneself married to an enigma.

Caroline thought I should aim for Douglas. My mother was in favor of Eddington. I myself rather favored Livingston (I have always liked a challenge). When my mother consulted Thorn, she said he was quite rude on the subject and told her I should take whomever I could get.

He probably thought I couldn't get any of them. Of course, this only fired me up to try even harder.

The husband hunt came to a climax in mid-May, at a garden party given by one of society's leading lights, the Duchess of Merton, at her beautiful home just outside of London. Merton House is situated on the Thames, with acres and acres of gardens and lawns and summerhouses and even a maze almost as large as the one at Hampton Court. The duchess apparently has this garden party every year and it is one of the highlights of the London Season. I can quite understand why. Everything about the day was perfect: the beautiful setting, the delicious food, the elegant company; even the weather cooperated by being warm and sunny. It must be nice to be a duchess, I thought, and so be able to order everything to your requirements.

Mother and Caroline and I all attended, and Thorn escorted us. He had been out of London for a week visiting a friend in Hampshire, but he had returned in time for the Duchess of Merton's garden party. Thorn had been a heroically good brother this Season, escorting Caroline to a large number of affairs that he obviously found very boring. He escorted me too, of course, but that was because I always went along with Caroline.

Truth to say, as the Season had advanced, Thorn's temper had noticeably deteriorated. As usual, he had taken his temper out on me. Even Caroline had commented upon his irritability.

"Every time Dinah opens her mouth, you jump all

over her," she had told him before he had left for Hampshire. "Whatever is the matter with you, Thorn? If London is preying on your nerves, please don't feel you must stay for my sake. Aunt Cecelia is a perfectly adequate chaperone, and you know that Robert and I have settled things between us. It is just the lawyers who must arrange about the settlements."

Released from duty, Thorn had promptly produced an invitation to visit a friend and had left for Hampshire two days later. We hadn't seen him until his arrival at Grosvenor Square the previous afternoon. He had insisted upon escorting us to the garden party, "to see what you have been up to in my absence," as he put it.

"Are you certain that it is not to see Rosamund Leighton?" Caroline teased. Rosamund Leighton was a girl who had, like Caroline and me, made her come-out this year. She was odiously beautiful, with smooth black hair and big blue eyes. She fawned all over Thorn, and he adored it. When I accused him of liking to be toad-eaten, he said it was a nice change to have a girl appreciate him instead of vilifying him all the time.

I hated Rosamund Leighton and her smooth black hair with a passion. She probably would be at the garden party, and the prospect of seeing her gazing worshipfully up at Thorn for the entire afternoon cast a pall of gloom upon the whole day for me. I can assure you, it was an utterly sickening sight for sensitive persons to be forced to behold.

It was hard to stay gloomy for long, however, when once I was out in the beauty of the duchess's gardens. My three suitors were supposed to be in attendance also, and I thought that if I saw all three of them in a countrylike setting, it might give me a chance to decide which one I liked best.

The program for a garden party is very simple. One strolls about the gardens, admires the views, eats and drinks in the dining room of the house, and talks to one's friends and acquaintances. On a warm mid-May afternoon it can be quite a delightful way to pass the time.

I spent the first hour we were at Merton House strolling about on the arm of Douglas MacLeod, who listened to every word I spoke with such an expression of intense interest that it depressed me unutterably.

Then I was claimed by Viscount Eddington. Viscount Eddington is a light-hearted young man, and I quite enjoyed the hour I spent walking about on his arm. If I had never seen the man on a horse I might have been more enthusiastic about him as a prospective husband. Unfortunately, I knew how he looked on a horse. The thought was inexpressibly discouraging.

Then I caught a glimpse of Thorn parading about with that odious Rosamund Leighton on his arm. The silly cowlike look on her face was enough to cast anyone into a fit of the dismals.

In fact, by the time I was claimed by Lord Livingston I was feeling very glum indeed. This business of suitors was not at all what it was cracked up to be, I thought. It was all very well to play games and make lists and gossip with one's friends about them, but the reality of having to spend one's entire life shackled to a strange man was . . . well, frightening.

Lord Livingston put my hand upon his arm and began to walk me firmly down a long path that I had not seen before. He chatted to me lightly, and I smiled and nodded without really listening.

Lord Livingston's looks are rather in the style of a romantic hero, which is one of the reasons he has broken so many hearts. His hair is dark and it dangles on his forehead in an unruly curl. His smile usually has a mocking edge to it. His conversation also had a mocking edge to it. It was that edge that so confused me. I never knew if he meant what he was saying or if he meant the opposite of what he was saying. He was rather exhausting company, if the truth be told.

"Lord Livingston," I said when we had reached a very pretty little arbor and he showed signs of wanting to stop, "don't you ever grin?"

His magnificent dark eyes widened with surprise. "Grin?" he said.

"Yes. You know—a big smile. A really *amused* smile. A smile that lets people know you are happy."

He lifted a well-marked black eyebrow. "I smile, little one."

"I know. But your smiles are so confusing," I said. "They never look happy."

He gave me one of those mocking smiles. "They don't?"

"*There*," I said, pointing to his mouth. "You just did it. That is not a happy smile, my lord. *This* is a happy smile," and I gave him a huge, radiant grin. "See?"

He was looking at me with a very odd expression on his face. He often looked at me like that. I never knew what it meant. Today was my day for clearing up mysteries, so I asked, "What are you thinking when you look at me like that?"

"I am thinking," he answered promptly, "that you are a most beautiful girl and that I want to kiss you." And then he did.

This was not at all like Signore Montelli's kiss. This kiss was serious business. Lord Livingston had me grasped firmly in one arm while his other hand held the back of my head so I couldn't pull it away. His mouth was hard and bruising. I couldn't breathe. I pushed against his shoulders with my hands, and couldn't move him. I was beginning to be frightened as well as disgusted, when a cold, furious voice ripped across the silence of the arbor.

"Get away from her, Livingston. Now."

It was Thorn.

Lord Livingston loosened his grip enough for me to pull away from him. I ran across the arbor to Thorn as if all the hounds of hell were at my heels.

"There's nothing to be upset about, Thornton," Lord Livingston said. His voice sounded oddly thick and he paused to clear his throat. Then he added, "I have every intention of marrying the girl."

Thorn turned to look down at me. "Is this true, Dinah?" he asked. "Did you agree to marry him?"

I stared up into his face. I had never seen Thorn look like this. His eyes were positively glittering with fury. There was a white line about his mouth. Even the tip of his nose looked white.

I shook my head so hard my hair floated. "No, Thorn," I said. I swallowed and then I whispered, "Please don't make me marry him."

I hate to admit it, but I sounded almost pitiable. But the thought of spending a lifetime submitting to that suffocating kiss! I shuddered at the very idea.

Thorn said to Lord Livingston, "If I ever find you within ten feet of my cousin again, I'll shoot you dead."

Lord Livingston was at least seven years older than Thorn, and certainly more a man of the world. However, it didn't surprise me at all when he decided not to pursue the discussion. The expression on Thorn's face was absolutely terrifying. After the briefest of hesitations, Lord Livingston turned on his heel and strode away.

We listened to the sound of his feet crunching on

the graveled path. Then he had passed out of our hearing.

Silence reigned in the arbor.

Finally Thorn said, "What the devil possessed you to come to this secluded place with a man of Livingston's stamp?"

"I didn't know he was taking me so far away from everyone," I protested.

"You have eyes, don't you?" He still sounded very angry.

I said, trying to introduce a note of humor into the atmosphere, "That is two men now who have kissed me, and you have threatened to shoot both of them."

He swung around so he was standing directly in front of me. "I never met the Italian dancing teacher," he said.

"Oh, that is right." I attempted a placating smile. I was uncomfortably aware of being in the wrong, and was doing my best to slide out of it. "*I* was the one who threatened that you would shoot Signore Montelli."

Thorn's blue eyes were searching my face. "Dinah . . ." he said. "*Were* you thinking of marrying Livingston?"

I don't know why, but I could feel tears begin to rise in the back of my throat. I shook my head.

"Then what of Eddington?" he asked. "Or MacLeod?"

I wet my lips with my tongue and tasted blood. That blackguard Livingston had cut my lip with his teeth!

"I am trying very hard to like them, Thorn," I said. "I know I must get married. Perhaps you had better make the choice. You know them better than I do."

There was a very long silence. Thorn's face was as unreadable as ever Lord Livingston's had been. Finally I said, "Do you have a hankerchief, Thorn? I fear that Lord Livingston cut my lip."

His eyes began to turn dark blue. Without speaking, he removed a square of white linen from inside his coat, took my chin into his hand, and dabbed the handkerchief gently against my lower lip. I stood very still and looked up at him. Then, after he had taken the handkerchief away and put it back into his pocket, he bent his head and very slowly, placed his lips lightly on mine.

Their touch was infinitely sweet. I think I must have swayed a little, for his hands came up to grip my shoulders and support me. The pressure of his lips increased. I tipped up my face and let my head fall against his shoulder. I know I closed my eyes.

And then we were kissing, deeply, intensely, our bodies pressed into each other, my arms around his waist, his hands spread on my back to hold me close. It was wonderful to be held so close to him. His long, lean body felt so strong against mine. I loved the familiar smell of him. After a while he moved one of his hands to touch my hip, my waist; it came to rest upon my breast.

I quivered with delight under his touch. His mouth was moving on mine, asking for something. . . . I opened my lips and felt his tongue come into my mouth.

I had never known kissing could be like this!

It was a rude awakening a few minutes later, to feel him take me once more by the shoulders and bodily lift me until I was set on my feet a good arm's length away from him. I blinked at the sudden separation.

"Dinah," he said in a rough-sounding voice, "this has got to stop or I won't answer for the consequences."

I stared at him. His hair was disordered and spangled his forehead with threads of gold (had I done that?), and his eyes were brilliantly, blazingly blue. "What consequences?" I asked.

"The consequence that you are likely to find yourself lying on the ground there with all your clothes off," he answered bluntly. "There is a reason, Dinah, for the rule that a young unmarried girl ought not to be alone with a man."

It sounded an attractive prospect to me, but I didn't dare say so. There was no humor about his mouth; in fact, he was looking oddly grim. A terrible fear smote my heart. Perhaps that was all it had been to him? The excitement of being alone with a girl? And now he was afraid I would take it to mean more than it did? I dropped my eyes and stared at the ground.

"You don't have to marry anyone you don't want to," he said. His voice was harsher than it usually was. "I never wanted you to think that."

I shrugged and still did not look at him.

"I thought you were enjoying yourself." Now he sounded as if he were accusing me of something.

I shrugged again. "I was just trying to do what was expected of me. It wasn't so bad at first. It was like a game. But then . . . when I realized that I would actually have to marry one of them . . . a man who was a stranger . . . a man I could never love . . ." To my horror, my voice had begun to shake. I stopped talking and drew a deep, long breath.

"Dinah," Thorn said. "Dinah, darling. Don't look like that." His feet crunched on the hard-packed dirt of the arbor and then he was taking me into his arms.

I huddled against him. I said into his shoulder, ". . . a man who wasn't you."

I felt his mouth on the top of my head. "All this Season I have been feeling like doing a murder," he said. "Isn't it amusing? I had no idea at all that I loved you until we came to London and I saw you dancing with another man. I wanted to go up to you, rip you out of his arms, and shout, 'Hands off. She's mine!' ''

I gave a delighted chuckle.

"I thought you thought I was an arrogant boor," he said into my hair.

"Well," I said, "I do." I lifted my face out of his shoulder and looked up at him. "I also think that you are wonderful. For years I have nearly killed myself trying to keep up with you, trying to get you to notice me. I've spent my entire life comparing other boys to you, and none of them ever began to measure up."

He looked fascinated. "Well, this is certainly news."

"This is very bad for you," I said. "You are spoiled enough by everyone else without my beginning to add to the problem."

The amusement left his face, to be replaced by a look of intent seriousness. "Spoil me, Dinah," he said softly. "I would love to have you spoil me." And he bent his head and kissed me again.

Ten minutes later he was towing me along the path toward the terrace of the house. "You are a menace, Red," he said as I bleated a protest that I needed to button the top of my gown, which had somehow come undone during the course of an extremely pleasant embrace.

"I?" I said with great indignation as I redid my buttons. "*I* am not the person who unbuttoned this dress, Thorn. It was you. Stop trying to blame me. You *always* try to blame me."

"It is usually your fault," he said. Then he grinned. "Stop flashing your eyes at me. It *is* your fault for being so damned irresistible. Now, be a good girl and come along before your mother and Caroline call up a search party to find us."

The following day, Thorn called a meeting of the family to tell them the news of our engagement. The general reaction was one of stunned stupefaction.

"*You are marrying Dinah?*" Uncle George said incredulously.

"Are you joking us, Thornton?" my mother asked doubtfully.

"But you two dislike each other!" Aunt Harriet said.

It was Caroline who was the surprise. She smiled and said, "Well, I am glad that is settled at last. I was beginning to wonder how long it would take you two to resolve matters."

Everyone, Thorn and I included, stared at her.

"Do you mean you expected us to become engaged?" I asked.

"I thought you might."

"And what brought you to that interesting conclusion?" Thorn asked in that odiously polite voice he uses when he doesn't believe a word you are saying.

"You have been like a bear with a sore toe ever since we came to London," his sister told him. "You have been consistently rude to all of Dinah's suitors. You were so rude that Douglas moved out of the house. And you watch Dinah all the time." She smiled at him. "I'm in love myself," she said, "so I noticed."

I hadn't noticed a thing.

"You made a list of suitors with me," I accused her, "and you never once mentioned Thorn!"

"She probably thought you'd laugh in her face," Thorn said.

Caroline looked at him with those smiling blue eyes. "Dinah has always worshiped the ground that you walk on," she said. "It wasn't Dinah's feelings that I was unsure of."

Now, in a deeply private moment I *might* perhaps be willing to admit such a thing to Thorn, but to have it said out loud, in front of all the family! I could feel my cheeks flaming.

There was a moment of amazed silence. Then my mother said, "I suppose we could have a double wedding."

"No," Caroline said immediately. "I love Dinah dearly, and have been very happy to have her company during the Season, but I will not be married with her. The only one who will look at me is Robert."

Caroline is such a generous girl, but even so, I thought it would take some time for me to forgive her for that remark about my worshiping the ground Thorn walked upon. He was looking overly pleased with himself at the moment.

"Dinah and I are going to be married immediately," he announced. "I see no need for the sort of delay Caroline is certain to insist upon. Dinah doesn't care about bride clothes and things like that."

This, of course, was perfectly true. It would have been nice to have been consulted, however.

Mother said, "Of course she must have bride clothes!"

Thorn said, "Dinah, come over here to me."

Normally, of course, I would never have jumped to his command. But there was a note of such heart-stopping tenderness in his voice . . . Well, I was beside him before I quite realized I had moved.

He put his arm around my shoulders and bent his head close to mine. "Are you missing Thornton Manor?" he asked softly. "Wouldn't you like to just go home and be married without any fuss?"

I think that was the first time the reality of what had happened really struck me. Home. Thornton Manor would be my home forever. I wouldn't have to leave my horses and my dogs and my friends in the stables and the kitchens. I would marry Thorn, and live with him, and perhaps have a flock of blue-eyed children, all with his beautiful hair. I sighed with the sheer bliss of it and smiled up at him.

"Yes, Thorn," I said meekly. "I would like that very much."